1·3·08

SPACECOYOTES

AND THE SECRET OF THE BLUE PLANET

JoJo was changing. The innocence and raw potential of the harian child she was, was about to be unlocked forever.

JoJo

PAUL FREDRICS

SpaceCoyotes

AND THE SECRET OF THE BLUE PLANET

5/100

LIMITED LARIAN EDITION

12·7·08

[signature]

Matador
9 De Montfort Mews
Leicester LE1 7FW, UK
Tel: (+44) 116 255 9311 / 9312
Email: books@troubador.co.uk
Web: www.troubador.co.uk/matador

ISBN 978 1906510 374

Typeset in 12pt Stempel Garamond by Troubador Publishing Ltd, Leicester, UK
Printed in the UK by The Cromwell Press Ltd, Trowbridge, Wilts, UK

Matador is an imprint of Troubador Publishing Ltd

*The problem with a secret, especially a big one,
is that there is always someone who wants to keep it exactly that.
Secret...*

Contents

ACKNOWLEDGEMENTS

Writing this book has been a true passion and there are a few people who have not only shared our passion but tolerated us as we went on and on and on and on about it. Never once did they threaten to have us locked away in a sanatorium for the terminally insane, although we are sure they all thought about it.

We are therefore eternally grateful to:

Cathy Creamer (Illustrator) for putting us on the right track and bringing the characters to life with her art.

Jean Fullbrook who spent many hours editing our book,

Maureen Nixon for her eagle eyes at spotting spelling mistakes.

Shelia McGovern who has been having her ear bent about the SpaceCoyotes for the last three years.

Lindsey Dodgson for giving us her true and honest support.

Linda Dotson, without whose continued faith in us, SpaceCoyotes may never have left Anilar.

Paul: To Annie, Aimie, Emily and Jessie, for whom all this is for.

Fredric: To Irmgard for her constant loving support over many years.

SHEB WOOLEY

This book is dedicated to our friend and fellow Larian, Sheb.

A multi-award winning actor, songwriter, recording artist and comedian. Sheb wrote and performed the massive global No 1 hit song *Purple People Eater*.

As well as starring in the long running TV series Rawhide, Sheb also starred in over 100 major Hollywood films including *The Hoosiers* with Gene Hackman, the Gary Cooper classic *High Noon*, *The Outlaw Josie Wales* with Clint Eastwood and as Jane Fonda's father in the classic *The Dollmaker*.

Sheb's first film *Rocky Mountain* was with legendary actor Errol Flynn. He also starred or co-starred in as well as hundreds of made for television movies and series.

Sheb encouraged and inspired us from the first day we met until his untimely departure for Anilar on September 16th, 2003. The original concept for this book was created in his house in Nashville, Tennessee.

CHAPTER 1

SECRET

All families have secrets. It's just that some are bigger, and far more secret than others. As fourteen year old JoJo sat cross-legged on her bedroom floor, rolling up the last of the fifteen carefully prepared StarCharts, she considered that perhaps her family had the biggest of them all.

She slid the chart into its protective container and popped the lid tight before stacking it alongside a gamut of other things she had collected for her forthcoming trip. There were compact food packets, high energy drink cartons, medi-kits, eyeglasses to protect from solar flares and most importantly, her hand-held PlasmaTab computer, without which she would be hopelessly lost. A few items such as the Oxyin 900, (a strange looking contraption which you placed over your mouth and nose and converted toxic atmospheric gases into fresh breathable oxygen), she hoped would not be needed, but it was always better to be safe than sorry.

Cramming everything except the PlasmaTab into her backpack, she opened a bedside drawer and retrieved a small, thin card about the size of matchbox.

In her hand, the card felt as light and insignificant as a leaf, but it was this tiny device that held the key to her missions success.

Printed across the top the words 'TeleCoy Inc. HOLOPAD' were emblazoned in electric blue text. Through the centre ran a pulsing golden band of colour.

She turned it over and slid a second even tinier card from its protective pouch. Carefully she checked its surface for dents or scratches, before gently wiping it free of dust and slipping it into position under her bed covers.

Whispering softly, she issued a command to her computer.

"JoJo. Holo program. Real," she said.

Immediately, her bedding began to swell as if a large balloon were being inflated under it. Bubbles of excitement burst in her stomach as a replica image of her own head appeared sedately from the covers like a tortoise emerging from its shell. Resting softly on her pillow, it began to breathe, the linen gently rising and falling in time to the soft purring emanating from its mouth. JoJo beamed satisfactorily. What she was looking at was her picture-perfect Holotrope. The minute fluctuations in her skin tone, the tiny scar above her left eye that Herman Gad had inflicted at her fourth birthday party, and the two huge red spots that she had woken to find bursting from her forehead this morning, were all perfectly represented in hozolium gas.*

Tenderly, JoJo brushed her hand over the holotrope's hair. It felt as real as if she were touching her own, which in a way of course she was.

*Note: A fascinating chemical, hozolium gas was discovered quite accidentally by a Dr. Hozol Libium when an experiment he was conducting into the extraction of water from sand went horribly wrong. He believed that by passing a massively charged neutron current through a pile of dry sand, it would be rendered instantly into drinking water, thus solving Anilar's desert dwellers any future problems. However, Dr Libium was not known for his rational thinking and rather than produce water, the current produced a rather large explosion along with several tonnes of thick viscous gas which bizarrely began trying to mimic its immediate environment. This trait was later honed and harnessed by other scientists into the Holotrope. Unfortunately, Dr. Libium never knew of his remarkable discovery due to the aforementioned explosion.

Even her greatest treasure, the family pendant that had belonged to her Grandmother, hung from its neck. JoJo involuntarily felt for the real one beneath her shirt.

It was better than looking in a mirror. When tomorrow the holotrope climbed out of bed and made its way to school, no one would be able to tell that it wasn't real. Not even her parents who never looked that closely anyway as long as she was where they expected her to be, which was usually in her room studying.

For the next two days this computer-generated clone was going to be JoJo and ensure no one missed her while she was away.

Satisfied, she left the holotrope to sleep and walked over to the window. Night had fallen and a slight pink haze hung over the city. She checked the Octavia time piece wrapped around her left wrist. The time to leave was rapidly approaching.

What a journey these last two years had been. She could never have believed so much would happen to her, but it was nothing compared to the journey on which she was about to embark. Soon her younger brother, 2B, would arrive and together they would set off from Anilar and travel across the galaxy in search of a secret that should never have been kept from her.

But for now she was content to stand in the comforting silence and think back to how it all began.

CHAPTER 2

LIP GLOSS

It was two years ago. JoJo had just turned twelve years old and, in the innocent way of all other twelve year olds, she considered herself to be a perfectly ordinary girl living a perfectly ordinary life. It was only in the summer when she changed schools that things began to go horribly wrong.

Her new school, Nexus Hall was big, very big and so noisy that JoJo could barely concentrate. Even in class it seemed that certain kids just could not keep their mouths shut for more than a minute. The teachers at St Gills, where she had spent seven happy years, would have been outraged. Not because St Gills had been strict. On the contrary, it was more that the lessons had been so interesting and challenging, that nobody had the time or inclination to chatter.

Nevertheless, she did her best to fit in at Nexus Hall. She made friends, worked out very quickly which teachers were cool and which were definitely not, and found the work refreshingly easy compared to the more advanced stuff she was used to at St Gills. Ironically however, that was when her problems began.

Apparently, some of her classmates did not think it normal to score top marks all the time in every subject, especially when you took more subjects than anyone else. Neither, they said, was it usual for a twelve-year-old girl to know in intricate detail, the inner functions of the hydrogen plasma accelerator, which JoJo did – and the teacher did ask didn't he? Maybe in hindsight, it would have also been wiser not to

4

have mentioned in front of the whole class that she had just applied to try out for the SpaceCoyote Pilot's Academy. When the laughter had died down, the mocking began.

"Are you stupid?" shouted one kid.

"You must have a screw loose," yelled another.

"Hasn't anyone told you that you've got to be at least sixteen to try out? They'll think you're an idiot."

JoJo was mortified at the humiliation. She had thought they would be pleased for her. How was she supposed to know pupils at Nexus Hall couldn't apply until they were sixteen? At St Gills you were encouraged to apply as soon as you felt ready. For JoJo, that time was now. So what was she to do about it? Withdraw her application and deliberately do badly in class just so she could fit in? That was about as likely to happen as a gas nebula suddenly developing ears.

What these 'no-brains' failed to understand was that becoming a SpaceCoyote was all JoJo had ever thought about since she was old enough to gaze upon the stars and wonder what they were. She spent every waking moment dreaming of being trained with the elite to fly missions throughout the galaxy, discovering new and uncharted worlds. It was her destiny, her birthright.

JoJo had taken her first flight with her father, a SpaceCoyote third class, when she was only seven. At nine she made her first solo orbit of Anilar and, at ten, she had accrued more space hours than many of the new graduates twice her age. On her eleventh birthday, she went through her first portal and back, travelling a distance of five hundred thousand light years, so she was certainly ready. She was more than ready.

This cut no ice with the kids of Nexus Hall however, and almost overnight JoJo gained some very potent enemies. Most notably a girl called Lip Smear. Lip was two years older than JoJo and notorious around the school. Most of the serious trouble could be traced back to Lip Smear and her bunch of hangers-on, the Lip Chix. Thankfully they were easy to spot and avoid as they all wore the same clothes – black tops, black bottoms and black make-up. The first time JoJo saw them she thought they were a bunch of undertakers. Only Lip herself stood out with the crimson red boots that she insisted on wearing everywhere. She even had a modified trainer version for gym class.

JoJo's first encounter with Lip came when she was ambushed outside school the day she let slip about the Pilot's Academy try out.

"Well, well, if it isn't the little 'chosen one,'" Lip snarled as she grabbed JoJo by the jacket and pinned her hard to the wall.

"My friends here tell me that you think you are better than us. Think that you're some kind of big shot fly girl, who wants to join the Academy and become a SpaceDog – oh I'm sorry – *Coyote*."

The Lip Chix sniggered collectively. JoJo was outraged, both at the sudden attack and at Lip's contemptuous attitude to the SpaceCoyotes, but JoJo wasn't stupid. Lip was much bigger than her, so she kept her mouth shut.

"Well we don't like big-heads around here, JoJo," continued Lip. "So you and I have to get one or two things straight, okay?"

Lip moved eyeball to eyeballl with JoJo. She had some of those new converter lenses in and they were changing colour from blue to green, violet to black and red to yellow. They were almost hypnotic, and set JoJo's teeth on edge. They made Lip look even more psycho than her personality suggested she was.

"I don't like you," Lip growled prodding JoJo hard in the chest. "Which unfortunately is bad news for you because it means the rest of your time at this school is going to be pretty miserable. From now on there will be certain rules by which you are going to have to abide. If you want to stay healthy that is. I'll let my Chix explain."

Squealing and shrieking like manic zombie Barbie dolls, the girls of the Lip Chix all started to push and shove JoJo between them as if they were playing pass the parcel.

"If Lip doesn't like what you wear, *you* have to go home and change," wailed one.

"If Lip wants something from the canteen, *you're* going to fetch it, chosen one," screeched another.

"If Lip doesn't want to see your face, then she won't see your face. Get it?" hissed yet another.

"Basically," said Lip, bringing the game of shove JoJo to a halt, "Whatever I say goes. Understand?"

JoJo hesitated, which was a mistake as it turned out. Viciously, Lip grabbed a hunk of JoJo's hair and yanked it downwards. JoJo cried out.

"Do you understand?" Lip snarled cruelly.

Twisted with pain, JoJo nodded, as best she could anyway, considering if she moved too much half her hair would be left in Lip's hand. Lip gave a final tug before pushing JoJo away.

"Glad we sorted that out. Now, get out of here."

JoJo limped off to lick her wounds as Lip smiled triumphantly and was engulfed by her cackling cronies.

From that day on the bullying became unrelenting and the teachers did nothing to stop it. Most of the time it was no more than name-calling and gentle pushing in the corridors, but once or twice JoJo found herself on the receiving end of one of the Chix fists, always in the back when she wasn't looking. She tried to pretend that it wasn't happening and didn't matter, but secretly longed to be back at St Gills where she had felt so at home and not different to everyone else.

After one particularly unpleasant morning, JoJo could stand it no more. She dashed home, locked herself in the bathroom and cried for a whole twenty minutes. When she eventually emerged, a lot angrier than when she went in, she had decided that if Lip Smear was all she had to look forward too every morning, then there was no way she was going back to Nexus Hall. Not that afternoon, not ever.

She had to get back to St Gills. It was just a matter of working out how.

CHAPTER 3

THE LETTER

A contact number – that is what she needed. If she could just get through to the principal of St Gills and explain the torrid situation at Nexus Hall, she was sure they would be only too pleased to welcome her back.

It took most of the afternoon searching, but finally she found a letter bearing the St Gills' crest in a drawer, in her fathers office. With much excitement, she scribbled down the number beneath the crest and would have replaced the letter exactly where she had found it had she not been first tempted to glance at its contents.

Maybe if she hadn't been so curious, her life would have taken a very different path and she may not now, two years on, be about to break nearly every law in the SpaceCoyote handbook. All the same, she did read it and, as she knew only too well from her lessons on quantum physics, time could not be turned backwards, not even for a second.

The letter was dated exactly one week before the end of her final term at St Gills and it read like a kick to the stomach.

Dear Sir,

I am writing to you with regard to your appeal against your daughter, JoJo's, permanent expulsion from our establishment. As we made perfectly clear in our earlier correspondence, the decision to withdraw her tuition was passed unanimously at our board meeting. This decision has not changed. We therefore regret to inform you that your appeal for leniency has been summarily rejected. May I add that such decisions are never taken lightly at St Gills. Here, we pride ourselves on taking the most difficult children if they are sufficiently gifted. However, a number of our members believe that the situation concerning JoJo has become untenable. I'm sure I do not need to remind you that we agreed to allow your daughter into our school not only at a great personal risk to our reputation, but very much on a temporary basis. We are Anilar's premier school of excellence and as such can no longer accommodate someone whose Grandfather has such an insalubrious history.

This decision is final and we do not expect to partake in any further discussions in this matter. As a gesture of goodwill, a place at Nexus Hall, beginning next term has been agreed,

Yours truly,

Saminian Dale
Principal Teacher. St Gills School for exceptionally gifted children.

The letter floated out of JoJo's hand onto the table. She could not believe what she had just read. She felt sick. It said she had been expelled! Expelled. Her! Why for heavens sake? She had never so much as had a detention, and what was all this nonsense about her Grandfather's 'insalubrious history.' What did that mean?

9

It must be some mistake. They must have sent the right letter to the wrong person or the wrong letter to the right person. Either way it was wrong. She snatched it up and searched for the telltale flaw, but there was none. That was definitely her name printed there in black and white. There were no other JoJo's at St Gills.

Before the shock could properly sink in, the door to the office was flung open. There, looking breathless and fraught stood JoJo's father. For a tense moment she thought he was going to explode with anger, but when he saw the letter in her hand he simply sagged.

"I'm so sorry," he said, apologetically. "I should have told you … sooner."

JoJo was dumbstruck. "It says I was expelled," she snapped thrusting the letter toward him.

JoJo's father nodded sadly. "You shouldn't have found out this way. It's my fault. Please, give it to me."

He made a move towards her, but JoJo pulled the paper to her chest protectively. Tears were welling up in her eyes.

"What did I do wrong, Dad?"

"You did nothing wrong JoJo. Please, I can explain."

"Explain? Yeah, why don't you explain," she sobbed. "Explain why I've been expelled from the best school in the world and sent to a horrible place where everyone thinks I'm some sort of freak. And you know what? If this letter is true, I am a freak. Why didn't you tell me St Gills was a school for special kids?"

"It is not for *freaks*, JoJo, it's for gifted children," he corrected her. "You went there because they wanted you. St Gills choose their pupils, not the other way around."

JoJo flourished the letter madly. "Not according to this they didn't. It says here that you practically had to beg them to take me."

"That's not true. It was they who came knocking on my door not the other way around. They came to me and your mother when you were four years old and said that a place had been reserved for you, no questions asked. You went the following year."

10

"And what, now they don't want me anymore, so they just expel me," said JoJo waspishly.

"They had no right doing what they did. Unfortunately, it seems that Saminian Dale would rather listen to his board members than his own teachers. All of them wanted you to stay."

JoJo huffed. That didn't make it better.

"So what's this about my Grandfather? You always told me he died on a mission. That he was a hero. This says that he's the reason they kicked me out."

"Your Grandfather *was* killed on a mission and it happened a long time ago, nearly forty years. It's history, not important." He said. "What is important is that you get your education. Just because you're no longer at St Gills doesn't mean you can slack off. Nexus Hall said you never returned after lunch. What's going on?"

JoJo wasn't about to be distracted. She didn't want to talk about Nexus Hall.

"Where was the mission to?" she asked.

"What mission?"

"The mission when Grandfather was killed. Where was he going? You've never told me."

JoJo's father turned suddenly stern. "I've never told you because it has nothing to do with you, so forget about it. All I want from you is a promise that tomorrow you will go back to school and that nothing like this will ever happen again."

JoJo ignored his words and persisted. "How can you say that it is nothing to do with me? It's a simple enough question. Why won't you tell me? It's not as though it could have been anywhere like the Blue Planet so–"

"JoJo. Enough," her father bellowed angrily. "There will be no more talk about this, ever. Do you understand? Your Grandfather is a closed subject. And don't give me that look. If I find out you've been snooping there'll be hell to pay, young lady."

Reluctantly, JoJo bit her tongue, but she knew she had hit a nerve.

Her dad wasn't given to sudden bursts of annoyance without good reason. Could her glib comment have actually been close to the mark she wondered? Could her Grandfather really been on his way to the Blue Planet when he was killed? She shivered at the thought.

The Blue Planet was infamous on Anilar. Known as 'Earth' by its inhabitants, it was the only planet ever discovered that had subsequently been banned under Admiralty law. SpaceCoyotes were forbidden from travelling there or making any kind of contact with it. The penalty was instant dismissal and being stripped of your SpaceCoyote status. Indeed, merely saying its name in normal conversation usually elicited a reaction very similar to the one her father had just demonstrated.

The details of why the Blue Planet was treated this way were sketchy, like it was a part of Larian history that would much rather be forgotten. It had been seen as a great discovery, that much was clear. A mission had been sent to investigate, but not all of the SpaceCoyotes who left Anilar made it back home. All of this happened forty years ago, around the same time her Grandfather was killed. Coincidence? Strangely, JoJo had never connected the two events before, but suddenly it seemed so blindingly obvious.

She considered pushing a little more, but the look on her father's face suggested it would be futile. Grudgingly, she changed tack.

"But Dad, it's not fair. I'll never get into the academy if I have to stay at Nexus Hall. They're not even allowed to apply until they're sixteen. I can't wait until then."

Her father hesitated, visibly mellowing. He reached into his top pocket and pulled out an envelope. "I was going to wait until your mother was here, but you may as well have this now. It arrived today."

JoJo took the envelope and cheered up immediately. The Admiralty crest shone across the front. This was the letter she had been waiting for.

She ripped it open eagerly and scanned the page.

'Thank you for submitting your application for the Academy

entrance examination. Obviously it is most unusual to receive one from someone so young ... blah, blah, blah, blah.' She read further.

'... exceptional grades...unparralled flying experience ...Therefore we are pleased to offer you a place on the 45th of this month...'

"YES!" She screamed joyously and jumped into her Dad's arms. He hugged her tight and kissed the top of her head.

"Well done. I'm so proud of you."

JoJo was so happy she could have stared at that letter for hours. This was it. Her big chance to get away from Nexus Hall, Lip Smear and St Gills if they didn't want her. Peering over his shoulder, she read the last line again; just to make sure she wasn't dreaming. The forty-fifth. That was soon. Very soon. It didn't give her much time to prepare, and she had so very much to do. Not least was to ignore her father's orders and go snooping. Despite him stating it was a closed subject, if what happened to her Grandfather came back and ruined her chances at the academy, just like it did at St Gills, she would be devastated.

Her father finally let her out of his clinch and looked at his timepiece. "Look, it's too late to go back to school now. Why don't you and I go and celebrate. We can grab some food at the SolarDome."

JoJo nodded smiling. That was her favourite.

"But tomorrow, you're going back to Nexus Hall where you will be staying the whole day, correct?"

JoJo nodded sourly.

"And no more talk of St Gills and your Grandfather," he added, guiding her out of the door.

JoJo was quick to agree, but this time, had her father looked more closely, he may have noticed there was a slight glint of rebellion in her eye.

Chapter 4

Axel F

It took JoJo less than a week to formulate her plan. It was daring and dangerous and hinged entirely on her ability to hack into a series of highly protected, top secret computer files that only six people on the planet had access too. For something so ambitious to work she would of course require help. Fortunately she knew the very person who could provide it.

That person was Axel Marx and, despite the ungodly hour of the morning (the sun had yet to rise), JoJo had just patched a call through to his personal communicator.

He answered on the fifth ring with a tired grunt.

"Axel, it's me. How are you doing?" she whispered excitedly.

"Ugh," came the unintelligible reply. JoJo tutted.

"Axel, it's me, JoJo, wake up."

The mention of her name penetrated his sleep haze like a bucket of cold water over the head. "JoJo. Wow. What do you want? I mean, er, hi, how are you? Great to hear from you, but do you know what time it is?" he garbled.

"Of course I know what time it is. I've been waiting ages to call you, so get your butt into gear you slouch."

JoJo heard the rustle of bedclothes as Axel sat up.

"Only you would call at this time and then tell me off for being asleep, JoJo."

JoJo smiled.

"And I suppose there is no way I dare put this communicator down without hearing what you've got to say is there?" Axel said.

"You had better not," JoJo said firmly.

Axel sighed. "Has anyone ever told you that you're a pain in the rear?"

"Not since yesterday," quipped JoJo, smiling.

She had missed talking to Axel. He was one of her best friends from St Gills. He wasn't her boyfriend or anything (although she had been told by more than one person that he wished he was) he was just someone who enjoyed talking about plasma injection engines and the differential thrust of Tutulium particles when subjected to cosmic heat radiation, and not boring war games. The fact that he happened to be a boy was a mere accident of genetics.

"So what do you want then?" Axel asked, coming around a little, "need some help with your stellar differential calculations do you?"

"As if," scoffed JoJo. "Maybe if I was still in a pushchair sucking a dummy. No, I need a favour. I want you to meet me tonight at St Gills in the old HoverBike hanger, after your lessons are over?"

"What for,"

"Sorry, no details over the communicator. Just say you'll meet me, Axel. Please"

"Well … I don't know if I can, I've got a SkyRider competition to practice for and …"

His voice tailed off. JoJo knew what was happening. This was always the way things went between the two of them. Axel would play hard to get, JoJo would call his bluff, and then Axel would cave in. JoJo smiled, ready to play her part.

"So you can't meet me?" she said.

"I'm just not sure…"

"Fine then," she huffed. "Don't bother. I'm sure I can find someone else who will be only too glad to. See you later Axel,"

Her finger hovered over the 'disconnect' button.

Sure enough, Axel said, "No, wait. Hang on. I didn't say I wouldn't come, did I? I suppose, for you, I could practice later."

15

"So you will be there?" urged JoJo.

Axel let out a deep breath. "Yeah, I'll meet you. Now can I go back to sleep."

"If you must. I'll see you later then. Don't be late."

"Oh don't worry, I wouldn't dare," concluded Axel.

JoJo flipped the communicator shut, suddenly buzzing. This was it. She could feel it. With Axel on board things were definitely looking up.

St Gills. South side storage area. HoverBike sheds.

JoJo doubted whether, as a recently expelled student, she would be welcome on St Gills' premises, so she was relieved to find the HoverBike sheds empty when she arrived. Tucked away from the main school buildings, they were completely hidden from view, with only a single dirt track leading to and from them. JoJo therefore had a perfect view of anyone approaching. That was of course the very reason she had chosen this place to meet.

She didn't have to wait long for Axel to arrive. He soon came speeding down the track on his AxeBlade SkyRider, billowing clouds of dust in his wake.

He was quite good looking in his own way, she thought as he brought the SkyRider to a halt and jumped off. He had what she guessed people would call a moon face: Round and cherubic. Fat, would be another way to put it, but that was rude and not entirely true. He was slim in every other place; his bones just hadn't quite grown into his head yet.

One thing Axel definitely was though was extremely well connected. His father was Adavan Marx, one of the six men of the Admiralty who ruled the planet of Anilar. This made Axel just about as close to royalty as a person could get. It also meant that the teachers at St Gills cut him a lot of slack because if you believed the stories, Adavan Marx was not a man to make an enemy of. If he got caught with JoJo they would almost certainly go easy on him.

"Hey, Axel," she said, jumping down from her elevated spying position as he strode through the entrance, SkyRider tucked under his arm.

He smiled. "Hey yourself. So come on, let's be knowing what all this cloak and dagger stuff is about."

JoJo smiled her best smile. "I want a favour, a big favour – something that could land you in a lot of trouble."

Axel sighed. "I thought as much, and here I was thinking you were going to ask me on a date because you missed me so much."

"Axel!" exclaimed JoJo, blushing furiously.

"Well, I can hope can't I? Come on then, divulge."

A little flustered, JoJo tried to regain some composure. "First things first. Did you know that St Gill's expelled me?"

Axel tried to look surprised, but he wasn't a good actor.

"You did," cried JoJo, punching him on the shoulder. "Why didn't you tell me?"

"We all thought you knew," Axel pleaded. "We thought that's why you haven't called anyone since you left, because you were embarrassed or something."

JoJo rounded on him. "Embarrassed? Hardly. Nobody even bothered to tell me I was expelled. They just packed me off to Nexus Hall without so much as a 'goodbye'. I only just found out."

Axel shook his head. "Wow, I'm sorry JoJo. Really I am. If I'd have known … I can't believe they did it to you. You hear rumours about people getting thrown out for not doing well in their tests, but you, you were the cleverest in the year."

JoJo leant back against a HoverBike.

"So why did you? Get expelled I mean," asked Axel.

JoJo shrugged. "I don't know that's why you're here. I want you to find out for me."

"Me, how?"

JoJo paused. This was going to be the difficult bit. "What do you know about the Blue Planet, Axel?" she asked.

Axel went white. "Okay, that's it. I'm outta here."

He turned and dropped his SkyRider to the ground where it hovered, waiting for him to jump aboard.

"No, wait, don't go," JoJo cried, grabbing him by the shoulder. "I need you to get me into the Admiralty Archives so I can see what's in there about the Blue Planet."

Axel spun round, eyes wide. "Oh is that all, well why didn't you say? Are – You – IN – SANE," he roared. "Do you have any idea what you're asking?"

"Well I did say it could get you into trouble."

Axel couldn't speak, so flabbergasted was he by her outrageous request, but JoJo was unrepentant.

"You only have to get me in, I'll do the rest," she urged.

Axel nearly swore. "JoJo, the Admiralty Archives are the most highly guarded computer vaults ever designed. You can't just open them up. There are passwords, key-codes, encrypted channels, hacker filters and cipher texts. Even if you could get through those, which you can't, you would only have about a minute before it traced your computer right back to you. So what use would it be? Do you have any idea how big the whole thing is? The entire history of Anilar is in those archives for goodness sake. You'd be locked up before you even read the front page. It's impossible, forget it."

"You're not keen then," said JoJo meekly.

"I'll say it again. You are insane. And I'm going."

Axel balanced one foot on the SkyRider.

"Axel please," begged JoJo desperately. "I don't know where else to go. I've been expelled from a school I love and sent to a place where all the kids think I'm a freak because I bother to work. They've even stopped me flying. My life is going down the toilet and all I know is that something happened on the Blue Planet forty years ago that's messing up my life now."

Axel looked at JoJo's pleading expression, but had little sympathy. "I'm sorry, I'm not helping you with your paranoid delusions. I can't. I won't. It's too dangerous. The whole world is not out to get you,

JoJo."

He kicked off the ground and with barely a wisp of dust his SkyRider soared out of the Hanger.

JoJo watched him go and then slumped to the ground, her head disconsolately buried in her hands.

Plan A, up in smoke.

CHAPTER 5

THE GAME

SpaceCoyote Gravitational Destabilisation Facility
The day of her Academy exam arrived without a single word from Axel. In the three weeks since their disastrous meeting at the HoverBike sheds, JoJo had made no progress whatsoever on finding out anything about the Blue Planet or her Grandfather, just as he had said she wouldn't. She hated it when someone else was right.

Now it was too late. All she could do was try her hardest to pass the exam and pray that an old prejudice would not rear its ugly head and prevent her from joining.

Right now though, thoughts of the Blue Planet were far from her mind. She was too busy trying to keep her lunch where it belonged, in her stomach.

She was sitting on the very tip of a metal platform little wider than a car tire. Not very frightening you may think until you know that below her was a two hundred and fifty metre drop, with nothing but a solid stone floor to break her fall. More likely, thought JoJo, any fall would break her – into a zillion pieces.

Her entire body was quivering, and not because she was cold, but because she was terrified.

A stark voice in her ear suddenly grabbed her attention.

"The exercise will begin in thirty seconds. Please take your starting position."

Thirty seconds! JoJo doubted she would be ready for this in thirty years.

This was the final test of a punishing day. She was tired, hungry and aching in places that she didn't even know she had. But, she was still standing.

There were now only ten candidates left and it was all going to come down to this. So far, she and the other applicants had been tested individually. Now, for the first time, JoJo could see who she was up against. Except she couldn't, because, quite apart from the fact that they were all wearing oxygen re-breather helmets with blacked out Plasma display visors, JoJo was simply too afraid to look around. All she had been told was that they were all male and aged between sixteen and seventeen.

The ten of them had been split into two groups of five. JoJo was in the Amber team. They had been pitted against the Jade team.

Separated by ten metres each, her four team-mates were off to her left, perched equally precariously on their own tiny platforms. She wondered if they were as petrified as her. She hoped so, but doubted it.

The examiners had described this test as 'a simple search and rescue simulation'. Huh! When all this was over, JoJo would have to congratulate them on their sense of humour.

Each team had to pretend they had landed on an unfamiliar planet in an unfriendly environment and had lost a vital piece of equipment. They had two hours to find it and return it, undamaged, to the examiners booth.

What the examiners had failed to describe to JoJo and the other nine hopefuls was the sheer hostility of the search environment. They would have no oxygen (hence the re-breathers), no motorized transport and the gravity in the building would be in constant flux, which meant GraviBibs were compulsory so they didn't float off into the air, or alternatively, slam into the ground bearing the weight of a small house of their shoulders. Neither did the examiners mention, (it must have slipped their minds), that the fifteen square miles of search terrain would be made up of mud encrusted swamps, raging ochre rivers, thick forest and, oh yes, an area affectionately known as 'dead man's plummet', which was what they were currently overlooking.

Dead man's plummet was a mile wide crater. At its deepest it touched half a mile. All (!!??) JoJo and her team had to do was get to the other side so their search could begin. To do this they had to use their GraviBib and a small set of boosters attached to their boots to '*fly*' across. One small miscalculation and they could end up miles out of their way.

With trembling hands, JoJo gripped the sides of her platform and rose slowly to her feet. Strong gravitational winds threatened to unbalance her as her head swam with vertigo. Whose mad idea was this anyway? Inside her helmet, her breathing was getting shallower and faster, her heart threatening to beat its way out of her chest.

She had to calm down or she wasn't going to be able to make the jump. (As it turned out, this needn't have worried her).

"*Fifteen seconds,*" said the voice in her ear.

She glanced anxiously across at her team-mates, their glowing amber chest bands the only light in the pitch darkness. The one on the far left, Amber One, had been nominated leader. He gave them all the thumbs up. JoJo flipped her hand out, before quickly returning it to her side. That was quite enough movement thank you.

"*Five seconds.*"

"Ohmygod, ohmygod, ohmygod," she chanted to herself, bending her chattering knees, poised to jump.

"*Candidates... You may go.*"

In the space of a heartbeat, the platform shot back from under JoJo's feet. She wasn't ready and fell like a stone. As the breath left her body and the black world whistled by, she realized they had misnamed this crater. It should have been called 'dead girl's plummet', because she was a girl, she was plummeting and she was surely going to die.

Her arms and legs flailed as panic enveloped her. Miraculously, her hand caught the stabilize button in the centre of her GraviBib. Small winglets blossomed out from under her arms, attaching themselves to the main jacket and her speed quickly slowed. Seconds later, the bib equalized her pressure and she came to a genteel, mid air stop.

Breathing faster than an asthmatic dog and suspended in complete darkness, she tried to gain some kind of bearing. Her visor display told her that she had fallen one hundred and ninety metres. She gasped. Another few seconds and she would have become a very permanent stain on the floor.

With more hope than expectation, she glanced up and around for her team-mates. There was no one. She knew she had been the only one unprepared for the platform's sudden disappearance. She felt so stupid.

She verbally instructed her visor to give her a three dimensional compass. It told her that at the moment she was floating horizontally. It was news to her. In such complete blackness, up, down, left and right meant nothing. Without the compass she could float around here aimlessly for a year and still not find her way to the top. She pushed her toes down firing the booster boots and swung herself backwards until her artificial horizon came level with her nose. Then she began her long ascent cursing herself all the way.

It took fifteen precious minutes to reach the rim of the crater. There, waiting for her were three of her team-mates. Even with their faces covered, she could tell from their demeanour that they were not happy.

"Finally the young grub decides to join us," sneered Amber One, hands on hips.

"Sorry," JoJo said feebly as he grabbed her hand and dragged her roughly onto the rocky surface.

"There's no time to be sorry," he barked gruffly. "We've lost precious time *and* Amber three. He was last seen heading eastwards, completely out of control. They've scratched him from the simulation, so there are only four of us now and you barely made it. Another minute and they would have scratched you too. If you ask me, it would have been better for us if they had."

His words hit JoJo like a hammer. She hated the thought of being the weak link, the one that could possibly let everybody down, so she dusted herself off and sounding more confident than she felt, said. "So what are we waiting for? Let's go."

Amber One huffed and stormed off followed closely by the other three. JoJo shrugged. It seemed she was on her own after all. Still, what else was new?

CHAPTER 6
RIVER DEEP, MOUNTAIN HIGH

Forty minutes later they were close to the rescue site. It had been tough going with the swamps proving the trickiest to negotiate. Amber Two had almost been sucked under when a crust of dried mud cracked under his feet. Just in time they had managed to pull him free, but his GraviBib had been damaged and he was now struggling to keep his feet on the ground. It was slowing them down and Amber One, whose tolerance was growing very thin, especially with JoJo who seemed to taking the blame for the whole thing, was berating him with every clumsy step.

From the swamps, their guidance computers had led them into a dense forest. Here, the gravity was noticeably lighter and had allowed huge towering plants, thick with vines and moss to rise like skyscrapers above them. Each one however seemed to possess some vile attribute bent on slowing them down. JoJo had never seen anything like it. Some dripped corrosive acid from their petals, whilst others had ten feet long spikes running up their stems. One (a huge brown thing with red flowers the size of dustbin lids), emitted a sap so sticky it was actually gluing pieces of their equipment together every time they touched one. Nevertheless, they were close to their prize, and even better, there was no sign of the Jade team anywhere.

Amber One stopped and held his hand up. "It's just beyond these bushes," he said. JoJo and the others clambered through the thorny, blue vegetation. Being the leanest, JoJo made it to the other side first. As she hacked away the final branch, she stopped dead and stepped back. The others bumped into her.

"What is it now, Grub?" growled Amber One.

JoJo stepped aside so he could see for himself.

They had emerged onto a ledge of purple slate-like rock that fell away vertically into a raging rust-coloured river. JoJo's stomach turned over as she watched the churning, crashing torrent. The word 'rapids' did not even begin to describe its immense ferocity.

"Don't tell me we have to go in there," said JoJo desperately.

Amber One pushed passed her. "What's the matter, Grub? Scared of getting wet are we?"

He peered over the ledge and smirked.

"Looks like it's your lucky day, it's down there, in that hole."

He pointed to tiny recess half way down the rock face in which there appeared to be a small glowing cube. "One of us is going to have to rappel down and get it."

He turned to JoJo and prodded his gloved finger into her chest. "You're the smallest and lightest, you can go. Maybe you can actually be of some use to us finally."

JoJo went white and stared hesitantly over the brink. Amber One sensed her apprehension. "What's the matter?" he mocked. "Scared? Wishing you'd stayed at home with your dollies? Because if you want to leave, be my guest. Believe me, you won't be missed."

He laughed, and the others joined in.

"I've never rappelled down anything before, that's all" she said worriedly.

Amber One snorted loudly. "Then you're going have to learn quickly aren't you, Grub? Either that or you'll be going for a swim."

JoJo shot him a stare. She didn't particularly want to shimmy fifty feet down a sheer rock face, but she certainly wasn't scared and she was getting quite sick of Amber One's constant macho attitude and being called Grub all the time.

Bunch of idiots, she thought. *I'll show them what they can do with their dollies.*

She turned and marched past Amber One, snatching a length of rope from his belt. Throwing one end to Amber Four she said. "Secure that to the tree, bonehead. You might like standing here listening to the sound of his voice, but it's giving me a headache and wasting our time."

As Amber Four caught the rope, he looked to Amber One, who nodded. Moments later, the rope was secured to the tree and JoJo's jacket and she was over the edge, heading towards the recess.

The rock face was like glass. There were no footholds to speak of and the lower she got, the more spray washed over her from the roaring river below. That was okay apart from when the water hit bare skin. Then it stung like having vinegar poured into an open cut. And all the while, Amber One kept up a constant nagging commentary on her progress.

"Step left. Swing. Now down, DOWN! Faster, come on. Watch out for that branch, Grub."

Her ears were humming with his droning voice. When she got back up she might just accidentally stick him to one of those blasted trees and leave him there.

Three more slippery steps and JoJo felt her right boot enter the recess. Relief flooded through her.

She let out another metre of rope until she was face to face with it – a small glowing cube of golden light. For all they had been through to get here, she had expected something a little more dramatic, none-the-less, they had at least beaten the Jade team to it.

Wasting no time, she took it in her hand.

"I've got it," she yelled. "Pull me up."

A sharp tug on her midriff followed, and slowly she began to rise.

She leaned back and let them do all the work. There was little she could do to help anyway with the rock face as slippery as a sheet of ice.

Inch by inch she rose, marveling at her strange surroundings as she went. To think that such a wondrous place had been built indoors. Everything from the fake sun and skyline to the mountains, swamps, forests and rivers had been artificially designed for its role in training the SpaceCoyotes. There was even a lake with an underwater section somewhere in here. Thankfully, JoJo had been spared that.

"Heads up, Grub," yelled Amber One.

JoJo looked up and glared angrily at the faceless visor that was staring down at her. Between gritted teeth she said, "Will you *please* quit calling me Grub!"

"Stop whining and pass me up the cube."

JoJo dutifully handed it over.

Amber One looked it over carefully. JoJo tugged impatiently on the rope.

"Hey, dung breath. What are you staring at it for? I'm dangling here, in case you hadn't noticed."

"Keep your mask on," he said tossing the cube to another teammate. "Just checking you hadn't damaged it on your way up."

"Just get on with it," she growled, offering her hand.

He leaned over. "Certainly, Grub. Here."

JoJo grabbed his outstretched arm and let go of the rope, but Amber One made no attempt to drag her onto the ledge. Instead he glanced over his shoulder to one of the others, "Free the rope. I've got her," he said.

"What?" squealed JoJo anxiously. "Why are you telling him to free the rope? Just get me up from here will you."

"No, I don't think I will," said Amber One, chillingly. "You see I'm taking an executive decision for the good of my team. I'm letting you go, Grub."

The rope made a whipping sound as it snaked past her head, coiling onto the rocks far below. JoJo made that breathy kind of laugh when you think something terrible is about to happen but you're not quite sure whether it's a joke or not.

Amber One cocked his head on one side. "You think this is funny

28

do you?" he said. "I certainly wouldn't be laughing if I was in your position right now. It doesn't look good does it?"

JoJo's fingers instinctively tightened around Amber One's wrist. As insane as it was, she realized Amber One was not fooling around. He was serious. She grasped at the rock with her free hand whilst scrabbling frenetically with her feet for some kind of purchase, but she may as well have been trying to walk up a wall of oiled marble.

She looked down, terrified. Amber One was right. It didn't look good. The fall. The rocks. The raging torrent of stinging water. *The rocks.* Surely he wouldn't be so stupid as to let her go. She could die. He must know that.

"Amber One, please," she pleaded desperately. "I know you don't like me because I'm a girl, but come on – this is crazy."

Amber One tutted derisorily.

"It is not because you are a girl that I don't like you, JoJo. Yes, I know who you are. We all know who you are. It's because you're his granddaughter. The betrayer. The murderer, and the only crazy thing around here is that they would ever consider *you* to be SpaceCoyote material."

He loosened his grip momentarily and JoJo dropped just a few inches. Her knees banged hard on the rock. Pain shot up her legs. If he was trying to frighten her, it was definitely working.

JoJo pleaded. "Look, I don't know what you are talking about. My Grandfather died a hero forty years ago. Now PULL ME UP."

"A hero?" Amber One yelled. "How dare you even say that?"

Amber One twisted his arm in such a way that JoJo's grip was torn from his wrist. She yelped as she was left totally at his mercy. The question was, did he have any?

"Tell me, JoJo. Can you can swim?" he said.

And he let go.

JoJo screamed as she fell from his grasp and tumbled backwards through the air. She hit the water hard like an upturned beetle and sank like a brick.

Unbelievably she had plunged into a deep-water eddy, missing the jagged rocks by centimetres. It was a miracle. Hitting just one would have smashed her spine as if it was made of cinder.

Beneath the raging dark river, JoJo was paralysed with fear. It's unerring strength lifted her off her backside and whipped her helplessly into the current. Mercifully, her visor knew what to do even if she did not, automatically forming a seal around her neck, preventing any water getting in.

Her hands and body grazed painfully along the river bed, smashing into stones and rocks as long, straggly plants, bent horizontal by the flow of water, whipped at her face. She made a grab at the slippery grey strands but she was moving far too fast. Even when she did manage to snare one, its anchoring roots snapped free.

The water was stinging horribly too. It was as though she'd been dropped in tank full of nettles. Even her suit was being penetrated. Every inch of her skin felt like it was being nipped. It was agony.

Suddenly the noise and power of the river increased and she was flipped head-over-heels over what must have been a small waterfall. As she splashed down into the water once more, she was consumed by a whirlpool of currents. Round and round she went. She was as helpless as a rag doll in the waters turbulent grip. Finally, JoJo was spat out six feet into the air landing once more with a heavy splash! But it was just as she hit the water that JoJo spotted a potential lifeline a little way down the winding river.

The sight of it invigorated her. Suddenly remembering her survival skills, she tucked her legs up to her chin and made herself into a ball. This was the best shape to protect her face, hands and legs as she bounced off the river bed.

She counted the seconds until finally, her speed began to pick up once again. Adrenaline pumped. This was it. She braced herself for what was to come.

The waterfalls edge came faster than last time. Over she went, tensing for what could be a hard impact. She slammed down and the whirlpool took control, and then …

… Just like last time, the water threw her into the air as if it were a giant mouth that had swallowed her whole and didn't like the way she tasted.

Wasting not a second, JoJo uncurled like a butterfly emerging from its chrysalis, slammed down the artificial pressure on her GraviBib so that she was no longer anchored to the ground, and pushed her toes forward, praying that the boosters in her boots would work despite being waterlogged.

They did, the winglets expanded and, astonishingly, she soared into the sky. Up and away from the orange, stinging river.

Her neck seals retracted and her suit dried in an instant. Mercifully as the water evaporated, the stinging went with it.

As soon as she was over more solid ground, she brought herself to a stop and savoured the relief. Somehow, against the odds she had survived. Now all she had to do was find her way back to the examiners' booth and finish this hellish exercise.

Searching the alien scape for a recognizable landmark, she saw none. Not the forests, nor the swamps. Anger welled up inside her as she realised just how far the river had taken her out of her way. That left her with only one option. Reluctantly she ordered her visor computer to do an emergency calculation of the quickest route home. It would lose her a lot of marks, she knew. Using the emergency maps was technically against the rules, but then JoJo was sure that trying to kill your team-mate was, as well, so she didn't give a damn. Only one thing mattered now. By whatever means, she was going to finish this game.

* * *

She arrived at the examiners' booth utterly exhausted and one hour late. Her booster boots had given up the ghost just fifteen minutes into her journey and she had pitched down on the wrong side of a craggy hill, still miles from home. The walk proved arduous especially when she found the other side of the hill was home to thousands of tenticular snakes. So named, according to her visor display, because of their ability to snare prey (and ankles as JoJo found out) with long tentacles attached to their heads.

At least though she had made it without having to be rescued. Of course she knew that she was sure to have been scratched, but winning was no longer important. The satisfaction of finishing, that was what she wanted, and that was what she had achieved.

There was only one solitary figure waiting for her when she arrived. She thought he may have been smiling at her as he left the booth to meet her. Or maybe he was grimacing. To be honest she hardly cared. Fatigue had finally won. She could barely stand. In fact, as her knees hit the ground, she realized that she couldn't stand. As the examiner rushed to her aid, and without a care for what may happen next, JoJo lay calmly on the floor and passed out.

CHAPTER 7

K.I.S.S.I.N.G

It was three days later. JoJo was recovering in an Admiralty hospital. It turned out that the river had had more of an adverse effect on her than she had realized at the time. She'd fractured a rib on the left side, but that had been healed with a bone binder – no problem. The rash however was proving trickier to cure. Toxins in the water had reacted badly with her skin, resulting in her entire body erupting in deep, purple welts. The medics assured her it wasn't too serious or permanent, but that didn't help much when you looked like an off- colour Dalmatian.

Today was the first day she was to be allowed proper visitors. Before that, she had been kept isolated in case the rash was infectious. It seemed it wasn't. Just very embarrassing.

Of course her mother, father and brother had been, but they had stayed behind a glass window and what with her room being very nearly soundproof, conversation had been limited to hand gestures and miming. There was only so much of that you could do before you started feeling ridiculous.

Now on day three, she was bored and frustrated. The least she had expected was a visit from someone at the SpaceCoyote Academy. She wanted answers. People weren't supposed to nearly die during a try out. No one had even asked her what had happened yet, or had the decency to apologize for it. They'd just brought here and left her, as if being thrown off a cliff was something that happened everyday. Well it didn't, not in JoJo's life anyway.

When her first visitor arrived shortly after breakfast, she had already worked herself into quite a temper and was more than ready to give whoever came through the frosted glass doors both barrels of her tongue. However, she had not expected it to be a rather awkward and guilty looking Axel Marx. Her anger dissipated immediately when she saw him.

"Axel, get in here," she urged, sitting up straight in bed.

Axel looked unsure but stepped in timorously, the doors sliding shut behind him.

"I can't stay long," he muttered looking at the floor. "I shouldn't really be here at all, but I had to know that you were alri- Jeez, you look awful, JoJo," he said finally facing her.

JoJo sagged. "Oh well thank you very much Axel. You still know how to smooth talk the girls then, I see."

"Sorry, I just wasn't expecting so many blotches. They said you had a bit of a rash that was all. But that's ridiculous."

He leaned in staring hard.

"Okay, Axel. I'm ghastly, you've made your point."

"Look at the size of some of those..."

"AXEL. I get it," JoJo snapped, pushing him away. "Gosh, anyone would think you'd never seen a hideously spotty girl before."

"Do they hurt?"

"Not as much as you're going to if you don't stop staring."

Axel reluctantly backed away.

"They itch a little sometimes, but nothing spectacular. So come on, tell me what's been happening and why you shouldn't be here?"

Axel's eyes hit the floor tiles once more. "Because of what happened of course," he said

JoJo looked at him puzzled.

"You do know what happened to you, don't you?" asked Axel

"If you mean, do I know that some moron dropped me into a poisonous river just for the hell of it – then yes, I do. It's the rash that gives it away funnily enough, but you had nothing to do with it so why shouldn't you see me?"

Axel looked at her quizzically then glanced behind him, furtively checking the door, before he spoke.

"It was to do with me though," he confessed. "You see, it was my brother who did the dropping,"

JoJo's mouth fell open. "Say that again, Axel. Your brother was Amber One?"

Axel nodded, and then spoke quickly like a man confessing his guilt. "It was all my fault. After I left the HoverBike sheds that night, I thought about what you'd said and, even though I still thought you were mad, I asked my Dad about the Blue Planet."

JoJo grimaced.

"I know, I know," said Axel. "I shouldn't have told him but I thought he would be able to put your mind at ease before you did anything stupid like trying to break into the archives."

"He didn't though, did he?" said JoJo knowingly.

Axel shook his head. "No, he went mental. He wanted to know why I was asking. I'm sorry, JoJo but I had to tell him about you. You don't know my Dad when he gets angry. When he finally finished shouting, he grounded me for a week and told me that I could never see you ever again. I think my brother overheard because the next thing, he was asking me all sorts of questions about you."

"Like what?"

Axel glanced at the door again.

"He wanted to know where you lived and how I knew you. I didn't tell him anything about you wanting to get into the Archives, honest. He knew that you were trying out for the academy though. I suppose Dad told him. Anyway, he said that St Gills had had the right idea when they expelled you, that a person like you shouldn't be allowed in the Academy and he was going to make sure you didn't get in. I thought he was just bluffing, he's an idiot most of the time."

"All of the time if you ask me," said JoJo, trying to take it all in.

Axel frowned. "I didn't think he'd go that far, JoJo. You do believe me don't you?"

JoJo didn't know what to believe. "I just want to know why everybody has got it in for me – that's all. It's not too much to ask is it?"

Silence descended between the two of them for a moment, then Axel produced a small bundle of papers from his jacket pocket.

"Here," he said, handing them to JoJo. "Memorise them and then destroy them. And if you get found out, you didn't get them from me."

JoJo took the papers cautiously. The first page was full of numbers in ten digit combinations. A bead of excitement caught in her chest. She flipped to another page. This had times written down the left hand side. Next to each was written a single word. *Passwords.*

"Are these what I think they are?" she asked.

"I couldn't possibly say. I don't see anything," replied Axel flatly.

JoJo understood. He couldn't be linked with them. "Fine," She began, "so if I were to accidentally type the numbers that *aren't* on the paper that *I haven't* got, into my computer, where would it take me?"

Axel shrugged. "If someone were to do that, which they can't of course because there is nothing there, then I would imagine they would end up in, say, the Admiralty Archives."

A smile lit JoJo's face. These were the passwords and keycodes she had asked him for. He had got them for her after all.

"Why?" she said simply. "You told me I was insane."

"I also thought you were paranoid and I was wrong about that too. The Academy is blaming you, you know. My brother told them that is was you who insisted on going down the rock face and that he did everything he could to get you up, but your inexperience made you panic and fall. The rest of the team backed him up and the Academy believed them."

"That's not true. They're lying," snapped JoJo angrily.

"I know. My brother told me what really happened. I guess he thought I'd find it funny. I pretended I did, so he would leave me alone, but I was so angry I went into Dad's computer system and copied them for you. I guess I owe you an apology. I was wrong, it seems the whole world is out to get you after all."

JoJo leaned forward and kissed him on the cheek. "Thank you," she said.

Axel blushed. "You made it onto all the news stations by the way, but I'm afraid they haven't been very kind."

JoJo cringed. She could imagine the field day they had. The youngest ever applicant to be offered a place at the exam turns out to be so dumb that she nearly kills herself. If there is anything reporters love more than a bad luck story, it's a very bad luck story.

"The worst part though," groaned Axel, "Is that my brother got in and you didn't. He starts next term."

JoJo's face dropped. She knew that her chances had been blown the moment she became separated from her teammates, but for him to be accepted! The injustice of it struck a raw nerve. Axel's brother didn't deserve to be a SpaceCoyote. If anything he should be dragged before the Admiralty for what he had done to her, but she was fast learning that people didn't always get what they deserved in life. Axel's brother had probably already been accepted before he turned up that day simply because of who his father was. She could see it in Axel's eyes that knew as much too.

"They're going to let you in the SpaceCubs School though," said Axel, trying to sound upbeat. JoJo flashed him a stare that would have soldered steel.

"The SpaceCubs," she sneered, "Are for kids who still wipe snot on their sleeves."

"At least they'll let you fly, and it's a way into the Academy. That has got to be something."

JoJo sank back onto her bed sulking.

Axel looked at his timer. "Look, I've got to go. Dad's still in a mood. I don't want to give him an excuse to ground me again." He turned to leave. As he reached the door, he said, "Just one more thing."

"What," JoJo huffed.

"If, by some miracle, those non-existent numbers on that non-existent paper, prove useful, you should know there's one code you'll have to get through by yourself. It's a hundred digits long and changes every hour. They call it the Kiss code because if you try and break in, it sends a silicon charge into your computer, and *wham*! You can kiss all your files goodbye."

"Great," quipped JoJo.

"If anyone can do it, you can," Axel encouraged as he headed for the door.

JoJo smiled, flattered by his confidence in her. She hoped it was well placed.

Before he hit the button to open the door, Axel turned. "You will be careful won't you?" he said seriously? "I'm helping you because I don't think it's right what's happened, not because I agree with what you're doing. The Blue Planet is a dangerous place, you shouldn't be messing with it."

JoJo smiled reassuringly. It was nice that he was concerned. He seemed to be the only one who was, but it wasn't going to stop her.

As the door swished closed behind Axel, JoJo gripped her fingers tightly around the bunch of papers and squeezed them protectively to her chest. *Plan A,* she thought. *Back on again.*

CHAPTER 8
THE END OF THE BEGINNING

A week later, JoJo was home, sitting in her bedroom hunched over the blue glow of her plasma filtron computer. Numbers fizzled and whirled like a thousand fly's were inside her screen trying to get out. This was 'Salvage' in action.

JoJo had been working on various code-breaker programs long before she ever came up with the idea of breaking into the Admiralty Archives. It was one of her pet projects. Salvage was the pinnacle. It crunched number and letter combinations at a rate of one million a second and could decipher the most randomly attributed passwords. So far however, even it was struggling against the Archives' many defenses. As far as JoJo could tell, there were ten gates she had to break down in order to access the main database. Axel's codes had got her through five. The rest, including the infamous 'kiss' code were under attack from Salvage, but they were proving more than a match.

She absentmindedly scratched at one of the welts on her arm. Thankfully, they were now down to the size of pinpricks, but she was still off school until they had disappeared completely. JoJo didn't mind. It gave her time to concentrate on the Archives.

A loud 'ding' snapped her attention to the screen. The words '*Gate number 6. Access granted*' was flashing in yellow text. JoJo's heart began to flutter, just a little. The numbers rolled again and almost immediately the words, '*Gate number 7, Access granted*' followed. Then gates eight and nine fell in quick succession.

"My God!" she exclaimed, "It's working."

Just one more to go, she thought. *Just one.* Then the numbers stopped rolling and the screen went blank. JoJo's heart sank.

"Damn it! Don't block me now."

She waited, her fingers poised hesitantly over the keypad, wondering if she had missed something important. Praying that she wasn't about to fall foul of yet another hidden barrier.

Finally, the words she had been waiting for appeared letter by letter across the top of the screen.

'Admiralty archive. Top secret. Access to authorized personnel only.'

Below that it said.

'Press any key to enter the database.'

Excitement flushed through her body like a tidal wave. She was in!

"Ohmygod," She said, taut with anticipation.

She typed furiously. Screen after screen popped up like flash cards, each one brimming with information.

The database was colossal, its treasures innumerable, but JoJo only had a limited time to get what she wanted. Axel's notes had proved invaluable detailing the many booby-traps and safeguards that were in place. She had used the information to design a sophisticated delay bug which would give her precious time, but would not hold them back forever. If she triggered any of the traps, the Admiralty would know precisely who she was and what she had been looking at. That could not be allowed to happen.

With no time to stop and read any of the files, she downloaded everything directly to a secret section on her Platitude Light Drive™. She could sort through them all later.

As the files, 'Benign mould life forms of Kessel' (Kessel being an extremely dull planet just a couple of light years away) and 'Catalogue of Sub-Sonic Quasons in the Unula Galaxy' were swallowed by the Light Drive's infinite storage, a timer appeared in the bottom left hand corner of the screen counting down from thirty, in one-second intervals. JoJo frowned. The delay timer had been activated. That meant she was half a minute away from being discovered, and she still hadn't got what she came for.

She urged her fingers to move faster on the keyboard. "Come on, come on!"

Twenty-five, twenty-four. "Wait! There."

Suddenly she saw it! The words, 'Blue Planet – Highly Confidential' sprung up on the screen. She clicked eagerly, but was stopped in her tracks. A flashing cursor infuriatingly informed her that yet another password was required to access these files. It took five costly seconds to find the correct letter and number combination. She supposed it was better than six.

Hundreds of pages blazed into view and were copied immediately to her Light Drive. Her excitement was immense, tempered only by her desperate wish for it all to go more quickly.

Finally she had them all. Now to get out.

The clock was ticking ... Ten, nine, eight.

"Go! Go! Go!" This was going to be close. Sweat poured from her brow.

Five, Four, three ...

She wasn't going to make it. She wasn't going to make it!

Two, one ...

She slammed a button and saw the word 'Goodbye' appear and then fade from the screen as the clock ticked to zero.

She slumped back, breathing heavily. That was too close. She looked at her hands. They were shaking. But it was worth it. There, trapped inside the Light Drive's optical fibres, were the answers she had been searching for. No longer would the Blue Planet keep its secrets from her. She had finally reached the beginning of the end.

Unfortunately, as it turned out, JoJo was quite mistaken on that point. She had not in fact reached the beginning of the end, rather, it was the end of the beginning.

CHAPTER 9

BREAKING THE LAW

JoJo's bedroom. Two years later. Present Day.

That was then. This is now.

Two years had passed. Two years of meticulous planning and preparation, all for tonight.

JoJo could never have imagined that when she sat down that night to read those first words from the Blue Planet files, she would have ended up here, about to …

The sound of her bedroom door swishing open made her start. Her brother, 2B entered nervously chewing the cuff of his shirt. She smiled at him. He did not smile back.

"Are you all right?" she asked gently.

2B nodded but without any real conviction. He looked fragile and as nervous as a kitten. She supposed she could not blame him. What she was asking him to do was at best illegal, at worst, life threatening, but there was no other way. The archives had given her so much, but ultimately left her with many more questions, the answers to which lay not in any computer system. So, tonight, they would be leaving the safety of Anilar and flying to the other side of the galaxy. Their destination, the Blue Planet.

She had of course fought with her conscience over whether taking 2B was the right thing to do. He was young and inexperienced. He had never even flown before, but in the end, this was not something she could to do alone and it was one of those situations when only family would do.

Of course, convincing him to fly to the most dangerous planet in the galaxy was not an easy sell, especially when, for his own protection, she couldn't divulge the real reason for going. Indeed, at one point so adamant was he that he was not going, he threatened to tell all to their parents. Not one to give up easily, JoJo resorted to her ace in the pack. It was called music.

She found it quite by accident, hidden deep in the Admiralty archives next to the words: '**Blue Planet audio files. Banned! Not to be played under any circumstances**'.

Obviously JoJo played them. What else could she do?

What she heard blew her mind. There was nothing even remotely like it on Anilar, and for the life of her, once she heard it, she could not understand why. It was fun, it was energetic, it was liberating!

The songs did things to her that she couldn't believe. Some made her cry, some touched her heart and some made her want to jump up and down and spin wildly round the room. The more she listened, the more she was hooked.

Alongside the audio files she found the blueprints for the construction of some device called a Photo Radio Receiver. Realising that this was the means by which the music had been collected, she set about building one. Then she let 2B in on the secret.

The effect was nothing short of staggering. Watching him throw himself around the room in total abandon was fantastic, if not a little disturbing. More importantly though, she knew she had him.

Rigging the receiver to cut out after just fifteen short minutes, JoJo cleverly ensured 2B was always left wanting more – much more. So much more in fact that he eventually agreed to accompany her to the Blue Planet on the pretence that she would collect as much music as he wanted once they settled into orbit. Sure it was manipulative, but at least if he was with her, he could not be at home telling people where she was.

"Come and sit down," she said, gesturing to the bed. "We can go through it all again if you want. We really can't afford any catastrophes, you know. It can't be like the time we tried to rescue that pet Teliping of yours, Erik was it, from Limpit Falls. I know you couldn't have predicted that thunderstorm, but being swept twenty miles down a river with no transport to get back, wasn't funny. So, if you have any problems, now is the time to say."

2B spat out the cuff. "I want to go, I just …" He sighed unsurely. "Just go through it, once more."

JoJo sat down beside him and flipped her hair off her shoulder. "Right, listen. Here's what's going to happen. To get to the Blue Planet and back again, we need two days. We can't afford to just disappear like last time, because Mum and Dad will go mental and send out the search parties. So, that's where the holotropes come in. They are going to take our places."

She showed him the holotropes abridged itinerary on her PlasmaTab.

"As you can see, yours will be going to school as usual, then over to Dom's house, where you'll be staying the night and playing at being intergalactic warriors or whatever it is that you boys do.

"While that's happening, my holotrope will be with Helix at a slumber party."

2B rolled his eyes.

"I know! But Mum bought it. On day two, Dom and Helix will take us, well them," she pointed at her sleeping holotrope, "to the Cyber Games Station, where you'll play on the space simulators and Helix can look at boys all afternoon. Of course, we'll be in full view of everyone, so no one will suspect that we're missing. Then we'll have tea at the SolarDome and head back home in time for bed."

2B looked unsure. "And you're sure nothing can stop them once they are turned on."

"Not a thing. Trust me."

"Promise on your flying license."

JoJo frowned. "All right, I admit. There is a small chance of a problem around heat, particularly fire, but it's negligible. For some reason it affects the holosphere – that's the space around them – and can, in a few cases, send them fuzzy."

"How fuzzy?" asked 2B nervously.

"Oh, hardly at all, really."

It was a lie. In fact, holotropes were notorious for getting caught out at parties such as bonfires, where they began to resemble walking shag pile carpets.

"And when we get there, we won't be landing will we? Because I'm not going if you are going to land."

JoJo tapped her first two fingers against her heart, "SpaceCub's honour."

"You hate being in the SpaceCubs," said 2B.

"Yeah, but I'm not lying, 2B. We're only going into orbit, I promise."

This time she really wasn't lying. JoJo was many things, but suicidal wasn't one of them. The Blue Planet hadn't been banned by the Admiralty for nothing. It was a treacherous and murderous place. If she hadn't quite believed it before, five minutes reading the archives certainly confirmed it. Every aspect of her plan had therefore been specifically designed so that everything could be done from a high orbit. Landing was not even an option she had considered.

"So are you cool with everything?" she asked shutting her PlasmaTab down.

2B nodded.

"Good. Now all we have to do is wait."

* * *

Their father's trademark snoring was the trigger to leave.

They each grabbed their backpacks and crept silently out of the house, running the half-mile to the local Hover Terminal. It was exactly half past midnight, just in time for the last transport craft of the night. Luckily, when it arrived the HoverFlo was all but empty. There were

45

three drunken Dobokis thugs in one carriage, but they were far too inebriated on Florin Juice to even open their thick, warty eyes, never mind cause any trouble.

Neither JoJo nor 2B spoke for the entire trip, their nerves jangling and minds racing. 2B's mainly wondering how on earth he had managed to get himself talked into such madness.

Twenty minutes later the HoverFlo delivered them to their destination. The magnificent Star Command SpaceDrome Centre.

It was a glorious place, beautifully designed out of plasmon glass and state of the art tutulium. The outer walls were adorned with vast moving images. Spacecraft rocketed from one side to the other, past beautifully coloured planets and through huge gaseous nebulae, whilst gigantic galaxies gently arced around the building in relentless orbits.

Everything about the place was vast, from the colossal doors leading into the reception area, to the hangers and offices contained within. It was the size of a small city and stood as a symbol to the Larian's complete mastery of the skies.

During a normal night the complex would still be a hive of activity. Workers would be organizing the next day's flights, setting schedules and a million other things, but tonight it stood virtually empty. That was because tonight was unique. Tonight, Anilar was celebrating its ten thousandth anniversary and the entire planet had shut down for a public holiday.

That was why JoJo had chosen it as the day to begin her mission.

Parties and celebrations had been raging all day and night. In the distance, JoJo could still see exotic laser shows dancing in the air, whilst the occasional loud explosion signaled another colourful display of 'moon dust fireworks.'

Only pilots above the rank of Grade Three SpaceCoyote, and a few unlucky space traffic controllers, were on call. But JoJo wasn't unduly worried. She had studied the worksheets and knew where each and every one of them would be at a given time. One of them happened to be her father, and he was at home sleeping.

All this, of course, meant that it was the perfect time to borrow an academy spacecraft, the Intergalactic Star Seeker.

JoJo led 2B through the unmanned entrance hall, down a long corridor, past dark deserted offices and into the main hanger. When he saw it, 2B gasped in wonder.

Nearly three football fields long and fifty metres high, the hanger was huge and intimidating. It was 2B's first time here so JoJo could imagine how he felt but even she, who had seen it a thousand times, felt her heart flutter at the sheer spectacle of it.

They were standing on a metal gantry, overlooking a scene that could only be described as magnificent. Below them, stretching from one end to the other, hovered row upon row of gleaming golden Star Seekers. Without counting JoJo knew there were exactly one hundred and twenty one rows, each containing fifty spacecraft, a total of six thousand and fifty Star Seekers. *Soon*, JoJo thought, *there would be six thousand and forty nine.*

Metal ramparts separated each row. They ran all the way to the back of the hanger, ending at a tunnel entrance. Above each tunnel, the words 'Launch Area' were written in green, holographic letters.

She guided 2B down some steps and onto the main hanger floor. To their left were the U1 Star Trainers. JoJo knew those well. However, this mission demanded something a little more sophisticated, a little less limiting, so she turned right and headed toward aisle number sixty three. There, bathed in crystal blue light, sat a row of fifty gleaming lustrous spacecraft. They were glorious. They were the X1 Star Seekers.

Its sleek and streamlined frame reminded JoJo of a shark. When it flew, the X1 was completely at one with the sky. The large elongated teardrop-shaped engines pushed out more power than four U1 put together. Granted, with no X1 flying time under her belt, she'd set herself a real challenge to pilot the pride of the SpaceCoyote fleet, but JoJo never did anything by half. For two years she had been studying every inch of the X1's capabilities. What she didn't know about it now, simply wasn't worth knowing.

2B followed furtively behind, feeling every inch a criminal about to be caught in the act. His eyes flicked continually from side to side, looking for the person he was convinced would, at any moment, step out and stop them in their tracks. But no one did. The entire facility really did seem deserted. Unbelievably, it appeared his sister truly did have it all planned out this time.

JoJo held out a hand at bay number seven. "This is it," she whispered. "This is the one."

She helped 2B into the spacecraft before he could change his mind and she followed.

Strapped into her chair, JoJo wrapped her right hand around the steering control lever. Her DNA was instantly analysed from skin cells on her palm and the cockpit suddenly came to life as all her personal settings were loaded into the on board computer. Now this X1 was hers.

She worked the controls as though she'd been flying it all her life. In under a minute, the pre-flight checks were complete, the engines were powered up in silent mode and the anti-gravity field, which kept the X1 suspended during shutdown, had been released.

As she eased the throttle gently forward, a wave of exhilaration tingled up her spine. The thrust pushed them into their seats as they lifted silently and smoothly into the air. As 2B's stomach fell away, he moaned anxiously, "Are you sure you know what we're doing? We're stealing an X1 Star Seeker JoJo! They're bound to miss it."

JoJo guided the Seeker forward. "Relax. We're only borrowing it. Anyway, I've doctored the command computer files, so anyone nosing around will think its down in the repair bays undergoing routine flight checks."

She said this as if she was simply ordering a pizza. 2B let out a groan of desperation. The very thought of anyone – especially his sister – messing with the command computer files, filled him with horror. Before he could argue, the exit tunnel loomed large before them and terror snatched his voice away.

With a diameter only slightly larger than the width of the Star Seeker, and lit only by thin neon green strip lights, to a non flyer like 2B, it seemed simply impossible that they could make their way down it without crashing into the sides. But JoJo accelerated smoothly without a care in the world, keeping her wings easily between the green markers. This was, after all, what she was born to do.

As the tunnel exit approached, she brought the Star Seeker to a halt. Beyond was the vast open space of the launch area.

Each tunnel had its own lane marked by strobing red lights which ran further than the eye could see. At the end of those lights was the outside world and outer space. Once she pushed the Seeker's nose out beyond the end of her tunnel, the launch would be completely automatic and out of her control. The SpaceCoyotes called it 'the slingshot.'

A prickle of anticipation ran through her. No one had ever attempted anything this daring before: An unauthorised flight to the most dangerous planet in the galaxy. She knew it was pure madness. But from that moment two years ago, when she read the Admiralty files on the Blue Planet, she knew this was the path on which her destiny lay.

Checking her Octavia timer, she noticed a trickle of sweat running over the back of her hand. She flicked it off. That was no problem. Nerves were good. They would keep her sharp.

Timing now was critical. It was two fourteen in the morning. At precisely two fifteen, the space traffic controllers swapped shifts. The whole procedure of clocking out and clocking in, took forty five seconds – forty five seconds when no one would be monitoring the night skies. That was her window of opportunity. If her maths (and her flying skills) were right, the launch would take twelve seconds, leaving her thirty-three seconds to fire through the atmosphere and out of radar range, before the new shift sat down and saw anything wrong. Of course, what she hadn't told 2B, was that the best anyone had ever done it before was thirty eight seconds, but that was just a mere technicality.

Her fingers drummed on the console. She checked again. Ten seconds had ticked by.

Her stomach trembled as she watched the timer tick down. She took hold of the control stick with a tense hand. "The first guard should be signing out of the computer ... now. Hold on to your hat little brother!"

She slammed the launch burners to maximum and was pinned to her seat as the X1 thundered out of the tunnel and crossed the red light. They were a smudge of gold against red as the slingshot propelled them to over twice the speed of sound in just five seconds. As the g-forces took hold and her breath was left somewhere back in the tunnel, you could just make out a beaming smile amongst the ripples of skin. 2B however could do nothing but hold on for dear life.

Exactly twelve seconds later they were spat out into the dark Larian sky like a bullet from a gun and JoJo was back in control.

With thirty three seconds to go, the race was on.

CHAPTER 10

ONE VISION

Doumas Gunz climbed the last of the half dozen steps to the control room and paused to catch his breath. Oh, how those six stairs were going to be the death of him one of these days.

He had just left a fabulous party where everybody had been very happily getting very happy. Now he was here, facing another long boring night of doing nothing but watch empty screens. It was taking all his willpower not to turn round and walk straight back out.

He stumbled over the threshold of the control room. There, on the other side, was a myriad of radar screens and control computers – and Yashin.

"My, my Doumas, are you all right?" said the terminally cheerful controller.

Doumas grimaced, "As a matter of fact...."

"Only, you're nearly two minutes early. It must be a record. Aha, aha."

Doumas let out a sigh. Yashin was a real 'jobsworth' and about as funny as gangrene. "Well Yashin, consider it a favour. I'm letting you go early," Doumas grunted.

Yashin looked aghast. "Oh no, I couldn't possibly. I've got my nightly log to complete and ..."

Doumas waved him off.

"Yadda, yadda, I'll just pretend you're not here then."

He clumsily shoved past Yashin and plonked himself in the controller's chair where he stretched out. Well, as far as he could anyway. Doumas was a big man, and getting bigger every day since they put him on these damn graveyard shifts. With nothing to do all night but watch empty launch areas, what was he supposed to do but fill his time (and stomach) with food – lots of food.

None of his uniforms fitted anymore and he had to admit that the chair was beginning to feel a bit … comfy. Even for Doumas this was getting ridiculous. *Maybe*, he thought as he stroked his bulging belly, *tonight, I should probably try and catch up on some sleep instead of gorging on snacks.* Yes. After all, all diets had to start somewhere didn't they?

Behind him, Yashin finally finished the sign out procedure on the computer and left; his attempt at goodbye was met with a big yawn from Doumas. He wasn't much of a conversationalist. His mouth was usually far too busy chewing food or swallowing drink to bother with idle chit-chat.

Checking he really had gone, Doumas reached eagerly into his pocket and retrieved a small golden flask. Unscrewing the lid, he greedily swigged a big gulp of Florin Juice before wedging his hefty behind further into the already straining chair.

"Ahhh, now that's better," he sighed.

Drinking on the job was strictly prohibited (Rule 68c paragraph IV. Doumas had been quoted it so many times, he knew it by heart), but he didn't care. He had always lived by the rule of what his bosses didn't know couldn't hurt them (or him for that matter). Besides, they were all no doubt currently sipping expensive Cabolbot Sap in their nice shiny suits, and not slaving away in the middle of the night like him, so who cared what they thought.

He put the flask on the console and stared at the gleaming golden vessel. He still couldn't believe his luck to have found such a beautiful thing lying in a rubbish tip. Well, that wasn't strictly true. *He* didn't actually find it in a rubbish tip. He stole it off the man who did. But hey, that was just nit picking. And it was beautiful. It would have been a crime not to steal it.

He shut his eyes. "Just forty winks," he mumbled to himself, as he hoisted his feet onto the console – no mean feat for a man like Doumas.

Unfortunately for him, he didn't even make the first wink.

A high pitched alarm noisily jerked him from his relaxation.

"Wassat?" he cried, knocking the flask on to the floor. On the console, a blue light flashed and message ran across the screen.

Tunnel twelve: flight prepared: checking permissions.

Doumas didn't understand (which in his case was not a great surprise). He hadn't been told of any flights out of here tonight. What was going on?

Grunting and straining (think of a champagne cork in a bottle) he prised himself out of his chair and stared down into the launch bay below. The booth's walls were made from glass, so from up here, he had a panoramic view. It was empty. He tapped the console hard with his fingers.

"Stupid machine, maybe you need some florin juice?"

The flashing light suddenly changed to red.

Flight permission granted. Ready for launch.

"What are you talking about!?" barked Doumas angrily. "Who's ready for launch? There's nobody even out there!"

How wrong he was. Suddenly tunnel twelve's red strobes began pulsating faster and brighter. Doumas could do nothing but gawp open mouthed as an X1 Star Seeker rocketed out into the night sky in less time than it took for him to blink.

"Shutlik!" he swore and instinctively reached for the emergency button. But he never made it.

"Pressing that button would not be the best idea you ever had in your life," a voice said.

Doumas spun around. There was a man standing behind him. Ye gods! He had never even heard the door open. The man smiled, but only with his lips, his eyes told Doumas a different story – one that did not look as if it would have a happy ending if Doumas didn't do as he was told. He didn't recognise the man who was thin and wiry and dressed in strange attire, like an assassin. Or, at least how Doumas imagined an assassin might look if he ever met one, which, unbeknown to him, he was just about to.

"Who are you? What do you want here?" barked Doumas.

"Who I am is no concern of yours. What I want is for you to take your hand away from that button. Right now."

Now, most people would agree that Doumas was a man with very few qualities. However, in the matter of self preservation, he was not altogether stupid. So what if regulations told him he should be pressing the emergency button. Here was a man who looked quite important or at least dangerous, who was telling him not to press the button. For Doumas, the decision was therefore easy.

He edged away from the console.

"So, are you going to tell me what this is all about – the flight that just left?" he asked.

"Was never there," replied the man bluntly, "And believe me when I tell you, that it is entirely in your best interest to forget you ever saw it. Or for that matter, that we are having this conversation."

Doumas looked blankly at the man.

"No flight?" Doumas asked.

"Correct."

"No conversation?"

"Also Correct."

Doumas nodded, smiling. "I get it," he said.

"Then we have an understanding," said the man. "Excellent. And I was informed that you were an imbecile."

Doumas smiled proudly then stopped, realising he may just have been insulted.

"Tell me," continued the man, sniffing the air, "Is that Florin Juice I can smell on your breath?"

Doumas paled. Damn.

"I, er. That is …"

"Only if it is, do you have any left? It has been a long day."

Doumas hesitated, wondering if he was being tricked. People had done that before, just to get him the sack.

"Don't worry," the man said, sensing his apprehension. "You are not in trouble if that's what you think."

Those were magic words to Doumas. Seeing as trouble usually followed him around like a lost puppy, determining whether he was, or was not in it, always needed clarification. Feeling much better, he picked the flask of illegal liquid off the floor and handed it over.

"It's good stuff," he said. "Cheap, as well. I don't go in for all that fancy expensive rubbish."

The man swallowed a large gulp and may well have wished he hadn't.

"Warms you right up doesn't it?" enthused Doumas.

The man had a small coughing fit. "You could say that."

He took another, more tentative sip and gazed at the flask.

"This is beautiful. I wouldn't have thought they paid you controllers enough to own such a precious thing as this."

"Er, belonged to my father. Heirloom. Passed it on to me years ago," Doumas lied.

"Hmm, then you are a very lucky man. Tell me, do they treat you well up here, Doumas?"

Doumas shrugged. "Not really and how do you know my name?"

"Ah, same everywhere," said the man, ignoring Doumas's question. "You give them your all everyday but do you get the thanks or the recognition you deserve? Do you hell. Am I right Doumas? Of course I am. I don't suppose any of your superiors offered to be sitting up here tonight did they?"

Doumas shook his head.

"I didn't think so." He beckoned Doumas over. "Come, take the weight off your feet, have a drink."

Doumas was more than little confused as to what was going on here but he had just heard three more of his magic words. He was in a chair, flask in hand, before the clock had time to tick.

The two of them sat like that for a while, Doumas drinking while the man asked questions. With every sip, Doumas's world seemed to get just a little bit brighter and happier. Eventually, when his words began to slur, his curiosity reached a zenith, and over-ruled his brain.

"So, that launch. What are we going to do about it?"

The man stared fixedly at Doumas. "Launch? What launch?"

"You know, the …" He stopped and paused as his mind did cartwheels. "Oh, right, I get it." Doumas tapped the side of his nose conspiratorially. "The launch that didn't happen, right? Can't possibly tell me about the flight that didn't leave here just now, can you."

The man sat back and steepled his fingers. "Well I could but I would have to kill you afterwards."

Doumas burst out laughing. He slapped the man on the leg.

"You. Have to kill me indeed. You know what? I'm starting to like you … what did you say your name was?"

The man sat forward. "I didn't but if you really want to know what is happening then I suppose … Can I trust you Doumas?"

Doumas sat straighter in his chair. "Sure," he urged, "You can trust me."

"You'll never believe me."

"I will, I will," cried Doumas eager to learn some really juicy gossip for the guys in the drinking dens.

"Well okay then, come close."

Doumas leaned in.

"The Star Seeker you saw flying out of here."

"The one that never went?"

"Precisely. Well, it was stolen."

Doumas gasped.

"By a fourteen year old girl no less," said the man.

56

"No," said Doumas.

"Yes – and not only that. Do you know where she is planning on taking it? Right now, she is on her way to … The Blue Planet."

That stopped Doumas in his tracks. Suddenly he felt very sober.

"The B-Blue Planet? But she can't be. That's n-not allowed. What they did, it's not allowed. She can't go there." He was shaking.

"I told you, you wouldn't believe me," said the man calmly.

"She'll die. Does she know what she is doing? You've got to stop her."

The man crossed his legs. "Oh don't you worry, she'll be stopped all right."

But Doumas wasn't listening. All he could think about was that an unauthorised, stolen, Star Seeker had left for the most deadly planet in the galaxy on *his* watch. He was going to be in so much trouble. In fact they would probably invent a new word for people who made the worst type of mess-ups. They would call it 'being a Doumas.'

He prized himself up and stumbled towards the console. A leg flicked out and blocked him. Doumas eyed the man.

"We need to press the alarm button," He protested. "We need to inform the Admiralty. Please."

"We don't need to do anything, Doumas apart from calm down. You said I could trust you, but you're getting a little bit hysterical aren't you?" The man rose to his feet.

Doumas backed away. "That was before. Before... Oh my."

The man inhaled impatiently. "Doumas," he began. "I'll tell you what I'll do. If it makes you feel better, I'll patch us through to someone who can reassure you that everything will be absolutely fine. Fetch me that communicator by the screen will you?"

Doumas spun around. "Yes, yes. Patch through. That's what we have to do."

After that everything happened so fast.

The moment Doumas turned his back the man flourished a length of black rope from a pocket. He aimed a kick into the base of Doumas's back, dumping him to his knees. As he fell, the man whipped the rope around the flabby skin of Doumas's neck tying it into a tight slip knot, before yanking hard.

Doumas gasped and choked as he was dragged unceremoniously backwards into a chair. Before he could even think about putting up a fight, his arms were secured behind the chair. He sat there, gasping for air. The man leaned close and whispered in his ear.

"Don't struggle. The more you struggle, the tighter it becomes around your neck and the faster you will die. And then, you will miss the ride."

Panicking, Doumas flailed like an injured animal. Sure enough the rope around his neck only choked him more.

"Now then," the man began. "Let me tell you what is going to happen. You, Doumas, are going to die a spectacular, but ultimately, very painful death. If it is any consolation, you were always going to die. I have only kept you alive this long so I could be absolutely sure you did nothing stupid before I arrived."

The man gazed at the large glass windows of the control room, settling upon one. With one hand controlling Doumas like a macabre puppeteer, he pulled a gun from his jacket pocket with the other and blasted the pane. Glass exploded outwards until there was not a splinter left. Air rushed in. Doumas scrunched his eyes against the gusting wind as everything in the room that wasn't nailed down blew into the air.

"Well, it has certainly not been a pleasure to meet you, Doumas," shouted the man above the gale.

Doumas felt his chair begin to move. Slowly, it rolled toward the open window and the enormous drop beyond.

"Oh god, please no!" he cried, coughing and spluttering desperately trying to force air down his strictured windpipe. He dug his heels into the floor, but it was no use, he just couldn't get enough purchase.

The edge inched closer. The front leg crossed the frame.

"Please. I won't tell anyone … I promise … Let me go … Please."

Now Doumas could see the drop and it made him want to throw up. It was so, so far down. His vision swam and his whole body shook violently with fear.

"Just one more thing," the man said, "Scream for me, Doumas."

He kicked the chair over the precipice, leaning forward to watch it plummet downwards. Doumas screamed like a stuck pig as he fell. The remaining rope uncoiled like a speedy snake revealing a grapple hook on the end. The three finger-like hooks shot forward and caught on the bottom window frame. The line pulled taut in an instant and snapped to a shuddering halt.

Moments later, the chair hit the floor of the launch area and smashed into a thousand pieces. The body of Doumas did not. It remained dangling on the end of the rope, swinging wildly half way down the drop.

"What a terrible way to go," the man commented to himself.

Then he turned and pressed a small button by the side of the window frame. Instantly, a fresh pane of glass sealed the hole, and him, in the control room.

Free from the noise of the rushing air, he made a call on his communicator. When it was picked up, he said. "She left exactly as planned. I will be following shortly."

He paused as the person on the other end spoke.

"I encountered a small problem, but nothing to concern you. Someone insisted on hanging around, so I obliged."

Another pause "No, I will not let you down, I promise."

He ended the call and placed the communicator in his pocket before heading for the door. The room was a mess, but someone else could come and tidy it up. He had more important things to do.

It was time to go flying.

It was time to go hunting.

CHAPTER 11

PLANET EARTH

JoJo had cleared Anilar's radar penetration with seven seconds to spare, which was impressive even for her, although if she was honest, she'd have to admit that her eyes had been closed for most of it.

From there, it had been a short run to the Endol portal where they had just spent three hours travelling one hundred million light years. Now they out and slowing rapidly to normal cruising speed. JoJo's vision swam and a wave of nausea hit her immediately as g-forces pushed her into her seat so powerfully she feared the hinge might snap.

She put her head in her hands and groaned. Portal jumps always did this to her. They were the one thing about space travel that she just could not get used to.

Travelling so far in such a short space of time played havoc with your body clock, as illustrated by 2B, who was curled up in his chair having slept through the whole thing. That often happened the first time. The brain can't cope and simply shuts itself down until it can figure out what the heck is happening. Apart from not knowing what day it was, or whether it was morning or night, 2B would be fine in a couple of hours. And so would JoJo, just as soon as she finished retching into the puke bucket.

* * *

When her stomach was well and truly empty, JoJo took a look outside. In the inky blackness of space, billions and billions of stars sparkled like fairy dust all around them. Just like always JoJo felt the hairs on the back of her arm stand on end. If there was a better sight in the whole universe, she couldn't think of it.

She checked her computer screens taking in all the information. Their speed was good, their position perfect, the flying conditions outside ideal and all the Star Seeker functions were running optimally. In short, things could not be better.

Excitedly she asked the computer to give her a visual on her final destination. An agonising few seconds passed before the image was finally projected on screen in full three dimensions. JoJo gasped.

There it was. The real thing. It was like gazing at an old friend. She knew its every facet, so familiar had it become from her studies of the archives. Her breath caught in her chest. For some inexplicable reason she felt as if she was looking at a priceless treasure. One she had been searching for all her life.

It wasn't that the Blue Planet was in any way more special than the other planets catalogued on the LarPlan list.* In fact if you were comparing size and chemistry it was pretty average, but really, who cared about chemistry. The Blue Planet was special in a way only one other planet was special. Like Anilar, it wasn't a mere lump of rock or gas spinning aimlessly around its Sun. It was an organic, living, breathing entity that was teeming with life.

JoJo still could not comprehend how such an incredible place had been ignored since its discovery forty years ago. It was easily the closest

*The LarPlan project was the very ambitious aim to catalogue every single planet in the galaxy. So far it had been running for about two thousand years and the number currently stood at 5,265,301. Of these, around fifty six thousand contained some form of life. It should be noted however that so terrified were the Admiralty of the Blue Planet, it does not exist on any of the official records of the LarPlan list.

thing to a sister planet Anilar had and the admiralty had done all they could to keep its existence hidden from the Larian public. That, JoJo thought, was the real tragedy of what happened all those years ago.

With the Blue Planet blazing like a real life screensaver, JoJo used another screen to access her private computer files. Clicking her way through folder after folder, she selected seven programs and ran them through a diagnostic check to ensure none had corrupted during the Portal jump.

Seconds later the seven file names appeared registering a clean bill of health. Beside each name was a graphical bar showing the current status of that particular program. Six of the bars were full, indicating the program was running. The seventh bar, whose file was named 'SCAN 16 Bp', was empty. A blinking orange light at the side told her it was in stand-by mode, not yet activated. JoJo was satisfied. That was as it should be.

SCAN 16 Bp was the most important computer file she had ever written. Probably the most important anyone on Anilar had ever written. It was known as a 'forget-me-file' (FMF), which simply meant that once inserted into the computer, nothing could stop it. No matter what, it would run automatically, carrying out whatever tasks were in the programming until they were complete. FMF's were the very latest technology. Engineers used them to run complex programs when they didn't want any outside interference. They were so advanced that even something as stupid as forgetting to switch the computer on was no handicap. FMF's had their own internal energy supply to keep the program running. Nothing could stop one. Nothing at all.

For obvious reasons their use on SpaceCoyote missions was banned. Having an unstoppable program running when you were a hundred million light years from home was something no SpaceCoyote wanted, but of course JoJo's program had not been anywhere near the appropriate channels for authorised use. If it had, it wouldn't be there. It was another huge risk she was taking, but then what was one Forget-me-File amongst everything else she was doing?

She wondered when it would begin to run. When she would see the results – results that could change her whole world. They would have to be closer to the Blue Planet that much she knew but the anticipation was already rising.

She closed down the screens and gazed at the serene blue orb. Unfortunately the serenity didn't last very long.

* * *

The pulsing green blip appeared on the Star Seekers radar screen like an unwelcome guest at a party. A loud warning alarm accompanied it, waking 2B from his slumber. A closer look told her whatever it was, it was moving toward them.

"Wassat!" 2B said looking this way and that. He spotted the radar screen and sat bolt upright. "Ohmygod! They've f-found us! They've already found us. I knew it. Didn't I tell you this would happen?" There was panic etched in every word.

"Calm down," said JoJo, moving quickly to silence the alarm and 2B. "It's just a Dimple probe that's all. Look, you can tell by its radar signature."

All 2B saw was a flashing green blip.

"It's absolutely nothing to worry about. There are hundreds of them flying around this solar system. They come to monitor the Blue Planet, not to look for invisible Star Seekers."

"A st- stolen, invisible Star Seeker you m-mean."

JoJo sighed. How many times had she been through this? "We've borrowed a Star Seeker 2B. *Borrowed*. We haven't stolen anything. Anyway, even if it was looking for us, with the cloaking device turned on were perfectly well hidden. It will just do its job, turn around and head back home. Simple as that."

Her words didn't console 2B.

"Simple as that you say. Well why didn't I know about *simple* dimple probes? I don't remember you saying anything about *simple* dimple probes."

JoJo gave her brother her best reassuring smile, reached into her pocket pulling out a sweet humba bar. She tossed it into his lap. "Here, chill. I didn't tell you because there was nothing to tell. They're harmless. Save you're worrying for when we get nearer the Blue Planet why don't you."

2B huffed, but thankfully for JoJo, was easily silenced by the promise of what lay in the humba bar's wrapper. It always helped when your co-pilot was so easily bought. With his attention successfully diverted JoJo cleared the radar screen of the dimple probe, set their course, balanced their speed and smiled at her brother.

"Next stop, The Blue Planet," she said. 2B didn't smile back.

* * *

2B was only two years younger than JoJo, but so far had lived every single day of his life firmly in her shadow. Where she'd been top of the class in every subject she had taken at school, he had languished somewhere between lower middle and bottom. When, last year, in a hail of publicity JoJo was honoured for passing her SpaceCub exams a whole year early, 2B was busy re-sitting a test he had already failed three times before. Indeed, he often complained that the only thing he seemed to excel at was being utterly rubbish at everything!

And things were only getting worse. Next year he finished his primaries and would graduate into one of the many 'Space Academy Cub' training schools. For most normal kids this was the most exciting time of their lives. The training schools were where it all happened. The pathway to the stars – quite literally. Places in the top schools were ultra competitive. Kids (if they had any sense) studied like crazy to get a chance. Most wouldn't make it, but for the chosen few, life would go intergalactic and never be the same again. For 2B it was simply going to be yet another massive anticlimax. He would of course be expected to take a route that would eventually lead to a shot at becoming a SpaceCoyote just like JoJo, his father and his Grandfather before that, but it wasn't going to happen.

So far 2B's applications to all the best schools, like Star Seeker Training School, Engine Designer School and Galaxy Navigator School had all been firmly rejected. His last and only option was a place offered to him at Trooper Maintenance School. The title sounded grand. The reality was so very different. Becoming a trainee maintenance captain was just a posh title for a 'trash man.' His days would be spent wiping inter-stellar space kill from the windshields of Star Seekers and making sure that the hundreds of different maintenance CoyoteBots were working properly. It would be dirty, smelly and most likely deadly boring but he would be in the SpaceCubs. That should at least go someway to gratifying his parents – he hoped.

This trip had come at the right time. He had convinced himself this was the opportunity to claw back some major respect. Sure it was most likely going to land him in so much trouble that even a seven ton RhondoPod would struggle to fight its way out, but how cool would he be? All the kids would want to be his friend. There would be no more teasing in the playground for him. Well, that was what he had convinced himself anyway. Now he was actually doing it, he wasn't so sure.

The last month had been one of constant nerves and worry. Everything was spooking him. The things he could see, like the dimple probes on the radar screen and the things he couldn't see that were lurking in the blackness of space.

Then of course there were JoJo's secrets. From the very start 2B had noticed a change in his sister. Despite his healthy record of proving otherwise, he wasn't stupid. He knew there was more to this trip than simply capturing music. JoJo after all, never put a foot wrong. It didn't make sense for her to suddenly rebel. Unless that is, she had a hidden agenda – a secret that she wasn't sharing.

In the end though it came down to trust, and 2B had no choice. He had to trust her because out here, she was all that he had and most of the time, he had to admit that she was cooler than liquid nitrogen.

"So when do we get there?" he asked, a little more relaxed as he chewed the humba bar and the sugar kicked in.

JoJo checked her computer screen. "Well, we have one more small portal jump to make which shouldn't take more than a few minutes and then about two hours."

2B grimaced. "Another portal jump?" he complained. "You said last night that the Endol Portal would take us right to it. You never said anything about two portal jumps."

JoJo tried to sound nonchalant with her reply. "I didn't tell you because I thought you might worry if you knew where the entrance was that's all."

2B sighed and felt a familiar feeling of portent prickle his nerves. "If your using words like 'that's all', it means something's up. So come on. Out with it. Where is this entrance?"

"It really isn't as bad as it looks," said JoJo rather too quickly.

She instructed the computer to recoil the black windscreen filter that had protected their eyes during the Portal jump. What 2B saw almost made his heart stop.

JoJo was very wrong – it really was as bad as it looked. In front of them was the largest, most terrifying asteroid belt 2B had ever seen and JoJo was flying straight towards it.

"You have g-got to be k-kidding. You're insane," he stuttered, the colour draining from his face like it had sprung a leak.

"Honestly," she said, urging him to calm down, "I admit it's not the most ideal place to have a portal entrance."

2B gave her a look of complete incredulity, "NOT IDEAL!"

"We don't have to go in. We just have to get close," added JoJo.

"Oh, well that's okay then," said 2B sarcastically. "They can put that on the gravestones can't they?" He wrote the imaginary words in the air. "'*We just had to get close.*' Brilliant."

JoJo shook her head. "This is exactly why I didn't tell you. I knew you'd over-react."

"Over-react? The only reason you didn't tell me is because you knew I'd have had you certified and locked up."

"Oh don't be ridiculous," cried JoJo. "Look, the portal entrance lies about two miles from the actual asteroids. Okay so they'll be a bit of debris spraying over us but it's nothing we can't handle. If we get the trajectory right, we'll be in and out the other side before you can say 'big, ugly stone.'"

Of course, JoJo always did have a habit of over simplifying things.

CHAPTER 12

SaRa

As they flew closer to the Saturnis asteroid belt, the atmosphere inside the cockpit began to change. 2B had been stony silent for a long while. Even JoJo was beginning to question the wisdom of this idea. Her calm exterior belied a stomach that was flipping cartwheels at the thought of skirting so close to an asteroid field.

The boulders of jet black rock stretched out for thousands of miles in a seemingly never ending sea of destruction. JoJo couldn't see where the top started or the bottom finished. There were asteroids the size of mountains as well as tiny, razor-sharp ones no bigger than the Star Seeker itself, all swirling and spinning, colliding with violent ferocity, spewing flames and dust out into space in dramatic displays of devastation. It was a vision of hell itself. *One small scrape,* she thought, *That's all it would take and the Star Seeker will be ripped open like a tin can.*

She sucked in a deep breath as her heart thumped like a jackhammer on overdrive. She simply could not get this wrong.

Blindly she reached above her head and flipped a switch before wiping a clammy hand down her suit. Above JoJo's main console a computer-generated head floating gossamer-like appeared from nowhere. It was female, coloured in varying shades of blue. Her name was SaRa. She spoke in a soft, gentle voice. "Auto pilot off. JoJo, you have control."

With trembling hands, JoJo gingerly took hold of the steering controls. "Thanks SaRa, how is everything looking?"

The head was quick to respond. "Well. If you are referring to the Star Seeker, then everything is fine. If however, you are referring to the view in front of us then I would have to say things are looking pretty terrible."

SaRa was an acronym. It stood for Seeker Auto Response Advisor and, thanks to the remarkable 'Arti-Inti' chip installed in her hardware, she was the most intelligent machine ever devised in the galaxy. She represented the absolute pinnacle of Larian engineering success. With true artificial intelligence, SaRa was the sole reason for the success of the LarPlan project. She could fly a Star Seeker single-handed anywhere in the galaxy, solve any problem she came up against and, if you so wished, tell you the time in three thousand four hundred and sixty two different languages (including Deerum which was less of an actual language and more of a series of grunts and whistles). Put simply, without her, it would be impossible for a two-man Coyote crew (or one boy and one girl for that matter) to travel the galaxy and return home in one piece.

Each SpaceCoyote had their own SaRa tailored to their individual personality. JoJo's was a girl of about eighteen with a shoulder length bob hair cut and a serious attitude – not least when it came to doing anything remotely risky. Every time JoJo attempted anything that wasn't written in the book of how to fly SpaceCoyote missions, she got 'the face.' She got it a lot.

In their two short years together they had already had some pretty spectacular arguments. JoJo had once been banned from flying for a week after throwing a cup at SaRa. It was a quite pointless act really seeing as SaRa is nothing more than a wonderfully constructed hologram and the cup sailed straight through her, damaging only her instructor's nose which happened to be behind it.

Since then they had tried their best to get along but in the end they were as incompatible as fish and deserts. JoJo lived to push back boundaries, fly beyond the conventional envelopes, take risks to get the job done. For SaRa, safety came first, second and third (there was no fourth. If there was, it would be safety!)

Right now 'The face' wasn't far away.

"Pardon me if I appear stupid," SaRa began "but you *are* aware of the impending asteroid belt and the dangers that it presents, are you not?"

"Of course I am," replied JoJo.

"Well can you please tell me then why you are taking this most preposterous route? Flying so close to an asteroid belt is at best exceptionally risky and at worst ... suicidal."

"Here, Here," said 2B, happy for an ally. JoJo shot him a monstrous stare.

She said, "We are taking this course because it is the only way to get to where we need to be."

"Oh but I beg to differ," retorted SaRa. "By far the safest course would be to turn round and head for the Sharamin Portal, twelve thousand miles north-west of us. That would bring us out on the inner side of the asteroid belt, approximately fifty thousand miles from Venus."

"FIFTY THOUSAND ... VENUS ... IMPOSSIBLE!" Yelled JoJo. "Do you know how long it would take to fly to the Blue Planet from Venus with no Portal jumps?"

SaRa responded like lightening, "Based upon top speed and taking into consideration the effect of solar flares when you're that close to the sun, I would say about –."

"*Stop*, it wasn't a literal question SaRa, I know the answer. The answer is – too long. We'd have to go home before we even get there."

"But we would at least, be alive."

JoJo sat straighter in her chair and looked first at 2B and then at SaRa. "Listen to me both of you. We are *not* going through any Sharamin portal. We *are* going through the Saturnis Portal. I haven't risked everything to turn around and go home empty handed. If I have to steer myself over an asteroid to get to the Blue Planet, believe me I will do it and *we will* get there."

Silence.

She pushed defiantly on the controls and banked the Star Seeker to the left, lining them up for the final portal jump. Don't know why they worry, she thought, what could possibly go wrong?

* * *

They were less than a thousand miles from the belt and at full portal entry speed when she found out what can go wrong.

Without warning and quite suddenly, the portal entrance disappeared. There was no bright flash, no ear-splitting boom, no indication it was about to happen. It simply vanished off the radar leaving them racing headlong towards a rock the size of a small city.

SaRa gasped. JoJo's whole world seemed to stop. She couldn't breath. She could hardly move. She was caught in a vice like grip of terror. Where had it gone? Why had it gone?

Although her body seemed paralysed, her acute brain instinctively played through the options. There were only two and both involved an extremely quick death. They could either abort or they could fly into the asteroids. Unfortunately, flying at portal entry speed meant aborting was next to impossible. The g-forces of deceleration would tear them apart, but flying into the asteroids … that was plainly suicidal.

"SaRa what do we do?" JoJo barked, fear coursing through her.

SaRa was dazed at the turn of events. After a long pause, she uttered the three words JoJo thought she would never hear. "I… I don't know."

SaRa – the computer who knew everything. SaRa – the computer who could solve any problem, didn't have an answer for their predicament and suddenly JoJo realised why. It was unsolvable. Whichever way you looked at it, there could be no favourable outcome to this scenario. SaRa had no solution to keep them alive because there wasn't one.

The realisation chilled her to the marrow.

As they raced closer to impact, panic and confusion gripped every fibre of JoJo's body. How could a portal just disappear? Her timing had been spot on. Sure, she knew Portal entrances were not always open. They behaved like the petals of a flower, opening and closing to a set rhythm. But she also knew Portals ran like clockwork. They never fluctuated and the Saturnis Portal was not due to close for another three days. Something had gone horribly wrong and JoJo ached to scream and shout in fury, but for 2B's sake she remained stoic, putting on her best 'I can fix this' face. Right now however, she couldn't imagine fixing anything.

She pulled back on the engine speed but it was no use. The gigantic granite and metal mass that lay ahead seemed to be engulfing them. They were now in the gravitational grip of the asteroid field and were being dragged unerringly on.

They only had seconds. "SaRa. Get me in highlighter mode and turn on every piece of avoidance software we have," she barked.

SaRa was aghast. "You cannot be seriously contemplating flying into the asteroids. The chances of survival are less than …...."

"I'm not arguing with you. Just do it."

Next to her, 2B sank a little further into his seat and gripped it a little tighter.

SaRa did as she was ordered and lowered the jet-black translucent panel down the windscreen. The whole sky sprang to life in a striking orange hue. The Highlighter screens job was simple – to brighten the sky, to accentuate any hidden dangers, to give them a chance. The problem was, in front of JoJo it seemed there was nothing but danger.

Trembling, JoJo said. "Count me down SaRa before I change my mind."

SaRa made her calculations. "Twenty Seconds," she said.

2B let out a squeal. JoJo glanced at him but said nothing. How do you reassure someone when you were about to fly into a mountain at Mach 8?

"You are making a terrible mistake," said SaRa.

"*Can it.* Just count."

"As you wish. Ten seconds."

The noise of the swirling rocks was building. Marble-sized chippings were beginning to clatter against the Star Seeker like hailstones on a tin roof.

"Eight seconds. Please don't do this JoJo." SaRa begged.

But it was too late. There could be no turning back.

JoJo counted the next three seconds herself then yanked back on the controls, sweeping them into a furious vertical climb. The Seeker shook violently. 2B screamed. JoJo held tight. The skin on her face stretched as her lips morphed into a manic g-force smile. Her teeth clattered together as the Seeker bounced brutally over the rough air like a pebble skimming across a pond. Then, as she caught sight of the asteroids tip high above her, she tensed every muscle in her body and began the countdown.

Five … four … three … two … one …

CHAPTER 13

SOLID AS A ROCK

JoJo leaned hard on the controls and felt the Seeker lurch. If SaRa had been programmed to scream she would have. 2B swore loudly as a shower of stones engulfed them. The noise was deafening. JoJo flung the Seeker hard left, then hard right, then hard right again.

"TURN THE DEFLECTOR SHEILDS TO FULL," she screamed.

"That will leave us exposed to detection," replied SaRa

"Just DO IT."

SaRa did. Silence fell. The stones still clattered around them but were now bouncing off an invisible shield inches from the Seeker's surface. It was a relief, but only a minor one. The shields would be useless against anything bigger than a football and there were millions of those.

The onslaught was relentless. JoJo swept the Seeker into high climbs and nose-dived like a missile through fire and explosions. Every turn brought fresh danger. Her muscles screamed at the exertion, begging her to stop but that was impossible.

Nausea grew thick in her throat as the aerial acrobatics took their toll. She could hardly see, she could hardly think. Every manoeuvre was pure instinct. Every rock evaded a triumph.

Seconds passed like hours as they diced with death. Hard left, then hard right before lurching into stomach-emptying dives. JoJo's fingers were raw and blistered from the iron grip she had on the controls. She could feel liquid trickling down her palm, was it blood? Whatever it was, it was horrible. She prayed for an end but there seemed none in sight.

Then she saw it. A mountain of an asteroid, fifty times their size shooting across their bow. Like a monstrous ravenous Pac-man, it blazed a trail through the smaller asteroids chewing them up and spitting their remains in all directions. But there, blown into the side was a huge, deep, black crater. Immediately her pounding head sensed an opportunity. If she could judge this right …

Without a second thought she fired the thrusters and started after the rock. 2B realised what she was attempting and closed his eyes, unable to look.

She caught the asteroid easily but had difficulty locating the crater. The collisions were knocking it into ever changing spins. JoJo twisted and turned, matching its rotation. Finally she came upon it. For a second as she gazed into the deep abyss she questioned her decision. It was so black, so unwelcoming, but what choice did she have?

Chewing her bottom lip in concentration, she cleared her mind of negative thoughts and began to lower the Star Seeker into the fissure…

Miraculously they bumped down on a rocky floor mere metres in. JoJo let her hands flop off the controls. She didn't know whether to laugh or cry.

"That … was unbelievable!" she said, looking at her brother.

He was deathly pale. The reason being, there was a large dollop of vomit pebble-dashed all over the radar screen in front of him.

"Oh well that's lovely," said JoJo grimly.

"I couldn't help it," he replied sullenly "I don't half feel ill."

"Well if you need to do that again, do it in a bag or something. That's horrible."

2B shot her a stare. "Well I'm very sorry," he snapped curtly. "Next time you're pulling three hundred and sixty degree turns and throwing us about in an asteroid belt I'll try not to be so inconsiderate." He hit the autotrash button a little harder than he should. A red glow shone in front of him and the screen cleared in seconds.

"Sorry," said JoJo, realising she should probably cut him a little slack. "I'm just so relieved we're out of that. I don't think I could have kept it up much longer. My arms are killing me."

For the first time she examined her hands. As she had half expected, bright red blood was trickling along her wrist and her palm was lined with blisters. Some had burst and the skin underneath rubbed raw. Now she had seen it, the stinging pain arrived in spades.

"So are we safe in here or what?" asked 2B looking out into the darkness of the cave.

"Safer than out there, that's for sure," replied JoJo, although of course that was an utter guess. She had no idea what dangers may be lurking for them in the blackness. What she did know however, was that by a sheer stroke of good fortune, the asteroid was heading in exactly the right direction to take them out of the belt. All they had to do was sit tight and it would carry them right through. For now she could almost enjoy the rest and save her energy for the final push. Maybe she could even relax.

* * *

Of course she should have known! SaRa, who was maintaining a constant countdown on their exit from the asteroid belt (one minute and counting), was affected first. Out of the corner of her eye JoJo saw the timer falter. It stopped, missed a second then corrected itself. Generally, something so trivial would be ignored but not where SaRa was concerned. Glitches like that just didn't happen with her. The hairs on the back of JoJo's neck immediately stood up. Danger.

It happened seconds later.

JoJo and 2B screamed as the explosion ripped through the sky like a hundred atom bombs exploding in unison. The Seeker shook to its very core. Only the asteroid protected them being annihilated.

All around was pandemonium. JoJo and 2B were thrown against

their belts before being catapulted back into their chairs with enough force to a knock out a rhinoceros. JoJo spat as she tasted blood.

A cacophony of alarms erupted around them. Doors and cupboards flung open spilling their contents everywhere. Debris flew from shelves and racks. Star charts spilled from their tubes unraveling across the instrument panel, as computer screens exploded, showering JoJo and 2B with thousands of tiny shards of glass.

As the worst of the buffeting subsided JoJo saw that they were no longer in the asteroid belt. Amazingly, it seemed the explosion had blown them out into space. It was nothing short of a miracle but before she could savour their success, her stomach dropped away and the Seeker lurched forward spinning out of control.

She grasped the controls to pull them out of the dive but nothing happened! The whole thing felt wrong. It was as if the Seeker had been turned into a huge child's toy that she couldn't control.

She instinctively turned to 2B for help and her heart sank.

His shoulder restraining belts had torn completely away. The only thing holding him into his chair was the strap round his waist, but it was the thin line of blood trickling out of the corner of his mouth that made her own blood run colder than ice.

"2B," she cried, reaching out to him. But the g-forces had her pinned in her seat. Just trying to move her arm felt like she was pushing through thick treacle.

"Karzig!" she swore, her hand falling back to the control stick.

Using energy she didn't know she had, she hauled the Star Seeker out of its deadly dive, drawing it level. As soon as it was, JoJo clamped her fingers around 2B's neck feeling for a pulse. Stupid. The Seeker was still shaking badly. It was impossible to feel such a delicate thing.

"SaRa," she cried desperately. "Please ... 2B. I can't find his pulse. Might be dead. Run a life scan for me." Tears were flowing freely down her cheeks.

SaRa ran the scan. There was a long, long pause. Longer than it should have be. SaRa was stalling. It was bad news, JoJo knew it.

Finally SaRa said "He's … alive. Unconscious, but alive."

JoJo almost burst with joy. Her little brother was alive. It was the sign she needed. A fresh impetus sparked inside her. They were going to get out of this mess. They were!

"SaRa, give me a damage report quickly," she asked.

SaRa's face turned grave. "We currently have problems in three grade A areas and four grade C areas."

"Karzig!" said JoJo. Grade A components were those essential for flight. "Give me options."

"Severely limited I'm afraid. We have damage to engine three and the landing thrusters. The navigation system has been virtually destroyed and the radar wouldn't spot a black troggle in the snow. However, all these pale into insignificance when you consider that the life support systems are no longer producing fresh oxygen."

JoJo's world tipped on its side. "Say again?"

"I said the life support systems are not producing oxygen. Really, I wish you would pay more attention."

JoJo couldn't speak. SaRa had just handed her and 2B a death sentence. With no oxygen, this trip was truly over – for good.

"It is my opinion that we have no other choice but to send an immediate mayday and await help," said SaRa finishing her assessment. With a whoosh, a silver panel opened in front of JoJo revealing the mayday call switch.

JoJo eyed it with something akin to defiance.

Only one other mayday call had ever been sent by a SpaceCoyote before. Forty years ago on a trip to the same planet. The irony didn't escape her.

It was the obvious thing to do, but somehow it felt like giving in, admitting defeat. It would also mean the end of her career.

JoJo placed a reluctant finger over the button. Pressing it would raise an alarm that would bring the entire fleet to her aid. They would locate her easily, but in the forbidden sky. She would be court-marshalled, stripped of her wings and probably serve time on Vanakin Island jail. But if it meant saving her brothers life …

With the button daring her to press it, she gently rested her finger on top...

But she couldn't push down.

"Are you sure there is no other way out of this SaRa?"

"None worth considering."

JoJo grasped at SaRa's words.

"That means there are some," she said hopefully

"There is one. But it is so preposterous, if it wasn't for the fact that I am unable to lie, I would never mention it at all."

JoJo sensed hope. "What is it? Come on, tell me. I order you."

"Very well. We have the option to land and repair. But of course, as I said, it is an utterly preposterous notion."

"Land where exactly?" asked JoJo.

SaRa looked at her feet (not that she had any, but if she had, that's where she would have looked) as if she couldn't quite bring herself to say the words.

"You don't mean the Blue Planet do you?" exclaimed JoJo answering her own question.

"I told you it was ridiculous, but the Blue Planet does have everything needed to sustain you while we attend to the repairs."

JoJo blew out her cheeks in exasperation. "Too right it's ridiculous and I thought I was the crazy one. Do you have any idea what would happen to us if we were found? We'd be destroyed! Just like last time. No. Absolutely not. I can't risk it. I won't risk."

"Well then," said SaRa calmly. "Press the mayday button."

But JoJo couldn't. She banged her fist frustratedly on the desk. "There must be another way."

"There isn't," said SaRa almost losing her temper. "I've tried running every possible permutation through the computers."

"Well try harder. Think. Use your powers. You're giving in too easily." JoJo shouted.

SaRa frowned. "And you're not listening. There are no other alternatives. You either hit that button, land on the Blue Planet, or sit here until we all die. You choose."

JoJo swore and cursed, which didn't help but made her feel better.

Suddenly from beside her, 2B coughed and spoke in a frail voice. "L-land …on…it."

JoJo turned. 2B moved painfully. A large lump was expanding on his forehead. JoJo winced at the sight of his wounds, but was overjoyed that he was awake. "Land on it!" he repeated hoarsely.

JoJo rubbed her tired eyes. "We can't," she said, almost to herself. "It would be going against everything we know."

2B gently touched his expanding bruise. "All I know is that it was your idea to come here and we've come this far and …" He grimaced in pain. "I need help JoJo. I can't wait for the fleet. My head hurts so much. And I…I can't see properly."

JoJo's heart was breaking. She was torn in two, being pulled apart by right and wrong. The right thing to do was to push the mayday button, own up to her recklessness and face the consequences. The wrong thing to do would be to fly to the Blue Planet.

She took a deep breath … and replaced the cover over the mayday button.

"SaRa, I'm going to switch over to autopilot. Get us down in one piece … Please."

CHAPTER 14

MISSING MISS WICKOWSKI

Totally oblivious to the turmoil that was occurring fifty thousand miles above the earth, Jimmy Green sat solemnly at his Grandma's kitchen table, slowly munching his way through his second slice of toast wondering if his life could sink any further into the mire. As he picked up the silver butter knife to begin his third round, he caught sight of his reflection.

"Ugh." He grunted twisting the blade in his fingers examining himself closely. He was shocked by what he saw. He looked a wreck. He plucked at that horrible sticky-out bit of chestnut hair which only appeared when it needed washing. That was just the start. His skin was slick and greasy and two plump whiteheads were erupting from his neck like pus-filled volcanoes. He had never had spots before. Never!

He could hardly believe that all this – his life and his complexion – had gone so wrong in the space of just two days. Two days that had taken him from feeling so high that had he looked down, his phobia for heights would have made him puke, to feeling so low that he felt there was no point going on at all.

And it was all because of a girl, Catrina Wickowski.

Cat Whiskers as she was known to her friends was easily the best thing that had ever happened to Jimmy. She was the reason that he prised himself out of his nice warm bed on cold winter mornings so he could walk with her to school. She was the reason that his heart beat faster than a hummingbird's at the very mention of her name and she was the person who yesterday walked out of his life never to return.

It was yet another deep trough in a life that, by most teenagers' standards, had seen far too many already.

His first fourteen years had not been exactly conventional. Through a series of twisted events he found himself currently living with his grandparents and their dog, Gunner, in a red brick farmhouse smack in the middle of the largest apple orchard in the world. He used to live with his Mum and Dad in the city, but that was before he fell into the first big proverbial trough.

* * *

It would be five years this December but he would always remember that Christmas Eve as if it were yesterday. He was nine years old and sitting in the back seat of the family car holding tight to a plastic army action figure he had been given by Santa Claus at the party. Of course it hadn't been the real Santa Claus, just one of his many helpers who happened this year, to be Henry Tuckson's Dad. Jimmy recognised him when his stick-on moustache peeled off during a particularly rumbunctious 'Ho, Ho, Ho.'

The night was a picture perfect Christmas card scene. Heavy snow had fallen during the party leaving the houses looking as though they had been dusted in fresh icing sugar. With fairy lights shining brightly everywhere you looked, all it needed for completion was the twelve reindeers to come flying over the chimneys.

Jimmy's Mum was driving, his Dad absent, working late as usual. It wasn't her fault. The fresh fall of snow and cold temperature had left the road like an ice rink.

Jimmy had just decided to name the plastic soldier 'Captain Frank', when a red sports car, travelling in the opposite direction, suddenly fishtailed across the road. Jimmy's Mum stood no chance. It smashed headlong into them.

Miraculously Jimmy was somehow thrown clear of the tangled wreck and escaped virtually injury free. His Mum wasn't so lucky. She bore the full, destructive force of the collision. Bones were crushed, seat belts were ripped from their moorings and metal twisted with metal shearing into a mangled heap.

In the end, Jimmy could do nothing but crawl to her and cradle her broken body in his arms as she passed away on the roadside. To this day, he had never forgiven himself for surviving when she hadn't.

It was three weeks later that Jimmy's father unceremoniously dumped him with his grandparents and left, never to be seen again (chalk up trough number two). He left a note saying that he just couldn't cope and that it would be better if he wasn't around while he tried to get himself back together. Better for him maybe thought Jimmy bitterly.

His Grandma was outraged. In her eyes, abandoning your own son was akin to cold-blooded murder. Grandad Bill, on the other hand thought it was utterly fantastic to have his grandson come and live with them. He had never hid his dislike of his son-in-law, nor his love for his only grandchild.

For Jimmy though, he couldn't begin to fathom what terrible thing he had done to deserve having both parents taken away from him so early in life.

Now, nearly five years on, Jimmy had long since learnt to adapt. Contact with his dad was through infrequent birthday and Christmas cards, which stand unopened on the mantelpiece, gathering dust just like Jimmy's memories of him.

So that was it. His story so far. He was now settled happily in Apple Valley where the summers were long, the country air clean and his friends the best in the world. In fact if his dad came back right now and asked him to move back home, Jimmy wouldn't go. He loved it here. Well, he had until yesterday. The day Cat left town.

✳ ✳ ✳

Jimmy had met Catrina at his twelfth birthday party. She had moved with her family into old man Clifton's house, five doors down from him, a couple of days before the party.

It had been his Grandma's idea that they invite her. "You can introduce her to all your friends." She had said enthusiastically.

For Jimmy, the prospect of being shackled to a new girl all day sounded simply revolting. The only saving grace was that Apple Valley birthday parties tended to involve all the neighbourhood kids whether they were your friends or not, so there was a reasonable chance he could ditch Catrina early on. That would then leave him free to talk to his best friend, Halfpint, about his one true passion, music.

Both he and Halfpint played guitar and had become inseparable since Jimmy moved into town.

When the day of Jimmy's birthday party arrived however, his well-laid plans were rudely shattered by the strangest sensation he had ever felt. It struck his body like a cannonball at precisely one fifteen on July the twelfth. The exact moment he first set eyes on Catrina Wickowski.

She was dressed in a flowing white dress that had little pink flowers embroidered all the way down the front. Her blonde hair was tied into two shoulder length pigtails and she wore slight heels that made her stand about an inch taller than Jimmy. Her deep turquoise eyes sparkled like precious jewels and, unlike all of the other girls who were heavily made-up trying look older than they were, Catrina wore only transparent varnish on her nails. Jimmy had never seen anyone so beautiful in all his life.

Deep in the pit of his stomach it felt like a thousand butterflies had suddenly burst free from their chrysalis cases and were fluttering madly in a bid for freedom and his poor heart began to beat so fast he feared it would burst out of his chest and land with a nasty splat on Catrina's dress.

After what seemed like an embarrassingly long time he finally managed to utter a very croaky, "Hi."

Catrina just smiled demurely and in that simple skyward movement of her lips, all the gently tickling butterflies turned into a single magnificent soaring eagle and Jimmy Green did something he had never done before. He fell in love.

The rest of the party became a wonderful blur. Catrina headed off and made new friends whilst Jimmy spent the whole time staring at this new, beautiful girl.

For two and a half years not much had changed. They became friends, helping each other with homework, going to the movies together and working side by side in the orchards during summer break. She even volunteered to be the singer when Edward and Jimmy formed a band.

They called themselves Applejuice (Cat's choice), recruited a drummer and a bass player – Paige Turner and Cornelius Wishbone the third (don't ask) and set about becoming the biggest band in the world – or in Apple Valley at least.

They had so very nearly made it too. Next week was the final of the very prestigious Apple Valley interschool Battle of the Bands competition. Held every three years, each of the four big schools in the Valley put forward a band to compete. Applejuice had won their heat and would represent Apple Valley High.

It was a great honour because not only would the winner be crowned 'best band in Apple Valley' but for this year only, they would be invited to play at the biggest event Apple Valley had ever seen – The Centenary Celebration Concert.

Celebrating one hundred years since the first apple tree was planted in the valley, an almighty party had been organised, with a huge pop concert as the finale. Already some of the top pop and rock bands in the world had agreed to play. To be a part of it was everything Jimmy had ever dreamed of and despite the fact that no band from Apple Valley High had won the competition for eighteen years, he knew they were good enough. Or at least they had been until Cat left.

Chewing a last mouthful of toast, his insides squirmed at the prospect of playing without her. He had a horrid emptiness inside. Like some vital part of him was missing. A guitar without strings. A drum kit without cymbals. Without Cat he was incomplete and he was angry for never having the guts to tell her how he felt. Maybe if he had, she would have stayed, and he wouldn't be feeling so bad right now.

Today was the first band rehearsal since Cat dropped the bombshell. It should have been a celebration of their semi final victory and planning for the final! But instead it was going to be a wake mourning the loss of their lead singer.

Worse than that, he just knew that the guys would be looking to him to explain how on earth they were going to play in front of four schools worth of students and teachers without Cat.

The trouble was, he didn't have an earthly clue.

CHAPTER 15

APPLEJUICE

Jimmy set out late for rehearsal, delaying as long as possible the inevitable conversation awaiting him.

The sun was blazing as he strapped his guitar to his back and climbed aboard his bicycle. The band practiced in his Grandad's old barn, which nestled on the edge of the orchard. As beads of sweat began to form on his brow he couldn't help thinking that on a day like today, the weather should do him a favour and not look so cheerful.

He sped off fast out through the houses and onto the dirt roads covering the three miles in no time. As he powered to the brow of the final descent, he skidded to a halt and gazed down at the barn.

It had once been the centre point of a large farm. A place where old machinery and vehicles were serviced and repaired. Then the farm was swallowed by the burgeoning orchard. Now the red paint peeled from the timbers and most of the windows were matte black with the grime of neglect. Still, it was where Applejuice called home and it had a special place in Jimmy's heart.

From his high vantage point, the orchards impact on the area was all too depressingly clear. Jimmy had only heard stories of the vast rolling meadows, the brilliant crystal blue lakes and the thousands of cattle that grazed on Thunder Ridge. Now it was miles and miles of apple trees, all in their perfectly ordered straight, boring lines. Jimmy hated it.

The Appleton Corporation who owned it all had started out with just a hundred trees, but had grown under Siegfried Dirt, son of the founder, out of all proportion.

Siegfried had been sent to the best schools and left knowing exactly what he wanted and who he was willing to trample on to get it. He had seen the future, and the future was genes.

He spent millions – if not billions – of his father's money developing the Corporation into pioneers of genetic science. In a few short years, Siegfried's team created such wonders as the TripleTrees™ that produced three crops a year and grew five times faster and bigger than normal apple trees. Then the ChompingTrees™ which bore fruit not only resistant to disease, but which actually fed upon the insects that once fed on them.

The trees success swelled the Appleton Corporation into a huge beast, annihilating the competition and taking global control of the apple market along with every piece of land within fifty miles of where Jimmy stood. Siegfried even had his own helicopter security force that jealously guarded his orchard's secrets.

Nevertheless, the old barn had survived this military style invasion and together the band decorated the walls with posters of their favourite bands and begged as much old furniture as they could. They christened it 'The Juice Pit' although Jimmy suggested 'The stink house' would be more appropriate since the stench of old, festering oil was ripe.

Sighing at the memory of happier days, Jimmy reluctantly picked up his feet and let the bike freewheel down the hill.

* * *

Paige, Edward and Cornelius had already arrived and the atmosphere was, as expected, darker than the inside of a cave.

They were all sulking. Paige was drawing circles on her snare drum with a drumstick. Cornelius, was leaning against an old tractor tyre running a fingertip up and down a worn groove, whilst Edward was fiddling with the back of his amp trying to keep out of the way.

The silence was awkward. Jimmy tried to break it.

"Anybody got any good ideas then?" he said in what he hoped was an optimistic tone.

Paige looked up, her face framed by two cymbals. "Did you know she was going?" she snapped. "Because if you did and kept quiet about it because you '*love her*' this drum stick is gonna end up in such a painful place…"

Jimmy held up his hands, not wishing to know where she had in mind. "Paige, I swear I found out at the same time as you. She didn't tell me a thing."

He was being truthful. The first he knew of it was right after the semi-final. Cat gathered them together and explained how her dad had been offered a new job, a too good to turn down job, and that she was leaving. Not leaving in a week or a month's time. Leaving the *following day*.

Words haven't yet been invented that could accurately describe what the news did to Jimmy's insides. It felt like some sort of primal scream of anguish. A completely unintelligible word, but very similar to that which is made when you get up in the night and accidentally stub your toe on the bed leg.

Paige faced Jimmy down. "So what the heck are we supposed to do? The finals next week! How are we supposed to find a singer at that short notice?" She thrust a stick at Jimmy. "*You* shouldn't have let her go. *You* should have done something."

Jimmy huffed. "What? What was I supposed to do?"

"Stop her. She's your girlfriend. You could have persuaded her not to go, told her that staying here was more important than going off to some foreign country."

Jimmy grimaced. "And where would she have lived, Paige? Here in the barn? No, exactly. And she was not my girlfriend."

"Well we're going to have to pull out, you know that don't you? There's no way we can play," stormed Paige sulking.

Cornelius stopped tracing the groove and slowly looked over at

Jimmy and Paige. He was a tall, muscular African American boy who could easily be mistaken for being athletic. That would be wrong. With Cornelius there were only two states of being – asleep and barely awake. Nothing was ever rushed with Cornelius. In fact snails viewed Cornelius as a kindred soul and a pretty cool guy. Enough said.

"I think we should all calm down a little," he said in a voice like winter treacle. "No-one says we have to pull out. We can find another singer. They don't have to learn many songs after all. We only have to play for twenty minutes."

Paige exasperation boiled over. She swore loudly in Mexican and hit her snare drum so hard, the drumstick bounced out of her hand and flew into the air catching Halfpints' nose on the way down. "Stupido." She screamed. "Where do you think we're going to find a singer who hasn't already been kicked out of the competition? All the bands from around a hundred miles entered and if the judges didn't think they were good enough then, why should they be good enough now. Face it. We have to pull out. We could have won, but now thanks to his girlfriend we have to quit." She turned her back on the others and slumped on her drum stool.

Jimmy looked across at Halfpint who had been keeping his head well down, during the exchange. "She wasn't my girlfriend," he said again.

Paige was always like this. She was an awesome drummer but had a tendency to be rather, what was the word, emotional.

He remembered the first time they met. It was in the schoolyard during break. Halfpint introduced them. Jimmy remembered it plainly because she had just delivered a beautiful right hook to the jaw of some kid who was at least twice her size. Jimmy was amazed, not least because with eyes as dark as plain chocolate, smooth olive toned skin and jet-black silky hair that cascaded all the way down her back, Paige was the spit for Disney's Pocahontas. Appearances it seemed could be very deceptive.

According to the enthusiastic onlookers it transpired that the big kid had been foolish enough to call one of Paige's six brothers something unpleasant. *More fool him*, thought Jimmy.

As the big kid limped off with a painful split lip and seriously dented pride, Jimmy wondered if Halfpint had deliberately forgotten to mention her predilection for hitting things other than her drum kit, or whether this was news to him too.

The interview – such as it was – was short and sweet. Jimmy carefully avoided any provocative words or gestures that may have resulted in a right hook, whilst Paige took no time in informing him that she *would* be playing drums in his band and that they had better be good or else she wouldn't be around very long. The rest, as they say, is history.

Back from his reverie, Paige's words swirled around his head. Maybe she was right. Trying to find another singer at this late stage was a stupid idea, but he couldn't bear to let the dream of holding aloft the Battle of the Bands trophy slip away. It wasn't fair. It wasn't fair at all.

With Paige sulking and the others at a loss for words, the silence in the barn became deafening. Up in the eaves you could actually hear the timber beams groaning in sympathy. Jimmy sighed and wondered if his day could possibly get any worse.

CHAPTER 16

DIRTY DEEDS

Of course as everybody knows, you should never wonder such things because you invariably get the answer you don't want.

After fifteen minutes of sulking silence, and not a single musical note played in anger, the sound of approaching quad bikes caught their attention.

Quad bikes themselves were not uncommon around Apple Valley. The orchard workers often used them as everyday vehicles and many of the rich kids had them as play-things, but Jimmy had never owned one and of those people he knew who did, he couldn't imagine any of them wanting to come to the Juicepit.

He looked over curiously at Halfpint as the engines of at least two bikes rumbled to a stop outside. A moment later the old barn door began to creak open.

When Jimmy saw the three figures silhouetted in the late afternoon sunshine (one very thin, two very thick) his heart sank down into his boots. He recognized them immediately. They were his least favourite people in the whole world, Damien Dirt and his two colossal henchmen, Kyle and Dominic Banner; the supersize twins. Damien stepped his wildly expensive looking trainers over the threshold and got straight down to business.

"My god this place stinks! Does it remind you all of your homes?"

His business was being obnoxious.

Jimmy tutted and huffed. As a come back it was pretty pathetic, but it was all he could muster.

Damien, as always was dressed in the latest designer clothes. And, as always, looked like a badly drawn tramp. His skinny bones poked through the sleeves like twigs in a sack and his legs would have shamed a crow. Somehow, for all the money spent, his body was just not equipped to fill the clothes he bought.

Not that it bothered Damien. As the only son of Siegfried Dirt, Damien held himself with the unwavering arrogance that only somebody born into money can have.

"Jimmy." He held out his hands and said it like "Jimmeyyyy."

"What the hell do you want here, Dirt?" Jimmy hissed.

Damien strutted forward. "Now, now Jimbo, calm yourself down. Is that any way to greet the person who has come to save your skin?' He smiled devilishly. It reminded Jimmy of predator just before it was about to sink its fangs into you.

'Save our skins? You couldn't save tokens for a free pizza. Now push off! Our skins don't need saving thank you very much."

"Ooh. Harsh words from somebody whose name is the colour of festering pond water. Not even a tad curious as to why I'm here *Green*?"

"My only curiosity where you're concerned is to know how high you would bounce if you were dropped from an airplane. Hopefully I wouldn't need a very long tape measure! And, for someone called 'Dirt' that last comment was a bit rich."

Cornelius smiled at that one. This was getting good.

"You've come to rub our noses in it," continued Jimmy, "to tell us that we're useless and don't stand a chance of winning the Battle of the Bands anyway. Well go ahead, take your best shot, do your gloating and then shove off!"

Damien brushed his hand through his black coiffured hair. "My, my, I am sensing some hostility Jimbo! A liddle bit grumpy wumpy since catty watty left are we?" he mocked. "I don't suppose it might ever occur to you that I might actually bring good news?"

"You're leaving the country as well then?" said Jimmy, quick as a flash.

Even quicker Kyle Banners hand shot out and smacked Jimmy on the side of the head. Jimmy never saw it coming and it stung. Silence descended.

"Really. Now you brought that on yourself," snarled Damien. "You really are very tedious you know."

Jimmy rubbed his face.

It had always been like this between the two of them. Ever since the day Jimmy prevented Damien from dropping a live frog into a jar of hydrochloric acid during a biology lesson, they had been archenemies.

It had been only Jimmy's second day at school and not a single kid in class had backed him up. They just looked at him as if he was insane. It didn't take him long to discover why.

Everyone was terrified of Damien Dirt.

Not because he was the biggest kid or because he was the toughest – certainly not, but because of who his dad was.

There was no-one in the Valley who didn't work for Siegfried Dirt in some capacity and boy didn't he – and his son – know it. If Siegfried had an unenviable reputation as a ruthless boss – once sacking his secretary for wearing a perfume that made him sneeze – his son was his equal as the playground bully. Knowing that he could not be touched no matter what he did or said (not if the parents wanted to keep their jobs anyway) Damien ran rough-shod over everybody.

Small kids frequently bore the brunt of his school dictatorship. Most days they were lucky if all he did was make them pay a tax on their dinner money.

Even the teachers didn't escape entirely. He chatted back relentlessly and never did homework, yet somehow still managed to secure top marks in every exam he sat. This despite one time never sitting the exam at all! And through it all the Banner twins guarded him like he was a member of the British royalty ensuring few reprisals.

In fact, Jimmy was the only person ever to have stood up to Damien and was generally regarded as being quite mad for doing so.

Their rivalry had reached a peak last year when Damien spread some truly ghastly rumors about Cat after she refused to go on a date with him. They took a long time to live down and Jimmy hadn't forgotten.

"Anyway, what was I saying?" said Damien. "Oh yes, good news about your little band. Obviously it's terrible that Catrina has had to leave. Left you in a terribly awkward situation. Very selfish. What do you say Jimbo?"

Jimmy said nothing.

"I always thought you really were scraping the barrel with her though Jimmy. I know you had a thing for her, but really … ugly doesn't even come close, and her voice, oh, don't get me started."

Dominic convulsed into guffaws of laughter. A large globule of green snot shot out of his nose and arched into the air, narrowly missing Jimmy's shoulder. Jimmy was too busy seething to notice. His fists were clenched so tight by his side that his nails were digging painfully into his palms. He was ready to explode.

"So that's why I'm here," informed Damien. "She was obviously too chicken to see it through. So say hello to your new singer."

Everyone's mouth's dropped open. Damien was clearly meaning himself and a new kind of silence swamped the barn. It was one where you expect tumbleweed to come billowing past at any moment.

Jimmy was first to find his voice. "You have got to be joking," he said, shaking his head firmly. "Absolutely no bloody way are you going to be the singer in this band."

"Oh I'm afraid I am Jimbo."

"Over my dead body you are."

"I don't think that will be quite necessary," smirked Damien. "But let me make it quite clear; I'm not asking, I'm telling you, I am your new singer."

Behind her drum kit, Paige leapt to her feet. "I'm not playing with him. It'd be like … be like …"

Damien locked eyes. "Sit down," he snarled.

Paige reared like an angry panther. Jimmy moved quickly to diffuse the situation.

"Er, I don't want to be in danger of stating the obvious Dirt, but you can't sing. In fact, you couldn't hold a tune if you had ten hands."

Damien snorted. "Oh ha, ha. Very funny, Green. Boys, pass me a brace, I think my sides have split."

Dominic actually *looked* for a brace.

"Green, you of all people should know that I never joke. If I want something, I get it. If I want someone to do something, they do it. It's not up for discussion so you'd better get used to it. And I *can* sing. Listen."

Damien launched into what could only be described as a musical train wreck. It was toe cringing. It was paper bags over the heads awful. It was the sound a whale would probably make if it were pulled through an industrial mincing machine backwards.

When he stopped the silence was deafening.

Damien carried on regardless. "My dad has already informed the competition judges of the change and they were only too happy to accept."

"I beg your pardon?" said Jimmy returning to his senses. "What do you mean your Dad has informed the judges? He can't do that without asking us first!"

Damien scoffed. "Of course he can. My dad can do anything he wants. He is funding the celebrations in case you had forgotten."

"Well you and your Dad can just think again, because there's no way we'll play with you. You'll have to sing on your own." Jimmy looked for support. Everyone nodded in agreement.

Damien smiled a very self satisfied smile. "Well of course I thought you would say that." He reached into his right trouser pocket and pulled out a stained piece of paper. It looked old, almost antique. He unfolded it and waved it provocatively under Jimmy's nose. "Do you know what this is, Green?"

Of course Jimmy didn't.

"This is a copy of the lease to your Grandfather's land. It covers the house, the fields, and indeed, the very barn that we are now standing in. And do you know what it says Jimbo?"

Jimmy grimaced. If Damien called him Jimbo one more time, he would take that piece of paper and shove it right up . . .!

"It says that the lease runs out on the last day of this month. The day of the concert in fact. Apparently, it turns out that my dad isn't too keen on renewing it. He has wanted to knock down your tatty house, street and barn for years so he can build a new sorting plant on the land, which would of course mean you would be homeless. That would be a shame wouldn't it?"

Jimmy's anger deflated like a popped balloon.

Damien smiled an acid smile. "Now, of course you must understand, seeing you out on the streets would be the last thing I would want, so I have taken it upon myself to have a word with my father and see if we couldn't come to some . . . arrangement."

Jimmy finally saw where this was heading. "You mean, I let you sing in the band and your dad lets my Grandad have his lease?"

Damien clicked his finger and thumb together above his head. "Bingo." He looked at Kyle and Dominic. "I told you this boy had brains didn't I? I will be more than happy to let father know that you agree to his terms."

"And what if we lose and don't get to play at the Centenary?"

Damien stepped forward menacingly placing his nose inches from Jimmy's. "Then the deal is *off*, understand. No Centenary concert, no lease. The diggers will move in and flatten your house the same night. You can live in the trees for all I care. Except you can't because that's my land and I'll have you arrested." He stepped back and gazed majestically into the rafters of the barn. "The Centenary is a commemoration of my families success; a celebration of ridding this place of those worthless cattle and creating the greatest apple orchard in the entire world. And I will be the crowning glory, Green. I will be the one that everyone will look at. The son and heir performing with the biggest bands in the world, what greater advertisement for the Dirt brand could there be?"

The next thing Jimmy saw was a blur of black hair and spinning fists speeding past him. It was Paige.

"You're a scumbag!" she screamed, launching a full-on attack. Damien faltered as the Mexican whirlwind landed perfectly on the balls of her feet and aimed an uppercut at Damien's chin. However, as her arm arched upwards, Kyle Banner whipped out a hand with uncharacteristic speed and caught her fist in his huge sweaty palm, then he started to squeeze.

Agony etched its way onto Paige's face. She let out a yelp, her knees buckled under the pain and she sank to the floor. Jimmy didn't know what to do. Paige always gave as good as she got, but this time she was beaten almost before she had begun. Damien smirked and quickly regained his composure. Kyle showed no mercy. His grip tightened until Paige could take no more and she screamed for him to let go. He did, pushing her sprawling across the floor.

Jimmy, Cornelius and Halfpint all stepped up ready for a showdown, but Dominic put himself right next to his brother and smirked. It was hopeless, like facing down two sumo wrestlers.

Damien straightened out his shirt and leaned over Paige who was gripping her injured hand. He pointed a bony finger right in her pained face, making her flinch.

"You should watch your temper, girl! We – don't – want – any – breakages – to – those – precious – little – fingers – do we?" He marked each word by slapping alternate sides of Paige's face. That was bad. Anyone else would be swallowing their teeth by now. But Paige looked defeated.

Damien cleared his throat, and as if nothing had happened began to head for the door. "Now, I'm sure you would like some time to think over my offer. Shall we say tomorrow after school? Because you are going to say yes, I will bring a list of the songs I want to sing and then I can see if you are good enough. Please don't even think about not turning up." He made a point of patting the pocket where the lease was.

With that, he and the twins left, but not before Kyle kicked over Jimmy's guitar case on his way out.

Jimmy and the guys were left stunned. Halfpint ran to Paige's aid.

"I don't believe that just happened," he said helping her up.

"Well it did," snarled Paige angrily rubbing her cheek. "And we're going to play right? Because when it's over, he's going to pay for that."

"Of course we'll do it," replied Halfpint looking at Cornelius for confirmation.

"Yeah man! We'll do it," he agreed. "If anyone can make that idiot sound good, it's us!"

Jimmy didn't say anything. He tried to smile but he felt sapped of energy. He knew that they would do it for him, because if the situation were reversed, he would do it for them too. They wouldn't allow Damien Dirt to make his family homeless, no matter what embarrassment they might have to suffer in the process. And to be sure, letting Damien Dirt sing in their band was going to cause them all immense embarrassment.

But, even with their magnanimous show of friendship, he couldn't help thinking that his day, had indeed, just got a lot worse.

CHAPTER 17

SPACE INVADER

**THE X1 STAR SEEKER. TEN MILES ABOVE THE SURFACE —
AND FALLING**

The landing was going well in the same way that the Titanic's maiden voyage went well. The Blue Planets ferocious outer atmospheres were battering the X1 Star Seeker relentlessly. The Seeker's engines were groaning under the strain and JoJo could barely grip the controls for more than a few seconds before her hands were shaken free.

"This is hopeless," she said, unbuckling herself from her chair. "We've got warning lights all over the place! Hold her steady SaRa, I need to check the stabilizers."

"Don't be long," replied SaRa fretfully. "Fuel pump to engine one is failing. I need you to work on it."

"Please be careful sis," groaned 2B.

JoJo clambered her way over the debris left by the earlier explosion, swearing as she stumbled her way to the back of the Seeker. Usually the stabilizers were locked away behind a metal panel, but upon reaching them she found the door swinging freely, its latch snapped clean off. That was not a good sign.

Lifting it high, thick, black smoke billowed out into her face. She coughed loudly as the stench of burning hit her throat. There was no need to waste her time here. The stabilizers were destroyed. No wonder she and 2B could feel every bump. She slammed the doors shut knowing they would just have to ride out the buffeting and pray that the Seeker held together until they landed.

She scrambled back to an increasingly panicky 2B.

"We're losing everything," he cried, desperately pushing any button he could find.

JoJo glared helplessly at the flickering cockpit monitors. One by one, all the lights were fading to black.

"Fuel pump out, radar system failing!" said SaRa. She was losing control.

"Oh for Karzig's sake," screamed JoJo, leaping into her seat and feeling the buckles tighten around her automatically. "I can't take anymore of this. Just try to hold whatever you can together. I'm taking us down!"

She held her breath, flipped off the autopilot, mentally crossed her fingers, dipped the nose and pushed the thrusters on full. With only two operational engines she was taking a huge risk. This amount of thrust could lead to one seriously big explosion, but enough was enough. It was time to put two feet firmly on the ground, even if that ground happened to be the Blue Planet.

The remaining engines whined horribly as they powered up. Faster and faster they went. Only when she hit top speed without being blown to pieces did she allow herself to breathe out.

Unfortunately, the high speeds made the Seeker even more unstable and JoJo had to pull some truly amazing manoeuvres to keep them on course.

For SaRa the strain of the last hour was taking its toll. JoJo prayed that she could hold it together just a little while longer because they would need her to make sure they didn't crash straight into a major city full of humans.

Finally, like molten metal pouring through treacle they thundered through the inner atmospheres and saw land for the first time. Even under these extreme circumstances JoJo felt a strong urge to look down at the Blue Planet. The temptation gnawed at her but she knew now was not the time for sightseeing. She gripped the controls tighter and focused all her energy on following SaRa's directions.

"Landing area sighted," SaRa said after several minutes of skirting the blue skies. Her voice seemed weak and sickly.

JoJo sighed with relief. "At last, I don't think she's going to hold on for much longer. The invisibility shields have about had it. We can't risk being seen SaRa. We just can't."

"I am doing my best. However I have taken the liberty of performing a life scan of the landing coordinates just in case and found no sign of human inhabitants."

"Then this is it. Let's get it over with and land before I change my mind."

As soon as she said the words and tilted the Seeker into its landing trajectory, the sheer enormity of what they were doing hit her like a wrecking ball to the guts. Was this truly the only way to save themselves? Every fibre of her being told her that to land on the Blue Planet was a mistake of cataclysmic proportions, but what choice did she have. It was this, or face certain death in the skies.

Poor 2B had no idea what they were about to face. JoJo had manipulated him from the start so he would come with her. She had told him everything was going to be all right. Clearly it wasn't.

Almost robotically, JoJo dropped the Seeker to its optimum landing height of two hundred feet from the ground and watched dazed as the green blurry landscape roared by her window. That was when she realized something was very wrong with the outside world. She strained forward in her chair looking from side to side concern etched on her face. "SaRa, where exactly is this landing site?"

"Four miles straight ahead."

"Then I suggest you reconfigure and do it quickly because there's nothing but trees for a hundred miles in every direction."

SaRa quickly reconfigured. "Are you sure? My computers tell me that we should be in an isolated valley of grassland and lakes. There should be no woodland below us at all."

Now it was JoJo's turn to panic. The strain had obviously pushed SaRa too far. She was malfunctioning! She had directed them to an area where they couldn't possibly land. It would take a recovery crew ten years to find all the pieces if they tried to touch down here. They had to find somewhere else. Quickly!

She reached for the abort button but never made it. Her finger was an inch away when it exploded in a puff of blue smoke. She screamed and pulled her blackened fingertip away sharply as the control panel lit up like a fireworks display. Lights flashed, buzzers buzzed and warning lamps came to life everywhere.

2B went whiter than chalk as the Seeker quivered and shook.

Then it started to fall.

It grazed a treetop, then another and another, skimming over the surface like a pebble on a pond. JoJo steered but the controls were useless in her hands. She braced herself for impact and urged 2B to do the same. Was this how it was going to end?

Reaching over, she took her baby brother's hand and squeezed it tight. No words could console him or express how sorry she was to have brought him here, so she didn't even bother trying. She just held on to him for all she was worth.

A high pitched whine was followed by a sudden and absolute silence. Both remaining engines were now dead. They were gliding.

Safety straps automatically shot from the chairs and wrapped tightly around their shoulders. 2B whimpered and squeezed JoJo's hand so tightly she thought one of her fingers might have snapped. The Seeker pounded against another tree throwing JoJo forward like a rag-doll. Leaves exploded into the air like confetti as branches whipped at the windscreen like knarred fingers scratching to get in.

Then they dropped right through the trees and slammed hard into the ground. The impact sent shock waves up JoJo's spine.

Now they were sliding out of control down what appeared to be a corridor of trees. The friction of Seeker against ground was finally slowing them down but it was going to be too little too late. In front of them was a solid wall of trees and a sharp left turn – a turn they couldn't possibly make. The trees were unavoidable, they were going to hit them, and they were going to hit them hard.

Closer and closer they came. Time seemed to stretch like elastic. Suddenly JoJo could see the entire scene as if it were being played out on a screen. She knew how it would all end.

As the trees loomed large she shut her eyes tight and prayed. For one last time they bounced off the dusty ground.

Then there was nothing but silence.

* * *

As JoJo and her Star Seeker lay, possibly fatally stricken on the surface of the Blue Planet, the man who had earlier so callously disposed of Doumas Gunz breathed deeply, lost in meditative thoughts as his own Spacecraft continued to travel along its low earth orbit.

Years of dedicated training had taught him that, much as he may want to, it would not serve him to get angry despite the turn of events he had just witnessed. Anger would only cloud his judgement as he considered his next move.

The instructions from his leader, his Arkhos had been clear. The girl must not be allowed to return to Anilar under any circumstances. How he achieved this had not been discussed. The consequences of his failure however, had been left in no doubt.

He speculated as to whether he could have possibly foreseen the girl's actions, but no. No one could have anticipated that she would land on the Blue Planet. Her file had more than one reference to her maverick approach to flying, but even so, failing to send the mayday alert had been an act of supreme stupidity. The consequences, not least for himself if his Arkhos found out, could be disastrous.

Therefore, he would sit here and think. There was still one surprise waiting for the girl if she had indeed survived; a little welcoming committee that he had arranged for such an unfortunate event as this. If she lived through that, which he dearly hoped she would not, then she was the luckiest girl alive, and he didn't believe in luck.

With a cursory glance at his plasmon screen to confirm that the tracker fitted to her Star Seeker was still functioning, he returned to his meditation and waited for her to die.

CHAPTER 18

HIDING PLACE

She wondered if she was dead. Every limb ached as though she'd been in a fight with a bad tempered Rhondopod and lost. Her head was swimming and she had the strangest sensation as if she was somehow floating. Tentatively opening her eyes, she found herself completely immersed in a thick blue viscous gel. It was all around her distorting her vision. She reached into the substance but her arm felt like it was attached to a bungee rope and it gently sprang back, the gel reforming behind it. She flexed a leg and the same thing happened. Where was she and what was this stuff?

Suddenly it came to her. *Croxy Gel, of course*, she thought. *A super saturated oxygen hydro-gel deployed automatically upon impact to cushion and protect the pilot from serious injury or trauma.* She recalled the first year lecture word for word, but this Croxy Gel was more than just cushioning her, it was enveloping her. It was up her nose, in her mouth and down the lining of her suit. Her hair was pinned to her head and her suit was pressed into creases of her body she didn't know she had, but amazingly it wasn't suffocating her. On the contrary, her breathing was quite normal. The gel felt comfortable and safe, as if she was stuffed inside a giant jelly. The only problem was she had no idea how to get out of the stuff.

For several minutes she sat trapped and frustrated, wondering what to do, then a loud hissing noise signaled the automatic gel extraction procedure and before her eyes it began to vanish into vents.

As it disappeared, the gel revealed 2B. He was blowing desperately out of his nose and twisting his fingers in his ears attempting to dislodge the gel. JoJo smiled. After him being knocked unconscious, it was a strange sort of relief to see him in distress.

"Feeling better then?" she said, wiping some gel out of her fringe. "You had me worried there for a minute."

2B kept on snorting like an angry bull.

"Just relax, it will dissolve on its own."

"S'orrible. Tastes like slopp repellant," he grunted grumpily.

"Well you're not supposed to eat it."

"Shurrup. When can we go 'ome?"

JoJo glanced around her. The Seeker was like a ghost ship. Not a single light, switch or monitor flickered with any sign of life.

She punched a few random computer keys but the screens remained resolutely blank. "I think it could be a while before we go anywhere. Why don't you go over to the bunks and see if you can find the first aid kit so I can tend to your head."

"Not my 'ed dat's the broblem," he snuffled unbuckling himself, "'dis flippin' gel up my dose dat's de broblem." He let out a snort sending a large globule of gel shooting from his nostrils. "Ahh. Now that's better," he said, breathing freely.

JoJo sighed. "You're cleaning that up you know," she said trying not to smile. 2B ignored her and slumped off to find the first aid kit.

JoJo turned her attention to the Star Seekers damage. "SaRa, how are you and what can you tell me?" she asked, fruitlessly trying more buttons.

SaRa's hologram appeared seemingly unscathed. "I have to say that I have been better. Croxy gel does nothing for my circuitry you know." She let out a tiny cough as if to illustrate the point. "It appears that the main computer system shut down before impact. I am immeasurably sorry for losing control of the engines. I can't tell you how embarrassed I feel, such a thing has never happened in over half a million intergalactic flights."

"Forget about it SaRa. We're alive, that's the main thing. Just tell me what we have functioning at the moment? Please tell me that we have some invisibility."

SaRa shook her head, "I'm afraid not. Without the main system operating it's totally impossible. I am running on my own reserve supply but it's not nearly enough to run any other programs as well."

JoJo slumped pessimistically back into her chair. This was the worst case scenario. Stranded alone on the most dangerous planet in the galaxy, completely vulnerable to attack or capture and there was not a damn thing she could do about it. How much time did they have before the humans found this big golden spaceship stranded in their midst? Surely it could not be long.

When 2B returned, JoJo washed and dressed his wound with a specially impregnated medi-plaster. It would at least help prevent any cross-species infections setting in. SaRa meanwhile set to work on the computer systems.

After several minutes she got it rebooted.

"Main system power back and working," she said proudly.

With a hiss and a click, the low cockpit hum returned like a familiar friend as a handful of lights and monitors flickered into life.

"Thank goodness. Now lets run a diagnostic check."

"I'm already doing it."

Lines of text began to scroll down JoJo's main monitor as every component in the Star Seeker was checked. It didn't look great. JoJo noticed many repetitions of words like 'damaged' and 'failed' written in the status column.

"I'll list the damage in order of priority for you," SaRa said as the check came to an end.

JoJo could hardly bring herself to look.

A huge amount of data came up on screen. JoJo's mouth dropped. "Maybe it would have been quicker to show me what is still working," she remarked quietly.

In all, there were one hundred and ten component faults. JoJo quickly scanned them all. Two in particular caught her eye. One would have to wait, but the other … "What's this about the life support system SaRa?"

SaRa grimaced. "As you know, the oxo generator was damaged during the original explosion in the asteroids. The crash has unfortunately completely destroyed it. My best calculations suggest that even if we switch to the reserve oxygen tanks, we will only have a space travel time of approximately one hour."

"One hour? How long to repair?"

"Days, I am afraid."

The news was like a kick from a Stone Toothed Largo. Without oxygen the return journey was impossible. An hour would barely get them to the Sharamin portal even if they ran at light speed which, with broken engines, was impossible anyway. But what were they going to do for *days*? She could feel her stress levels rising again. Why was it that every little success brought with it a huge problem? She looked at 2B who appeared pensive.

"Don't worry," she reassured, "at least we're safe in the Star Seeker. Nothing can get in and we're certainly not going out."

SaRa coughed. "Unfortunately," she said, "that may not be entirely your decision. Motion sensors are indicating that we have company in Engine bay number four."

"COMPANY? What do you mean company?" shrieked JoJo.

"I mean that I have detected movement of unknown origin."

"What!" JoJo jumped to her feet. "It must be a mistake. Check again. The crash must have caused it to go off accidentally."

"That won't be necessary. The motion sensors are one of the few things still in full working order."

'Karzig,' thought JoJo, if the sensors weren't faulty then what was in the engine bay? A human? Surely not. She couldn't be that unlucky, could she?

The engine covers were situated at the very rear of the Star Seeker. JoJo had no choice but investigate.

She moved slowly and carefully in the dim glow of the emergency lighting. All around her lamps flickered and crackled testing her nerves to the limit. Not that she was afraid of the dark; oh no, it was the things she couldn't see in the dark that worried JoJo.

Once at the covers, she blindly patted the wall until she located the keypad that would open the doors. Wrapping her hand around it so she would not lose it, she typed six of the seven necessary digits, then paused. What if she was about to let a human loose into the Star Seeker? Punching that last number could be the last thing she ever did.

She swallowed her fear and pushed the button.

With barely a hiss, the cover slid open.

Silence. The hatch was just large enough to push her head through, but she didn't feel that brave. Rather, she placed her left ear as close to the opening as she dared and tapped on the metal shaft. Nothing responded and she wondered if SaRa really had got it wrong.

Just above her head, an emergency flashlight was secured in a recess. She yanked it from its mount and turned it on. Finally some light. Cautiously she shone the torch into the bay and shook it from side to side hoping whatever was in there would be startled enough to make a noise.

Still the only sound was the electric crackle above her head. This was getting he nowhere. Taking a deep breath, she bravely pushed her head inside shining the torch into the bowels of the engine.

A deafening screech wailed like a siren, resonating riotously off the metal sides. JoJo jumped and dropped the flashlight. She watched helplessly as it bounced out of reach.

Another screech followed, much louder this time. JoJo thought her ears had burst. She yanked her head out, whacking her skull on the top of the opening as she did so. She swore. It hurt like hell but just wanted away from the noise. A noise she recognized only too well. Flailing in the dark, she slammed the keypad to shut the cover.

But it barely moved a few inches before it jammed.

From down in the bay came frantic scratching and scurrying sounds. Oh no, it was heading for the hatch!

She smacked the keypad again. Still the panel gaped open.

"Karzig! Karzig! Karzig!" She screamed, hitting it with each expletive. On the last hit the cover mercifully freed itself and slid shut. The instant it sealed, the stowaway slammed against the panel and began pummeling it.

"GO AWAY!" screamed JoJo and kicked the cover with the sole of her boot. That only seemed to antagonize the thing. The cover took a massive hit so JoJo kicked harder.

It seemed to work. The scurrying sped away, deeper into the bay. Her relief however was short lived. The terrible screeching was replaced by an equally earsplitting, brain-piercing squeal of teeth against metal. It rammed her senses like someone was trying to thread a knitting needle through her head.

She cupped her hands to her ears and rushed blindly away stumbling across fallen debris.

In the cockpit, the noise was still loud enough to battle a drill for the most annoying sound award. JoJo had to shout to be heard. "What cameras do we have working SaRa?"

"Only rear facing."

"That'll do." JoJo urged. "Show me the feed."

A live picture of the outside flashed up on her monitor. 2B peered over her shoulder, his hands over his ears. 'What is it? What are we looking for?'

She ignored him, concentrating on the screen. "Pan around so I can see engine four. Quickly, I think it's trying to eat its way out."

The camera panned around. To her horror, she could see a jagged gash in the metal. The scratching stopped.

"He's done it! He's only gone and done it."

Out of the newly ruptured tear a vile looking creature about the size of a cat dropped to the ground with a thrump. Three more of its kind followed.

"Oh my good god," exclaimed JoJo.

"What? What is it?" urged 2B.

Each creature landed gracefully, shook itself and then voided its stomach contents all over the floor. From both ends, if you get the picture.

"Urrghh! That's gross!" said 2B, and he was right. The creatures were truly hideous things. A true Larian nightmare and all male if she wasn't mistaken.

She watched the beasts stalk around sniffing the air. They appeared quite unperturbed by their new, unfamiliar surroundings.

"This is not good. Not good at all," whined JoJo.

She looked hard at 2B who read instantly what was on her mind "No!" he said firmly, "absolutely no way!"

"We have no choice. You know we don't; we have to go outside. That is a serious grommet problem!"

Chapter 19

Hunting the Hunter

The motto of the SpaceCoyotes is simple. 'Wherever you've been, keep it clean.' In a nutshell that meant that a planet visited by a Larian should be left as it was found – as though they had never been there. They even had tools to help them. What they didn't have however, was a magic wand which got rid of grommets and if she wasn't careful, JoJo was about to become the first person ever to cause an interplanetary cross-species spread. Not a title to strive for.

JoJo hated grommets. Ever since a baby one tried to bite her foot off during a cub training exercise, they had been at the top of her most despised creature list. They resembled an unearthly cross between a hairy slug and a vampire bat and were fast, tough, ugly and very, very deadly.

Hundreds of thousands of years ago grommets had been relatively placid creatures dwelling in large burrows deep in the jungles. It was not until a small population found themselves trapped in the highly radioactive underground planetary heating ducts that they changed. In only a few years they advanced and evolved into voracious, mean-tempered, metal chomping eating machines which devoured anything that got in their way, including Larians and, if she wasn't careful, humans.

JoJo dashed to the weapons store and thrust a finger in the DNA lock. A tiny sliver of skin cells were sloughed off and their DNA matched with JoJo's unique authorization code. The door swished open.

She jammed a Salton Five Disabler into her inner jacket pocket and tossed 2B an explorer jacket. Finally she unclipped a MKII tetra Harpoon from its mounting and began readying it.

"Stupid, stupid, stupid," moaned 2B as he slid an arm into a sleeve. "We'll be killed for sure. We'll be killed then eaten. No we won't, we'll be eaten before they kill us. We'll be-."

"Okay enough with the doom and gloom," interrupted JoJo. "Just put your jacket on."

2B huffed. "How did grommets get in here in the first place anyway?"

JoJo clicked a freshly charged cartridge into the Tetra Harpoon and peered down the sight. "I have no idea. It is common knowledge that they love engine bays, they've even been found nesting in them during the breeding season. Lots of expeditions were cancelled in the old days because of them chewing up the wiring, but nowadays all Star Seekers are checked every night before lockdown."

She pressed the touch sensitive targeting screen, making the gun hum into life.

"Maybe it was my fault," she mused. "By changing the command computer, it must have missed being checked or something." She looked her brother straight in the eye. "Whatever happened, we have to get out there and get them back before it's too late."

Locked and loaded she swung the tetra harpoon over her shoulder.

"Where's my weapon?" asked 2B.

JoJo snorted. "Ha, you've got to be joking. Do you know what damage these can do? Now shush and listen up."

2B frowned as he pulled his jacket around him.

"Put that jacket on full protection mode. You know how dangerous grommets are, don't you? They can see in almost complete darkness, their sense of smell is over two million times stronger than yours or mine and their stomach can digest three times their own body weight in under an hour."

2B's colour paled.

"They crave anything metallic and rather than excrete it as waste … pooh it out 2B. It means they pooh it out."

"Oh."

"They recycle it as a thin black carapace that stretches all the way down their backs. When you shoot them you have to be really careful not to hit it. Even a tetra harpoon spike will bounce straight off. It can go anywhere. Including in you! In fact grommet's are virtually impossible to kill."

As pep talks go, this one wasn't having the desired effect on an increasingly nauseous looking 2B.

"And I haven't even mentioned the teeth;" she continued bluntly, "four rows of razor sharp venomous blades sitting on a huge jaw. The jaw can be unhinged like this," She kept her elbows together and pulled her hands wide apart. "Get the picture? I've seen one take down a crimson pukkaloo before now. Snap." She slapped her hands together making 2B jump. "But the most horrible thing is that they don't kill you before they eat you. They inject a paralyzing toxin into the bite wound. Then, while you lay there unable to move, they eat you alive."

2B had heard enough. He began to unzip his jacket. "Forget it. I'm not going. You must be mad. Why would you even tell me that stuff?"

"I'm telling you so you know exactly what we're up against. Now come here." She brushed his hands off the zip and yanked it up to the very top.

SpaceCoyote explorer jackets came with three levels of personal protection; low, medium and high. The high level was like having the equivalent of a suit of armour strapped to your chest, but armour made from a fabric as light as a feather. It would easily protect him against a grommet bite but there was a downside. Its protective fibres were organic and powered by the person's own energy. All very well if you were feeling tip top, not so great if you were stressed and injured. The more stressed the body, the more energy the jacket needed. It was a vicious cycle and meant it could only be used at that level for short periods of time.

JoJo had seen the effects when they had been left on too long. They weren't pretty. Within an hour a person could be turned into a gaunt quivering wreck, incapable of complex movement or communication. It could last for days, sometimes weeks. With 2B's stress levels already high, she would have been lying if she had said she wasn't worried.

Moving faster now, JoJo reached in her pocket and took out two small cylindrical containers. She handed one to 2B.

"Put that in your left eye, it's a retinator. It's getting dark outside and it'll help us see what's happening and hopefully stay one step ahead."

2B struggled to pull the top off his container. JoJo unscrewed hers as it should be done and then did his. The lid revealed a transparent lens sitting on a thin layer of sponge. She held the container a centimeter from her open left eye and, as if attracted by a magnet, the lens shot off the sponge and embedded itself painlessly into her cornea. A single tear slid down her cheek.

2B blinked sympathetically.

"It modifies the optic nerve." JoJo explained. "In low light it'll stimulate the photo sensitive cells so your brain will think it's much brighter. If it gets too bright, it does the opposite."

She held 2B's retinator against his eye.

"Ouch," he said, and adjusted his vision as the lens sucked in.

She waited until he had blinked away the tear, and then enveloped him in a big bear hug. "Don't forget to tell me the instant that suit starts to affect you all right? No playing the hero."

He nodded into her chest.

"You ready then?" she said, releasing him.

"No," he replied flatly.

"Good. Let's go then."

They walked to the exit hatch. It opened automatically as they approached.

Below them, the Blue Planet surface slowly appeared inch by inch. Her heart hammered with a strange mix of apprehension and excitement. The Blue Planet. She couldn't believe it. Her toes were twitching nervously in her boots. Was she really about to set foot on the surface?

With one hand gripping the tetra harpoon and the other squeezing 2B's hand, she took what she hoped wouldn't be her last look around the Seeker.

"If anything goes wrong you get back here okay. Don't worry about me. Just get back here to SaRa."

2B nodded anxiously. JoJo took a deep breath.

And then they jumped.

CHAPTER 20

ALIENS IN THE ORCHARD!

APPLE VALLEY. SOUTH ORCHARD

So much had happened in the last twenty minutes it was hard to make sense of it. Trembling with a heady mixture of excitement and terror, Jimmy, sticky and sweaty from the heat, was crouched behind a large apple tree. Halfpint was glued to his side like a conjoined twin, eyes as wide as dinner plates. Cornelius and Paige were in similar states, ten feet away behind a large tree of their own. None of them could quite believe what they were seeing.

Only ten minutes earlier everything had been so different. They had been in the barn dreaming up increasingly painful things to do to Damien Dirt when a distant explosion rocked the barn and them in it.

Paige was convinced it was a bomb. Cornelius insisted they were in the middle of an earthquake and Halfpint thought the end of the world had arrived. None of them were right. None of them were even close.

Fuelled by adrenaline they burst out into the early evening dusk, eager to see what had happened.

From the barn they had uninterrupted views across the valley. At first glance everything appeared normal. The never-ending lines of trees stretched out like soldiers on parade as they always did. The lazy contours of Thunder Hill across the far side of the valley still resembled a fat man sleeping, and in the far, far distance billowing smoke rose from the Appleton power stations. But there was a difference. Something subtle had changed.

It began at the Cattle Bridge Canal. The 'Cattle Bridge' was the longest of a hundred water canals that criss-crossed throughout the length and breadth of Apple Valley. It was five miles from the barn to the canal. Jimmy knew that because he cycled it often.

From the bridge, *something* had smashed its way through the trees, breaking the tight formations and cutting a scar through the perfectly parallel lines. The wound continued for about four miles until it stopped abruptly. The reason for the sudden stop was obvious. The '*something*' had crashed – embedded itself in one of the largest trees in the whole orchard.

Jimmy looked at Paige, who looked at Cornelius who looked at Halfpint. Each was thinking the same thing. They had to get closer.

Jimmy wasted no time. Despite the fading light he broke into a run leading the gang excitedly into the orchard. It wasn't long before the dense foliage of the orchard consumed and the barn disappeared from view.

Adrenaline flowed in gallons and nerves prickled Jimmy's body as they flitted carefully between the looming trees. Jimmy hated the orchard at night. It was a merciless place, so vast and unrelenting. Every view was the same and every step treacherous. Thick, bulbous tree roots tried to trip you. Fallen apples from the Triple Trees lay in wait like so many tennis balls in your path, whilst low hanging branches continually flashed sharp twigs in your face.

He hadn't even considered how they were going to find their way out again.

Two minutes later Jimmy heard the faint crackling and popping of burning wood. Panting, he slowed to walking pace and rounded the next tree. Halfpint, Paige and Cornelius lined up behind him. At once they knew. They had found what they were looking for.

It was the most incredible scene Jimmy had ever witnessed. Branches and twigs littered the floor as though a lumberjack had gone mental with a chainsaw. Several small fires were smouldering and there, bathed in the amber glow of the flames was … A UFO!

It had to be a UFO; there was no other rational explanation. Certainly no human could ever have built such a fantastic machine – that was for sure.

Most of the craft was hanging precariously in the upper branches of a huge Triple Tree. It looked likely to fall at any second.

It had no wings to speak of. Instead there was what could only be described as two stretched-out teardrops. They swept back, curving and tapering to sharp points behind the tail. A series of vents were sliced into the sides mimicking sharks' gill flaps.

The main body was smaller, more streamlined and had a large 'X1' engraved into its side. Jimmy stared in wonder as the last of the daylight shimmered off its golden surface. The whole thing was beautiful but how it flew was anyone's guess. It was like nothing he had ever seen before.

The spell of discovery was broken when all of a sudden a cone of turquoise light appeared from beneath the craft like liquid treacle pouring from a glass. It stretched through the branches to the valley floor and for a second flickered sharply. Then out of the glow walked two people. Two alien people!

Jimmy and the guys scattered like mice in the face of an angry cat. With his heart pounding, Jimmy dived behind a tree where he lay perfectly still. Halfpint joined him. Paige and Cornelius remained together behind a different tree. Completely breathless they all sat like statues, not a single muscle twitching between them, trying desperately to merge with the scenery and praying they would go unnoticed by whoever it was had just landed on their planet.

※ ※ ※

In the command and control centre of a top secret military base one hundred miles away, the strange radar anomaly had been spotted and traced the second it entered the earth's atmosphere.

No-one knew what it was or where it had come from.

Except for one man. He alone recognised its true identity, but wasn't about to admit it. Instead he excused himself and calmly exited the control area into a room with a private telephone line. There, he placed a call which he had been waiting forty years to make.

Back in the command room, the radar operative followed the anomaly with increasing consternation as it passed close to a populated area before dropping thousands of feet in a matter of seconds. Finally it disappeared in what was the vast Apple Valley Orchards.

It took only seconds for the rough co-ordinates of the landing site to be handed to the commanding officer.

"Probably nothing, a stray weather balloon or such like. Send up a spotter," he said brusquely to his subordinate.

Within five minutes a helicopter had been scrambled from the reconnaissance squadron and was heading out to the middle of Apple Valley. Little did the pilot know four kids had already beaten him to it.

CHAPTER 21

HOLDING OUT FOR A HERO!

Jimmy sat with back his against the trunk facing down the long length of trees. His world was in meltdown. He couldn't stop his hands shaking and his knees felt like they were made of rubber bands.

Beside him, Halfpint to was shaking, "What are we going to do?" he moaned in a quiet, desperate whisper.

Jimmy shrugged, "I don't know but I don't like it sitting here. Trust it to land in a bloody TripleTree zone."

The TripleTree zones were specially designed areas of the orchard. Here, the corridors between the trees were extra wide (at least the width of a road) to accommodate their vast upper branches. That meant as hiding places go, it was pretty poor. Even a short sighted mole wouldn't take that long to spot them.

"We could make a run for it," Jimmy ventured hopefully.

Halfpint's head nearly came off at the neck with the ferocity of shaking it from side to side.

"Okay, bad idea," agreed Jimmy. "Let me take a look then."

He peered around the trunk. The aliens were crouching low as they walked, glancing left and right. Jimmy got the impression they were searching for something. He hoped it wasn't them. There was one thing about them that surprised him though.

"They're just kids," he whispered to Halfpint. "It's a boy and a girl I think. She looks the same age as us. They're so … human."

"No way," said Halfpint emphatically. "They're not human.

They're aliens. I know it and if we're not careful they'll be sucking our brains out and keeping them in jars."

Jimmy frowned. "Don't be ridiculous. Look for yourself. They're just kids."

"They could be in disguise Jimmy," argued Halfpint. "Mimicking us, to blend in. We shouldn't have come. We shouldn't be anywhere near here." His tone was becoming increasingly desperate.

"I agree, but they're right in the middle of the track. We wouldn't get ten yards. We've no choice but to sit it out and hope they turn back."

Halfpint groaned. Jimmy knew how he felt. The longer they sat here, the darker it was becoming. That meant the prospects of escaping the orchard tonight were getting slimmer by the second.

Jimmy watched the boy and girl. Silently he was urging them to head back to the UFO, but secretly he found himself enraptured at the sight. He wanted to take it all in so he would never forget. How dazzling the Spacecraft was. How amazingly human-like the two aliens were and just how big that gun slung round the girl's shoulder was. That brought him back to reality with a bump.

Then, from high above the trees, a low whoosh cut through the air and the situation changed dramatically.

Instantly the girl was on the balls of her feet, gun drawn, twisting in rapid circles, scanning the orchard. Suddenly her eyes locked on an area of sky. She shoved the boy toward the cover of a tree but he wouldn't go. Screaming, she pushed harder making it clear she wasn't taking no for an answer.

Jimmy was clammy with sweat He didn't like the girl's demeanour one bit. She was seriously spooked which meant he was seriously spooked. He searched the sky for himself but saw nothing unusual. But that sound, like a missile speeding its way toward a target...

He found himself involuntarily hugging the huge trunk, perhaps hoping to draw some sort of protective comfort from its size and strength. For now that's all he had.

* * *

JoJo felt like a fly which had just landed in a frog infested pond. The shhhhushing sound as the grommets scythed their way through the air was unmistakably terrifying and sent a veritable avalanche of shivers up her spine.

As her eyes and gun hit the sky, she cursed. Of all the stupid things, she had forgotten that male grommet's fly! In the Cubs they were only ever allowed to study females because the males were too aggressive. If she had remembered that, she would never have come out here. Against an airborne grommet they stood about as much chance as a one winged moth against a bat.

She thought of grabbing 2B and sprinting back to the Seeker but it would be too late. Grommets were fast and furious … and now they were raining down towards her like guided missiles.

She pushed 2B away. He screamed to stay, but she screamed louder and won. She focused and took aim. Two of their hideous contorted faces filled her sights.

Then, with her finger poised to squeeze the trigger, just like with the formation of a rain droplet, it all went pear-shaped.

* * *

They were four of the most fearsome looking monsters Jimmy had ever set eyes on. They plummeted through the upper branches of the TripleTrees in a tight formation dropping into the corridor, heading straight at the girl. Jimmy watched breathlessly as the two outer beasts peeled off like jet fighters and disappeared into the depths of the trees. The remaining pair honed in like living breathing tomahawk missiles. The girl would only get one shot at each. To miss either meant certain death. Jimmy shuffled to the side for a better look, willing her to fire true.

As he moved a dry branch snapped noisily beneath his right foot. His heart froze. In the still air it sounded like a firecracker had exploded.

The girl whipped her head around in his direction. It killed her concentration. That split second was enough. Jimmy dropped his head in despair.

When the girl turned back, the creatures were only feet from her. Her finger instinctively squeezed the trigger and she got lucky, vaporizing one in mid air.

But she could do nothing about the second.

She twisted sharply as the creature slammed hard into her right shoulder. It was as if she had been hit by a juggernaut. Bone crunched and blood sprayed from the wound! She pirouetted twice before hitting the ground like a puppet with its strings cut.

Pandemonium ensued. The surviving creature soared back into the air where it screamed in triumph and was quickly joined from the orchard by the remaining two. Together they began to circle the grisly scene from on high, biding their time.

The boy sprinted out from behind his tree towards the girl screaming his lungs out. That was a big mistake.

Behind his tree Jimmy puked his guts up.

By stepping on that branch and distracting her, he had killed her as sure as putting a gun to her head and pulling the trigger.

Wiping his mouth he turned and watched in desperation as the boy, jabbering hysterically, groped at the girl. His howls though were nothing compared to the new and terrifying sound from on high.

The creatures had begun to communicate.

A mixture of low, guttural growls and high-pitched squeals filled the air with horror movie sound effects.

Like phantoms they appeared again, three abreast between the trees. Jimmy followed the silhouettes. They split as before, but this time the two swept around re-joining the attack from the side. Their target – the boy.

Isolated and out in the open he was a sitting duck.

And it was then that something truly monumental happened to Jimmy. Not really thinking, his heart pounding like a steam train, he leapt out from behind the tree and sprinted as if his life depended on it.

"Nooo!" Yelled Halfpint lunging desperately to stop him, but he grabbed only air.

As the creatures wailed and Jimmy's legs pumped, he saw the central creature drop into the corridor. Knowing the others would be close, he channeled every ounce of energy into his muscles urging them to go faster than they ever had before.

With twenty yards to go Jimmy knew he wasn't going to make it. He simply wasn't fast enough.

Then miraculously the front creature jolted in mid air. Jimmy's presence on the scene had confused it. With a vicious roar it readjusted its position and lost time. The moment of hesitation gave Jimmy his chance and he took it. Re-invigorated, his feet kicked on through the dust.

Five yards from the boy and Jimmy could smell the creature's vile stench at his side, but he didn't dare look.

The boy saw what was coming at him and was frozen to the spot. He had the eyes of a condemned man. Jimmy wondered which strange creature terrified him more, the beast from Hell or the teenager from earth.

With no time for subtleties, Jimmy leapt into the air tackling the boy hard in the midriff. They tumbled over the stricken girl and rolled in a heap on the floor.

As his face painfully scraped the dirt and soil, the two creatures attacking from either side reached the point where the boy should have been. With no time to take evasive action they slammed headfirst into each other with bone crunching force. The sound was sickening but Jimmy felt a sense of triumph as the creatures slumped to the floor, their heads twisted at impossible angles. After a few involuntary twitches they lay still and lifeless.

There was no time for celebration though, because having narrowly avoided the collision itself, the remaining creature had swept into the trees. No doubt to re-evaluate its tactics.

But it would be back. Jimmy had no doubt about that.

He grabbed hold of the boy by the jacket and tried to drag him away. If they could get to the trees it would at least make the creature's life difficult, but the boy fought him, kicking and yelling until Jimmy had no choice but to let him go. "Come on," he urged angrily. "Don't be stupid. It *will* come back."

But the boy wouldn't leave the girl. Jimmy supposed he could understand, but there was nothing either of them could do for her and under the circumstances it was pure madness to stay out in the open. He briefly considered the possibility of dragging her with them, but it would weigh them down too much.

Above, the screeching began again. This time though, it sounded even more pained. It grew louder and louder, boring into Jimmy's head like a sonic drill. He cupped his hands over his ears but it made no difference. The pain was excruciating.

Blinding white light swept in from the edges of his vision like an onrushing migraine. The orchard was disappearing before him. He panicked, gripping his temples to try and stop his head from exploding!

Then the noise stopped, but Jimmy's pain didn't.

Fear ripped through him as he found his eyesight all but useless and realised that the noise had been a deliberate ploy on the creature's part. Blinding and weakening him, leaving him isolated and defenseless. He staggered to his knees desperate to get away, but he didn't even know in which direction to go.

Within his milky vision, a blurry image began to form. Was it a woman? Yes, definitely a woman. The features were fuzzy but he got a sense of slow, graceful movements. The gossamer figure was reaching out to him. His heart almost stopped beating in his chest as he thought he saw …

* * *

Halfpint, Paige and Cornelius screamed in unison as they watched the drama unfold. Everything about this night had been too shocking to

126

comprehend. Paige was the only one who watched the creature descending towards their best friend. Halfpint and Cornelius had their heads buried in their hands, too scared to look.

She alone would be the witness of what would happen next.

* * *

"Mum, is that you?" Jimmy said, knowing how stupid it must sound, but yet ... it seemed so right. She was waiting to guide him to the other side, he was sure.

He reached out and a feeling of utter bliss enveloped him as he felt her touch for the first time in five years. He almost cried.

Then he was hit hard in the chest and he knew it was over. He collapsed backwards, no longer fearing what would happen because he knew the pain wouldn't last if his Mum was there.

... But Jimmy's Mum never came.

Instead of a warm comforting embrace, he felt a jet of hot, thick slimy fluid cover him from head to foot. He gagged at the stench and spat warm wet fluid out of his mouth.

His world came quickly back into focus after that.

The noise had stopped. The orchard was calm once more. He rubbed slime out of his eyes as beside him he saw ... the girl. Incredibly she was alive!

She looked like hell, covered in the same festering mess as him, with blood oozing from a vicious rip in her shoulder, but she was alive! And so was he.

Instinctively he knew that she must have blown the creature to pieces and what they were covered in was its remains. The fact that he had half a bloodied eyeball stuck to his shirt also gave him a clue.

He also realised that the hazy figure he had seen and touched had not been his mother offering to guide him into the after-life, but rather the girl reaching out to push him out of the way.

She had saved his life.

Barely conscious, she nodded toward the alien boy a couple of feet away who was curled in a ball, whimpering. "Jacket…" she said, barely audibly.

Jimmy shook his head, not understanding.

Her deep blue eyes pleaded with Jimmy willing him to understand, but before she could connect another syllable, the weapon dropped from her hands, her eyes closed and she slumped to the floor unconscious.

CHAPTER 22

THE TURQUOISE BEAM

With the danger seemingly over, Halfpint, Paige and Cornelius raced to Jimmy's side. Paige thumped him hard on the shoulder.

"Ouch!"

"Stupido," she yelled, "What were you thinking? You could have been killed. If it hadn't been for her we'd have been taking you home in pieces."

Jimmy rubbed his arm.

"And why didn't you move? You just sat there like a fool with that … that monster coming towards you."

Jimmy dazedly explained about the paralysing blinding light. Seemingly no-one else had been affected. Paige thumped him again, same place, even harder. "Stupido!" She sniffed the air with a disgusted look on her face, "and you stink."

"Thanks very much," moaned Jimmy.

"What's the matter with him?" asked Cornelius, nodding toward the boy, who was rocking from side to side, paler than a glass of milk with seemingly no concept of where he was or that there were even other people around him.

"Must be shock or something," said Jimmy getting gingerly to his feet and waving a hand in front of the boy's inert face. "That's going to make it more difficult."

"Going to make what more difficult?" asked Halfpint.

Jimmy pointed to the spaceship. "Getting them back in there, of course," he replied, wiping something quite revolting off the front of his trousers.

Halfpint swallowed hard. "You're joking aren't you? You can't seriously want to hang around here after what you've just been through. Paige is right. You were about an inch away from being totalled by that thing. We're going right now."

Jimmy pointed out the gashes in the girls shoulder. "We can't just leave her here like that."

"Of course we can," argued Halfpint. "We didn't ask them to come here and those *things* they brought with them could have done us all in. It's her own fault she's ended up like that."

Jimmy looked bemused. "If it wasn't for her I'd be dead," he said.

"It was because of her you nearly were dead."

Jimmy couldn't understand why he was even arguing about this. "It was my fault she got hit by that thing, Halfpint. She would have shot them easily if I hadn't have snapped that twig. The least we can do is to get her somewhere safe."

Halfpint's white complexion turned pink with anger. "The least we can do is leave them here. If we stay any longer, we'll be stuck and I, for one, don't want to spend the night in this orchard."

Jimmy glared at his best friend. "You mean to say that she's laying here with her arm half off and all you're bothered about is getting home before bedtime?" He looked at Paige and Cornelius accusingly. "Do you guys think the same huh? Are you happy to just walk away and leave them?"

Cornelius looked at his feet

Sensing triumph, Halfpint put his hand on Jimmy's shoulder. "Face it," he said, "you're not thinking straight. You're in shock. It's understandable. That thing nearly killed you. But you just can't go walking inside a spaceship. It would be mental."

Jimmy shrugged Halfpint off. "I'm not arguing with you. She needs help. So I'm going to help."

Halfpint stomped his foot and turned away muttering under his breath. "Idiot. Just because he couldn't save his Mum."

"What did you just say?" growled Jimmy, stepping towards his best friend. "You didn't just say what I think you did. Did you?"

Halfpint turned and screamed at Jimmy. "Yes I did. Ever since I've known you you've been on some big saviour kick. Like you've got to try and help anyone or anything all the time. Well she is not your Mum, and just because you couldn't save her doesn't mean you have to try and save everybody else."

There, he had got it off his chest. He felt better, but only momentarily.

Jimmy snapped. He shoved Halfpint hard in the chest. "You haven't got a clue what you're talking about little man. My Mum has got nothing to do with this. This is all about you being a coward!"

He pushed him harder. Halfpint fell onto his backside where Jimmy stood over him, bunching his fists. Paige quickly stepped between them. "That's enough. Arguing isn't going to solve anything. Now back off him Jimmy. Back off I said." She guided him away before helping a hurt looking Halfpint to his feet.

Jimmy huffed and turned to the girl. His anger and frustration felt like a volcano waiting to blow, not least because Halfpint had struck a nerve.

It was true that ever since the accident Jimmy had gone out of his way to prevent anything else from dying. Even to the extreme of not letting anyone squash a spider while he was around, but none of that was relevant here. At least, he didn't think so.

"I know you all think I need a shrink," he said irritably. "But I am going to do something to help her. If you want to go, then just go, all of you. Leave me here. I couldn't care less one way or the other."

Of course he could. The thought of being left alone in the orchard terrified him but he wasn't about to let them see that. So he knelt by the girl's side and tried desperately to figure out what to do next.

Thankfully Paige sighed and shook her head. "I'm not leaving," she said. "When we go, we go together."

Cornelius hesitated but then reluctantly agreed, "Paige is right, Halfpint. I say we stay."

Halfpint said nothing.

"That's settled then," said Paige, "now let's make this quick, because if I don't get home and get my beauty sleep, somebody's going to pay."

* * *

Jimmy's first-aid knowledge was limited. A one-hour crash course before a school abseiling trip was the extent of his training. Even then the sling he tied on Halfpint fell off after only five minutes. It didn't take a genius therefore to see that the girl's wound was going to be way beyond Jimmy's capabilities.

It was as if five sharp blades had been drawn across the top of her shoulder and chest. Her jacket was in tatters. Flecks of the blue material were matted together with her flesh and the largest gash was still bleeding freely. The wounds needed cleaning and stitching at the very least, but taking her to a hospital was clearly out of the question. Even if they could have navigated their way out of the orchard, how would they have explained it?

All Jimmy could think to do was strip off his outer shirt and fashion a clumsy looking bandage out of it. Carefully – and with Paige's help – he peeled off the girl's jacket and tied the makeshift dressing as tight as he could. He was pleased when it appeared to stem the blood loss. "Right, come on. Cornelius, you give me a hand here; Paige, you and Halfpint get the boy."

Halfpint muttered under his breath. Jimmy ignored it.

Once they both had a hold of their respective alien, Cornelius said, "Are you sure this is a good idea?"

"No," replied Jimmy testily, "but look, that's her spaceship right?

She'll feel safe in there and if she feels safe when she wakes up there'll be less chance of her freaking out."

"And what about if there are more of those creatures in there," pointed out Halfpint.

Jimmy shook his head. "She was out here trying to kill them wasn't she? I don't think they were pets."

"This might be a stupid question," said Paige, staring up at the UFO, "but how do we get in it? It must be seventy feet in the air, and if you say we have to climb, I'm going to pound you."

Jimmy had thought about that. "We won't have to climb," he said confidently. "That turquoise beam must have something to do with it. They came out of it so I reckon we can go in it."

"You reckon?" she said.

Jimmy shrugged.

Paige shook her head. "We're going to end up climbing I just know it."

* * *

They had carried the bodies about half distance when a distant rumble stopped them dead in their tracks.

"Is that what I think it is?" said Paige looking up at the now dark sky.

"A helicopter, or more than one," said Cornelius.

Jimmy agreed. The low growl was unmistakable. Although he was keen to see it through, Jimmy wasn't stupid. Helicopters over the orchard at this time of night could mean only one thing. They weren't the only ones to know this spaceship had landed.

"What do you think?" Jimmy asked, looking to the others.

"We've come this far," said Paige, "may as well see it through to the end."

Cornelius nodded. Even Halfpint agreed (albeit half-heartedly).

"All for one and one for all," sang Paige, punching a fist in the air.

That broke the tension and all four of them smiled.

"This isn't a game though," Jimmy said. "Things could get totally screwed up from here on."

"Like today has been all too ordinary already," muttered Halfpint.

He had a point. How much worse could things get.

So together they re-gathered their charges and hurried for the turquoise beam.

CHAPTER 23

TAKE MY BREATH AWAY

When they reached the strangely opalescent blue light, all four of them were breathing heavily. Jimmy's arm and shoulder ached from supporting the girl and his legs felt as if he'd run a marathon.

Now that he saw it, all that effort didn't seem like such a great idea anymore.

It was just a light. He didn't know what he was expecting exactly, but he hoped it would look a little more special than a blue one hundred watt bulb shining on the ground. This didn't look as though it could transport them anywhere. But with a helicopter honing in on the scene, the thought of being caught covered in foul smelling slime and helping aliens into a spaceship, spurred him on to at least try.

"Are you ready?" he asked a panting Cornelius.

"Let's just get it over with shall we."

Overhead, the heavy Spaceship creaked as the branches strained under its weight.

Jimmy motioned to Halfpint. "That thing looks pretty unstable so you two wait and see what happens to us. If it looks all right follow us in. If not, make a run for it and forget about us."

"Not a chance," Paige protested.

"But-."

"NO! If we're going, then we all go together."

Jimmy sighed. There was no time to argue.

"All right – after three, we step in." He took a breath, closed his eyes, "one, two … three." He moved forwards dragging the girl and a reluctant Cornelius with him. Halfpint and Paige followed behind.

The change from dark to light was immediate. Jimmy opened his eyes and gazed around him. Cornelius was scrunched up, his shoulders tense and brow beaded with sweat. Paige and Halfpint were awkwardly hugging each other whilst trying to keep hold of the boy. But the girl – Wow! She had changed beyond all recognition. Her head was no longer slumped limply against her chest but was facing the UFO high above their heads, her eyes wide open. She looked serene, angelic almost.

Jimmy followed her gaze upwards. And there it was. A hatch. An entrance into the spaceship.

As soon as he saw it he felt his entire body tremble and become lighter. His stomach lurched as if they'd dipped over the summit of a speeding rollercoaster and the light began to dance in front of his eyes. First it was blue then green, before fading to iridescent violets and pinks.

"What's happening?" cried Halfpint nervously, "I don't like it."

Jimmy could only describe it later as like having your belly tickled from the inside.

He gripped the girl tightly. If she was working it, he sure wasn't going to be left behind.

And then in a heartbeat, everything sucked back to normal. A sudden white light forced him to squint.

They were no longer in the orchard, but in a stark white empty corridor that ran about thirty feet in both directions. At one end was a sealed door.

Instinctively he looked down. He wished he hadn't. Far below through the tangle of branches was the orchard floor with nothing between it and him. Like a cartoon character which had just sprinted off a cliff edge and was in that frozen moment before the fall, Jimmy panicked and leapt onto the solid corridor, quickly followed by the others.

He breathed deep. They had made it. They were in the spaceship.

* * *

The first thing Jimmy noticed was how much more unstable the Spaceship seemed now he was in it. It was shifting from side to side like a boat moored in a harbour. The groans of the struggling wood beneath were all too apparent and very off-putting. Whatever they were going to do, he figured they better make it quick before the whole thing lost its battle against gravity.

Jimmy didn't want to just dump the boy and girl in the corridor, so they dragged them to the door at the end of the corridor.

There was no handle, just some kind of sensor recessed into the wall at the side. The size of an iPod, the sensor had a blinking red light in the centre. Jimmy pressed it but the door remained firmly closed. "Oh this just gets better by the minute," he complained, pressing it again and again, the only effect being on his waning patience. "Any bright ideas?" he asked.

Everyone was blank. "Shame you can't wake her up," Halfpint said looking at the girl, "bet if she pressed it, it would open."

That gave Jimmy an idea. He took her limp hand and held her index finger firmly against the sensor. Instantly the red light rippled outwards, turned green and the door swished open.

"Genius," congratulated Cornelius.

"Lucky guess more like," said Paige.

Jimmy was first into the room and it was like walking onto a movie set.

The cockpit was huge, terrifically huge. Far too huge to be real! From the outside dimensions Jimmy estimated it would be like a large jet's cockpit, but it was at least the size of a spacious living room. Truly the King of all cockpits.

It was something else as well – a mess. It was as if some giant hand had picked it up and shook it. There were things smashed, bits of wall hanging off and the floor was littered with debris that had, at one time, presumably been hidden away. And the whole place smelt like burning electricity.

"You know what," said Cornelius, touching the wall as if it couldn't possibly exist. "If I couldn't feel my arms aching so much, I'd swear this was a dream. It can't be right. It just can't be."

The walls were scorched, but mostly white with the occasional accent in blue. They were covered with lights, buttons, switches and computer screens. Twenty feet in front of them was a massive control console which arched under the triangular window, following the contour of the ship's nose. That too was alive with yet more computer screens, holographic images and pulsing lights. Behind it, two plush chairs hovered in mid-air! Actually, one was more stuttering than hovering, but the effect was equally impressive.

The only area which had remained undamaged was against the far wall where a huge glass tank was bubbling with a sparkling clear liquid. Swimming in the liquid were hundreds of penny sized multi-coloured insects. They corkscrewed through the water squirting jets of fluid behind them. For Jimmy it was all quite simply too incredible to comprehend.

But the room didn't end there. It stretched on behind them where it was subdivided into what appeared to be storage areas on the right and sleeping quarters to the left. With clothes strewn about the floor, it had the all too familiar look of his own bedroom about it.

Beyond even that, yet another corridor stretched away with doors spaced every few feet.

With the wonder of it all, it took Halfpint losing his grip and almost dropping the boy, for them to remember why they were here and eventually they managed to haul the boy and girl over to the beds.

With the girl laid down, and once a squeamish Cornelius and Halfpint had bolted out of the way, Jimmy unwrapped the make-do bandage to assess any further damage caused by the journey. Paige, for what it was worth, sat with the dazed and vacant boy.

The bandage peeled away remarkably easily. Jimmy winced, preparing himself for what lay underneath, but to his utter astonishment, all he saw was a relatively healthy looking shoulder.

Impossibly, the largest of the gashes which had so made Jimmy cringe earlier, was now nothing more than a thin raised red scar. All the others had virtually disappeared, leaving only tiny scratch marks. How could this have happened? It was a miracle. She was healing faster than humanly possible!

He turned to Paige, who opened her mouth to say something, when Cornelius yelled out a warning from the cockpit window.

* * *

JoJo felt the human touching her. She had never been so terrified in all her life. Inside she squirmed with every touch. It took all her strength not to pull away. She desperately wanted to scream but held it in. She had to stay focused and strong for what she had to do next.

In truth, she couldn't believe she was even still alive after taking such a hit from a grommet. There *had* to be at least one wound. The human had just removed some kind of wrapping from her shoulder, which intimated some kind of cut, but that was impossible. An adult grommet bite would already be gangrenous. She would be in the most terrible pain and without the proper medical attention, only hours from death. But other than a dull, heavy throbbing, she felt amazingly fine. She just hoped she wasn't hallucinating and, in actuality, on the brink of death!

Right now though, it was best if she put the grommet out of her mind and concentrated on the current problem.

When one of the humans shouted, she risked a look. Both humans nearest her were looking away. Perfect.

Very discreetly, she slid her hand between the bed and the wall feeling blindly for something she had spotted when they laid her down. When her fingers grasped it, adrenaline flowed giving her renewed vigor. Gently she flexed the muscles of her good arm to check all was well. It was. She was ready.

With lightening speed and total confidence in what she was about to do, she sat up and struck hard and decisively.

The gun was pointing at Jimmy's head before he knew what was happening.

"Get that jacket off my brother!" JoJo growled angrily at Paige. "Get it off him, or this one dies, right now."

Jimmy was frozen to the spot, not daring to move.

"I'll count to three" said JoJo, shaking now. "You humans do know how to count don't you? One …" She cocked the trigger.

That did the trick. Paige ripped roughly at the boy's jacket dragging it off his back before tossing it at JoJo. "There. Point that thing somewhere else, or I swear you'll regret it," she hissed.

"I don't think you're in a position to be giving out threats, human. Now move away from him – slowly."

Paige inched away. The gun never moved. Jimmy tried desperately to look for a way out, but there was none. He felt helpless and, if he were honest, more than a little underappreciated. He had just saved that boy and this was the thanks he got. He stared at the girl trying to show her without words that neither he, nor anyone else, was a threat, but all he saw in return were two eyes filled with fear and anger. He sagged, praying that he hadn't just led his friends to their deaths.

* * *

JoJo could not believe she was face to face with the enemy.

Her emotions were all over the place. She was petrified for 2B. His jacket had been on for far too long. Who knew what damage had been done and she was scared for herself. Four against one with an injured arm didn't give her much of a chance. Most of all she was scared because, right now, her understanding of the world had been turned on its head by the actions of this human boy.

Everything she thought she knew about humans – their depravity and selfishness – had been contradicted. He had acted selflessly and risked his own life to save 2B from certain death. This was not the behaviour of an evil and barbaric animal. This was somebody with compassion and kindness. Somebody with the true Larian spirit.

She looked into his eyes and saw the primal fear of survival reflected back at her. She didn't want to become a killer. She desperately wanted to lower the gun, to trust that things would be all right, but what if she were wrong?

For the second time today she felt a paralysing doubt. It was something she had hoped not to be repeating so often.

CHAPTER 24

CoyoteBots and Helicopters

The next few seconds saw the situation turn on its head.

It started as a slight tremor beneath their feet. Then, as quickly as a TV switches stations, the whole Spaceship dropped and slid backwards several heart wrenching feet, before jamming to a halt on a thick, gnarled branch.

Everyone stumbled. Halfpint fell over. More importantly for Jimmy, JoJo fell sideways. The gun jolted from her grasp and was sent skidding across the floor. It was all the encouragement he needed. He dived for the gun before JoJo could regain her balance, but Paige beat him to it. Spinning round, she leapt up and pointed it firmly in the girl's direction.

Situation reversed.

"What did you do that for, you cow?" she yelled angrily. "You could've killed him."

JoJo stared at the gun in terror. "I ... wouldn't press that trigger if I were you," she said unsurely.

Paige – who was acting a whole lot braver than she felt – smiled and said, "Well you're not me, are you and seeing as you …...." She frowned at the gun. "Wait a minute ... what the?"

JoJo's head sank a little.

Paige turned and pointed the gun harmlessly at the wall beside her. She pulled the trigger.

Across the room, Halfpint dived for cover.

He needn't have worried. All that happened was creamy coloured liquid, as thick as condensed soup, oozed from the barrel. Paige lifted it to her nose and sniffed it.

"Well unless you come from a place where they kill each other with Jojoba, this is not a real gun."

She looked accusingly at JoJo who bowed her head sorrowfully.

"It's hair conditioner," she admitted. "It's a novelty bottle of hair conditioner. I just thought that … Oh I don't know what I thought."

She broke down in tears. "I'm sorry. I'm so sorry. I didn't mean it," she sobbed.

From his position on the floor, Halfpint looked confused. "What the bloody hell's Jojoba?" he asked Cornelius, who shrugged.

Suddenly, SaRa's blue holographic head appeared from the console, making everyone jump. "JoJo, we have a radar warning of an unidentified airborne human craft approaching our position."

JoJo groaned mournfully, burying her head in her hands. "I knew it," she said. "It's happening all over again, just like last time."

Well Jimmy didn't know or care what was happening again. This was all getting well out of hand. All he wanted was to be away from here. He could see it all now. *UFO lands in orchard. People spot UFO. People send an aircraft to locate UFO. People find UFO stuck in a tree. People find Jimmy and the band in the UFO with two aliens.*

He wished he had known how fast these aliens healed before setting off, then he could have listened to Halfpint. But that was irrelevant. There was only one way out of this mess now.

"Will this thing fly?" he barked at JoJo.

All the others stared at him as if he was mad.

"There's no way we can make a run for it," he added. "It's the only way."

"Oh, it can't be the *only* way," complained Halfpint worriedly.

JoJo said nothing, her sobs growing deeper.

"Will this thing FLY?" Jimmy repeated as forcefully as he dare.

"I don't know," JoJo yelled back, spittle and tears showering him. "I don't know."

"Then find out, because I'm getting pretty bored with near-death experiences tonight. I don't want to be put in prison trying to explain why I happened to be found covered in alien slime in a spaceship. So please, pretty please. *Get us out of here!*"

* * *

The human's words seemed to strike a cord in JoJo's brain. He was right. She couldn't just sit here and let them come for her. That would be a disservice to the memory of those SpaceCoyotes lost forty years ago. But without shields or engines what could she do?

With a concerned glance at 2B, she slid off the bed and rushed to the main console. Picking up her PlasmaTab, she thrust it at Jimmy. "Take this and sit next to me," she ordered. "Do you think you can you work it if I tell you what to do?"

Jimmy looked it over in his hands. "What is it?"

"It's called a PlasmaTab. You don't have anything like it here, so don't even try to work it out. Just do exactly as I say and nothing more," she replied brusquely.

Jimmy nodded unsurely and looked behind him at Paige. She mimed an action, asking whether he wanted her to try and take the girl out. Jimmy shook his head. For the time being, they had to trust her.

As if sensing what had just happened, JoJo said, "Don't think about trying anything stupid. That gun may have been a fake but this isn't."

She pulled something from the console and held it for him to see. It looked a bit like a tiny bottle of deodorant.

"Don't tell me, as well as threatening to give your captives shiny hair, you can also make their arm-pits smell nice?" said Jimmy.

She gave him a look that suggested he was only one more quip away from having an alien fist in his mouth.

"This is a Salton five disabler," she said. "One press of this button and you're in suspended animation until I give you the antidote." She stuffed the weapon into her belt, "and you're not my captives. You brought me here remember. Please feel free to leave whenever you like." She glanced at the door.

"Let's just go shall we?" said Jimmy.

"Fine."

"Fine," snapped Jimmy, smiling despite himself.

He was beginning to like her.

* * *

The PlasmaTab was bizarre. It looked a bit like one of those palm computers except the screen was circular and kind of glowed in three dimensions.

JoJo switched it on and Jimmy jumped as a large Coyote's head (wearing an astronaut's helmet!) sprang from the screen and began to rotate inches from his nose. Every three hundred and sixty degrees it looked to the sky and let out a howl. "This day just gets weirder," he said, shaking his head.

Now free to work the main computers, JoJo quickly accessed the Seeker's main system and began to fix the damage caused by the crash. Out in the orchard the helicopter could just be made out. It appeared to be scanning the orchard bottom with bright halogen lights. They didn't have much time. "SaRa, give me the priorities to get us airborne."

"Fuel lines need attention, as do the solar boosters and the vertical take off system, and if you're planning to go above the A-line, you'll need to reconfigure the oxogens."

The 'A-line' was coyote-speak for going through a planet's atmosphere and into space.

"Oxogens won't be necessary. What about invisibility?

"We would be running at eighty percent if we turned it on now."

JoJo shook her head. "Eighty percent is no good, SaRa. Human radar will see us at eighty percent. Keep working on it and don't activate it until it's at least ninety five percent ready."

She rested the palms of her hands on her forehead, thinking. There was something else wasn't there? Of course, the hole in the engine bay left by the grommets.

"SaRa, how are the CoyoteBots doing fixing the engine bay?"

SaRa frowned. "Huh. Don't get me started on those reprobates."

"And what's that supposed to mean?"

"It means, that if you had brought me some rather more experienced CoyoteBots, as opposed to the hotchpotch of metal and screws I'm working with, maybe we'd have been in the air already."

JoJo sighed. "Not this again. Will you please stop going on about it. Ever since we set off, it's been nothing but whinge, whinge, whinge. I brought what I could get okay! It's not easy commandeering top line C-Bots without good reason you know."

SaRa's raised her eyebrows "Well, maybe you should have thought of that before you decided to steal an Admiralty Star Seeker and crash it into the only forbidden planet in the galaxy!" she said haughtily.

JoJo slammed her fist on the console. "SaRa, PLEASE! Now is not the time! Just tell me how they are doing."

"It will take another twenty minutes, minimum," replied SaRa.

JoJo let out a little cry of desperation. "That's way too long. You've got to impress upon them just how important fixing that hole is. Until it is airtight we can't risk putting power into any of the engines, and while you're telling them that, ask Pulp to come up here will you. I've got a job for him."

"Pulp is far too busy," said SaRa firmly.

"Well I need him up here, SaRa," insisted JoJo

"Taking him away from his duties will only increase the delay in fixing the hole. Is that what you want?"

"Of course it's not what I want," growled JoJo, her temper rising. "But I need him up here. The others will just have to work harder, won't they? What is it with you anyway? Are you deliberately trying to aggravate me or something?"

SaRa stuck her nose in the air. "I am merely offering you the benefit of my considerable experience. However, if you choose once again, to disregard my advice then ...."

"SARA," JoJo interrupted. "I really don't have time for another lecture. Could you just get me Pulp up here? Pretty please, with sugar on top."

SaRa huffed something about being childish, but made the call nevertheless. "I must once again register my disapproval at your constant and flagrant ..."

JoJo raised her hand at the console as if to say '*I'm not listening.*'

"Is it always like this with you two?" asked Jimmy.

"Not always," replied JoJo. "Sometimes we really don't get on. Now, are you ready to help me get this thing in the air?"

Jimmy nodded.

"Right then, here's what I want you to do."

* * *

Although he didn't have a clue what was happening, Jimmy did everything JoJo asked of him. It wasn't easy; the PlasmaTab took some getting used to. The lack of a keyboard meant all manipulations of pictures or data were achieved either by moving a finger over the small built-in screen and speaking the command you wanted, or by pushing and pulling 3D holographic displays as if they were solid. JoJo showed him how to operate specific components and change settings just by manipulating them in the right place. It was amazing but he couldn't help worrying that by having to have everything explained to him, it was seriously delaying proceedings.

In between guiding Jimmy, JoJo maintained a running commentary on every button she pressed or calculation she altered.

By the time they had finished, Jimmy had an insight into SaRa, all seven of the on board CoyoteBots, the inner workings of cryo-nucleogenic plasma reactors!!??? Oh yes – and they introduced themselves.

"Right," she said, tapping a key with an air of finality, "that's all we can do."

Jimmy was relieved. Sweat was pouring off him from the concentration.

"So what happens now?" asked Halfpint.

"We wait," answered JoJo. "We wait and hope that the CoyoteBots are doing their job down in the engine bay."

CHAPTER 25

PULP FRICTION

ENGINE BAY NUMBER THREE

Unfortunately, deep in the bowels of engine bay number three, all was not well. Without Pulp to retain order, the six remaining CoyoteBots (Pyro, Occular, Prickle, Arachno, Janitox and the new trainee, ScatterBot) were undergoing what may be loosely termed an 'industrial dispute.' More accurately, they were slipping into all-out warfare!

Self-appointed leader Prickle – the operative word there being 'self' – was, as usual, the catalyst for the discord. Janitox was already refusing to do any more work for the spiky C-Bot (Prickle resembled a small sea mine with eyes), when he rounded on Occular. "You're wrong, so wrong! If you put that there you're going to set us back at least fifteen minutes. You lot really are the poorest excuses for CoyoteBots I have ever encountered. Why won't you listen to me? If you just – Umphh"

The end of his sentence will forever remain a mystery because it was at that precise moment, one of Arachno's eight metal arms shot out faster than a pneumatic drill, grabbed Prickle by the midriff and pinned him to the engine bay wall with a satisfying clang. "Will someone please shut this tin-can up!" Arachno said in a voice deeper than most oceans. "I can't hear myself think here."

"Well, I never," protested an indignant Prickle. "I hope you know that committing actual physical violence against a fellow CoyoteBot is against regulation three hundred and sixty seven of the Artificial intelligence charter. I shall ...."

"Yadda, yadda, yadda," mocked Arachno.

"*I shall* therefore be submitting a formal complaint upon our return. And let me add, I have never been, nor will I ever be a 'tin-can', insect-boy."

A veil of silence descended. ScatterBot shot into the corner cowering, Janitox and Occular smiled at each other. Trouble was brewing.

Arachno's eyes glowed red with rage. Like harpoons propelled by pistons, three more arms bulleted their way towards the pinned Prickle and gripped him tight enough to crush steel.

Pyro intervened just in time "Hey, easy there spidey! You don't want to do that."

Arachno hesitated, "I don't?"

Prickle looked as though he'd just been reprieved from death row.

"Nah, you want to let me melt his silicon." Pyro raised an arm and flicked on a blazing, blue flame. "Then we can plug the hole with his big fat mouth. What do you think my multi-appendaged buddy?"

Prickle let out a whimper.

"Tempting," drawled Arachno, "but I think I have a better, less terminal, idea." Quick as a flash, arm number five shot out and squeezed Prickle right in the oil tubes – an act that was guaranteed to silence any male CoyoteBot, or at the very least, raise his voice a few octaves. Arachno dropped the whimpering Prickle like a used oilcan. "Now, shall we get on?" he said and headed back to the hole.

* * *

Pulp, or CoyoteBot HP-76 Class 3A as he is officially known, came flying into the cockpit about the same time Prickle hit the floor.

Pulp was a chunky, dull metallic sphere about the size of a large grapefruit and was flying so fast that most of the time, all Jimmy saw was a grey blur. Finally he came to a halt by JoJo's left shoulder, beeping manically. Jimmy watched, amazed as two slots opened like curtains to reveal deep blue penetrating eyes, whilst a thin black line in the metal curled to form a large crescent-shaped smile.

"Hello, Pulp" said JoJo. Pulp beeped back joyously. If he had a tail to wag, Jimmy figured it would be fanning him about now.

Out of a drawer in the console, JoJo pulled out six gobstopper sized golden glowing spheres. "Open up," she said to Pulp. A small trap door slid open on the underneath of Pulp, revealing a hollow store. JoJo placed the six balls carefully inside.

"That's six cleaner bombs Pulp. Don't waste them. Use your common sense and spread them out evenly."

She then retrieved a thin translucent micro-disc from her pocket, which she inserted into a hairline slot below Pulp's mouth. "We're hoping not to be here when you get back. This 'nav' chip will help you find your way to us. Okay?"

Pulp beeped again. JoJo flicked her head. "So what are you waiting for? Get out of here."

With a flourish of beeps, Pulp turned and shot out of the doorway.

JoJo couldn't help but smile as she watched him go. She loved Pulp. It was all very well SaRa being pompous about the quality of the CoyoteBots on board, but the truth was JoJo much preferred the older models. Take the latest Occular 9000, with the extra supple telescopic eye and state of the art platinum stabilisation wings. Shiny it may be, but it was notorious for breaking down. It had already popped its vents twice during her training runs alone. Pulp on the other hand wasn't particularly clever or dexterous but, what he lacked in technical wizardry, he more than made up for with good old-fashioned brute force and guile. With a series of hidden pulleys, chains and wires, his tiny frame could lift, winch and pull things hundreds of times his own weight and he never, ever broke down. Most importantly however, he was fearless.

* * *

Pulp's progress was followed via the 'Bot Cam.'

"All CoyoteBots have remote cameras attached." JoJo explained, as Pulp dropped the first cleaner bomb beneath the Star Seeker. "They're automatically activated as soon as they leave the Seeker so we can track them. Hopefully if he does his job right, no one will ever know we were here."

Apart from the slight rumble under their feet, nothing obvious seemed to happen as a result of dropping the first cleaner bomb, so Jimmy took to watching Pulp ride the treetops as he made his way to the second drop point. Sometimes though, Pulp's journey took him through the trees rather than over them.

Through the audio feed Jimmy learnt several CoyoteBot expletives when the ride got a little hairy.

The second cleaner bomb detonated in a patch of ruined orchard about a mile from the Seeker. This time Jimmy saw the full astounding effect.

The ground exploded into a torrent of swirling magenta light. It radiated fifty feet outwards like ripples in a pond, before spectacularly shooting high into the night sky.

Jimmy must have looked panicked by the dramatic display because JoJo smiled and said, "Don't worry. The only reason you can see it is because you're watching it through the Seeker's windscreen. It's totally invisible to the naked eye."

The swirling light suddenly split into hundreds of individual rays dancing in a ballet of colour. Jimmy watched as each ray carried with it a single broken branch pulled from the orchard floor. Like fish on the end of taut lines, branches flicked and fought in the air, whilst down below the gashes and gouges on the injured trunks began to repair before his eyes. Loud cracks and long creaks pierced the night as the wood regained its original shape. Once the trees were whole again, fresh young leaves sprouted from the tips of the branches and white blossom bloomed from thousands upon thousands of newly born buds. Within seconds the blossom turned to fruit and the emerging apples grew fat and ripe.

The entire process took only thirty or forty seconds and was like watching time-lapse photography. Pulp, meanwhile had released four more cleaner bombs at strategic points along the trail of devastation, where the whole process was repeated.

"I've got to get me one of those for my bedroom," said Halfpint.

All this though, was a mere diversion from the real problem of still being helplessly stuck in the tree.

The invisibility shields were still below the ninety five percent JoJo had insisted they reach before she would take off, but when they reached ninety three percent, her patience evaporated. The helicopter (for now they could all see that's what it was), was so close it was making the floor of the cockpit vibrate.

JoJo tapped her finger nervously on the console and said, "This is ridiculous SaRa. As soon as we get news from the C-Bots, we have to go whether the shields are ready or not."

She ran her hands through her hair – which was difficult considering all the grommet guts congealed in it – and prayed it wouldn't be long.

* * *

Finally the news they had been waiting for arrived. The hole in engine bay number three was fixed and all the CoyoteBots were clear of the area. JoJo clapped her hands together, "At last," she said, urgently flipping buttons and switches on the console.

"SaRa, fire one and three up to three quarter power, give me some vertical thrust and void through the plasma fuel line. Oh and turn the invisibility on."

Turning to Halfpint, Cornelius and Paige she said, "You might want to find somewhere to strap yourself in. This could get a little bumpy. The sleeping areas are good."

Halfpint paled.

"What's up with you?" asked Paige as they dashed to the bunks.

"I, er, didn't think she would really do it," he mumbled, as Paige pulled a sheet off the bed and tied it first round a pole, then herself.

"Do what?" said Paige. "Fly? Of course. C'mon grab onto something, this should be wicked."

Halfpint still wasn't keen.

"Er, excuse me for asking a dumb question, but if your invisibility shields are on, why can't we just wait here? The helicopter will soon leave. We don't have to go anywhere."

JoJo stared at him.

"Nice try human, but I am not hanging around here being a sitting target. If anything goes wrong, I want to be up in the air where I can do something about it."

Halfpint sighed and looked pleadingly at Paige for some moral support. No luck. Paige just urged him to get secured.

"Do I stay here?" Jimmy asked JoJo

"You stay there," JoJo answered firmly, and activated the one remaining seat strap before he could think about leaving.

The thrup, thrup, thrup of the helicopter rotors scything through the air was joined suddenly by another, new and indescribable noise. The Star Seeker engines.

To Jimmy they sounded like nothing on earth. Their resonance spread through him like a low electric current. It rose up his legs and into his chest. Adrenaline surged as he realised that they really were about to *fly* in a spaceship.

He grasped the chair, bracing himself for whatever came next.

The thrust was building like a fighter jet heading down a runway for takeoff. JoJo gripped a small joystick and began to pull back. The nose started to lift slowly but jerkily, groaning under the pressure. The branches, it seemed, did not wish to release their catch so easily.

Suddenly, the Seeker lurched and tipped forward and they slid further into the tree. Jimmy's nails dug deep into the leather-like material of the chair as JoJo swore and corrected the tip.

Biting her lip she tried again, this time managing to get the nose to move up more steadily. It had gone probably two feet when, without warning, SaRa killed all the thrust and seized control of the Star Seeker bringing it to an abrupt halt. JoJo looked ready to kill.

"What the hell are you doing?" she screamed. "Have you lost your silicon mind? Give me back control right now."

"Do you wish to crash?" said SaRa firmly.

"What?" JoJo yelled.

"Take a look outside."

JoJo strained against the belts and gasped loudly when she saw how incredibly close the Helicopter was. SaRa had been right. If she had lifted off just then with the shields turned on, the chopper would have unknowingly flown straight into her.

"Maybe you could try being a little more observant next time." SaRa said, raising her eyebrows.

"Oh can it." Shot back JoJo, more upset with herself than SaRa.

The olive green helicopter moved over them, its spotlights sweeping into the cockpit. Instinctively, JoJo thrust her hand into Jimmy's, interlocking her fingers and squeezing tightly.

It was unexpected but, scared as he was, Jimmy was comforted by the gesture.

Everyone held their breath. The only sound louder than the thundering rotor blades was that of Jimmy's heart pounding against his ribs.

The seconds seemed to stretch into days as they waited for the helicopter to pass.

For a moment Jimmy thought it had hesitated, but to everyone's relief it went on its way. The shields had worked. Everyone breathed a big sigh of relief.

JoJo and Jimmy grinned at each other before looking down at their hands and dragging them apart as if they were on fire.

"Ahem – right – let's get out of here," said JoJo, regaining her composure.

This time the lift-off was easier. There was only one moment when the Star Seeker strained against a particularly tough branch, but with a carefully calculated thrust of the engines, they broke free and paused, hovering several feet above the tallest branch.

JoJo savoured the feeling of freedom. Now she could finally power up the engines to flight speed. "Okay. Hang on," she said.

They did. And they were off.

The sensation was incredible. It was like sitting astride a missile, albeit a missile with a very comfy seat.

They rocketed high into the sky at speeds Jimmy didn't even know existed. Unfortunately, although the rest of his body went up, his stomach was left firmly on the ground. He didn't know whether to laugh or scream. At their highest they seemed to be skirting the very edge of space. The billions of stars shined brighter than he had ever seen them before and the crescent moon looked so close he could have reached out and hung a coat on it. Down below the orchard seemed miniscule, like a scale model built for a film. Jimmy could not wipe the smile from his face. He wished they could stay up here forever. This must have been the feeling his Grandad got every time he flew a jet fighter. How he envied him.

As she banked left, Jimmy watched the final swirls of the magenta cleaner bombs fading into the night. Tomorrow all trace of JoJo and 2B landing in the orchard would be gone, but he would never be able to wipe away the memory as easily. This was something that would live with them forever.

JoJo banked around three hundred and sixty degrees. "So, where are we going?"

"Why are you asking me?" replied Jimmy, surprised.

"Well it is your planet. Got any bright ideas where I can hide a Star Seeker?"

Jimmy considered for a moment, and then realised the obviousness of the solution. "Well there is one place, not too far from here as it happens, but ..."

"No buts. We've come too far for buts. All I need to know is, is it safe?"

"I suppose–."

"Then tell me where."

Jimmy quickly explained his idea and, when presented with an on-screen map of the entire Apple Valley perimeter, showed her exactly where to go.

Moments later they were speeding toward Juicepit barn.

CHAPTER 26

AFTER THE COPTERS

Jimmy returned home extremely late that night. Exactly what time it was he had no idea because his watch had stopped working about the same time it got covered in grommet guts. He just knew it was late because the only human being he saw on his way home was a madman in a speeding car which came around a corner so fast it nearly ran him off the road. After a flurry of curse words, Jimmy was glad to get into the house.

He had hoped to sneak in unnoticed, but waiting for him as he opened the door was his Grandad. For about a second, Jimmy was glad it wasn't his Grandma but then he saw his Grandad's face.

He was pacing the floor whilst twisting what appeared to be a necklace, manically between his fingers. He looked like one of those worried looking old ladies you see on the TV after a major disaster, clutching a bunch of rosary beads in their hands. Jimmy tried a half-hearted smile. It was met with an unusually stern look.

"Very nice of you to finally come home, Jimmy. Where have you been?" The voice was flat and emotionless.

"Just at the barn, practicing. I know it's late, sorry. We just didn't realise the time."

Jimmy waited for a response. When he got none, he carried on

"Yeah, what with Cat having to leave and all, we had a lot to talk about. You know, who's going to be singing, what songs we can play, that sort of thing."

Okay, so it wasn't a very good lie, but it was all he could come up with. His Grandad continued to pace agitatedly.

"So you must have got a lot sorted out then? A productive night?"

"Yeah, loads of things."

"Never thought to phone?"

"What?"

His Grandad stopped pacing. "Phone. You know that thing with numbers on. Dial the right ones and you get to talk to someone on the other end. Useful to let people know what is happening."

"Oh, er sorry – just didn't think with everything going on."

His Grandad suddenly slammed a fist into the table making the salt and pepper pot jump into the air. The necklace he had been holding flew out of his hand, landing by a pile of napkins.

"Don't lie to me," he bellowed. "Do you think I'm an idiot? When you didn't come home I went looking for you. The first place I went was the barn."

Jimmy's stomach flipped.

"And what do you think I found there?"

Jimmy said nothing.

"Well I didn't find you did I? So where were you? And please, no more lies, you're in enough trouble."

Jimmy stumbled on his words. He wasn't a good liar, his face showed guilt too easily, but unless his Grandad was bluffing – and he had no reason to think he was – he was in a corner. He opted for a half truth.

"Er, we thought we saw a fire," he began tentatively, "in the orchard, not far in – honest. So we went to have a look. I know it was probably stupid but we did. I'm sorry."

"And was there?"

"Was there what?"

"A fire, Jimmy. You just said you thought you saw a fire."

"Oh, yeah, it was a bunch of kids messing about, setting light to some old boxes. We chased them off. It was no big deal really."

He tried to sound relaxed and convincing but inside his heart was pounding.

"These kids, did you recognise them? Setting fires in the orchard is pretty serious stuff."

"I, er, no. They were already running when we got there."

He felt his Grandad's eyes studying him hard, looking for the tell-tale signs of guilt.

He was a difficult man to lie to. One of those men who command immediate respect the minute they walk into a room, without anyone knowing quite why. If he asked you to run in front of a bus, most people's response would be, 'how fast?' Jimmy felt himself shrinking under his gaze.

A part of him wanted to blurt out the truth and get the night's adventure off his chest, but he knew he couldn't. The truth was simply too preposterous.

Finally, his Grandad shook his head sorrowfully. His face was drawn and tired.

"You know what son," he began, "I don't believe a word you just said. You're too much like your mother and she was a terrible liar. So I'll tell you what I used to tell her, shall I? I'm not in the business of making threats and I won't make you tell me what happened tonight if you don't want to, although I could and you know I could. Trust and honesty goes both ways Jimmy, and without honesty there can be no trust. Do you understand me?"

Jimmy nodded weakly. He felt less than an inch tall. He wondered why his Grandad was being so tough. He had only been late home. It wasn't as though he'd murdered anyone or anything. It was a good job Jimmy had kept the truth hidden. If his Grandad knew the real reason he was late, he would have a serious reason to be angry.

"You know where I'll be if you want to talk," said his Grandad. "Now I think bed would be a good option, don't you, you've got school in the morning."

Jimmy could feel the disappointment radiating out of him. As he passed the table, he reached across and retrieved the necklace. It looked old and had some sort of initial on it. He didn't recognize it, in fact it looked broken. Nevertheless, it seemed to be important to his Grandad, so Jimmy handed it to him as a sort of peace offering. It was not received as such.

Jimmy slumped off. He had never felt more rotten in his life, but how could he possibly ever tell anyone the truth?

Unsurprisingly, Jimmy found sleep impossible. With everything that had happened, his brain just would not flip into neutral. At one fifty, to take the monotony out of staring at the ceiling, he switched on his mobile phone only to find six text messages waiting for him. All were from Halfpint; all checking that there were no hard feelings between them after their argument in the orchard. Jimmy smiled – finally some good news. He hated fighting with Halfpint and if ever there was a time when you needed a best friend to talk to, it was now. He checked the time of the texts. The last one had been sent only a minute ago.

Jimmy replied immediately, apologising for almost getting them killed. Halfpint responded saying that he wouldn't have missed the ride in the Star Seeker for anything, but could have lived without the exploding grommet.

Friends again, they continued texting well into the early morning as they relived the night's action.

* * *

The flight to the barn had been unforgettable. As soon as the helicopters had left the scene JoJo had swept them into a stomach churning dive. A manoeuvre Jimmy suspected she had done on purpose, because she was smirking all the way. Within seconds they exploded toward the orchard touching the treetops before coming to a halt right outside the barn.

It took a bit of negotiating and some very careful flying, but the Star

Seeker eventually nestled perfectly in the huge back storage area. With its nose a few feet above Paige's drums, hovering genteelly above the bits of old tractor and truck parts, it looked as if it had been made to fit.

Shortly afterwards Pulp returned, whizzing happily through an open barn window, his blue eyes shining brighter than when he left – his mission totally successful. The only clue that a Star Seeker had passed through would be the slightly sweeter taste to the apples grown as a result of the cleaner bombs – a side effect of being formed in several seconds rather than several weeks.

As far as JoJo was concerned, the hiding place was perfect. With the invisibility shields finally on full power, she would be able to work on the Seeker unhindered and have time to nurse 2B back to full fitness, whilst the barn could be used as normal. (Jimmy hadn't told her about band practice yet.)

Once settled and with a still catatonic 2B safely in bed, JoJo dragged Jimmy to a small glass cubicle, pushed him in, shut the door and told him to close his eyes.

"Wh – What are you doing?" he stuttered nervously as the door locked.

"I presume you don't want to go home stinking like a cess pit?" said JoJo, peering through the glass.

Jimmy looked down at the congealing fetid grommet viscera dangling from his clothes. He looked like an extra from a bad zombie movie. "Point taken. What are you going to do?"

"Close your eyes and wait and see."

She pressed a button that activated a series of dry chemical sprays. Jimmy shut his eyes tight, and waited for the hissing to subside. When he opened them again his clothes were as clean as when he'd first put them on (probably cleaner actually).

"Now, you can go home," said JoJo, opening the door.

Jimmy and the guys took the hint.

* * *

Halfpint must have eventually dropped off to sleep from text fatigue because Jimmy's final transmission never received a response.

With their friendship restored, Jimmy soon succumbed himself, dreaming sweet dreams of spaceships, rockets and alien girls. Indeed when he woke the next morning he wondered if the whole thing might have been a fanciful dream. It was only when he saw his Grandad's stern face at breakfast he knew it had really happened. Happy that he wasn't one cello short of a string quartet, he left for school itching to get down to the barn.

By nine o clock, Jimmy's day was looking up. He and Halfpint arrived at the school gates only to find the whole place cordoned off with yellow plastic warning tape and hundreds of confused kids milling around. A sixth form prefect trying his best to shout above the general hub-bub informed them that a major gas leak had occurred in the boiler room over the weekend and with only one week of term left before the holidays and the repairs set to take two days, the headmistress, Miss Witherspoon, was closing the school and starting summer early. Once Jimmy had established that there would be no disruption to the battle of the bands, he and Halfpint found Cornelius and Paige and rushed directly to the Juicepit.

* * *

It was exactly as they had left it, which is to say either the Star Seeker was still invisible or it wasn't there.

"Do you think they have gone?" said Halfpint quietly.

Jimmy shrugged his shoulders. "I don't know I ..."

Suddenly, from the space behind Paige's drum kit jumped a remarkably rejuvenated 2B.

"Do you play these?" he screamed, pointing at the instruments, oblivious to the fact that he'd just scared at least five years off each of the guys lives.

Jimmy was utterly puzzled. The last time they saw him, this boy

163

had been a gibbering wreck. Now he looked like he'd had one too many 'e' numbers in his diet.

Before Jimmy could answer, JoJo appeared and grabbed a handful of 2B's coat.

"Come back here, I told you not to go out there," she growled. Then to Jimmy, "I'm sorry about him. He's been like this ever since he saw all this stuff this morning."

"But … I …Yesterday …" Stuttered Jimmy, master raconteur.

"He's fine," interrupted JoJo, struggling to keep hold of her eager brother. "I told you he only needed rest. Look, WILL YOU PACK IT IN!"

Jimmy shook his head unbelievingly. First there was JoJo. The cuts on her shoulder had healed within a matter of minutes and now 2B, back, presumably to his normal self. The curative capacity of these aliens was just phenomenal.

"Do you play these instruments?" 2B persisted, getting more agitated at being held back by his sister. "Please tell me you play."

"Yes we play," nodded Jimmy. "We're a band called Applejuice. But how do you …?"

"Music is why we came here, isn't it JoJo?" 2B blurted out. "We can't get it back home – music, that is. I don't think anyone has ever heard any actually, but JoJo, she found a way of getting it using a photon radio receiver."

JoJo deflated. 2B's inability to keep his big mouth shut was, unfortunately, legendary.

"A photon what?" asked Halfpint.

"A Photon Radio receiver. It was completely illegal to build it of course, but…"

"2B!" yelled a horrified JoJo, yanking his collar hard. "Why don't you just tell them everything for goodness sake."

"I trying!" he grumbled, missing the sarcasm, "anyway it could capture sounds all the way from this planet. She let me listen and it was fantastic. But you couldn't listen a lot because the radio only had a limited span or something. So now we've come to record a whole lot more and take it home, except we weren't supposed to land here. That was a big mistake." He looked accusingly at JoJo. JoJo shot daggers back, "but since we did, are you going to play something for us? Please."

Cornelius scratched his head. "You mean to say that you came all the way from another planet *just* to listen to music?" he asked unbelievingly.

JoJo shrugged, looking almost embarrassed to admit it. When it was said like that, it did sound a pretty ridiculous thing to have done.

"You must be mad," said Paige shaking her head, where was it you came from again? The planet *Insania*?"

"It's called Anilar actually," snapped JoJo defensively.

"Well you must have really liked what you heard to do something like that, Jeez," said Paige

"Play something then," insisted 2B, gazing longingly at the instruments.

"2B," admonished JoJo through gritted teeth, "I'm sure they would much rather be left alone, wouldn't you?"

Once again 2B ignored his sister. "This here is a bum kit isn't it? How do you play it?"

Everyone burst out laughing, except JoJo. "You're such a numbskull 2B. It's a *drum* kit. Not a 'bum kit.'"

2B blushed scarlet. "Well I was nearly right. Who plays it anyway? Can you show me how to do it?"

Paige stepped forward grinning at the eager 2B. His faux pas certainly broke the ice between the six of them. The atmosphere had in an instant changed from being rather awkward to almost relaxed.

"Come on then little man. Let's see you hit something," encouraged Paige.

JoJo wore a look of concern as 2B finally broke free from her grasp and scurried off to Paige. A bit like a mother the first time she leaves her child at playgroup, except this wasn't playgroup. This was sending 2B

165

into the company of humans and it was difficult for her to feel anything but unease at the prospect.

* * *

As the others joined Paige and perhaps sensing JoJo's disquiet, Jimmy walked over to her. He was quite certain that she didn't want him there, but figured the opportunity to talk to an alien might never happen again so he ought to at least make the effort. Besides, quite unexpectedly he was finding himself attracted to her in a way that felt was quite wrong when you considered he was a human and well ... she wasn't. She was pretty, no doubt about it, but there was more to her than that. She had a steely confidence that he'd never seen in a girl his own age before. Then there were her eyes, an unearthly blue and totally mesmerising. *A boy could really get lost in eyes like that,* he thought.

At least they would have something to talk about. If she liked music, then Jimmy could converse about that all day, which was good considering his woeful track record of talking and being interesting around pretty girls. The last one had just left the country, for heavens sake.

His problem had never been thinking of something to say. Rather the fact that the words were always bypassed through his brain's '*will she think I'm stupid if I say this*' filter, first. The result was lots of inane questions and far too many monosyllabic grunts.

As it turned out he needn't have worried. When she finally relaxed a little, Jimmy found JoJo the type of person who liked to talk a lot, pause briefly for breath (no longer than half a second as far as Jimmy could tell) and then talk some more. After twenty minutes he was actually fighting for a space, just to get a few words in.

It also became amazingly apparent that JoJo was not only aware of lots of the popular bands here on earth, but that she liked most of the same ones he did. It was downright amazing really. He wondered how the bands would feel if they knew their fan base extended to one hundred million light years.

"I guess that proves teenagers really aren't that different no matter where you come from," Jimmy said.

Eventually, as the guys continued to show an overawed 2B the other instruments, their conversation culminated in a guided tour of the Star Seeker.

JoJo introduced him properly to SaRa who wowed him with some of the things she could do, including being able to mimic any voice that she heard. Jimmy found it very disconcerting to have a conversation with something that was responding to you in your own voice.

She showed him where they exercised and kept fit during long missions (an entire room full of bizarre looking gym equipment), the medical room and the portable laboratory where they could run all kinds of tests if they needed to.

She showed him the star charts and how to use the special pen that made the stars move, and then explained about Space Portals.

Apparently humans knew about portals, but completely misunderstood them.

"You call them black holes," JoJo said. "You think they are some sort of dead star that's collapsed in on itself, but they're not. They are like interstellar short cuts. Imagine you're at one side of a huge lake and you want to get to the other. You can either walk all the way around which would take, lets say a day, or you can cross a bridge, which would take about ten minutes. A portal is like the bridge. You enter them at one part of the galaxy and come out in a completely different part in a fraction of the time."

According to JoJo there were millions of them scattered throughout the galaxy, each with a specific route. By choosing the right combination you could go virtually anywhere you wanted and travel hundreds of millions of light years in mere hours.

The tour finished with the hydrobugs. These were the little red and gold insects Jimmy had noticed swimming in the vertical tank of water yesterday. Up close they were flat and oval shaped with a single eye at the front and a tiny hole at the back.

"They purify all the water on board," JoJo explained. "You see how they move? Like a jet? That's clean water shooting out of the back."

Jimmy peered in as the hydrobugs blasted from one side of the glass tank to the other.

"They feed on any impurities, then they get rid of what they don't want. Fortunately, what they don't want is exactly what we do want."

"You mean you *drink* hydrobug wee?" Jimmy asked, turning up his nose.

"In a manner of speaking. Its more poo than wee but you'll never get a more pure water than that which has passed through a hydrobug," JoJo said.

Jimmy grimaced and made a mental note – don't accept any offer of a drink from JoJo.

After leaving the Star Seeker they perched on the rusty old Jeep and watched 2B attempt to play Cornelius's bass guitar, which was taller than him. As they did, Jimmy told JoJo his and the bands story. It was funny, yesterday morning he would have sworn that no one had any worse problems than himself. Next to flying through asteroid belts and crash landing one hundred million light years from home however, his troubles about Cat and Damien Dirt sounded pretty lame in comparison and he began to wonder why he was even bothering.

Reaching over Jimmy, JoJo plucked a pink baseball cap from the seat opposite. On it, it read. *'Beware, this kitten's got claws.'* "So, is this Cat's?" she asked.

Jimmy blushed at the memory. "Yeah, that's hers." He had bought it for her last Christmas. "Must have forgotten to pack it I guess," he said hopefully. The thought that she had deliberately left it behind pierced his heart like a lance.

"She sounds a pretty special girl."

Jimmy shrugged. "She's all right, y'know. So this trip of yours," he said, quickly changing the subject, "is it official? I mean were you sent here?"

JoJo laughed. "No way. Trust me I don't even want to think about what will happen if I get found out. The least they'll do is kick me out of the academy and never let me near a Star Seeker again."

"You really risked all that, just so you could hear music?"

JoJo shrugged. "What do you think, Jimmy?"

"I think you'd have to be crazy and you don't strike me as being crazy – a little odd maybe," he smiled. "So what did you come here for?"

JoJo looked out at the rest of the band. "Don't you think you ought to go and rescue the others before 2B does irreparable damage to that guitar? I know how clumsy he can be."

Jimmy watched 2B topple sideways as he tried to take the entire weight of the bass himself.

"Go," she said. "I'm dying to hear what all the fuss is about anyway."

Jimmy knew a hint when he heard it. JoJo wasn't ready to talk about her reasons for coming just yet. *Ah well*, he thought, *there's plenty of time.*

CHAPTER 27

COSMIC BOOMS

JoJo listened to two songs but her heart wasn't in it. The band was good but she longed for the solitude of the Star Seeker.

As soon as she breathed in its purified and familiar air, tiredness overwhelmed her. Last night the after-effects of the Grommet's kiss put pay to any thoughts of sleep she may have had. Her shoulder had throbbed continually and no matter what position she got herself into, she could not get comfortable. Consequently, most of the evening was spent staring at the ceiling compiling mental lists of things to do. Lists that quickly grew to the point where she had to subdivide them into smaller lists just to keep them all in her head.

Top of the first list had been to send a secured StarMail to Helix back on Anilar. With her mission timetable in tatters and little hope of getting home soon, something would have to be done to ensure the Holotropes continued unhindered.

She'd set them for a life of forty-eight hours. After that they would simply dissolve into their original micro-chip form. That meant they needed re-programming from scratch, which was easy enough. She could do it from here but only Helix could ensure the holotropes spent as much time out of the house and as little time with JoJo's parents as possible.

She would not expect a reply to her StarMail. Transmissions of any kind to the Blue Planet were banned under Anilar law. Even secure Mailings were not immune to the Admiralty's relentless paranoia of all things Blue Planet. However, as they had no reason to expect StarMails *from* the Blue Planet, she hoped hers would slip through unnoticed.

With that done, she moved on to item number two, fixing the Star Seeker toilets.

Thankfully JoJo was getting more help now. Pulp's return to the Seeker had coincided with a dramatic increase in CoyoteBot activity. It seemed the prospect of being hoisted up in the air by your lateral vents and flung butt first into the plasma reactor was more than enough incentive to stop the arguing. Cleaning gloopy radioactive slop from the plasma reactors was usually the job of an unmanned stink probe. To a highly intelligent specialised CoyoteBot, being placed 'in the tank' was the ultimate insult.

At four o clock in the morning, with JoJo's eyes finally shutting, SaRa got word that they could be 'space' ready within forty-eight hours. JoJo smiled contentedly. "At last, some good news."

She was fast asleep within a minute.

Now, twelve hours later, with 2B otherwise occupied, it was time to find out just how close they really were to going home.

"SaRa have you got those figures I asked you for last night?" JoJo asked.

"Of course."

A long list appeared on a screen in front of JoJo. Unfortunately, as she had suspected, none of them made good reading.

"Are these numbers correct?"

"To the nearest zero point zero one percent. I can of course check them again for you if you wish," said SaRa, a little indignantly at having her maths questioned.

"No, no. It's just …" JoJo shook her head despondently.

What she was looking at was a series of calculations that showed her all the inner workings of the Star Seeker. Similar to those pages full of numbers which no-one really understands at the back of computer manuals. The figure that caught her attention was labeled 'X1: T.O. detonation points.' The T.O. stood for 'Take Off.' and the figures adjacent represented the minimum speed the Star Seeker had to reach in order to break through planetary atmospheres and avoid melting the outer tutulium shell of the Star Seeker. Or put more simply, stop them turning into a massive fireball. Obviously each planet had a different minimum speed due to the variable consistency of atmospheres. The speed needed to get off the Blue Planet was beyond belief. If it was true – and she had no reason to doubt SaRa – they had a real problem. Last night when they were checking the damage along with the failure of the oxo generators, there had been one more catastrophic failure which JoJo had noticed. She had tried to put it out of her mind, but these figures meant she had to ask.

"SaRa, how is the repair to the accelerator coming along?"

"Ahh."

"And what's 'Ahh' supposed to mean precisely?"

"It means that it is going badly, JoJo. In fact, at this moment I am unsure if it can be fixed at all."

JoJo's heart sank. She pointed at the figure she had been studying. "How am we supposed to generate that much power without an accelerator or a launcher, SaRa? It's impossible. Were shutliked."*

"I'm afraid your eloquent summary of the situation is indeed correct," said SaRa calmly. "There is no human technology that could propel us to such speeds. Plasma burners haven't even been thought of yet."

"But … but that means we're stuck here."

"It would appear to be the case, yes."

JoJo frowned. "Well pardon me for saying SaRa, but you seem to be taking this news rather well."

SaRa's lip curled ever so slightly. It was the first time JoJo had ever seen her attempt a smile.

"For the first time in our short, but rather tempestuous relationship, JoJo, it appears that I know something you don't."

*Please note that the literal translation of this word into English would curl most granny's' toes, therefore we will stick to the Larian.

That got JoJo sitting up straight. "What are you talking about, SaRa?"

"I'm talking about a potential answer to our problem that you have failed to consider."

So smug did she look that if she'd have had hands, SaRa would have been carefully inspecting her nails for blemishes.

"Well ..." JoJo said impatiently.

"Well what?"

"Oh stop playing games. Tell me what you know."

"Oh please allow me to bask in the glory for a while, JoJo. This is a rare event. I can feel a surge in my circuits already."

JoJo narrowed her eyes. "You'll certainly feel a surge soon. Now tell me what I've missed before I pull your wires out."

"Oh very well, our problem is simple. In the vacuum of space, Star Seekers use a very high-energy fuel to propel them to their maximum speeds. On the atmospheric planets however, such fuels cannot be used for fear of a devastating environmental disaster. Therefore we require some alternative way of launching into space. On Anilar we use the slingshot. On other planets we use the accelerator which, as I just said, we probably, will not have."

JoJo frowned, "SaRa, this is kindergarten stuff. Get to the point."

"Very well, tell me, what do you know about Cosmic Booms?"

"Cosmic booms. Er ..." JoJo searched her mental files. "Cosmic booms are incredibly rare but dramatic effects caused by sonic disturbances during galaxial superstorms," she said, dragging the information up from goodness knows which recesses in her brain. "The superstorms generate winds that can reach speeds of, I think, over two thousand miles per hour. When that happens, giant spacedust tornados, hundreds of miles wide are formed. There have been reports that Star Seekers caught in the storms have inexplicably been subject to massive short-term speed increases. Velocities up to fifty times normal cruising speeds have been logged. Am I close?" she said, knowing full well she was.

"Very good, JoJo. The sudden and violent acceleration causes a loud crack in space that carries for hundreds of thousands of miles, hence the name, cosmic boom," SaRa finished for her.

"But, some people don't believe they even exist."

"Oh, I can assure you that they exist all right," said SaRa expertly. "Larian engineers spent years designing baffles to counteract the tornado's effects. They're fitted as standard on all X1 Star Seekers."

"They are? I had no idea," said JoJo, genuinely surprised.

"And you also had no idea I suppose, that we encountered such a phenomenon, not an hour ago."

"What, a cosmic boom!" cried JoJo, smiling incredulously. "Don't be ridiculous. Have you been drinking the high density oil again? Forgive me for being thick, but I think I would have noticed a two thousand mile an hour wind blowing through here."

SaRa shook her blue holographic head. "You are assuming that a cosmic boom is solely a result of the storm winds," said SaRa.

"Well isn't it?"

SaRa smiled a self satisfied smile. She was loving playing the teacher for a change. "Actually, for many years that was thought to be the case, but no longer. Research discovered that when the winds reach two thousand miles per hour, a sound frequency is produced which interferes with the plasma injectors and it is *that* which causes the acceleration – nothing at all to do with the speed of the wind."

"A sound frequency?" exclaimed JoJo.

"Precisely. One high pitched note that occurs in space only when the storms are raging at their most dramatic.

"Are you sure?" said JoJo, shaking her head. This was the first she had ever heard of musical notes in space.

"I am absolutely positive, and if you had known about this, you would have known that the very same note was played by one of those human's musical instruments."

JoJo's mouthed dropped open. "Wait, let me get this straight. You're saying that this Star Seeker underwent a cosmic boom because one of the humans played a guitar riff?"

"Well, it was more of a cosmic-pop, but yes, that is essentially what happened."

"So why didn't we shoot through the barn at ten thousand miles per hour."

SaRa raised her eyebrows at JoJo. "Perhaps because the engines are not turned on." She said slowly.

JoJo looked embarrassed. "Oh, right," she said.

"Of course the note generated would not have been nearly loud enough to induce the full blown effect. But nevertheless the frequency was correct and the plasma injectors would certainly have received a significant power boost. In fact, I believe it may be enough…"

"To blast us through the atmosphere," interrupted JoJo suddenly getting it. "SaRa, you're a genius? How much louder? How much longer would it need to be?"

"Oh considerably more on both counts. I don't believe the capabilities lie within this barn."

JoJo's brain went into overdrive. "You know what we need SaRa? We need Jimmy."

* * *

Buzzing with excitement, she gathered the band and 2B for a meeting in the Star Seeker. It was incredible really when she thought about it. The Blue Planet was vast. They could have landed anywhere, yet fate had delivered them to this very place. A place which could possibly hold the key for her return home.

She began by quickly explaining cosmic booms and how the simplicity of playing a single note on a guitar could, in theory, induce such an extreme reaction. Everybody listened utterly transfixed. It was only when she mentioned the volume required that Jimmy stopped her.

"Urm, we can't play any louder than we are at the moment. Our amplifiers won't do it."

"But it is possible to play louder? I mean, humans do have the capability of producing more volume than that don't they?"

"Oh sure," nodded Halfpint. "You ought to be here for the Centenary concert, it's gonna be a definite ear protection zone."

JoJo looked quizzically at Jimmy. "The Centenary Celebrations, that's where the winner of this Battle of the Bands play, correct?"

"Yes but…."

"So you could do it? If you played there, you could hit that note again loud enough to make a cosmic boom?"

"I suppose so, if we played there, but…."

"What about it SaRa? Would it be feasible?" interjected JoJo excitedly.

"Well, it would be extremely risky. The volume and duration would have to be absolutely precise. Any failure of one or the other and I'm afraid we would fly into the atmosphere far too slowly, but in theory … I suppose it would."

JoJo clapped her hands together and looked around at all the others. "That's it then. It's a chance we have to take. Will you do it?"

"Er guys," said Jimmy, trying to get their attention.

"What about those baffle things?" asked Paige. "Didn't you say they stopped it happening?"

"Oh Karzig," said JoJo, "she's right SaRa. Is there anything we can do?"

"I have already taken the liberty of instructing Arachno to begin their removal."

JoJo beamed. "Such a clever girl."

"Er Guys," said Jimmy a little louder as the air of excitement grew.

"This is just the best news. I can't tell you what it means that you're going to help us. Are you sure you want to do it?"

"Are you kidding?" beamed Halfpint, "how many guitarists can say that their playing actually blasted a rocket into outer space. It's the stuff of legends."

"GUYS," yelled Jimmy and finally everyone turned. "This all sounds absolutely fantastic and believe me, I would love nothing more than to help you out, JoJo, but I think you're forgetting something. If all this depends on us winning the Battle of the Bands, then we have a major, major problem.

CHAPTER 28

MORE DIRTY DEEDS

The major problem arrived shortly afterwards. Damien Dirt strutted into his first rehearsal with all the pomp and ego of a fully-fledged platinum selling rock star. With him he brought the ever-present Banner twins and a list of songs he insisted he was going to sing whether the band liked them or not.

Jimmy almost wrapped his guitar around the buffoon's head before he had played a single note.

"Let's just get this over with," he whispered to Halfpint as he turned his guitar up full, filling the barn with an electronic hum of anticipation.

One song in and Damien's voice left Jimmy wondering if some new musical notes had been invented that he hadn't been told about. He also wondered just what JoJo and 2B were making of it.

* * *

Safely tucked away in the Star Seeker, the two Larian's were watching the proceedings with increasing anguish.

"He must be ill," grumbled 2B as he clamped his hands over his ears. "Either that or dying. This is nothing like what we heard on your radio JoJo. It's awful!"

JoJo agreed. Damien Dirt had the worst voice she had ever heard. Admittedly her experience of music was limited, but even she knew rubbish when she heard it and this was definitely rubbish! More amazing was that for some unfathomable reason Damien Dirt seemed to think he sounded fantastic.

2B jammed some bits of sponge in his ears. "They are so never going to win that competition. They've got more chance of juggling dust."

JoJo had already resigned herself to this fact. The tiny crumb of optimism she had felt thirty minutes ago when discussing the cosmic boom had vanished. She hadn't quite believed Jimmy's view on Damien's awfulness. Perhaps she hadn't wanted to, but everything he had said had turned out to be true.

Down below Damien screeched another ear-splitting note.

"Oh boy! He needs a voice transplant. It's his only hope. That or a tetra-harpoon up the -"

"*2B!*"

2B slumped forward, encasing his head in his folded arms. "Well, what can you expect? That's our way home going up in smoke out there. Who knows how long we'll have to wait for another chance like this. I don't want to stay stuck in this Star Seeker forever, JoJo. I want to go home. I want ... JoJo ... are you listening?"

She wasn't. Something he just said had caught a hold in her mind like a fish suddenly taking the bait pierced on a hook. Two words played over in her mind. *Voice transplant. Voice transplant.* Could it work?

All at once a tiny spark of a plan caught hold and ignited. This was how it always happened with JoJo. Ideas didn't bubble gently to the boil like water in a kettle, they burst forth in great gushes like champagne from a shaken bottle. A flood of adrenaline flowed through her body like gasoline fuelling the flames and within seconds she had the answer to their problem completely mapped out in her head.

She would of course have to be careful – and do some reading. Lots of reading. And SaRa. She would definitely have to consult SaRa. Although such a thing was technically out of her sphere of expertise,

JoJo was sure she could be of some help. It would be difficult and probably very dangerous, but – oh if it worked! If she could pull it off.

She looked at her sullen brother, sponge sticking out of his ears. He didn't know it but he had just solved their problem. There was a way to get home after all.

Now all she had to do was convince Jimmy it was a good idea.

CHAPTER 29

THE BEST LAID PLANS

It was a bad idea. The worst idea in fact since the guy who believed the ejector seat would be a good addition to a helicopter.

It was the morning of the Battle of The Bands. Standing backstage at Apple Valley High nervously watching the band from Winesap High soundcheck their equipment, Jimmy massaged his temples. Somewhere beneath his fingers he could feel the mother of all headaches bubbling threateningly.

Three long days of rehearsals with Damien had passed with little to show for their endeavours other than frayed tempers and ears that needed a good syringing if they ever wanted to be the same again.

Then last night, JoJo had told them of her 'plan.'

Vocalosis. That's what she had called it. Swapping the quality of someone's voice with that of another was how she described it. Barmy was what Jimmy had said.

Was this really what it had come down to? Was he really going to walk out onto this stage in a few hours time in front of nearly two thousand people and trust his credibility *and* his Grandad's lease to a magic trick that sounded not only improbable but downright impossible?

It seemed that JoJo's grand plan and their success (or failure) in the competition would come down to a few strands of hair she had found trapped in the Velcro fastening of Cat's baseball cap. Somehow she was going to use these to transfer Cat's voice over to Damien. Every time he

180

thought about it, it sounded more ludicrous.

His headache inched a little closer.

How on earth had he got himself into such a ridiculous situation? The love of his life had flown off to another country never to return. His number one enemy was holding him to ransom. His relationship with his Grandad had deteriorated to the point where they were no longer talking, and all that stood between him losing his home and living happily ever after was an alien and a wispy knot of blonde hair.

The complicated explanation JoJo offered as to how Vocalosis worked had washed over him like river water over a pebble.

"Its all to do with DNA," she said holding Cat's hat. "Everybody has a different voice right? That's because of a lot of factors such as the shape of your mouth, the position of your teeth, the size and shape of your vocal cords and the contours of your lips, and all these things are determined by your DNA."

She had looked at Jimmy, Paige, Cornelius and Halfpint like they should be offering her the nobel prize for science for this remarkable piece of deduction. When their faces remained blank she said, "Cat's DNA is in these hairs here. They probably got pulled from her head when she last took the cap off. So all we have to do is use Vocalosis to temporarily transfer all of Cat's attributes over to Damien and we will have ourselves a singer."

"You mean he'll sound like a girl?" asked Cornelius dumbly.

"I'd pay to see that," smiled Halfpint.

"No he won't," assured JoJo. "At least I don't think he will. I've done a whole lot of reading on the subject and SaRa thinks it's certainly possible. His voice will just be better because he will be using Cat's 'vocal machinery.'

Vocal machinery, mused Jimmy. It sounded amazing. It sounded as likely to work as a bicycle with no wheels! But what did they have to lose? Whatever JoJo thought she could do to Damien's voice she couldn't make it any worse, so at this late juncture anything was worth a try.

Of course, things never being entirely simple, there was a problem. In order for it to work, JoJo would have to maintain eye contact with Damien the whole time. This meant not only did she have to be in the crowd during the performance, she had to be close enough to see him clearly. It hadn't escaped Jimmy's memory that when they first met, JoJo had been none too pleased about spending time with humans and as far as he knew this hadn't changed. She hadn't even so much as stepped foot outside the barn since the aftermath of the crash. This worried Jimmy. Being thrown in amongst nearly two thousand hyped-up children and adults at what would effectively be a rock concert, could be an ordeal for anyone. For all her protestations to the contrary, he wasn't sure she quite knew what she was letting herself in for. Even if she could get here unscathed and get the vocalosis to work, losing her nerve – and eye contact – at any point during the show would prove disastrous – not just for the band. The very last thing JoJo needed was to draw attention to herself because the truth was, no matter how much she might resemble a human being, she wasn't one. She was a Larian – an Alien, and the more time Jimmy spent with her, the more he was beginning to notice subtle differences between the two species. It was more to do with the aura that surrounded her than her actual physical looks. It was something subtle, yet distinctive. Many tiny differences that added up to great whole. She was different. There was no getting away from it. What if people started asking questions she couldn't answer? She might panic. She might do something stupid. She might really use that gun on somebody!

In the end though, JoJo persuaded them that it was the only way.

Between them they had concocted a persona for her to use if anybody started making conversation. For today JoJo would become Joanne, Jimmy's cousin visiting from overseas. That would nicely get around her accent, which sounded like it came from nowhere in particular, and the fact that she didn't know her way around Apple Valley. He also briefed her on a few of this year's slang words so she might stand a chance if she heard them, but there was only so much time and Jimmy felt they were sending her into a battle armed only with a toothpick.

"Some of the kids are rough, especially the Gravenstein lot," stressed Jimmy trying to make her realise what she was letting herself in for.

"I can handle myself," argued JoJo

"They can smell a new kid a mile off. They'll try to make your life a misery."

JoJo wasn't listening. As far as she was concerned this was the only way. If she didn't do it, Jimmy wouldn't get his lease and she wouldn't get home. Everyone would lose. And as we know, she didn't like to lose. She would, she insisted, be absolutely fine.

* * *

Pacing around the Star Seeker cockpit chewing on an already chewed nail, listening to the clock tick-tock inexorably along, JoJo could only conclude that this had to be the most stupid thing she had ever considered doing. Her heart was racing. Sweat was pouring down her temples as though she had a raging fever and her legs had nearly buckled twice already. Madness!

The mere thought of being in such close proximity to so many humans made her head spin like a Catherine wheel. She must have been delusional to have even suggested it – caught up in the moment somehow. She'd never even performed Vocalosis on a real person before for heavens sake.

Sure she had managed to swap the grunt of a Hairy yuka with the high pitched squeal of a Golden kittlebird, but that was in class under her teacher's supervision. And she'd had the entire animal to go at. This time she was supposed to do it on a full grown human with nothing but some manky bits of hair. Strange how it had seemed such a good idea at the time.

She thought of Jimmy. He would be at the school now, waiting in the wings ready to play, with all his hopes pinned on her. God she was stupid sometimes. Why didn't she ever just do the simple thing? Surely it would have been easier to fly to this place called France, pick up Cat and bring her back for the competition. She was sure they could have done something to get the Deeds back from Damien. SaRa knew all kinds of mind-warping tricks. Shame that idea hadn't occurred until after she'd enthused about Vocalosis. Now it was too late.

She checked the clock for the hundredth time, took a final look at herself in the full length mirror and groaned.

She couldn't get the feel of these clothes at all. They had been borrowed from Paige and, while Jimmy insisted she looked fine, JoJo was not convinced. The red top she could deal with. It was pretty much just a T-shirt with a few extra frills and a slash cut in the midriff, but the denim skirt and black leather ankle boots made her feel, well, like a girl. And that hadn't happened in a long time. And Paige was at least two inches shorter than she was so everything felt small.

She shimmied her hips trying to shuffle the skirt down her thighs a little more. It was no use. She felt like she was five years old playing dress up. The only thing missing were her Mum's over-size shoes.

How she longed for her Cub's Uniform. Maybe with that on she wouldn't feel so nervous. Maybe then she could give the bathroom a well needed break from her presence!

At least 2B wasn't giving her any grief. He had kicked up a real stink when she told him he couldn't go and in the end she had to resort to incentives to get him to stay. At the moment he was playing a game of electro-tag hide and seek with Pulp, Occular and Arachno.

The game was simple. Think of tag-team hide and seek but with electric phase batons to spice it up a bit and you'll have the general idea. 'Get found and get buzzed' was the motto. The effects weren't permanent but definitely painful. JoJo could hear them scurrying about and was watching the proceedings via some live feeds on one of the big screens in the cockpit. At the moment 2B had zapped Occular inside one of the toilets. Arachno meanwhile had managed to take Pulp out of the game, sticking him to the wall near the relaxation room. That left 2B seeking out Arachno, but they were miles apart. Arachno was just about to hide inside one of the food bins whilst 2B was way down near the engine bays about to peek into the Plasma reactor chamber.

JoJo grinned. Boys!

She checked her watch again (one hundred and one times now). It really was time she made a move. She took a deep breath trying to calm down. '*Really,*' she told herself, '*there's nothing to worry about. All the directions are programmed into my watch so I can't get lost. SaRa's right there if I need her. I've got the cap and Jimmy will be there. Piece of cake.*'

That's when all the alarms went ballistic and 2B screamed.

CHAPTER 30

THE SURPRISE PACKAGE

At first she thought Arachno had found 2B and zapped him in a rather painful place. Phase shocks in the wrong anatomical area can certainly make a young boy scream, but the horror of the computer monitor told her different.

She followed the sound and skidded to a halt, panting, outside the door of the Plasma Reactor Chamber. Inside, 2B stood, back to the wall, hands aloft, eyes on stalks.

"I swear on my life that I didn't touch a thing," he shouted. "I just walked in looking for Arachno and everything went off."

Everything was going off all right. Warning signs were flashing on all the walls, a claxon was sounding somewhere overhead and a red emergency light was circling outside the door in tandem with yet another alarm. JoJo quickly scanned the room.

The Plasma Reactor Chamber was, like all rooms in the Star Seeker, much bigger inside than it could possibly truly be. About the size of a badminton court, it housed a single computer terminal and twenty-five equally spaced, transparent circular tubes. Each tube ran from floor to ceiling and bore a large luminous warning label. They were filled with a gently flickering blue and pink liquid. The pink part swirled from top to bottom in constantly shrinking and expanding globules like huge larva lamps. This stuff was Plasma. The Star Seeker's main fuel.

At the ceiling, the tubes branched into hundreds of smaller pipes that cris-crossed their way in all directions before exiting through the walls, heading for the cyro-nuclear reactors.

After solids, liquids and gases, plasma is the fourth state of matter. JoJo had learnt bucket loads about it during her first year in the Cub's but at this moment only two points seemed worthy of recall.

The first was just how incredibly unstable and volatile it was. In Star Seekers it was blended together with a cocktail of liquids and known as *plaque*. Plaque was stable and safe enough to stick your hand in, if you were crazy enough to want to!

However, point number two of what she remembered was what happened if the plasma ever managed to escape from the plaque.

If you ignored the enormous energy burst that would instantly vaporise any living thing within a twenty mile radius, then you couldn't ignore the radioactivity it would leave behind. As one teacher put it – *'It's enough to melt your brain at spitting distance'*. Well JoJo couldn't spit very far and having a melting brain was not top of her list of priorities, so this was nerve racking. All that radioactivity didn't go away quickly either. If a plasma spill occurred here on the Blue Planet, you could forget about growing apples around here for at least the next thousand years.

Of course, worrying about such things would only be necessary if the plaque somehow managed to leak from its cylinders, wouldn't it? Only then would there be a real risk of the plaque separating and becoming plasma. Unfortunately, that was exactly what was happening. That's what had set off the alarms. There, flowing in its gloopy state down cylinder number twenty-three was a stream of plaque.

JoJo stared at the plaque, then at the floor. She stamped down hard with her foot. Shutlik! The floor was coated with tutulium. That was bad. Very bad. When plaque came into contact with any kind of metal, the reaction binding the plasma together with its safe chemicals was reversed. Once that happened there would be no stopping it. JoJo, 2B, the Star Seeker and everything around them would be turned to a molten globule within a matter of seconds.

Her mind reeled. What sort of idiot engineer would put tutulium on the floor of a plasma reactor chamber?

Quickly she located the source of the leak high up in the ceiling amongst the smaller transfer pipes. One of them had ruptured and was venting the stuff like a fresh water spring.

Luckily for her, the split pipe had fallen fortuitously against its neighbour, which was now acting as a channel along which the thick plaque could run. From there it flowed straight to cylinder twenty three and down, down, down towards the floor.

"2B. Get out of here now," she urged staring at the broken pipe. "Fetch something to catch this stuff in."

2B looked at her blankly.

"A cloth, a sponge, a towel, a bucket. Anything. Just go. And hurry. It's halfway to the floor already."

Much to JoJo's exasperation, 2B didn't appear to understand the finer points of plasma and plaque.

"Why are we bothered if it's on the floor? It doesn't look dangerous, can't we just mop it up?" he said.

JoJo eyed him like an angry bull. "I don't look dangerous right now either, 2B, but trust me, if you don't go and fetch something right now, then that's going to change. Very fast."

2B held up his hands. "Fine, keep your spacesuit on. I'm going"

As he left, JoJo snatched the phase baton out of his hand. "I'll take that thank you."

2B muttered something rude and carried on.

JoJo wasted no more time. She leapt onto the computer table and kicked the monitor out of the way. She reached up as far as she could but it was no use. The transfer pipes were too high and the broken one too far away. There was only one thing for it.

Bending her knees and breathing deep, she sprang off the table and grasped for one of the unbroken pipes. As her fingers gripped, the phase baton slipped. She snatched at it and just managed to scrape a hold of it before it fell. This time she jammed it in her mouth and bit hard with her teeth, then she began to shimmy along the pipe.

It was about twelve feet to the break. She didn't look down or look to see how far the plaque had moved down the cylinder. If she slipped and fell there wouldn't be time for another attempt anyway.

Below her, 2B arrived back carrying a length of hose, a pump usually used for cleaning out the lavatories, some towels and several self-sealing eco-disposal bags. JoJo frowned.

"It's a plaque vac," he said, smiling and holding it up for her to see.

Something told her that her brother still hadn't quite grasped the gravitas of the situation. However, maybe …

"strab de 'ag to da tuu," she muttered.

"You what?"

JoJo sighed, let go with one hand and pulled the phase baton from her mouth. "I said strap the bag to the tube, it'll self-seal. Then use the pump to suck the plaque off the cylinders. Don't fill the bags too full and don't, whatever you do, let any touch the ground. I mean it 2B. It'll be the last thing you ever do and if you kill me, I swear I'll spend eternity kicking your ghostly butt. You can put the bags in that plastic box in the corridor. Now do it."

2B finally seemed to get the message and set about his task.

The noise of the alarms continued to attack their senses, but JoJo was not going to be beaten. One hand went over the other as she inched her way across the pipes. They strained dangerously under her weight. If one snapped …

And where were the CoyoteBots when she needed them? Alarms were supposed to summon them immediately. Not even Arachno, 2B's partner in the game, had arrived to help. She was going to be having some serious words when this was all over.

It took one more swing and JoJo finally reached the gushing pipe.

She gasped. The cut was perfectly clean. It could not have possibly happened by accident. Who … who would deliberately cut a plasma pipe knowing the consequences?

Anger boiled in her, but recriminations would have to wait.

Her idea for stemming the flow of plaque was simple. Electric currents caused plaque to solidify. At least she thought that's what she remembered. Sure, technically speaking the current applied should be far greater than that packed into the phase baton, but with a sustained blast, she hoped the effect would be much the same. If not … well, it would just have to be wouldn't it.

Slowly she released one hand, took the baton back out of her mouth and pushed the tip into the flowing pink plaque careful not to drip any.

"Here goes nothing," she said and pulled the trigger.

The result was spectacular. Not least for the fact that the ensuing cascade of purple sparks revealed the culprit of the crime hiding behind tube twenty five.

"ScatterBot," she gasped as the youngest and current trainee CoyoteBot shot from his hidey hole like a pebble from a catapult.

JoJo jumped. The Phase Baton slipped from her grasp and clanged to the floor.

Her heart almost stopped.

Above her head, a small portion of the plaque had turned to a jelly-like gloop. She knew it wasn't going to be enough to stop the tide. And it wasn't.

Almost immediately the trickle of the plaque again began flowing over the jelly as though it wasn't even there. JoJo swore loudly.

Meanwhile ScatterBot was making a bid for freedom. She was helpless, hanging in mid-air. There was nothing she could do. The little metal terrorist was going to get away.

But then the cavalry arrived in the shape of Arachno and Pulp. With his blue eyes sparkling like azure stars and a look of complete faith in what he was about to do, Pulp tore through the door and battered headlong into the hapless ScatterBot sending him hurtling back the way he had just gone. 2B had to duck as he flew past, smashing painfully into the wall behind JoJo.

Arachno meanwhile made a run for the Phase baton, scooped it up and flew it to JoJo.

Re-invigorated, JoJo thrust the baton back into the plaque and squeezed the fire button again. Within seconds the flow began to subside as the jellifying plaque formed a solid plug in the end of the pipe. She hardly dared believe it was working.

Pulp glanced back and beeped joyously at the success, presumably happy that he could concentrate his attention on the traitor who had limped off into the far corner. JoJo could no longer see ScatterBot, her view obscured by plasma cylinders, but Pulp knew exactly where he was. Arachno rushed to join him, but a harsh bleep from Pulp warned him to stay away. This treacherous turncoat belonged only to him.

If it had been any other situation, JoJo would have probably stopped him from dishing out his own justice, but for some unfathomable reason she couldn't even begin to understand, ScatterBot had tried to kill them all. For that he probably deserved everything he was about to get – and then some.

When they came, the pain ridden squeals of ScatterBot rang out even above the alarms. JoJo tried to block them out as she continued to pump phase after phase into the Plaque, but it was difficult.

Then it happened. Just as the plaque was *almost* entirely solid – just as 2B had *almost* sucked up every drop into his bag – just when they were seconds away from safety – the world unraveled before JoJo's eyes.

Somehow ScatterBot had broken free and was racing around wildly. Several cylinders took direct hits as the tiny C-Bot bounced off them trying to make good his escape. He was smaller and lighter with greater agility than Pulp and Pulp was losing him.

JoJo turned as ScatterBot whipped around a corner aiming straight for her. His eyes were red and manic. JoJo had never seen anything like it.

He was attacking her.

Instinctively she pulled the phase baton out of the plaque and swung it, finger firmly on the trigger. It was all she could do to protect herself but it was a mistake.

The strike landed plum between ScatterBot's eyes sending him into violent convulsions. He dropped to the floor like a rock where he lay still and unmoving, yellow sparks igniting in his crimson pupils.

She had defeated him, but at what cost? On the tip of the phase baton was a tiny droplet of liquid plaque hanging by the flimsiest of stringy threads. It must have stuck there when she yanked it from the pipe.

As carefully as a surgeon would manipulate his instruments, she attempted to pull the baton to her but the plaque was like cheese on a slice of pizza, stretching all the time, shrinking thinner and thinner.

She screamed as the inevitable globule dripped, heading straight for the tutulium floor.

It was a cliché, but bits of her life flashed before her eyes and time seemed to slow to a crawl.

As the milliseconds moved like minutes, her eyes traced the drop of pink death down and down. Or was the floor rising to meet it? She could no longer tell. Whatever, the outcome would be the same. Instant death.

From nowhere Pulp appeared, still searching out ScatterBot. *Too late*, she thought. Out of the corner of her eye he thundered by at tremendous speed. He swept in a big arc under her legs, opening his cheerful mouth to smile at her.

She knew then what he was going to do.

He swallowed the plaque.

Pulp came to a sudden and grinding halt and began to spasm like he was undergoing some brutal epileptic seizure. Yellow sparks shot from his mouth as slivers of his metal coating began to peel away like dead skin from an ailing body.

Then he screamed. A blood-curdling, bone chilling scream of such utter pain that it made JoJo spin away in tears. She couldn't even imagine what torture the little CoyoteBot must be going through as the plaque dissolved his body from the inside.

A blinding silver flash followed by a loud sucking wind signaled the end. A calm like no other suddenly descended.

Pulp was gone. Not a trace of him left – only memories to know that he even existed.

With the Plaque solid in the tube, JoJo let go of the pipe and dropped to the floor inconsolable with grief. At her feet, ScatterBot lay twitching like some toy whose batteries had faded. Nevertheless, he was alive … and Pulp wasn't.

Rage overtook her. She snatched up the helpless body and glared at him with utter contempt. He was a killer, a murderer.

She released a mechanism that opened a hatch on his front. Inside glowed the beating red soul of the little C-Bot, his life-force – his heart. It mocked JoJo. ScatterBot was alive and Pulp was dead. Life was about balance and the balance here was uneven. It had to be corrected.

She knew it was an act of pure evil to take the life-force from a CoyoteBot. An act against the very oath she made to uphold all life in whatever circumstance and form, but her grief was uncontrollable and someone had to pay.

Beside her 2B knew what she was about to do, and looked away.

Reaching inside, she closed her eyes and felt the anger of the last few minutes rise to a crescendo within her as the life-force beat between her fingers.

"For Pulp," she said, and pulled.

CHAPTER 31

DIRTY DEALS

Completely unaware of the new threat to their Battle of the Bands success, and with showtime inching ever closer, Jimmy stalked the backstage area at Apple Valley High.

Much had happened since Applejuice had finished soundchecking. A draw had been made to decide the order in which the bands would take to the stage – Applejuice would play last – and the trickle of people entering the hall had become a torrent, yet worryingly, neither Damien nor JoJo had so far turned up.

Halfpint, Cornelius and Paige were equally uneasy and JoJo's no show. As the backstage area filled with people all excitedly changing clothes and giving each other encouraging pep talks, they remained quiet and worried. They hadn't spoken a single word to each other in the last thirty minutes and right now the only thing keeping Jimmy here was the thought of losing his Grandad's lease – and the atmosphere in the school hall.

There was no denying it. The hum emanating from the excited crowd was electric. Nearly two thousand pupils from all four of the competing schools were squashed together arguing and shouting about who was going to win.

The girls were fiercely contesting chanting and screaming competitions, whilst the boys stood back and checked out the girls who were chanting and screaming. Amongst them, the much outnumbered teachers and parents were trying without much success to keep it all under control.

Luckily it was good-natured. Only the Gravenstein contingent threatened to spoil the day by turning nasty. Their band, the Pips, had been equal favourites to win along with Applejuice, but of course that was when Cat had been singing. Since the news had spread through the school jungle drums that she had left, Gravenstein's confidence had grown to atmospheric proportions and they were not exactly shy at letting people know it was now *they* who would be crowned winners in a few hours.

Watching their pupils snarl and show off, Jimmy couldn't help wondering why Damien didn't go to Gravenstein. He would fit right in.

That's when he heard him. "Get out of my way man. Do you not know who I am? There is a competition that cannot start without me so it would be wise of you not to get in my way again."

Damien pushed the hapless teacher aside and marched through the backstage doors. As is usually the way with Damien, the teacher was too stunned to say anything back.

All the guys rushed him. "Where the hell have you been?" Jimmy cried, trying his best to contain his anger.

"Conducting some band business." He replied.

"You should have been here," growled Jimmy.

"Really? Why? Can't you even manage to soundcheck without me? If you must know I've been having a fascinating chat with a man who's very interested in signing the winning band to a management deal. Of course I told him he was talking to the right man in me. I've invited him around after the show to talk figures."

"You've done what?" screamed Jimmy. "You can't make decisions like that without asking us first. Who is this man?"

Damien put his hand on Jimmy's shoulder and smiled facetiously. "Oh Green, Green, Green. Who this man is, is no concern of yours. When will you get it through your skull that you don't make the decisions any more? Your opinion counts for less than my pet goldfish and he's dead. So please stop having these delusions that Applejuice is still somehow your band. This is my band now. Whatever I say goes. No compromises, no debates, no arguing. Capiche. And please, what is that you are wearing?"

Jimmy's mouth dropped open, but no words came.

"That will have to go," continued Dirt, pointing at Jimmy's shirt and walking off.

Miss Witherspoon chose that precise moment to step onto the stage amidst the noise from the crowd and cough loudly into the microphone. Any noise abruptly ceased as people jumped out of their skins.

Miss Witherspoon was a tall, no nonsense woman who had the unerring charm of looking like everyone's Grandmother. She cleared her throat genteelly.

"Ahem. Welcome everyone. Thank you for coming to what promises to be a most exciting Battle of the Bands competition. How wonderful it is to see so many people here to cheer on their schools band."

There was much whooping and cheering from the audience. She let it die down before continuing.

"To the rules. The bands will play in the following order. First, Mass Apeel from Winesap High." Large cheers came from their contingent. "Second, Earth's Core from Macintosh High." More cheers. "Third, The Pips from Gravenstein, and finally from Apple Valley High, Applejuice." Their name brought the loudest cheers from the home turf. "Each band will play four songs." She continued. "Once Applejuice have finished their songs, the judges will retire to deliberate on their decision. And…" her face grew stern, "… let me make it quite clear that there will be absolutely no more attempts at bribery *Mr. Blackstock*, or blackmail for that matter, *Miss Coops*. The judge's decision will be final. The winner will then be invited to play at Saturday's Centennial Celebrations."

The hall erupted. Jimmy felt a tingle run up his spine. He couldn't help it, the thought of playing on that Centennial stage was so stirring he couldn't put it into words. He'd tried to put it out of his mind. Not daring to dream he'd be standing here still able to play. Still in with a chance…

"So, without further ado, I will now invite the first band to take to the stage."

"Oh my god," said Halfpint. "This is it."

Jimmy and the others suddenly found themselves being ushered deep into the wings by teachers. Over on the other side of the stage Mass Apeel had their guitars slung around their necks ready to make their entrance. Their singer was tapping his microphone nervously against his palm. The drummer was beating a rhythm against his right thigh. They looked uptight. *Good* Jimmy thought, *uptight was good*.

The lights went down in the hall. A hush of anticipation descended on the crowd. A single spotlight lit Miss Witherspoon on the stage. "And now, Ladies and Gentlemen, boys and girls, would you please welcome MASS APEEL."

The place erupted. The band walked out.

The Battle of the Bands had begun.

CHAPTER 32

PEEL, CORES AND PIPS

Jimmy watched raptly from the side. He hated to admit it, but Mass Apeel were good.

The early nerves Jimmy hoped might be their undoing did not materialize and, despite himself, he found his foot tapping along enthusiastically.

"These may well give Gravenstein a run for their money," he shouted to Halfpint as the third song kicked in. Halfpint nodded, seemingly in agreement. Applejuice were definitely going to need JoJo and her Vocalosis to pull this one off. Which reminded him, where was she for goodness sake?

Mass Apeel finished to a huge cheer. The crowd called for more, but that wasn't in the rules so they left the stage all smiles. Jimmy noticed the lead singer of The Pips, Tarquin Jones, whispering spitefully to one of his band mates. It seemed Mass Apeel had also caught them by surprise.

In the dressing room, Halfpint, Paige and Cornelius used the interval to change their clothes before heading back with Jimmy to see the next band. Damien didn't join them. He remained by himself meditating in the corner.

"At least he's not practicing his singing," whispered Halfpint to Jimmy as they pushed past the Banner twins, who had been posted like sentry's outside the door.

"Maybe he's expecting a rush of girls clamouring for autographs!"

Smirked Halfpint. Jimmy merely tutted.

Miss Witherspoon introduced the next band from Macintosh High, a punk rock band called Earth's Core.

They stormed out with their distorted guitars blazing like fuzzy thunder. Jimmy and Halfpint grimaced. "Jeez, do you think that their amplifiers go all the way to eleven?" quipped Jimmy over the noise.

This was a band that was certainly out to make an impression. Unfortunately, for reasons completely unrelated to their songs, they were to make sure no one would forget them in a hurry.

It began to go wrong when their lead singer, a rather portly lad called Austin Foley, got a little over exuberant during the first chorus. Whilst making a mad dash from one side of the stage to the other, he tripped on a stray wire. His microphone flew out of his hand and into the crowd where it howled screechy feedback. With unstoppable momentum, Austin piled head first into the guitarist who could do nothing to get out of the way. The combined weight of the now flying twosome didn't stop until they had taken out three amplifiers, two microphone stands and half the drum kit. The whole thing sounded like a kitchen falling down some stairs.

The pupils from Gravenstein thought all their birthdays had come at once and barracked the band with jeers and catcalls. Two boys were laughing so much that they had to be forcibly ejected by Miss Witherspoon.

Eventually, when everything was put back together, a very embarrassed and far less energetic Earth's Core returned to finish their set. Unfortunately, their chances of winning had gone.

With only The Pips to go before Applejuice, Jimmy studied the bulging crowd for any sign of JoJo. Maybe she was out there keeping a low profile, maybe something had gone wrong, or she had decided it was a bad idea after all? It was the not knowing that was driving him crazy.

He had spotted his Grandma and Grandad alongside Halfpint's parents on the far side of the hall. His Grandma looked pretty excited, chatting freely with Halfpint's Mum. His Grandad however looked miserable. As though he wanted to be anywhere else but standing there. Jimmy shrugged. The last few days had seen their relationship seriously deteriorate. He knew it was his fault. He was keeping secrets. Big secrets. There was the lease and there was JoJo. But what was he supposed to do? The lease thing would only cause his Grandad to worry and where on earth did you start with JoJo? Hopefully when all this was over they could get back to some kind of normality because in truth, he missed his Grandad terribly.

"What are we going to do if she doesn't show?" asked Paige sensing who Jimmy was looking for.

Jimmy kept scanning the faces. "I guess we just play. What else can we do? Maybe Dirt has bribed the judges; I wouldn't put it past him. Although I don't fancy our chances of getting past that lot if he's rigged it."

Not far away the Gravenstein pupils were causing all sorts of trouble, shoving people out of their way as they rushed to the front in anticipation of The Pips performance. One girl had to be dragged onto the stage to prevent her being crushed against it.

"Set of morons," said Paige scathingly.

Jimmy glanced across at Tarquin Jones who was joking with the other band members and generally behaving as if they had already won. Tarquin's eyes met Jimmy's across the stage. Tarquin smiled, then raised a hand to his forehead making a losers 'L' shape with his finger and thumb. Jimmy turned away and looked again for JoJo.

"Where are you?" he said to himself.

CHAPTER 33

ShowTime

The Pip's had gone down a storm. As soon as the opening number began, Jimmy knew that Applejuice was in trouble. The entire hall was on its feet dancing and singing, and as much as he wanted to hate The Pips, he couldn't. They were good – very good. Their stage act was well rehearsed, they played well and never fluffed any lines. Against an Applejuice with Damien singing, there was no contest. The Pips would win. A heavy, sinking feeling took hold in Jimmy guts as he was forced to watch with a grudging admiration.

By the looks on their faces it seemed Paige, Cornelius and Halfpint all thought the same. Their dreams of a Centenary appearance were slipping away faster than a bobsleigh down a track.

* * *

"We have to forget about what they just did," said Jimmy as Applejuice were given a fifteen-minute warning. "We can't give up. We have to believe that JoJo is going to turn up. Don't lets go out there thinking Damien is going to be terrible, or else we'll hold back, and we can't afford to."

Halfpint, Cornelius and Paige all nodded in agreement. *Great*, thought Jimmy. *I've convinced them, now who is going to convince me.*

* * *

The stage curtains had been closed, and throughout the hall, the buzz was louder than a swarm of bees homing in on a honey pot. Backstage, all the talk was about the ending to The Pips show.

As the last note had been struck, a huge pyrotechnic explosion had erupted from behind the drum kit. It had showered the stage with bright yellow sparks whilst simultaneously spraying thousands of tiny pieces of confetti over the audience. It was a dramatic and fantastic finale that no one had expected and cemented them as clear leaders.

Stood alone, isolated from the crowd, a guitar around his neck, Jimmy watched as a sixth former huffed and puffed his way onto stage carrying the last of Paige's cymbals.

"Bloody heavy these – never told me they were so heavy when I volunteered," he moaned to himself. Jimmy ignored him.

It was odd just how cut off from everybody Jimmy felt up here. Like an athlete who had been told to take his marks, his concentration was utterly focused on the next twenty minutes of his life. A nervous energy had appeared from nowhere and suddenly he was alert to everything happening around him. In his mind he plotted the exact dimensions of the stage. The position of the four monitors along the front, the arrangement of amplifiers at the back, Halfpint and Cornelius' starting places. All were fixed in his mind like grid references on a map. That way, when they began, he could navigate the stage without having to worry about tripping over or bumping into anyone.

He ran his hand up and down the smooth neck of his guitar. Goose bumps rose on his arms like little mountains and his mouth ran dry. The wood and metal was a part of him. It felt so right. Like Mickey and Minnie or Wallace and Grommet, Jimmy and his guitar were meant to be together. When he played, no one could touch him or hurt him and for the next four songs that had to be the case. If the Vocalosis didn't happen the band would cop a lot of flak, not merely from all the other schools but from Apple Valley High who believed this to be their best chance of winning the trophy in twenty years. So, for the next twenty minutes Applejuice had to become the mega-million selling rock stars they dreamed of being. They had to convince everyone out there that they were watching something special. They could do nothing about Damien. His fate seemed to be in the hands of the Gods.

He shouted for the guys to gather in a huddle.

"Right," Jimmy began in a whisper. "We know how well we can really play. We're good. In fact, we're great and this is our chance to prove it to everybody. So let's play for each other. We play for Applejuice and we play for Cat. This is only one day and when Dirt is a bad memory, Applejuice will still be going strong. Agreed?'

"Agreed," they said in unison.

"Okay then." Jimmy offered his right hand in the middle of the circle. Everyone put theirs on top. "For Cat and Applejuice," he said.

"For Cat and Applejuice," they repeated and thrust their hands in the air with a big shout.

Miss Witherspoon interrupted, tapping Jimmy on the shoulder.

"Are you ready?" she asked politely.

Jimmy nodded, "I think so. Is it time?"

"It's time. So run off to side stage," she said, shooing them along. Then she was gone, striding off to centre stage.

"You nervous?" Jimmy asked Halfpint as Miss Witherspoon took a hold of the microphone.

"Papping my pants," replied Halfpint.

The curtains opened. "Good," Jimmy said, "I thought I was the only one."

CHAPTER 34

VOCALOSIS

JoJo was sprinting as if her life depended on it. In a way, it did. If she didn't get to the Battle of the Bands before Applejuice began playing, they wouldn't win and she wouldn't be going home. Simple as that.

The journey was proving arduous however. Once out of the orchard and past the few sparse houses that skirted the trees, she had hit the town of Apple Valley. It was bigger than she thought with roads meandering in all directions. She was constantly having to stop and check that she was going the right way and running in Paige's boots had given her a blister that was rubbing her heel raw.

Flying by her side – not that she could see him as he was cloaking – was Arachno. After Pulp's sad demise, SaRa had insisted JoJo not go out into the human population alone. With 2B a none starter another CoyoteBot was the only alternative.

All of them volunteered, but Arachno was chosen because his was the only cloaking device working correctly. Although she hadn't voiced her fears at the time, JoJo had concerns. ScatterBot's traitorous turn had shocked her and had muddied her thinking about the rest of the C-Bots. What had happened to him? Had any of the others been similarly affected? Was she really any safer with Arachno by her side? No doubt she would discover the answers to these questions shortly.

The next corner saw her locate her destination. The school was just as Jimmy had described. One large old stone building that looked as though it belonged to a different time, surrounded by lots of smaller wooden structures.

Long stone steps led up to the main building, from which rose a huge gothic bell tower. That was where Jimmy told her to go. The hall was directly below it.

Closing her mind to the sharp, stinging pain that sliced into her heel with every step, JoJo set off through the wrought iron gates and headed over the deserted sports field. As she ran she listened carefully for music, unable to shake the desperate feeling that she might have missed Applejuice.

At the top of the fifteen steps (she counted them on the way up), she stopped. From inside the school the muffled voice of a woman could be heard. JoJo cocked her head and listened attentively.

Please, she thought, *please don't let me have missed Applejuice.*

* * *

The crowd erupted as Miss Witherspoon finished her introductions. Jimmy and the guys rushed onto the stage and took their positions. With the bright spotlights blazing in their eyes, Jimmy could only see a few rows in. That was enough. The faces looked eager and expectant.

He placed his hands on the guitar, drinking in the heightened sense of anticipation amongst the rest of the band and the crowd as they waited for him to begin the song. Slowly, he turned the volume knob to full, savoring the guttural hum that emanated from the powerful amplifiers behind him. Then, gripping his plectrum tight between his finger and thumb, he struck the opening riff to the first song.

Any nerves left him as soon as the music hit his ears. It surrounded his soul like an angel's comforting hug. The lights, the crowd, the loud guitars, this was all he had ever wanted to do and it was wonderful. He stared out over the smiling, dancing faces and felt a hot, exhilarating glow fill his entire being. It was then that he realized Damien could never really take his home away from him. This was his home – on stage, playing in a band.

On cue, Paige, Cornelius and Halfpint kicked in effortlessly and they sounded fantastic. The crowd was dancing and Applejuice were rocking. A broad smile swept over his face and for a brief moment he was in heaven. He wondered if JoJo was somewhere watching.

Then Damien opened his mouth to sing.

* * *

JoJo's heart leapt. The voice definitely had said Applejuice. She hadn't missed them, she still had time.

The doors clattered into the walls as she raced down the corridor like a demented cheetah. Ahead of her the sound of Jimmy's guitar flooded her ears. She recognised the song from Apple Juice's rehearsals. A rapid mental calculation told her she didn't have long before Damien started singing.

Following the music JoJo quickly reached the main hall. A sign above the doors read 'PUSH'. JoJo obeyed, but shockingly she bounced back sprawling to the floor. She stared in disbelief. Her mouth ran dry. They were locked. The damn doors were locked.

She pulled herself up and stared desperately through the glass cupping her hands to her eyes. There was Jimmy. There was Damien. But her view was obscured by bodies. Lots of bodies.

She rattled the door hard, but it wouldn't budge. One of the obscuring bodies, a man turned to see what all the fuss was about. JoJo jumped at the sight of him. He wore wore black sunglasses, which although entirely uneccessary in such a darkened hall, were clearly hiding some form of disfigurement. A thick scar ran from his cheek to his chin.

JoJo pointed at the handle, urging the man to let her in. But he didn't move. She repeated the gesture more deliberately this time, but still the man refused to help. JoJo frowned. This was wasting precious seconds. Frustratedly she rattled on the handle and gave him her best 'let me in, bonehead' glare. It was a mistake. The man simply raised his eyebrows, smiled conceitedly and turned his back on her. JoJo slammed the pane with her fists.

"Idiot. What's your problem anyway?" she screamed. But it did no good. '*Black specs*' was not going to turn back around in a hurry.

The band was in full flow now. She knew she had only seconds left. Suddenly, from above her, Arachno whistled. He'd uncloaked halfway up a staircase that JoJo guessed led to the bell tower. He beeped twice, beckoning her. JoJo didn't hesitate. She took the stairs three at a time following him up and up.

Two flights later she arrived at a break in the staircase. Ahead of her lay a gangway with lights suspended beneath it. More steps ascended to her left, leading to another doorway, but JoJo did not need to climb anymore. The reason Arachno had brought her here was clear. The wooden gangway ran the full length of the hall. She had emerged about halfway along. Perfect viewing for the stage show. And perfect as well, because up here she would be completely alone while she worked.

She dropped to her knees ripping the baseball cap off her head urgently. Below her, Damien's lips were touching the microphone.

Grasping the strands of hair in her left hand, she focused hard on Damien's eyes and tried to clear her mind.

Whether it was the exigency of the situation or merely the fact that she had had no time to wind herself up into a state about the Vocalosis, she found the energy flowed easily.

It was hard for her to explain what happened when she performed Vocalosis. Her teachers back home would insist that only by preparing the mind to enter a highly complex altered state of awareness could it be performed successfully. This mysterious state could take years to achieve apparently. Well JoJo didn't know about any of that. To her it was like daydreaming, but using someone else's thoughts and desires rather than your own. The times she had done it successfully was when she had become one with the object in her hand. Felt its energy flow first into her, then out into the recipient like sitting in an ocean wave that gently retreats to the sea only to wash over you once more. That was what was happening right now. Usually it took several minutes – even hours – to find the correct place in her mind, but today it seemed to be there without even looking.

Though her eyes were fixed intently on Damien's, in her mind she could see only a blonde-haired girl standing tall before a microphone. The girl was singing her heart out.

It was Cat.

JoJo could hear her beautiful voice filling her senses. It was as if Cat was singing only to her. *Wow*. She thought. *Now that's singing.* Between her fingers, tiny pink sparks crackled and danced from the strands of hair.

JoJo cordoned Cat off into one half of her brain.

Now for Damien. Tuning into him seemed harder somehow, more draining. Her affinity with him was strained and distant. *It's his aura*, she thought. *His aura is the worst I've ever come across.* He just oozed rottenness from his very being, illustrated perfectly by the dirty, gun-metal gray sparks now firing throughout the pink.

With much effort she dragged Damien in. It was not nice, but she kept hold of him. She now had them both. Cat and Damien.

Like two opposing ends of a magnet she joined the two aura's together in her mind completing the connection.

A surge of energy flooded her body. It took her breath away and made her back arch in a spasm. The power was strong. She had done well.

All she could do now was hope and pray it worked.

CHAPTER 35

DAMIEN SINGS THE BLUES

The first line of the song was terrible. Worse, it was painful. All around Apple Valley cats were jamming their paws into their ears. Jimmy turned to Paige, his back to the audience, and swore at the top of his voice. When he turned back around he noticed the front few rows of the crowd had stopped dancing. Some kids were sniggering. Most just looked bewildered.

Off stage to his left, Tarquin Jones was bent double, laughing so hard that snot was hanging from his nose like a mucus stalactite.

The second line was even worse – if that were possible. The cats were now leaving town just to get away from the wretched sound. Jimmy felt like the eyes of the entire world were staring at his band – and laughing.

He strummed and picked his guitar harder and louder hoping to drown Damien out with extra volume. It didn't work.

Jimmy wanted to get off the stage. He wanted to pull the plug, run away and never come back, but he knew in his heart it would only make matters worse. Running away would make him a coward. He had to see this through to the very, very bitter end.

Then, as they approached the end of the verse, something changed. To be more precise, Damien's voice changed. Not dramatically – not at first. It sounded like the vocal equivalent of Jimmy and Halfpint tuning their guitars. As they turned the peg on the head of the guitar, so the note changed in pitch. Well, someone was tuning Damien. With every note his voice moved a little closer to where it should be. Jimmy dared not believe it was really happening. He glanced across at Halfpint who had noticed it too – so had Cornelius. The only person who hadn't sensed the change was Damien himself. Not a flicker of recognition was passing over his contorted face. He was too busy making google eyes at a girl in the front row. She looked ready to puke in his face. Could he really be so vain and so self-delusional that he didn't even notice? Of course he could. This was Damien Dirt. Normal rules didn't apply.

As the chorus reached its end, it was amazing. Jimmy could not believe it possible, but Damien sounded every bit like a proper singer.

When a little later they crashed out the final note to that first song, the crowd cheered louder than they had for any of the other bands. Jimmy flooded with pride. Halfpint, Cornelius and Paige had smiles wider than a crocodiles. Now this was what it was all about. This was why they did it. The glory, the adulation.

Before the bubble burst, Jimmy launched into the second song with a new found belief beating in his heart.

Now they were rocking.

Whenever Jimmy faced Paige it was like watching a maniac. He pitied the poor drum kit, which was being hit so hard you'd have thought it had insulted her brother. As for Cornelius and Halfpint, they played like only they could. All the old fancy stage moves came back with a flourish as their inhibitions were cast aside like yesterday's fashions.

Time flew by in a haze. An extremely fast moving haze.

When they sounded the final crescendo to the last song, Jimmy couldn't believe it was over. He was pumped. He could have played on for hours.

As one, the band struck the last note and the blare of amplifiers was replaced by the deafening roar from the crowd. It hit them like a tidal wave and caught Jimmy totally by surprise. It was overwhelming. He swallowed hard, past the lump that was forming in his throat.

In fact – mortified as he was to admit it – it had almost felt as good as when Cat sang with them. Of course he knew in a way she had. Sure, the clipped tones were Damien all right, but the essence of that voice, its soul, was pure Catrina Wickowski and that was all down to JoJo, wherever she was.

Jimmy, Cornelius, Halfpint and Paige all joined hands and took a bow. Damien stayed by himself making the most of the acclamation.

"Just how big do you think his head's gonna be after this?" shouted Halfpint to Jimmy.

"I think they'll have to take the side off the building if they want to get him out of here," replied Jimmy. Halfpint laughed.

With the cheers seemingly never-ending, Miss Witherspoon took it upon herself to restore some calm.

"Thank you … THANK YOU … QUIIIIETTTT!" She yelled. The hollering stopped. "That is better. Thank you. Now, I'm sure you'll agree, Applejuice gave us a most fantastic end to what has been a wonderful, wonderful competition. All the bands have made this very special Battle of the Bands a competition to remember."

More cheers.

"There will now be a short thirty-minute break to catch our breath, in which time the judges will deliberate upon a champion. Please feel free to move quietly into the canteen where refreshments will be served. Be sure to be back here at four o clock prompt though when we will announce who will be playing at the Apple Valley Centenary Celebrations."

Swathes of people began to move, noisily. Not all left the hall, some headed for the stage. Caught unawares by the sudden surge, Applejuice quickly found themselves being bombarded by complete strangers slapping them on the back and telling them how fantastic they were and that they should win easily.

One first year, a tiny red headed girl with pigtails, who Jimmy had never seen before in his entire life, even asked for his autograph and then told him that she loved him. Jimmy's cheeks instantly turned the

211

colour of the girl's hair, which she thought was a huge compliment. He quickly signed his name on her school bag, hoping that she would go away and leave him alone. Nearby Paige was wetting herself laughing.

Damien of course was in his element. He was holding court with a gaggle of girls who appeared to be hanging on his every word, cooing over him like he was the next big thing. Girls, Jimmy noted, who only yesterday would probably not have handed him a band-aid if he were bleeding to death.

"Well, I've been telling them for months they were wasting their time with anyone other than me," Jimmy heard him say to one doe-eyed brunette. "I am, without a doubt, the best singer ever to have emerged from Apple Valley and now everyone knows it. I only hope that the judges recognize real talent."

Jimmy simulated throwing up by sticking his fingers down his throat. Halfpint sniggered.

Just then, two hands covered Jimmy's eyes catching him by surprise.

"Guess Who?"

Jimmy whipped around. It was JoJo. His heart leapt at the sight of her. Before he knew what he was doing, he pulled her close and hugged her tight. She didn't try to pull away and several young girls who had been plucking up the courage to talk to him slipped away devastated.

"You're a genius," said Jimmy, oblivious to the heartbreak he'd just caused. "An absolute bloody genius. For a few minutes there, even I forgot he's a complete moron."

JoJo smiled as Jimmy let go. He noticed she looked pale and exhausted.

"Sounded all right didn't he?" she said tiredly.

"He sounded a little bit more than all right, JoJo."

"Well, you have Cat to thank for that. Not me."

Jimmy felt a twist in his heart at hearing Cat's name, but it subsided quickly. More quickly than it had yesterday, which had indeed been quicker than the day before that. Could it be that he was getting over her? Jimmy felt guilty at the idea. He didn't want to be over her. Not yet. It was too soon.

"If you want to know the truth," JoJo continued, "I can't believe it worked so well. I was too scared to tell you before but that's the first time I've ever done it on something larger than a rat."

Jimmy looked shocked, then laughed. "Well, you got the 'rat' part right anyway."

"Do you think he really believes his voice is that good?" said JoJo nodding towards Damien.

"Oh absolutely, I don't think he even knows anything happened. I told you, he's not all there. There are normal people, there are idiots and then there's Damien Dirt. I think he was dropped on his head as a baby or something."

She laughed. It was nice.

Just then, Paige and Halfpint arrived looking fraught. Yet more kids were trailing behind them. This lot was staring as Halfpint's guitar, but judging by the amount of whispering and shaking of heads that was going on, none of them wanted to be the one to ask him for a closer look.

Paige sensed an opportunity to escape and dragged JoJo off further backstage.

"Thanks." Shouted Halfpint sarcastically as all the kids gathered around expectantly. Paige turned and smiled.

But Jimmy could not take his eyes off JoJo. He marveled at her skills, her remarkable gifts that were unlike anything a human possessed. 'Vocalosis.' Really. Who would have believed it? It was like something dreamt up for a Hollywood movie. Yet it had happened. It was real.

She caught him staring and smiling, but he wasn't the least bit embarrassed. What with Cat's baseball cap turned back to front, the red vest top, short skirt and pair of black boots, Jimmy figured he would like to stare at her all day.

When she returned his smile, he suddenly felt a rather uncomfortable shudder in his guts. A shudder that he had only felt once before in his life and had certainly not expected to feel so soon after Cat's departure. Luckily for him, Miss Witherspoon's voice suddenly blared through the speakers saving him from any deep analysis of the feelings.

He quickly turned around and felt his stomach drop for an entirely different reason.

They were about to announce the winner.

CHAPTER 36

THE DUKE OF EARL

It was funny how life played out sometimes. There were moments where time just seemed to drag on endlessly, moving no quicker than a tortoise with a broken leg. Then there were times when you felt as if you were trapped in a video with someone pressing the fast forward button. Jimmy was definitely in a fast forward moment now.

The sixth formers had worked fast and cleared the stage of hangers-on in minutes. Thankfully, JoJo had stayed close to Paige which meant she was going nowhere. Not even the sixth years messed with Paige Turner.

All four bands had been lined up across the front of the stage. Miss Witherspoon stood in the middle, a large red envelope clutched tightly in her hands. The results.

As the crowd shuffled excitedly, Jimmy glanced up and down the line. Earth's Core at the far right looked completely uninterested. No doubt resigned to the fact that their chances of winning were currently lying somewhere between 'never' and 'not if you were the only band left on the planet.'

Mass Apeel on the other hand looked fidgety and apprehensive. They definitely thought they were in with a shot. Jimmy didn't share their optimism. He was sure this competition was between themselves and The Pips, which brought him to Tarquin who provided no surprises. Shy and retiring were not two words that would be ever used in a sentence about Tarquin Jones. The swagger was intact meaning

215

Damien's surprise vocal performance had done little to dent his confidence.

Jimmy himself required only one word to sum up how he felt. Nervous. So much was riding on what was written on the piece of paper in the red envelope that it wasn't even funny. No longer was it just about winning or getting to play in front of tens of thousands of people. It was about securing a home. It was about a girl and her brother who were pinning their hopes on Applejuice being at those Centenary Celebrations. A girl, whom it seemed as every day went by, meant more and more to him.

Miss Witherspoon finally spoke. "Let me first begin by once again thanking all of the bands. Without them, today would have been oh so very ... Quiet"

The hall laughed.

"This is an old competition." She said more seriously. "It dates back to before most of you were even born. Back to when there were only two schools in Apple Valley. Gravenstein and Apple Valley High. I think if I'm not mistaken I even recognise some of the parents in the audience who have competed on this very stage themselves in the past."

Jimmy saw several dads smile and nod as memories flooded back.

"And at the end of every competition someone stands here and says how they wish every band could win. I am no different but, unfortunately, there can be only one winner. So without further chatter from me..." She slid her finger under the flap of the envelope and tore it open. Jimmy's stomach flipped. Tarquin grinned smugly.

Slowly, Miss Witherspoon plucked the piece of paper from the envelope, dragging out the tension. She teased everybody by rolling the paper in her hand but leaving it folded.

"I understand that the judges have had an extremely difficult time in choosing their champion. In fact, please could we have a round of applause for our four judges, Mr. Marchbanks from Apple Valley, Miss Hutton from Winesap, Mrs. Yardley from Macintosh and Mr. Hugo Kyte from Gravenstein."

People clapped but their hearts really weren't in it. They, like Jimmy, just wanted to know who had won.

But Miss Witherspoon was not done teasing. "In order to reach a decision, the judges awarded points out of ten for overall stage craft, musicianship, songs and that all-important but intangible quality – the 'X' Factor, giving a total score out of forty."

As she talked Jimmy silently muttered 'come on, come on,' to himself.

"So, in fourth place, with nineteen points – Earth's Core."

No surprises there. Jimmy glanced at where JoJo was hiding behind one of the huge curtains and nodded. One down.

"In third place, with a very respectable twenty eight points. A tremendous performance I thought. Lets here it for … Mass Apeel."

Lots of cheering ensued with a handful of boos from the Macintosh area of the crowd, clearly unhappy with the score. Mass Apeel saluted the crowd. They had done well but disappointment was etched on their faces.

So this was it – the final two. Applejuice versus The Pips.

The crowd was chanting. Apple Valley trying to out-shout Gravenstein. Gravenstein trying to out-shout Apple Valley. Jimmy smiled, crossed his fingers and glanced at JoJo. She looked as anxious as he, her eyes wide, her fingernails getting shorter by the second.

The hall quietened, but only to a vibrant edge of the seat buzz. Miss Witherspoon took a deep breath. "This has been the closest decision ever in the history of the competition. In fact," she paused again, "the judges unanimously agreed that Applejuice and The Pips could not be split. They each scored a massive thirty eight points. We have a tie!"

The crowd roared and instantly dropped to a confused murmur, unsure as to what had just happened or what it meant.

"However," continued Miss Witherspoon, "as I have said, only one band can play at the Centenary and upon due deliberation and a check of the Battle of the Bands regulations, it became clear that one of the bands had in fact broken the rules."

Jimmy's heart ground to a halt in his chest as a dramatic 'ooohhhh' went up from the crowd. His first thought was that they had found out about the Vocalosis. His second thought was *Don't be stupid. How could they possibly know about that?*

"According to the judges, a break in the rules accrues a five point deduction. Therefore the winning band, with thirty eight points to thirty three is …

… Applejuice."

The hall erupted with cheers. On the ceiling the light fittings shook. Jimmy almost collapsed with relief. Halfpint screamed and jumped high in the air, landing on Paige's back. Cornelius buried his hands in his face. Damien just looked like Damien, thoroughly smug.

Tarquin however was having none of it. "WHAT RULES? He bellowed at Miss Witherspoon. "We didn't break any rules! This is a fix – a rotten fix."

Miss Witherspoon kept calm as all around her people went crazy, either utterly elated or steaming mad.

"I'm afraid young man it clearly states that the use of any unauthorised pyrotechnic displays is banned in this competition. You broke the rules, pure and simple. Now if you'll excuse me."

Tarquin was about to complain further, but Miss Witherspoon wrapped Jimmy him up in a hug. "Well done. Well done indeed," she shouted over the din. "They'll be talking about this for years. If you want the truth, I was more than a little worried when I found out who you'd chosen to replace Catrina." She pulled even tighter. "But you obviously knew something we all didn't. Great job. Really. A great job. The school is so proud of you."

Then she was off and Jimmy suddenly disappeared under a pile of friends screaming "We did it. We did it." at the top of their voices.

Jimmy felt ecstatic. They really had won. Despite everything, all the set-backs, they *were* going to play at the Centenary. JoJo *did* have a chance of getting home and Jimmy *would* get his Grandad's lease back. He could hardly believe it was true.

From behind her curtain JoJo watched the band celebrate. It was fantastic to see them so happy. The sheer pleasure on their faces was contagious.

For the first time since they met, JoJo felt a real bond of friendship between them. They weren't just a bunch of humans who happened to be helping her out, but friends whom she could talk to and confide in – who she could laugh and joke with.

For the first time she saw them as people. And people should not be judged by what planet they happen to come from, but judged on what they did with their lives. How they acted. How they treated others. That, she realized, was where the Admiralty had got things so wrong. They had not given this planet a chance.

Forty years ago something had gone terribly wrong and they chose to not only close the book, but to throw it away and never look at it again. That was a mistake. If they had just taken the time, they would surely have found people like Jimmy, Paige, Cornelius and Halfpint. People who were willing to do anything for anybody if it meant helping them out. JoJo doubted whether she would have been willing to stand on that stage and let Damien Dirt sing with his normal voice. Halfpint, Paige and Cornelius had been prepared to if it meant getting the lease back for Jimmy. That was real friendship.

Finally, Jimmy beckoned her over.

That was when she felt the chill, like a shiver of ice cold dread it spread throughout her entire body in milliseconds. Her smile faltered, her breath quickened. Something caught in her throat. What was happening?

From when she was little, JoJo had always been told she had a sensitive soul, that she could sense the good or bad in people. Well, a wave of something so bad had just hit her that it had stopped her dead.

Her eyes darted, searching for the source of her feelings. There were boys and girls, teachers and parents but none had the blackness she sensed.

Then he swept past her and she swore her blood froze in her veins.

Still and silent she watched as the man made his way across the stage. He seemed to glide like a ghost, effortlessly graceful. There was something ethereal about him. But more than anything, there was something evil about him. Suddenly she didn't feel safe, but what was it she feared so?

She caught Jimmy's eye. Once more he beckoned, but her face was set like stone. The man was now next to Jimmy. All her hairs stood on end. Jimmy was in danger. It sounded ridiculous, but somehow she was sure. Desperately she tried to send him a signal, a warning through her eyes, but it all was too late. Jimmy was no longer looking at her – he was taking something from the man's hand.

* * *

Jimmy didn't see the man until he was right on top of him. From out of nowhere, a hand was suddenly there for him to shake.

"Jimmy Green, I presume – Guitarist Extraordinaire."

Jimmy turned and grimaced. He didn't mean to, he just couldn't help it. The hand in front of him looked unreal. The bones were too twisted, the skin too rough, the nails too long and the man it was attached to, almost skeletal.

He wore, well … black. Everything from his socks up to his sunglasses was the colour of night. Even the leather lace that was keeping a small plait of hair locked in a pony-tail was devoid of colour. Strangely though, his voice was soft and quiet, much friendlier than his appearance would suggest. Jimmy still did not shake hands though.

Not at all offended, as if people always had this reaction to him, he turned to Paige, "And you young lady must be Paige Turner. Let me tell you, the way you hit that kit. Woo! Makes me glad I'm not a drum."

Paige stepped forward, half smiling at the compliment.

"Please allow me to introduce myself," the man said. He withdrew his hand, reached into an inside jacket pocket and plucked out a small rectangular business card. With one hand he offered the card to Jimmy. The other he offered once more to shake. "The name is Cobs. Earl Cobs. Artist management and representation. I talked to your singer earlier. He may have mentioned …"

Jimmy took the card.

"I didn't know talent scouts were allowed in the competition," said Halfpint. Earl Cobs ignored him.

"Good boy that Damien. An extremely confident young man. I like that. The most important thing in a rock singer is confidence, wouldn't you say, Jimmy."

Jimmy found himself nodding despite himself.

"And I must say I'm surprised your victory wasn't more decisive. I've been in this business all my life and let me tell you, those other bands weren't even close."

Over his shoulder, Jimmy caught sight of his Grandad standing behind JoJo. As was usual these days he seemed to be somewhere else entirely. He wasn't even looking at Jimmy.

Well, Jimmy was sick of the moods. If he couldn't be happy now they had won and were getting attention from real music people, then too bad.

Jimmy smiled, grasped Earl Cobs' hand and shook it firmly.

"What can we do for you Mr. Cobs?" Jimmy asked. Out of the corner of his eye he watched his Grandad turn and walk away.

"Mr. Cobs? Why so formal, Mr. Green? Please call me Earl and I'll call you Jimmy. And it is not what you can do for me, rather what I can do for you."

Earl Cobs grinned. It wasn't pretty. His mouth resembled a slash in his face. He leaned in close. A little too close for Jimmy's liking. "You ever thought about a recording contract Jimmy?"

Jimmy's ears pricked up. "A recording contract?"

"Certainly. Playing at the Centenary Celebrations is a fantastic opportunity. Do you realise the bands you'll be playing with? Believe me, with the publicity it will generate, a man like me can have you signed to a record label like that." He snapped his thumb and forefinger together. "First single out within eight weeks. An album before Christmas, possibly a tour. Sound good? Of course it sounds good. It's what you've always dreamed of am I right?" He looked at Halfpint, Cornelius and Paige. Like Jimmy, they too were hooked on his smooth patter. "I can see you guys work hard. That's all it takes. Hard work and the right contacts. Well, I've got the contacts if you've got the hard work. What do you say?"

Jimmy looked bedazzled. Record contracts and tours. Earl Cobs had said the magic words. Jimmy definitely wanted a bit of that. Earl however took his disbelief as doubt.

"I'm moving too fast," he said stepping back looking concerned that he may have upset Jimmy. "I'm sure a band as good as yours is going to have many other offers. You must of course take your time and do what is best for you, but I'll tell you this, Earl Cobs gets things done. Earl Cobs can take you to the top because Earl Cobs believes in you and cares about you." He put one hand on Jimmy's shoulder and pressed the card firmly into his hand with the other. "Keep the card Jimmy. I know we'll be seeing each other again. I just know it."

With that he swept off, making a beeline for Damien.

As soon as he was gone, JoJo ran over. "Who was that? What did he want?" she asked worriedly.

Jimmy turned and smiled. "He wants to make us stars," he said.

CHAPTER 37

PHOTOGRAPH

The celebrations continued all the way back to the barn and into the early evening. JoJo and the band (minus Damien) were joined by 2B and the CoyoteBots who were desperate to know everything that had happened.

JoJo had, of course, explained to the band about the ScatterBot incident and Pulp's selfless sacrifice to save their lives. Much to her delight, Jimmy suggested they have a little ceremony in his honour, so, utilising remnants of the old jeep, they lovingly crafted a junkyard shrine to him in one corner of the barn.

"He would have loved it. Thank you," said a tearful JoJo.

After that they put on some music, cracked open some bottles of coke and relaxed.

For a couple of hours everybody forgot the problems which had led them to this place and just rejoiced in the fact that finally, things had gone their way.

Of course there were still problems to face. For one thing, Jimmy hadn't been given the lease. Damien had slipped away with the Banner twins before he'd had the chance to challenge him about them.

Then there was Earl Cobs. JoJo had made it very clear she didn't like the look of him, but in Jimmy's eyes, this was a man who had promised them a recording contract. Who cared what he looked like?

However, so caught up in Earl's sales pitch had Jimmy been, he hadn't even considered what would happen when Earl Cobs heard the real Damien Dirt.

The equation was simple enough. Damien couldn't sing without JoJo. JoJo was going home therefore, Damien minus JoJo equalled… earache for everyone.

At first, Jimmy felt downhearted, but then had a most wonderful thought. Was it not the band and the songs that Earl Cobs had liked so much? He had said as much hadn't he? If that were the case, then maybe they didn't need Damien at all. Perhaps the promise of a recording contract could be used to lure Cat back from France. He was sure Earl Cobs wouldn't take much persuading when he heard Damien's genuine voice against Cat's that was for sure.

No, despite JoJo's reservations, the more he thought about it, the more he decided that Earl Cobs coming into their lives was a very good thing indeed.

* * *

As the evening wore on, the inevitability of having to go home crept nearer and nearer.

Home, Jimmy thought. Where was that exactly? It was ironic but after all he had been through to secure the lease, that house didn't feel much like home anymore. What with his Grandad acting as if he hated the sight of Jimmy, it felt more a battlefield of silence and moods.

Once again Jimmy couldn't help but feel abandoned by the ones he loved and upset that they really didn't seem to care what happened in his life very much at all. Neither his Grandma nor his Grandad had even congratulated him on winning. Perhaps this was how his life was destined to be forever. First his Mum, then his Dad, then Cat and now his Grandad. Even JoJo would be leaving soon.

Somebody (a well meaning aunt Jimmy seemed to recall) once told him, just after his Dad left actually, that God only gave people the burdens and pain they could handle, and that Jimmy must be an extremely strong and special boy to be handling so much, so young. Well, Jimmy hadn't felt particularly special back then and he certainly didn't feel special now either. If there was indeed a God – for a while now Jimmy had not been so sure that there was – then he wanted to tell him to stop! That he had had quite enough burden and pain thank-you very much and it was time to pick on someone else for a change.

"Anyone for an Applejuice cocktail before we call it a night?" shouted Halfpint from behind the open fridge door. "We're all out of coke."

An Applejuice cocktail was a sweet mix of fruit juice, lemonade and ice cream. It could rot your teeth just by looking at it. Jimmy loved it, but declined and excused himself. He wasn't in a cocktail mood.

He stepped outside, welcoming the cool night air flowing into his lungs. Actually it was a little too cool. The weather had drawn in and from a beautiful summer's day, the sky had turned battleship grey and a storm looked imminent.

Nevertheless, he took a seat on what had once been the front scooper of a large digger. It was now half buried in the ground.

From his back pocket, he pulled out a brown leather wallet and clicked open the snap fastener. He sighed. Another reminder. The wallet had been a present from Cat. His name was embossed along the front, a nice touch. As gifts go this was one of the better ones. Not because it was particularly grand, but because of why she had bought it him. One day, in passing Jimmy had happened to mention how he was looking for something to keep a photograph in. Something a little sturdier than the material of his back trouser pocket. Cat had presented him with the wallet two days later.

He unfolded the creaky leather revealing the corner of the photograph he had so wanted to protect. There was nothing else in the wallet. Just the photo.

No one, except maybe Cat, knew how much this simple picture meant to him. He treasured it. It was the most precious thing in the whole world.

He lifted it out. The shot was of a woman taken many years ago at an open air music concert. The type where you take a tent and sleep overnight in some muddy wet field just to catch a glimpse of your favourite band.

The sun was shining in the background and the woman was smiling at the photographer as if she didn't have a care in the world. It was a smile Jimmy recognised every time he looked in the mirror. It was his smile. The woman was his Mum.

His heart ached for her. He couldn't begin to describe how much he missed her. She had been his rock and his best friend. They had shared a bond that he just knew was different to everybody else. Even from his earliest age they had been like one person tied together in an extraordinary love. Each knew what the other was thinking before they had said it. If he woke at night, scared by a bad dream, his Mum would already be there waiting to comfort him. If he hurt himself at school, she would be on the phone to the teacher before they even had a chance to patch him up and let her know. They used to joke that they were telepathic. Maybe they were. She would certainly have understood just how much todays victory meant to him.

And now, this photograph was pretty much all he had left of her. None of her possessions had been retained. His father had seen to that, throwing it all out before the funeral had even taken place, and although his grandparents had many photographs for him to look at, most were of her as a young girl. That was someone Jimmy didn't know. This here, this was *his* Mum.

As he stared into the photograph, longing to reach out and touch the smiling face within, he didn't hear the barn door creak open or see JoJo walk over and stand beside him.

He only had eyes for one woman.

CHAPTER 38

A KIND OF MAGIC

JoJo said nothing as she tiptoed to Jimmy's side. She was concerned and had come to check that he was okay. Clearly he was not and judging by his demeanour, he obviously didn't want to be disturbed. He looked utterly lost; completely unreachable.

She gazed over his shoulder at the picture. The woman in the photograph that had Jimmy so entranced was beautiful. It did not take a genius to work out who it was. The eyes, the smile, they were unmistakably Jimmy and she was unquestionably his mother.

Then the strangest thing happened. As she stared into the eyes of Jimmy's dead mother, a sharp blast of pain pierced her chest like a steel blade. Grief poured into her heart from nowhere overwhelming her and making her feel unbelievably mournful. Like the twisting roots of a plant, the grief wound itself around her body, smothering it in agony until there wasn't an inch of her that did not feel it. More than anything in the world JoJo wanted to cry there and then, but she did not. She could not because as real as it felt, this wasn't her pain.

She knew without knowing that what she was experiencing was Jimmy's pain. Jimmy's hurt.

She desperately wanted it to stop. It felt wrong to be intruding on a person's emotions like this. *There are some things you shouldn't know*, she thought darkly, fighting the agony.

Frantically she tried to drag her eyes away from the photograph but couldn't. Some uncontrollable force was drawing her in deeper and deeper.

Memories, not hers but Jimmy's, began to flash and fade in her mind. Flash and fade. Flash and fade. Scenes and people, places and events all played out in her head.

She knew them all. Even though they were all foreign to her, she could put names to the faces, locations to the places. She saw tragedy and despair and fun and laughter in equal measure. She thought she was going mad. It was all too much, overloading her brain.

The memories and emotions threatened to engulf her, drag her to a place from which she may never return. But she held fast against the tide of heartache that crashed all around her and absorbed it all.

Finally, without warning she was back, her mind once more her own. She breathed hard. In what could have been no more than a minute, JoJo had seen deeper into the life and mind of Jimmy Green than anyone had a right to.

Before she had time to make sense of it, something even more surprising happened. She began to fall.

Not literally. But the world around her tipped and turned like some weird and wonderful fairground ride and foolishly she found herself stumbling for balance even though her rational brain knew that both her feet were planted firmly on the ground.

As she descended through a darkening void to goodness-knows where, JoJo encountered what can only be termed as an epiphany.

In the beat of a bee's wing, all her fear and uncertainty vanished like a pricked soap bubble. In that briefest of moments she saw in crystal clear clarity, the destiny that lay in front of her.

JoJo was changing. The innocence and raw potential of the Larian child that she was, was about to be unlocked forever. Unleashed from its chains would be the power and promise of the young adult she was soon to become.

Surprisingly knowing all that held little fear for her.

Like all Larian children, this was a pre-ordained time. There could be no stopping it and nor would she want to.

JoJo was coming of age.

* * *

Her journey complete, she stepped out of the blackness into a completely different world. But it was a world she knew despite never having visited it before in her life.

She was in the middle of a massive field. In the sky the sun was as bright as she had ever seen it. All around her, tens of thousands of people danced and sang and screamed. In the distance a stage loomed large and music blared out at a volume comparable to an exploding bomb. It was amazing.

She stepped forward and yelled at the top of her voice. As she suspected, no one showed her the slightest bit of attention. No one could hear her. No one could even see her. Although everything around her was, to all intents and purposes, real, JoJo knew that it wasn't. There was no actual field, no sun, no people. JoJo was in fact *inside* Jimmy's photograph. She was picture walking and that could mean only one thing.

JoJo was a 'seer'.

* * *

All Larians were born special. Every child had within them a dormant, but wonderous gift that would, at a preordained time bestow a great power. In days gone by it was believed that a mysterious god gave them the gifts, but that was wholly inaccurate. The gifts were nothing but pure science.

A unique chromosome, number forty seven – imaginatively given the name 'the gift set' – was solely responsible for coming of age. It was this 'gift set' that placed Larian's apart from humans.

The thousands of genes on chromosome forty-seven could

combine in any number of ways producing gifts that were immensely varied and highly unpredictable. No one in fact knew what they would become until that special day arrived when they were first expressed. Some gifts, such as increased acuity of one or more of the senses were relatively common. Others, such as that of the Seer were much rarer.

The ability to read a person's thoughts, to peer into the darkest recesses of their mind and, with the correct training and guidance, be able to influence those thoughts, had belonged to very few. Now JoJo had joined the ranks – early as well. You weren't expected to come of age until after your fifteenth year. But like everything it seemed, JoJo was ahead of her time.

In a way it was a shame to have happened in this manner. Coming of age was a huge event. It was a time of much trepidation and excitement, shared and welcomed by the whole family. She had missed out on the parties and celebrations, the wise words from parents and grandparents who had been through it all and more importantly, the guidance of her teachers in how to use her gift. All that would have to wait until she returned home. For now she was on her own. She alone would have to figure out how this new and powerful gift worked. She just hoped she was up to it.

She tried to take stock. Although she wasn't scared exactly, being transported inside a photograph for the first time was more than a little disconcerting, especially when you weren't precisely sure how to get out.

Picture walking was a 'trick' unique to those gifted as seers. That's how she could be so sure she was one. However, that pitiful bit of information, was all she knew of how the process worked in reality. Was she actually, physically in the photograph? Or was it just her mind projecting her inside? She could certainly feel the solid floor beneath her feet and if she looked up at the sun, yes, it hurt her eyes. So maybe this was more than just a simple trick of the mind.

She glanced about her surroundings. The stage was two hundred yards away. That, she believed was where her destiny lay. Why?

Because he would be there. JoJo had not made this journey alone. Someone close had been dragged along too, and at all costs she must find him or risk leaving him here forever.

* * *

Jimmy instantly knew where he was. He had gazed at that photograph a million times, so this place was as familiar to him as his own hand.

Although the falling sensation had been rather unpleasant and his initial shock at finding himself here had rendered him speechless, he had never felt more energised. Even if the whole thing turned out to be an elaborate conjuring trick, or if his mind had finally snapped and this was his own madness he was looking at, he knew that somewhere amongst this sea of people – maybe only a few feet away from him – was his Mum.

That thought, that anticipation filled every cell in his body with a crackling, positive energy. It was as if there was now no other purpose in his life other than to glimpse a sight of her.

He moved fast through the throngs of people. Nobody bothered him. It was as though he didn't exist. Whichever turn he took a path seemed to open up for him and allow him through. As he began to canter, he tried to visualise where she would stand. Think, think, did she ever talk about the picture? About the concert? He cursed under his breath. He couldn't remember.

The music was getting louder. The band had begun another song. Jimmy listened. That song, that intro. *Dum, de-dum, dah. Dum, de-dum, dah* – he recognised it. Like a forgotten memory that had been held back behind an impenetrable dam, the rocks were suddenly shattered and it all came flooding back. This was the song his Mum was always humming and singing. This was the song that was playing on the car stereo when ... when the car crashed.

She was near the front row. He knew that now. She had told him about it when he was seven or eight.

He dashed for the stage, warily stepping around the screaming people, apologising as he went.

"It's all right, they can't see you."

Jimmy spun around. JoJo. She was out of breath, but smiling.

"You," said Jimmy. "You did this."

JoJo nodded. "I don't think I meant to. I'm not quite sure what's happened actually."

Jimmy shushed her. "My Mum, she's here. She was here watching this band somewhere near the front row. I …"

"Go," said JoJo, "I'll follow. Just pretend the people are not there."

That was easier said than done, but as they set off, the people did indeed part like waves before them. He got within about ten rows back … and deflated. It was huge. He could run around in these crowds all day and never find her. He had to get higher. He had to be able to look down on the many faces.

He had to get onto that stage.

Jimmy sprinted through the crowd, past the security guards and roadies and climbed the steps until he was standing behind the massive amplifiers. Here peered around. There was the band. There was the crowd. It seemed so strange to consider walking out in front of so many people, but he had to do it to find his Mum.

"Just go," said JoJo who had caught up and was pushing him in the back. "Trust me they won't know we're there."

She took the lead and stepped out in front of the hordes. Jimmy remained hesitant. He watched JoJo walk straight past the singer – who ignored her completely – to the front of the stage and start scanning the faces.   His confidence was suddenly buoyed and out he ran, his eyes everywhere.

Then he saw her.

Six or seven rows back, wearing the cream coloured top and pink alice-band that he recognised from the photograph.

His heart melted and exploded all at the same time. His emotions were besieged, unable to cope with the vision before him. Tears tracked down his cheeks and his legs felt like they had no supporting bones at all. JoJo tenderly held his hand.

"She was really beautiful Jimmy." She said.

Jimmy wiped his sleeve across his running nose. It was all too much. So many times he had asked God and anyone else who may have been listening for the chance to see his Mum, but now, now it had been granted, he realised why such a thing was never meant to be.

In a second, or a minute, or in an hour, he would have to leave and when he did his heart was going to break all over again. Only this time the pain would be a hundred times worse. To wish for something so badly and then be granted it for just a fragment of time, Jimmy realised was far worse than never having being granted the wish in the first place.

He gazed into his Mum's hazel eyes and she stared back – but not at him. To her, he didn't exist. He wasn't there. It was agony and ecstasy all rolled into one. He longed to dive off the stage, grab hold of her and never let her go but he knew it was impossible. JoJo sensed his heartache and tried to concentrate on blocking the pain for him but her new-found powers seemed to have no effect.

Jimmy traced every inch of his Mum's face; burning it into his memory so he would never, ever … The crowd parted just a little and Jimmy saw the most amazing thing. There was something different about her … She was … fat. It took a second for the realisation to dawn … Not fat … pregnant.

He looked feverishly around. Behind the band a large sign suspended across the full width of the stage told him what he was looking for. This concert took place just over fourteen years ago. So that meant the person in his Mum's swollen tummy was … him. He was looking at himself before he had been born. He laughed through his tears. The absolute bizarreness of the situation was incredible. He turned to JoJo who was staring into the distance, seemingly lost in her own thoughts.

"This is so amaz …" he began, but never got to finish his sentence.

He felt a wrench in his stomach as if someone had lassoed him around the waist and was dragging him away from the scene.

"Noooo!" he screamed, but it was no use. The pull was relentless.

With a Whuump! He and JoJo were back at the barn, him sitting in the digger's bucket, she by his side but now with a face paler than snow. And it was raining.

"JoJo, are you okay?" he asked squinting against the dreadful weather.

JoJo didn't answer. She was in a trance.

"JoJo, what's the matter?" He stood and took hold of her by the shoulders. "Talk to me please. What's wrong?"

Her eyes met Jimmy's and he thought he saw them burn with a strange, distant fire. Shrugging him off, she said, "You and I need to talk," and she marched into the barn.

CHAPTER 39

'FIRST CONTACT'

JoJo didn't say another word until she was in the Star Seeker sitting before SaRa. Jimmy had followed without a clue what was going on. As they had passed the others in the barn, Jimmy gave Halfpint a look to say he was all right but they should leave them be for a while. Halfpint nodded his understanding.

When Jimmy reached the cockpit, JoJo was already calling up files from SaRa's databank, organising them around the screen with her fingertips. All the while her expression remained flat and dark.

"I'm going to show you something that I think you need to see," she began as the screen faded to black. "But first, its time I told you a story." She swiveled her chair to look Jimmy square in the eyes. "Do you know why I came here?" she asked.

Jimmy shrugged. "Well I know it wasn't to collect music."

"You're right. I could see in your eyes that you didn't believe it the first time we met."

Jimmy shrugged. It was true. He'd never bought that.

"How come you never asked me the real reason?" JoJo asked.

"I don't know," Jimmy said genuinely. "I just figured you'd tell me if you wanted me to know. It wasn't any of my business anyway."

JoJo looked at him funnily. "Is that really the reason? Are you sure it wasn't because you already *knew* why I'd come here?"

Jimmy frowned. "How could I know anything about why you came here? Look, what's all this about? One minute we're somehow transported fourteen years into the past, standing on a stage looking at my Mum – which by the way you are really going to have to explain – and the next you're acting all weird, storming off and asking stupid questions."

JoJo ignored Jimmy's rant and turned to face the computer screen. "Okay," she said. "I'll play along, you know nothing, I get it."

Jimmy screwed his face up. What was happening?

She brought the screen to life with a picture of earth.

"So," began JoJo. "The story begins just over forty-five years ago when we first found this planet. It was a miracle really because it lies in a part of the galaxy known as the black zone. That's a vast area of space we can't fly to because there are no portals into or out of it – or so we thought. Quite by accident we found a portal that led us straight to this solar system.

"Dimple probes were initially sent to investigate. Everything about your planet was catalogued and studied and the more information that came in, the more excited the people on Anilar got. You have to understand, finding this place was the most significant event in our history. It caught everyone's imagination. Here was this tiny planet, all the way on the other side of the galaxy, which had living breathing people just like us. So the Admiralty, that's the people that run our planet, formed a mission codenamed 'first contact.'"

Jimmy thought about that. "You've been here before," he said softly to himself as the realisation hit home.

"A crew was hand picked by the Admiralty itself. Two Star Seekers, each carrying three men. They were top pilots, the absolute best of the best."

On the screen, the Solar System was replaced by a posed photograph of five men. Three were standing while two sat in front. All were dressed in an aged version of the spacesuit JoJo had been wearing when she first crashed.

Easily the most striking member of the crew was a tall thin man standing in the middle at the back. His eyes, which could hardly be described as eyes at all, were deep jet-black pools of oil. "Who's that?" asked Jimmy.

"Obel Scar," replied JoJo flatly. "The younger man to his left is his brother, Mathius."

Jimmy was surprised to see Mathius was not much older than JoJo or himself.

"The others are Ratan Stol, Com Standish and Sakuro Mantos."

"Why are there only five? You said two crews of three were chosen. That's six men."

JoJo once again ignored his question. It seemed she was working to her own agenda and would not deviate from it.

"It took five years of study and preparation until they were ready to begin their mission. Forty years ago tomorrow they took off from Anilar to come here."

"That's amazing," said Jimmy, edging forward to get a closer look.

"It would have been if everything had gone okay," said JoJo.

Jimmy turned. "They crashed too?"

"Oh no, the landings went totally smoothly but they didn't know about your people waiting for them. Humans. Lots of humans with very bad weapons and even worse intentions," said JoJo forebodingly.

"The military?" asked Jimmy.

JoJo nodded. "That's what you call them. They were waiting in numbers you would normally only amass for a war, not a peaceful visit from a friendly planet. If nothing else this should have warned the crew to fly straight back out as fast as possible, but they didn't."

Jimmy wrinkled his brow. "What did they do?"

JoJo breathed deeply. "There's only one account of the events which took place after the landing because only one person survived."

Jimmy gasped.

"I'm going to show it to you, and be clear, what you're about to read has not been seen by many people on Anilar, never mind a human. But its time someone saw it. Its time *you* did."

She emphasised the word 'you' as if Jimmy was somehow

237

personally involved. He didn't say anything. Just let her get whatever it was off her chest.

She began her fingertip dance with the computer files once more, explaining as she did so all about hacking into the Admiralty archives and how she'd spent the last two years examining the files trying to piece together a story that had effectively been kept secret from the Larian people for an entire generation.

As the files came up on the screen Jimmy felt a strange mix of apprehension and anticipation. He wasn't sure – for reasons he could not explain – that he was going to like what he was about to read. However, neither could he draw his eyes away from the words and what they may contain.

The first document was entitled.

'Mission: First Contact.
Witness Statement: Obel Scar.'

Intrigued, Jimmy began to read.

CHAPTER 40

EXPERIMENT 456

It was like reading a scene straight out of a horror movie. Only, in a reversal of the usual roles, Jimmy quickly realised that the good guys were the aliens and the humans were most definitely the villains.

He read Obel Scar's statement slowly, taking in every word of the horrific events. It made uncomfortable reading. It was graphic and explicit but absolutely compulsive.

JoJo had been correct, the flight to earth and the landing went perfectly smoothly for the six SpaceCoyotes, but when they touched down they found themselves encircled by what sounded like an entire battalion of soldiers. Obel described armoured personnel carriers, helicopters and tanks, their guns all trained on the alien crafts.

The SpaceCoyotes didn't stand a chance. They had not come prepared for a fight, they had come offering the hand of friendship and were completely overwhelmed by the force that greeted them.

After a very one sided struggle, which saw Ratan Stol and Mathius injured, they were forced to submit and were taken prisoner. They were blindfolded, their hands and feet bound together and bundled into trucks to be taken away.

At their destination (unknown or not mentioned) the six men were stripped of their clothes and belongings, separated and thrown into sterile, windowless rooms containing only a toilet and a bed. For three days their only contact with a human was via a video camera which followed their every move in the tiny white walled prison. They were given no food just the occasional glass of water to keep them alive.

On the fourth day, Experiment 456, led by a man Obel would only call 'the savage' began.

Obel described how the six SpaceCoyotes were man-handled out of their cells to a large white hanger where they were strapped into wooden chairs. He said it was *'a terrifying cross between a madman's laboratory and a torture chamber.'* All the walls were white and the entire place stank of disinfectant and sterility. Even the humans (who still refused to communicate) wore white disposable overalls, plastic gloves, rubber boots and goggles as if fearful of catching some terrible disease off the Larians.

The hanger had been divided into rooms by means of huge transparent plastic sheets hanging from long metal runners. Each makeshift room was equipped differently. One contained a bank of monitors and archaic medical equipment whilst another housed a massive tank of pink liquid. Yet another had what Obel described as *'frightening steel contraptions with all manner of pulleys, levers and spikes.'*

However, it was his description of the young SpaceCoyote Mathius that touched Jimmy the most.

'He was so unbelievably weak. Barely able to speak or move. It was obvious that nothing had been done to treat his wounds and that they were now badly infected. The humans prodded and poked their way around him, making notes but doing nothing to ease his pain. I begged them to treat him, to at least clean his injuries and give him a chance to live but they ignored me. I knew I was watching him die.'

Jimmy could barely believe the cruelty. But it was to get worse. Much, much worse.

* * *

Sakuro Mantos was the first to be 'tested'. As the others were forced to watch he was placed on a metal gurney, his arms and legs secured at the four corners. Wires and electrodes were attached to every part of his

240

body. Beginning with his legs, Obel described in gut-wrenching detail how the humans sent wave after wave of high voltage electricity through him.

'*Each bolt arched his back until I thought his spine would snap. He was screaming in pain, vomiting and retching with every blast, begging them to stop, but the humans did not relent. On and on they went until his entire body was burnt and scorched from electrocution. How he survived I will never know.*'

Jimmy felt sick. How could they have done this to people they hadn't even tried to get to know. It seemed insane and barbaric. He looked at JoJo. She remained impassive as he read, but he realised now why she had been so scared and wary the night of the crash. If this was her only experience of human beings she had every right to feel scared. Right now Jimmy was ashamed to call himself a human.

The torture and experimentation continued every third day. The human captors would choose just one of the six to be the guinea pig whilst the others watched.

The first time they chose Ratan Stol, he was hung from a beam ten feet in the air by his arms and whipped with razor sharp wire until not a sliver of skin remained on his back.

Com Standish had to withstand burning flames as the humans measured how long it took for his skin to blister and melt. Mathius had his hands and feet strapped down whilst a multitude of chemicals were dripped into cuts inflicted by the humans.

Jimmy could not even begin to imagine the agony those men must have gone through.

Experiment 456 continued for weeks. The SpaceCoyotes grew weak and each time they were tested, a little more life drained out of them.

Inevitably, it was not long after their third week began that Sakuro Mantos underwent what was to be his final experiment. He died in freezing cold water at the bottom of a giant glass tank. He had been stripped naked and weights attached to his legs before being dropped in without air. It was a test to measure for how long he could hold his breath.

He managed to cling onto life for thirty five minutes. His lifeless body was then dragged out and taken away. None of the SpaceCoyotes saw him again.

After Sakuro, the others succumbed quickly. Ratan Stol (killed by being force fed poisons) and Com Standish (shot at close range) both died on the same day – before the humans turned their attention to Mathius. Jimmy read Obel's words:-

'There was no way I was going to let him die at the hands of those savages whilst I still had breath in my body. On the day they dragged us out I knew one of us would be killed. It seemed that the experiment 456 was coming to a close. The laboratory had been mostly stripped of its torturous devices. They were shutting everything down and that meant us too. Many of the humans who had been so keen on monitoring our pain had left.

'But he was still there.

'The human savage who had led the whole operation, the man who had stolen our belongings and shared them out as trinkets, the man who reveled in our pain. He still remained to watch his final two playthings destroyed. But they had made a mistake. They believed me to be a beaten man. They believed me to be harmless. They thought the few men they had left were enough, but they were wrong, dead wrong.

'I attacked as they dragged Mathius off his chair. He was so weak he could barely stand and it took all the remaining humans to lift him. This worked in my favour as for a moment they left me alone. I had already worked free of the shackles and had the element of surprise. I wasted no time.

'Three of the five humans were dead before they even realised I had escaped. I fought the other two and after a long battle finally overcame them. I can't say I am proud of what I did. For any Larian, taking a life is the most contemptible act, but I cannot say either that I regret it. My only remorse is that I did not act sooner because it was *clear as soon as we were free that Mathius was so close to death, there was little hope he would live through the day. His last wish was to be returned home. A wish I intended to fulfil.'*

"He made it back two days later carrying the dead body of his brother out of the Star Seeker," said JoJo as Jimmy finished reading.

Jimmy was shell-shocked. "I don't get it. Why did you want me to read this? Do you want me to apologize for what they did?"

"No I don't want you to apologize, Jimmy," she snapped angrily. "I want you to tell me the truth. I want you to look me in the eye and tell me that you had no idea who we were or where we had come from when you stepped in and saved my brother from that grommet. I want to know that our friendship has not just been a horrible game to you."

Jimmy blew out his cheeks in frustration. "Here you go again with that crazy talk. How on earth could I possibly have known who you were? You've just flown goodness knows how many million, billion miles to get here and I'm supposed to have known you were coming. I don't even know all the people who live on my street never mind on another planet. As for Obel Scar's story, that's the first time I've read or heard anything about it, I swear."

She studied Jimmy's face for any sign of a lie. He seemed to be telling the truth, but humans were good liars and right now, she didn't know what to believe.

"Why, all of a sudden do you think I knew all about this anyway?" asked Jimmy.

"Because of your Grandad," JoJo replied cryptically.

"My Grandad, what's he got to do with any of this?"

She took a deep breath. It was hard, but he had to know. If he was telling the truth, he deserved to know. If he wasn't, then this was all a game anyway and he already knew. "Your Grandad," she said flatly, "and the man Obel Scar talks of as 'the savage.'"

"Yes?" said Jimmy.

JoJo locked eyes with him. "…They are the same person."

243

CHAPTER 41

THE UNBREAKABLE RULE

Jimmy was dumbfounded. JoJo was wrong. So wrong in fact that she had gone off the scale of being wrong.

"Let me get this straight," he said stomping to his feet. "You're saying that forty years ago my Grandad, a man you've never met by the way, led the torture and murder of those SpaceCoyotes?"

"Yes I am," replied JoJo firmly.

Jimmy shook his head flabbergasted. "Where do you get off saying something like that? My Grandad's a good man, an honest man. He's been more of a father to me than my own Dad ever was and you're calling him a murderer."

JoJo looked unmoved. "I know it must be hard for you to accept."

Jimmy pounced. "Don't patronise me. You don't know anything about me and you certainly don't know anything about my Grandad if you think he did that. He isn't capable of doing those things; he just isn't."

"Not now maybe," countered JoJo.

"What's that supposed to mean?"

"Well, you say that I don't know him, and you're right, I don't. But neither did you forty years ago."

"Well duh!" Said Jimmy fuming. "Okay, if you're so sure, prove it, and it better be good or else I'm out of here and I won't be coming back."

JoJo nodded. "Just give me five minutes and if you still don't believe what I say, then I'll keep away from you until we've gone. You won't have to talk to me again."

Jimmy sat back down in the chair. This should be good.

"Okay," began JoJo, "Everything fits too well for it not to be true. Your Grandad was in the military and he was stationed here, you told me that yourself, and you admit that you've never had a clue what he did because his job was so top secret."

Jimmy crossed his arms defensively. "That doesn't prove a thing, JoJo. How do you even know those SpaceCoyotes landed anywhere near here? Earth is a big place. It could have been anywhere. Those transcripts don't tell you anything."

"No, they don't, your right. Actually, the landing site has never been revealed, not even in the archives but I figured it out."

"Of course you did," Jimmy murmured under his breath.

"When I came into land, nothing was functioning properly and SaRa was stretched beyond her capacity just trying to stop us from crashing. I told her to find us a place to land and she brought us here to Apple Valley. The problem was, she miscalculated. For some reason she thought we should have been flying over miles and miles of empty fields, not an orchard. At first I put her error down to being so over worked and under pressure but now I think I did her a disservice. I think she got it right after all."

Jimmy shook his head. "Explain."

"Well, you see under normal landing conditions we would scan an entire planet's surface for an optimal landing site but in emergencies SaRa would automatically switch to a pre-existing alternate. That means bypassing the scans altogether and – as long as you've visited the planet before – reverting to the last known landing site. Well the only previous trip here was ..."

"Forty years ago," Jimmy finished for her.

"Precisely, as soon as you told me how this whole place had changed over the years, I knew that had to be it."

Jimmy thought about it. "Okay, so you can put the SpaceCoyotes

245

and my Grandad in the same place forty years ago. That still doesn't mean he had anything to do with what happened to them."

"Agreed,"

A thought suddenly came to Jimmy. "Is this a revenge mission you are on? Are you planning to kill my Grandad? Because I know what happened to those men was terrible, but you've risked a hell of a lot for five men who died before you were even born."

"Four men," corrected JoJo.

"I beg your pardon?"

"Four men. There were two survivors. And no, I haven't come to kill your Grandad."

Jimmy frowned. "But Obel was the only survivor."

"Not necessarily. Think back to the beginning of his transcript. Obel talks of all six SpaceCoyotes being taken by the humans, but later he describes the deaths of only four men: Sakuro Mantos, Com Standish, Ratan Stol and Mathius."

"So the other…" Mused Jimmy.

"Lived, I'm positive of it. Not only that, but I believe he remained on your planet and that your Grandad knows all about it."

Jimmy wanted so much to disbelieve JoJo and put an end to this conversation, but a part of him had been drawn in to the story and had to see it through. He took a deep breath.

"You've had four minutes. Get to the point of how you know all this," he said.

JoJo smiled softly and faced her screen, pulling up yet more files. "It's complicated so bear with me. When I first started going through the archives, I knew there was something odd about them; something I couldn't quite put my finger on. Then one day I realised – the communication logs between SaRa and Anilar. I couldn't find any anywhere."

"Why is that unusual?"

"Because SaRa continually stores all the data of the mission so it can be reviewed at a later date. Such was the importance of 'first contact', it would be inconceivable that SaRa wasn't involved all the way."

"Couldn't they have switched her off or something?" asked Jimmy.

JoJo shook her head. "You can't switch SaRa off. The most you can do is to re-route her transmissions so they don't feed back to the main base computer."

"Is that what you've done? Re-route them so they don't know you're here?" Jimmy asked knowingly.

"Yeah, but I'm trying to hide, they weren't."

Jimmy nodded. That made sense. "Okay, so what happened to them?"

"Somebody deleted them, that's what happened. Somebody who didn't want anyone finding out what I found out. I trailed through thousands upon thousands of files before I found their footprints."

Jimmy rolled his eyes. "Footprints?"

"It's hackers' slang," she said expertly. "I don't know what the computer systems here are like, but on Anilar it's virtually impossible to delete a file entirely once it's written. We save to light drives and there's always some remnant left. It might just be a tiny fragment; a word, a number, a sentence, but, if you're careful and you know what you're looking for, you can find them.

"We call them footprints because that's exactly what they are like. Think about it. If you see a footprint on the road, you have no idea what the person who made it looks like, sounds like or dresses like, but you can tell certain things and guess at others. Such as whether it's a boy or a girl, a man or a woman or how tall they are likely to be. Do you see?"

Jimmy did, but he didn't see how any of this proved his Grandad murdered some SpaceCoyotes.

"So what did you find in these footprints?" he asked.

"For a start I found all of SaRa's correspondence, and this."

She highlighted a line of text on the screen. Jimmy read it, then re-read it.

"It's a Mayday call made four days *after* Obel Scar returned to Anilar," confirmed JoJo.

Jimmy narrowed his eyes. "A Mayday call from here?"

JoJo nodded, grinning. "Only a SpaceCoyote can make a Mayday call. It requires a scan of their *living* DNA."

"Bloody hell," Jimmy exclaimed. "But that means …"

"As I said, someone survived," she finished for him.

Now Jimmy was hooked. "So who was it?"

JoJo brought back onto the screen the photograph of the five SpaceCoyotes she had shown Jimmy earlier, only now there was a sixth figure, his face and body blacked out of the image.

"That's him. His name is Willum Havelok. He was the leader of the expedition."

Jimmy thought back to what he had read. "I don't remember Obel mentioning that name?"

JoJo shook her head. "That's right," she said. "Willum is the big mystery in all of this. You see back on Anilar, he took the blame for everything that happened. The story goes that Willum desperately wanted to be the leader of the Admiralty. In order for that to happen, he needed to see them discredited and saw 'first contact' as the perfect opportunity. According to the archives, it was he who ordered both Star Seekers to fly onto the Blue Planet without shields or invisibility. When they were captured and he realized what the humans planned to do to them, he offered them a deal. He would give them valuable technological information, they would grant him his freedom. Ultimately, he believed that such a tragedy would terminally weaken the Admiralty back home. Because of all that, his name has virtually disappeared from Larian history, wiped away as if he never existed. I wouldn't put it past the Admiralty to have edited Obel's testimony so it had no reference to Willum at all."

Jimmy scratched his head. "So you came here to find Willum? But why if he did those terrible things?"

"Because he sent a Mayday call and it was ignored" JoJo said sternly. "He asked for help and they pretended it didn't exist."

"But why would you care if he's a traitor."

JoJo blanched. "Firstly," she said, holding up her index finger, "a Mayday call from a SpaceCoyote, no matter what the circumstances, is never ignored. It's an unbreakable rule. Secondly, I don't for a minute believe that is what actually happened. There are too many anomalies to the story and thirdly," she paused holding up three fingers. Her voice grew suddenly quiet. "And thirdly ... Havelok is my mother's family name. Willum is my Grandfather."

CHAPTER 42

MISSING

Jimmy searched for the right words but none came. His mouth hung open wondering how many more twists lay in store before this night was out. For a brief moment, thoughts of his own Grandad and JoJo's insistence that he was somehow involved with the barbaric events of forty years ago had drifted from his mind. He remembered how it felt when he saw his mother earlier and knew exactly what had driven JoJo to come here and find her family.

"Does 2B know?" he asked softly.

"No," she replied anxiously, "and I don't want him too either. You have to promise me that you'll not say anything."

Jimmy did. It was none of his business anyway and he had no wish to betray her confidence.

"So how were you planning on finding him in two days? It doesn't sound like a two day job to me. Even if he did survive there's no reason why he'd stay around here. He could have traveled anywhere in forty years. He might even be dead."

"True, but you're forgetting that I was supposed to be ten miles up safely orbiting this planet, not stuck in a barn unable to fly anywhere. I'd written a computer program which would have performed a life scan of the entire surface. Every living thing would have been accounted for and had its DNA compared with mine."

JoJo quickly explained about the 'gift set' chromosome and how it was not found in any human being.

"Wow," said Jimmy impressed, "sounds complicated."

"It is, or rather it was," she said smiling rather coyly. "If you discount myself and 2B, there should be no Larian DNA on this planet, so a positive match would have to be Willum. Simple."

"So what happened? Why haven't you done it?"

"ScatterBot happened. It turns out that he did a lot more than just slice through that pipe and try to kill us all. He also trashed half the programs I had running, including that one. He shouldn't have been able to do to, but somehow the little traitor did."

"Bummer," said Jimmy, the master of the understatement. "It would have been amazing for you to find your Grandfather after all these years."

JoJo smiled coyly at Jimmy. "Well, there may still be a way of finding out, if someone was willing to help, that is."

From the big doe eyes JoJo was suddenly fluttering, Jimmy got the hint that he was the one who was going to get volunteered to do the helping and he had a good idea what she had in mind. "You think my Grandad can somehow help you find Willum don't you?"

JoJo raised her eyebrows. "It may have crossed my mind."

Suddenly Jimmy's impatience re-surfaced. "You're not listening to me. I'm telling you that he had nothing to do with what happened to your Grandfather forty years ago."

"And I say he did."

Jimmy screwed his face in frustration. "Ahhhhh. This is insane. Why, all of a sudden are you sooo convinced? You didn't think he was involved yesterday and you didn't think he was involved this morning, so why now?"

JoJo reached around the back of her neck and unclasped a necklace that Jimmy had not even been aware she was wearing. She held it in her palm for him to see.

Jimmy was struck dumb.

"This belonged to my Grandmother. It was passed down to me by my Mother. It's called a union charm."

A neon blue pendant dripped from the silver necklace. A crimson 'C' had been carved expertly into its face. Shaped like a slightly distorted teardrop, it reminded Jimmy of one portion of the Chinese yin-yang symbol.

"It's called a union charm because it's really two pieces in one. The other half to this has an 'S' on it. You're supposed to give one half to someone special and keep the other half yourself as a symbol of your love for them and their's for you."

Jimmy reached out and gently brushed his finger along the contours of the red 'C.' he could feel the blood pumping in his ears.

"The night before he left for the Blue Planet, Willum gave this half to my Grandmother," continued JoJo. "He kept the other half. Days later my Grandmother discovered that she was pregnant. Willum never knew he was going to be a father. When Obel returned and Willum was classified dead, it was given to my Mother as a reminder of the Father she never knew. That's how I know your Grandad was involved because … Jimmy, I saw the other half tonight, when we were picture walking. Your Mum had it round her neck."

CHAPTER 43

TREASURES AND TRINKETS

Jimmy bolted for the door like a startled animal, his world collapsing around him. He leapt into the turquoise transporter, ran headlong past the startled Halfpint, Cornelius, Paige and 2B and didn't stop until he had powered his bike home and was standing outside the garden gate.

The rain was pelting down. The back of his legs were soaked and splattered with mud from the ride home and his hair was pinned flat to his forehead. The dark miserable skies matched his mood perfectly.

As he stared at the pretty house which, only this afternoon, he had fought so hard to secure from Damien, his mind reeled with the words of Obel Scar. *'They stripped us of all our belongings sharing them out as treasures and trinkets.'*

Treasures and trinkets. Sadly it all made sense.

As soon as Jimmy saw the half pendant dangling from JoJo's hand and she told him of its origins, he knew. Its colour and shape was as distinctive as McDonalds' golden arches. He could easily picture the other half, the half with the crimson 'S', because he had seen it with his own eyes. Seen it in his own hands the night JoJo crash-landed. It was the pendant his Grandad had thrown across the table in anger.

The conclusions were obvious. JoJo was right. His Grandad had been a part of experiment 456. There was still no way JoJo or anybody else would convince him that he had been 'the savage', but being in possession of a necklace owned by Willum Havelok was pretty damning evidence for the prosecution.

On the ride home Jimmy had hypothesised a hundred innocent explanations as to how the pendant could have come into his Grandad's possession. Unfortunately all of them sounded as weak as a large cup of milky tea. There was only one convincing explanation. Jimmy just didn't like it. His Grandad must have been there. He *must* have taken the pendant and then passed it on later.

Every time he thought of what his Grandad had been a part of, he felt a knife twist in his guts. He had always been a hero to Jimmy.

How different the truth was turning out to be.

Jimmy swung the gate open and marched down the path to the front door. With time to think on the ride home, he had worked up a quite an anger, but little in the way of a plan. He intended to get some answers for sure but more importantly, he wanted to reclaim the pendant for JoJo. After travelling so far and carrying so many secrets with her, all to find a man who more than likely was now dead, she at least deserved to go home with that.

How exactly he was going to get the pendant was a different matter. He would have to be careful not to alert his Grandad to JoJo and 2B's presence on earth because he would never forgive himself if he put their lives in danger. One thing was for sure though, he wasn't coming out of this house without it.

* * *

In the few minutes Jimmy had stood outside of the house working through his next move, he never once paid any attention to the dark green car parked twenty or so metres across the street. If he had he may well have had some vague recollection of the gentleman sat behind the wheel.

The man was dressed casually in a brown leather jacket and jeans. Slowly he raised a thick cigar to his lips and inhaled. As the lit end glowed it sent a glimmer of light across his face highlighting a thick white scar that ran from his eye to his chin.

This was the fifth straight night he had been on stakeout. So far there had been little for him to get excited about, but there was something in the air that told him tonight might just be different. For tonight was the first time Jimmy's nightly procedure had changed. Firstly, he had left the barn in a mighty hurry and alone. That had never happened. Secondly he had dropped his bike to the ground rather than storing it away in the shed like normal. A small detail perhaps, but then he was trained to look for small details. And thirdly, Jimmy had now been standing by the front door in the pouring rain for over five minutes. That was the behaviour of a person with something on his mind.

It was time to move.

Ever since the landing, his instructions had been crystal clear. *There could be no mistakes.* If there was even a hint that Jimmy had discovered the truth about the events of forty years ago, then decisive action was to be taken. The stakes were too high – far too high. It didn't matter that he had known the boy since he was born. The time for sentiment had passed.

By the time Jimmy had entered the house, the scarred man was already making his way to the gate, his cigar extinguished and saved for later. His instincts were tingling like a blow to the funny bone and those instincts had never let him down before.

There could be no mistakes. The words went round in his head like a carousel.

With his body hunched slightly forward and a hat pulled low over his face to both shelter from the rain and hide his appearance from any nosey neighbours, he listened by the front door. When he was sure Jimmy had left the hallway, the scarred man gently twisted the handle and made his way inside the house.

* * *

JoJo followed Jimmy out of the barn but was too late to stop him speeding away. As she watched him disappear over the brow of the hill, her head felt muddled with feelings of confusion and guilt.

She had been too hard on him she knew. How did she expect him to react after accusing his Grandfather of being a murderer? Even for JoJo, the lack of subtlety was surprising.

Now she thought about it, she wasn't even sure why it was she had felt the need to unburden all her secrets to Jimmy. Maybe it had been the shock of suddenly finding herself picture walking, or the equally strange feelings of embryonic power that had stumbled through her veins like a toddler taking its first clumsy steps. Everything had been so clear in her mind after she saw Jimmy's mother wearing the missing half of *her* pendant. Like reading the final chapter of a book, the missing parts of the story had all seemed to come together. As she watched Jimmy ride out of sight, there was a slight nagging doubt in the back of her mind that maybe, just maybe, she had mis-read some of the earlier pages.

There was something else too – something she had not told Jimmy. During the picture walking she had felt something pretty cataclysmic happen between the two of them. There had been a closeness, a bond of such strength and depth that it had shocked her. For the briefest of moments it was like a door had opened into both their subconscious minds and their thoughts had become one. During those fleeting seconds, she knew that Jimmy had glimpsed into her mind just as easily as she had seen into his.

And that connection had not completely closed. Right now she could feel Jimmy was cycling into mortal danger. As clearly as if the words were painted on a big red neon sign in front of her, she knew it to be true.

So it seemed it was time to pay back some favours.

CHAPTER 44
SECRETS AND LIES

Jimmy's house was empty. He peeled off his saturated coat and flung it over a kitchen chair. Where was everyone? There was no scribbled note pinned to the cork-board and no message on the answer machine. He reached into his pocket and checked his mobile phone. It had one missed call listed, but no number. He shouted out as he made his way to the stairs. No one answered. Not even Gunner came to greet him.

For a moment he felt cheated. He had been ready for a doozy of an argument with his Grandad, and had been denied it. On the flip side, a wonderful opportunity had presented itself. If the house was empty he could search for the pendant without interruption or interference, and he thought he knew exactly where to start looking.

Taking the stairs two at a time he burst into his Grandma and Grandad's bedroom, flicked the light switch and closed the curtains before diving into the nearest drawer. The guilt of trespassing into his grandparents' personal belongings weighed heavy on his mind but he just kept thinking of the secrets and lies that had been told over the past forty years and ploughed on. After all, if his Grandad had done those things JoJo said, then he deserved to have his private possessions invaded and if he didn't, then snooping around was surely worth it to prove his innocence.

Three drawers and two cupboards later and Jimmy had drawn a big fat blank. There was no pendant. Not even a sign of an empty box which may hint such a pendant existed. There was however something about the atmosphere within the room. The longer he stood there, the more he was sure that this was where the answer lay. Of course that sounded ridiculous. How could he be sure of something like that? But he just did. He reasoned that because the pendant had belonged to his Mum, he could feel its … well, energy for want of a better word and that energy was definitely telling him that he was in the right place. Cat would have said it was psychic mumbo jumbo and a few days ago he would have probably agreed but when you've seen the things he had in the last seventy-two hours, he was willing to try anything.

So, feeling more than a little silly, he stood bolt upright in the middle of the room, closed his eyes and tried to summon up the force.

After a minute or two of looking as if he needed the toilet, he gave up. The only thing he felt – apart from a pain in his head from squinting too hard – was a desperate need to get out of his wet clothes.

That's when the silver glint of light reflecting off the corner of a picture frame curiously drew his eye.

The frame was on his Grandma's dresser. It had been stuffed between an old heart shaped music box and a vanity mirror obscuring the picture within. He found that odd. Why hide a photograph? He walked over and picked it up. A smile lit his face. He'd found what he was looking for.

* * *

At the foot of the stairs the scarred man breathed heavily. The boy was searching for something. He just knew it. He prayed that his instincts were wrong, that it was just some misplaced item of vital importance to a teenager – like his zit cream or something. But when Jimmy bolted out of his grandparents' bedroom clutching two keys in his hand, he knew what must be done.

* * *

In the photograph Jimmy could have been no more than one year old. His Mum, who was laughing joyfully, was holding him whilst his Grandad posed proudly by their side. Jimmy had never seen the picture before in his life, but he certainly recognised the pendant hanging loosely from his Mum's neck and the outhouse in the background. The picture had been taken here in his Grandad's very yard. It was the clue Jimmy needed.

When you're little – and even when you think you've grown up as Jimmy did now – there is always a place, be it a room, a locked cupboard or a secret box or drawer, that adults disliked kids nosing around in. The outhouse at the back of the garden was just such a place.

Tucked away and mostly hidden from view by two large willow trees that draped over it in a kind of living veil, it was the one place Jimmy had never been allowed into, either alone or with his Grandad present. Jimmy had always wondered why. Unfortunately he was pretty sure he now knew.

It wasn't just the extraordinary amount of secrecy that convinced him the outhouse held the answers. Neither was it the presence of the two keys he had found Velcroed to the back of the picture frame – keys which would no doubt fit the two huge padlocks visible in the photograph. Rather, it was the number painted on a little plaque nailed to the door in an attempt to make it look like a house number. An hour ago he wouldn't have given it any thought but now a shiver of ice that had nothing to do with his cold wet clothes, ran down his back. It couldn't possibly be coincidence. The chances were infinitesimal.

The number was 456.

CHAPTER 45

BLAME IT ON THE WEATHERMAN

It was dark – correction, it was very dark and quite frankly, with the rain beating a tattoo on the roof and the wind whistling through the branches of the willow trees like the songs of ghosts, Jimmy was having serious bravery issues.

456, the number of the experiment. The answers had to be in here.

He was also having lock problems. The keys were in his fingers, the padlock was right in front of him, but could he get one to go in the other?

"Bloody hell," he cursed as the key slipped out of his wet fingers for the fifth consecutive time. He blinked the rain out of his eyes and looked anxiously behind him. "Just calm down," he told himself. "This is the same garden you've been in a thousand times before. Now get a grip."

He tried again and this time the key went in and the lock pinged open.

Water was now pouring from his fringe in a constant stream and he just knew that tomorrow he'd have a cold and be sneezing as if he'd fallen in a pepper pot.

He dislodged the padlock and slid open the bolt it had been holding back but the door wouldn't budge. Damn. Then he remembered – the other key.

He fished it out of his sopping pocket and searched for the lock but it wasn't in an obvious place. *Why didn't I bring a torch? That would have been the sensible thing to do.*

Ten more seconds of being pelted with rain followed before he located the lock an inch from the top of the door frame. He reached up and heard a satisfying click as the lock turned and the door swung open. He was in.

The first thing he saw was absolutely nothing. It was pitch black. The kind of black where it seems light is just too scared to come anywhere near and it smelt fusty like fresh air hadn't been invited in for a long, long time.

He ran his hand up and down the walls to his left and right and located what he hoped was a light switch. He flicked it and breathed easy as a fluorescent tube began to splutter and strobe as if it had been woken from a good sleep and was complaining bitterly about it.

When it finally settled, Jimmy stepped out of the rain and into a whole lot more trouble.

✣ ✣ ✣

The scarred man was entirely sick of the storm. He hated the wind, he hated the rain but not as much as he hated wind and rain together.

He'd let Jimmy approach the outhouse partly out of curiosity, but mostly to put off as long as possible what he had to do next.

If Jimmy knew about the outhouse, then the secret was out and forty years of covering up was about to unravel before his very eyes. He couldn't allow that to happen.

It didn't please him to know his instincts had been correct because it meant having to deal with the boy but there had already been so much sacrifice.

He waited until Jimmy found the light switch then he made his move.

✣ ✣ ✣

At the barn, JoJo and 2B were finally alone. Halfpint, Paige and Cornelius had called it a night soon after the rain started.

Several times 2B had tried to ask his sister what was wrong (because something clearly was) only to be met each time with a shake of the head.

"Has it got something to do with going home?" he ventured.

JoJo said nothing.

"Don't you want to go or something?"

"Of course I want to go home. It's just …"

"Just what? Is it Jimmy? You two spent a lot of time on your own tonight." He paused, thinking. Making two and two make sixteen. "Do you fancy him or something?"

JoJo laughed. "2B, for goodness sake. Just because I spend some time with a boy doesn't automatically mean I fancy him. We were discussing something private if you must know."

"That's a 'yes' then," he said quietly.

"What? No! It's a 'no'. Definitely a no."

2B rolled his eyes and shook his head. "Huh, fancying a human. Gross."

"I said. I do not fancy any human," JoJo said sternly.

"Uh Huh. If you say it enough times you might even believe it."

"Oh shut up," she barked.

"There. Told you," 2B said in a superior tone. "Very defensive. You wouldn't be nearly as bothered if you didn't want to *snog* him."

JoJo put her head in her hands and screamed. Little brothers. Good for nothing except using as the occasional punch bag.

"If you must know, I think he's in trouble." she said, getting up and beginning to pace the floor.

That made 2B stop. "What sort of trouble. Is that why he ran out of here so quickly? Is it to do with Damien Dirt?"

JoJo shook her head. "I don't know what sort of trouble, or why he ran out of here – not exactly, anyway. But it's nothing to do with that twerp Dirt that's for sure."

2B jumped to his feet. "So are we going to help him?"

JoJo turned. "I am, yes," she said.

2B jumped to his feet.

"Oh. No. You're not leaving me here," he snapped.

"Oh, I so am."

"No way," 2B argued. "He saved my life and yours. If he is in trouble then I want to help."

"It's too dangerous. I can't protect you. I don't even know where he's gone precisely."

"Then I can help look."

"No," she said firmly.

For a moment, she thought she had got through to him then he exploded with rage.

"Do you know what, I hate you. You always do this. When you want someone's help, its all, *'oh please, trust me, it'll be all right, I can't possibly do it without you'* and people do, because you're JoJo, and JoJo's a bloody genius who can't do any wrong. But, when someone else wants to do something, you're all, *'No, you can't possibly do that, because it's far too dangerous and you might get yourself killed.'* Well, answer me this, JoJo. How much more dangerous can what you're going to do be, than chasing down a grommet."

JoJo gazed at 2B, somewhat shocked. Then she sighed. She had no argument. He was right. She did manipulate people. She had manipulated him to come here in the first place, hadn't she? But sometimes, when you were good at getting your own way, it was difficult to change.

"Fine," she said eventually. "Grab your coat. We've got a human to save."

2B clapped his hands together. "Yes! Finally a chance to get out of this place."

JoJo huffed, "Yeah, well don't get too excited. You haven't seen the weather yet."

* * *

The outhouse was about twenty five feet long. Benches ran down either side and shelves lined the walls. There was not a single window and the only entrance and exit was the door through which Jimmy had just walked. Slowly he stepped in, the hairs on his arms standing on end. It was as if the entire room was charged with the same energy as he had felt in the bedroom.

There were boxes everywhere. Pushed against walls, balanced three high under the benches and filling the entire shelves. Some were sealed shut with brown parcel tape whilst others lay open, papers spilling out onto the floor. It was as if someone had put their entire life into cardboard and then locked them in here. He picked out one of the papers at random. Stamped across the top in red ink were four words.

Top Secret. Restricted Access.

He reached down and plucked another one from a different box. Same four words.

The letterheads were definitely military (two swords crossing an eagle). The documents were reports of UFO sightings dated twenty or so years ago, one in Italy, the other in Texas USA.

Jimmy's heart was sinking. It was not what he had hoped to find. He kept telling himself that bits of paper on their own didn't prove a thing, but he was fast losing the battle with his own common sense.

He walked in a daze to the far end of the building where a large corkboard filled the wall. It was so crammed with newspaper clippings, maps, pencil diagrams, letters, photographs and scribbled notes that there was actually no cork left to be seen. He sighed. It would take days to go through everything here. Days he didn't have. He glanced at a few random pieces, but none of it meant a thing except…

…There was one photograph. It was an old grainy black and white image pinned beneath three scrawled pencil notes. He unpinned it and stared for several seconds before the full enormity of what he was looking at sank in. When it did, it sank with the force of a ten tonne barrel of lead.

Two men stared back at him. One, dressed in what appeared to be a military uniform, he didn't recognise, but the second he knew only too well. Yes he was younger, yes he had more hair, but there could be no doubt. It was his Grandad.

The photograph had been taken from a gantry overlooking what appeared to be a large aircraft hanger. Below the men, in the background only just visible, was the distinctive teardrop shape of an X1 Star Seeker engine. Worse, round his Grandad's neck was the trophy Jimmy was now searching for forty years on. The missing half of the union necklace.

The photograph slipped from Jimmy's hand. It was the irrefutable proof he'd been dreading. Everything JoJo said had been true. His Grandad was a kidnapper, a thief, a murderer.

He felt a sudden and desperate need to be out of this place. It was as if the whole room and its contents had suddenly focused into perspective. And it was horrible.

Over there on a shelf Jimmy saw the charred and blackened remains of a burnt out PlasmaTab. Over here a locked silver box labelled 'Anilar. Confidential.'

Now he looked with eyes untainted by the need to prove his Grandad's innocence, he realised that everything in this place related to the SpaceCoyotes and experiment 456. It was sick and depraved.

The most chilling of the rooms hideous collection were the six boxes lined up on a shelf to Jimmy's left. Their labels sent chills through his body.

'Ratan Stol', 'Mathius Scar', 'Sakuro Mantos', 'Com Standish', Obel Scar and 'Willum Havelok.'

A box for each of the SpaceCoyotes.

In an almost trance-like state Jimmy found himself moving towards the box of Willum Havelok. On tiptoes, he retrieved it from the shelf. He placed it on the table and slit the parcel tape holding its top together. Hardly daring to breathe, he slowly folded the brown box lid over and peered inside.

There was no necklace, only Willum's blue five star uniform neatly folded in the bottom, a name badge bearing his rank and title, a cap and an envelope. Jimmy looked again. *The envelope.* Scribbled on the back was a name. It read, Jimmy.

He snatched it out, gazing in disbelief at his name. Why would there be a letter addressed to him in the box of Willum Havelok's belongings?

He tucked his finger roughly under one corner and made to rip it open but the sound of a rubber sole squelching on concrete made him stop. He spun around and let out a funny breathless squeak.

A man, a horribly scarred man, stood in the doorway, dripping like a melting shadow.

The man stepped forward, the light illuminating his face further. Impossible as it sounded, Jimmy knew him. Or his face at least. Like his Grandad, he was much older now, but the distinctive scar hadn't changed in forty years. This was the man stood to his Grandad's right in the photograph over-looking the Star Seeker. This man had been part of it too. Every nerve in Jimmy's body began to tingle.

As coolly as you like, the scarred man tipped his hat forward emptying the brim of water before reaching into his jacket pocket and retrieving something small and very, very sharp. Jimmy gasped and the light glinted like a solitary star off the tip of a hypodermic needle.

With the precision of a doctor, the scarred man ejected a small quantity of liquid from the syringe and said, "I'm sorry Jimmy. I really am," his voice hoarse like a roller skate riding over a gravel path.

Jimmy didn't know what to do. He stuffed the envelope into his back pocket and began to back away. What was the man going to be sorry about? What did he want? Where was his Grandad?

Jimmy glanced around nervously searching for a way out. But the man was blocking his only exit. So what now? He could fight, but Jimmy was not exactly built for hand to hand combat against an adult (not even against someone his own age if the truth be told) and without any kind of a weapon, his options were as limited as a dog's vocabulary.

In the absence of anything resembling a brain-wave, he took what most people would consider the most cowardly, but ultimately, most sensible decision.

He ran. Fast. He ran with purpose and determination and with his head down like a battering ram.

As he drew closer Jimmy hurled Willum Havelok's box blindly from under his arm as hard as he could but the scarred man was ready and dodged easily. What the man wasn't ready for, however, was the very wet patch of mud, deposited earlier by Jimmy's right trainer, he had just stepped in. It had left that patch of ground with less traction than a banana skin on an ice-rink.

Just as Jimmy got within striking distance of the needle, the scarred man's legs went from under him. One slid under the table, the other caught under the weight of his falling body. He went down hard with a painful yell.

Jimmy hurdled over him, landing with a splash on the wet grass outside. He chanced a glance back. The scarred man lay unmoving, but groaning. Curiosity being what it is Jimmy leant forward for a closer look. He gasped. The syringe had snapped clean in two. Unfortunately for the scarred man, the half containing the needle was sticking out of his right thigh muscle with half of its contents injected.

"Serves you right." Jimmy shouted through the wind and rain.

He flicked off the light and slammed the door shut, quickly locking the padlocks. Then he set off running.

It was clear now that they – whoever 'they' were – knew about JoJo, 2B, the landing and Jimmy's part in it. It also stood to reason that if they were scared of having experiment 456 exposed, JoJo would be the next obvious target, if she hadn't been targeted already.

With the storm still raging in all its glory, Jimmy splashed to the front gate, grabbed his bicycle and pedaled for all he was worth. He just hoped he would make it in time.

CHAPTER 46

RIDERS ON THE STORM

JoJo and 2B didn't so much walk as trudge and slosh their way from the barn. Water streamed past them, cutting furrows in the softening ground as the wind lashed angry raindrops into their faces like lead shot from a gun.

"Great weather they have here," shouted JoJo sarcastically over the gale. "Remind me to come here more often."

2B kept his head down.

By their side, Arachno flew a watching patrol but even he was having difficulty maintaining a straight line and keeping a check that the route ahead was clear. Water was never the perfect partner for sophisticated nano-engineering and wind played absolute havoc with his micro pneumatic vertical stabilizers.

They had walked barely fifty metres from the barn when Arachno's senses alerted him to some movement behind them. He turned (with difficulty) in mid air. He saw nothing except a wall of rain. He scanned the immediate area. The noise was there again and whatever it was, it was getting closer but he still couldn't pinpoint anything. He frowned. If CoyoteBots had the capacity to get nervous, this would be one of those times.

He turned to warn JoJo, but she had moved on, unaware of the potential problem. He jetted off after her but didn't make it very far.

From out of nowhere a quad bike rocketed into their path moving so fast it left the ground. Mud and sludge sprayed everywhere. Arachno was engulfed. His sensors were blinded instantly.

He flew on but almost immediately collided with something solid and dropped to the ground. As the filthy black mud began to wash over him, a systems check revealed at least two of his eight arms were broken. Unable to gain enough purchase to lever himself out of the sticky ground it took only a matter of seconds for him to be swallowed by gushing torrent.

* * *

JoJo never saw the attack coming. The whistling and whining of the wind blocked out the noise of the three quad bike engines and the blackness of the night had camouflaged them perfectly behind the trees.

The shock of the assault stunned her. She screamed and pulled 2B close as the bikes circled them like angry orcas gathering in their prey.

The riders wore black clothes and black helmets. They looked like blurry shadows as the screaming engines revved with animal ferocity. Earth and mud sprayed up in the air as exhaust fumes blended with the rain creating a grey wet smoke screen.

Suddenly the front bike peeled off and the second rider chanced his arm, swerving in close and aiming a kick at 2B. As JoJo tried to cover her brother she was suddenly slammed in the back by something – or someone – very big and heavy. 2B was popped from her grasp as she was flattened face first into the mud.

Her assailant, who must have been twice her body weight pinned her in the sludge. The breath left her body as though it was escaping from a high-pressure valve and she yelped in agony as her left arm was jerked up her back.

She lifted her head from the mucky water and desperately yelled out, "2B!" With great relief she saw his feet sploshing through the bouncing rain running back towards the barn. "Goooo," she screamed "get away." A punch was slammed into her kidneys for her trouble. If she could have doubled up in pain she would have.

Two more followed. The last one was harder than she had ever been hit before and it took the last bit of fight from her. She sank into the mud coughing and wretching, resigned to her fate.

A heavy black boot stepped down in front of her nose. It splashed dirty mud into her face which she spat away. The person in the boot squatted till their black visored face was mere inches from her own.

"Greetings," it said in a muffled, male tone. "Terrible weather for the time of year, don't you think? Never mind though, I can assure you that it won't bother you for very much longer. Not where you're going."

JoJo gritted her teeth. She wanted nothing more than to reach inside that visor and poke the guy's eyes out.

"And don't think about resisting anymore. We know where your brother is hiding." His eyes indicated the barn. "It would be a real shame if he were to have a nasty accident while you're away. All those rusty bits of sharp metal. Brrrrrrr." He pretended to tremble.

JoJo bucked, but the heavy thug just held her tighter.

The guy in front of her put a gloved hand to his visor and slid it up.

"Shall we go then?" he said.

When JoJo saw who was behind the tinted plastic, not for the first time this week, she felt her whole world tip on its axis and slide off in some unknown, but very unpleasant direction.

* * *

With a squeal of brakes, Jimmy skidded to a halt at the top of the hill overlooking the barn. He couldn't see a lot through the weather, but he could see at least two or three quad bikes buzzing around the huddled figures of JoJo and 2B like malicious bluebottles. His heart sank. He was too late. They had found her and they had come mob handed.

His wiped the rain from his eyes and felt nothing but anger as he watched the drama unfold. He saw 2B make his escape then watched as JoJo's captors laid their fists into her. Jimmy felt every punch as if it had landed on his own body.

There was nothing for it. There was absolutely no way he was going to sit back and let them take her and do to her what they had done to the other SpaceCoyotes.

He picked up his feet and set off through the mud, his head reeling with ideas of what to do.

By the bottom of the hill, he had a plan.

* * *

The three bikers clearly weren't expecting trouble because they weren't rushing. This worked in Jimmy's favour.

At the bottom off the hill, rather than simply wading straight in with an attack which would be doomed to failure, he used the cover of the rainfall to sneak up behind a large tree. Just by chance, it happened to be next to where one of the attackers had left their quad bike idling away.

The attacker whose visor was up, seemed to be directing the other two. Jimmy made a mental note that he was most likely the leader.

They manhandled JoJo forcibly to her feet, where a gag was tied around her mouth. Amazingly her arms and legs were left unbound. But JoJo didn't make a move against them and he wondered why.

With reluctance and anger burning in her eyes, she climbed onto the bike behind the man who had attacked her, and despondently wrapped her arms around him as he revved his engine.

The leader approached her and said something. The noise of the rain prevented Jimmy hearing it but he certainly saw the needle in his hand, and saw him stab JoJo in the thigh with it. *Just like the scarred man at the outhouse,* Jimmy thought.

JoJo yelled a swear word and went to kick out, but slumped unconscious against her rider before her leg was halfway towards its intended target.

Jimmy resisted the temptation to bolt out and try to free her. One against three was poor odds. He had to stick to his original plan, although with JoJo unconscious, it did change things.

271

Soon all the bikes had a rider, including the one next to Jimmy.

Tight behind the tree Jimmy heard the engines rev and smelt the pungent gasoline.

This was it.

The leader accelerated in front and was followed closely by the one with JoJo. Jimmy, let them go.

He was targeting the third quad bike.

His adrenaline pumping, Jimmy took hold of a low branch and as the bike set off, swung his whole body up into the air in an arc around the tree. His idea was to become a human sledgehammer, his body the handle, his feet the hammer.

He timed it to perfection. At the apex of the arc, his feet connected with the helmet of the quad bike rider, knocking him clean off into the mud. The bike, still in gear, continued forward bouncing through the mud. Jimmy chased the bike and vaulted over its rear two wheels landing squarely on the seat.

He panted desperately as he pulled back on the throttle, careful not to show himself in the mirrors of the other riders. He hoped that the weather would help keep him hidden.

As he rode, he found his mobile phone in his pocket and speed dialed Halfpint. There was no answer. He quickly left a message explaining what had happened leaving out every detail apart from the essentials. JoJo had been captured and was in danger, 2B was alone in the barn. Under the circumstances, Jimmy thought that would be enough to get Halfpint's attention. He just prayed that he picked up the message in time.

With the storm continuing to growl as if the sky had a bad case of stomach ache, Jimmy laid himself low on the bike protecting his body from the worst of it and followed the others to who knew where.

CHAPTER 47

WITHOUT THE GIRL

Wherever Jimmy thought the riders' final destination would be, this wasn't it. Not even close.

For the first mile or so Jimmy had struggled to keep up because he couldn't figure out how to change gears on the bike. It appeared to be an expensive custom model and unlike anything Jimmy had seen before. Only when he had mastered the basics did he turn his mind to what exactly he was getting himself into and where he might be heading.

His biggest fear was that JoJo would be transferred onto some other vehicle that would prove impossible to follow, or worse, driven to some top-secret compound with fifty foot walls of flesh-ripping razor wire. In fact pretty much anywhere wouldn't have caused as much surprise as when the bikes turned into Apple Valley High School and parked by a side entrance close to the gym block.

Maybe what he did next was stupid. He could have called the police and let them handle it but he didn't trust anybody right now except himself and there was no way he was going anywhere without JoJo. So he followed them in.

Dumping his bike out of sight he trailed the riders on foot. The school grounds were eerily quiet as he splashed his way over the playing fields, his trainers sodden, probably ruined.

Once inside the school, following the riders' path proved easy. Wet footprints and the unmistakable squeak of wet shoes on polished tiles conveniently betrayed their every step. Jimmy pulled off his own shoes,

Tied the shoelaces together and hung them round his neck so as not to make the same mistake. As he ran he couldn't help but think how different the corridors had been earlier that afternoon, full of kids, full of life. Now they seemed dark and forbidding.

He caught the kidnappers as they were pushing through the double doors into the science labs. Jimmy held back, peering around the wall. JoJo was being carried fireman's lift style over the shoulder of the second bike rider. She was still out cold, her arms flopping to the rhythm of the biker's movements. Anger once again welled inside him at the injustice of it all.

He trailed them down the dark corridors passing changing rooms, which even after a week, still stunk of sweaty sports shirts and even sweatier socks.

Finally, after another set of double doors the puddles stopped at the door of classroom B12 – one of the biology laboratories.

For a long while he hid and waited. Eventually when no-one came out, he crouched low and tip-toed forward, nervous of making any tell-tale noises. There was a square window two thirds of the way up the door. He pressed his ear to the varnished wood just below it, listening for … something, anything. All was quiet. Slowly, like a tortoise testing the air outside its shell, Jimmy raised himself level with the glass pane and peered in.

Moonlight glinted off the glass test tubes, conical flasks and assorted beakers which were lined up along the benches ready for the new term. In the far corner he saw her. JoJo, trussed to a chair, her head hanging limply on her chest. Crucially though, she seemed to be alone. He wondered why. Like all the school laboratories, room B12 had two doors – just in case. After all, chemicals and school children together in the same room often resulted in unexpected minor fires and explosions. B12's emergency exit led into a different corridor, unseen from this vantage point. Maybe Jimmy was in luck and they had left through that door and gone in search of the third rider. They must be missing him by now.

Jimmy could feel his heart rate quicken as he sensed his chance to free JoJo. He let his eyes drift to the floor while he took a few breaths to psyche himself up. That is when he noticed his mistake, a mistake that in all probability could well turn out to be his last.

He'd been so stupid. Two pairs of footprints had come up the corridor. If he'd have taken the time to look properly, he would have seen that only one pair had made it as far as the laboratory.

That meant …

… He looked up straight into the face – or rather the helmet – of one of the riders. Dressed entirely in black leather, he looked like Jimmy's shadow come to life. His visor was down. Droplets of rain had collected on its surface and now sparkled like stars in a space vista. At another time Jimmy might have seen the irony in that but not now because, although there was nothing to see of the man beneath it, Jimmy was certain he was grinning.

Before he could react, the door to the laboratory swung open and the second biker stepped out. Jimmy was caught in a rat trap. The second, thinner biker (the leader) tilted his head at Jimmy and raised a finger ticking it in a left, right motion as if to indicate that Jimmy had been a naughty boy. Something about the way he did it struck Jimmy as familiar …

… Then, with a sharp *crack*, that would have made a rutting stag wince, the first biker's helmet connected with the side of Jimmy's skull like a tea spoon smashing the top of a boiled egg. Pain like he'd never known pierced his head and in that briefest of moments before he blacked out and crashed to the floor, he thought not only of how he had failed JoJo, but how he was sure that his head had just been split cleanly in two.

CHAPTER 48

AN INNOCENT MAN

There were no words to describe the pain throbbing in Jimmy's skull when he woke. If there was, it would probably read something like '*/@".!.!#' and make the sound of a drum kit falling out of a window; although that would in no way do it full justice.

As Jimmy attempted to prise open his eyelids, which for all the world felt like they had been glued together with 'Uhu', he sensed three things. Firstly he was tied up – his arms were bound behind the chair in which he was sitting. Secondly, bright sunshine was streaming through the windows meaning he had been unconscious for at least the entire night. Thirdly, despite the daylight making the whole eye-opening thing doubly bloody difficult, he knew someone was staring at him.

"Finally!", the someone exclaimed irritably. "At last he wakes up."

"Uh," mumbled Jimmy.

"You've been asleep for hours. C'mon, snap out of it." The person gave the chair a shove. Jimmy numbly tried to acclimatise himself to the surroundings. His bruised synapses flickered gently, beginning to gradually join the dots of the previous night's memories. Unfortunately a torrent of nightmares quickly followed behind. His Mum at the concert. The outhouse with all those boxes of dead men's things. His Grandad the murderer. The scarred man with the syringe and JoJo being whisked away by leather clad kidnappers …… JoJo!

"You're here," Jimmy said softly so as not to detonate his head.

"Of course I'm here," JoJo snapped. "I've been here for hours, although unlike you, I've been awake!"

Jimmy squinted through the yellow light at her. She was by his side in an identical chair, identically strapped to it. She did not look happy.

"They headbutted me," Jimmy said weakly.

"Arrrhh. How tewwibul. Did widdel Jimmy get a bangy wangy on his heady weady. Well tough! They stuck a bloody needle in me I'll have you know. I hate needles, the Sineoks!*

"I was trying to rescue you," argued Jimmy.

"Well you didn't do a very good job did you?", replied JoJo ungratefully.

"Well I'm very sorry for only getting my head bust open for you. Next time I'll try and lose a limb shall I?"

"Oh don't be stupid. What I meant was that I'd have preferred you not to get caught at all. Anyway, there's no blood so he couldn't have hit you that hard."

"Not Hard!" Jimmy huffed. "I was head butted with a crash helmet. Do you know how tough those things are? It could have given me serious brain damage."

"I doubt it."

"Look, what's your problem?" spat Jimmy, feeling that his efforts weren't exactly being appreciated in quite the way he would have hoped.

JoJo's exasperation boiled over. "My problem? I'll tell you my problem shall I? It's the day of the concert, the day when I'm supposed to be going home. But I'm not going home am I? No. Instead I've been stabbed, drugged, kidnapped, tied-up god-only-knows where. My little brother is alone, probably scared witless worrying about what's happened to me and the only person who knows where I am and could have done something about it, is sitting by my side trussed up like a

---

*Again, the literal meaning of this colourful Larian word has been omitted so as not to offend readers of a sensitive nature. Suffice to say, it is not a term of endearment.

Jiggle bird. Oh yeah, and your pocket has been vibrating, every five minutes for the past two hours, and it's really starting to freak me out."

Silence descended. Jimmy glanced at his pocket. His mobile phone was in there. No doubt it would be Halfpint wondering what the hell was happening.

"Point taken," said Jimmy calming down. "I'm sorry I botched the rescue okay. Now, will you stop shouting? My head feels like it's going to explode."

"I'm sorry too," said JoJo, "but this is so frustrating. And I'll tell you this much. If I ever see Damien Dirt again, I'm gonna kick his spoilt butt to the Vibex peninsula and back."

Jimmy's brow wrinkled at Damien's name. "What's he got to do with any of this?"

"What do you mean *'what's he got to do with any of this?'* Everything. That's what. It was Damien Dirt and those stupid hooligan monkeys of his that put us here. Don't tell me you didn't know."

Jimmy was dumbstruck. "But … I thought … I mean … Damien Dirt! Are you sure?"

"Positive. We had a little chat before he stuck me with that needle." She jiggled on the chair trying to get comfy. "The moron has somehow got it into his thick skull that we were planning on replacing him as singer … with me!"

Jimmy was incredulous. "But I thought it was them that had found you. You know, just like forty years ago."

"So did I," said JoJo angrily, "until I saw Damien's ugly mug under that visor."

Jimmy shook his head. "Damien Dirt … But that's fantastic," he said, breaking out into a smile.

"Oh yeah, fantastic. If you like being tied to a chair it's your lucky day."

"No you don't understand. When I saw them taking you, I kept thinking back to those transcripts you showed me. I had visions of them doing awful things to you – experimenting on you. To find out it's all because Dirt is scared he won't be singing at the Centenary Celebrations … well, it's such a relief. I don't think I could have handled it if anything had happened to you."

For a moment JoJo mellowed – a little.

"You know what," she said, "that's the nicest thing a human has ever said to me."

Jimmy blushed slightly. "That's not saying a lot is it? You've only ever talked to five."

"It doesn't matter," she said earnestly. "It was still a nice thing to say."

"Yeah well."

Jimmy gazed around the lab, almost nostalgically.

"I haven't been in here for years you know," he said. "It's ironic actually. But this is the same lab where I stopped Dirt killing that frog. This is where it all started between him and me."

"Fascinating. It's a shame you couldn't have avoided that crash helmet, then maybe you could have ended it here as well. Lets just save the reminisces and try to figure a way of getting out of here shall we."

Jimmy sighed. "Your nice side didn't last very long."

JoJo flashed him a cold stare.

"Fair enough," said Jimmy and began testing the strength of his bindings. They were tight, very tight. They felt like those plastic bag ties which the police use nowadays instead of the metal handcuffs. There was no way he would be able to snap them or slide his hands out. Whatever Damien was up to, he certainly didn't intend for them to escape any time soon. He huffed and wriggled into his chair to take the pressure off his shoulders which were beginning to ache. He had the feeling it was going to be a long, long day.

* * *

The morning wore on to midday. Time moved slower than a plough being pulled by an arthritic ox.

Together Jimmy and JoJo passed the time struggling endlessly against their ties and talking an awful lot.

"So you're a what … A seer?" said Jimmy, after JoJo explained once again to him about coming of age and the gift set of genes.

"It appears so, yes."

"So you can see into my mind?"

JoJo shifted uncomfortably. She supposed this was a question she was going to get asked a lot now. But it was tricky. She didn't particularly like the idea that someone may be able to read her mind. What if she really hated that persons guts, but was pretending she didn't. They would see the truth. In the same way, she doubted whether other people would like it too. There was just nowhere to hide when someone was reading your mind. Her reply therefore erred on the side of caution, (i.e. she lied)

"No I can't," she said flatly.

"I bet you can. What am I thinking right now?" Jimmy persisted.

"That you wish we could get out of here probably," said JoJo non-committaly.

"Lucky guess," smiled Jimmy. He knew that she could read his mind. He had felt her in there when they had been on the stage during the picture walking. It seemed for her own reasons though, it was something she didn't want to discuss so he changed subject.

"So picture walking is like dreaming then – only on foot?"

"Um, yes and no. I believe we really went into that picture. Not literally obviously, but in every other way. In our minds and in our hearts it was as if we were truly there so the experience was real enough."

"Awesome. And it can work with any picture then?"

"I don't know. I guess so. As long as it's a real photo I think, not a drawing or anything. But it's never happened to me before so it's all new to me too."

"Wow," he said contemplating the possibilities. "Imagine. If only they'd have invented cameras earlier, History homework would have been a breeze."

* * *

Not too far away in the doorway of the outhouse in Jimmy's garden, the scarred man was being shaken roughly by the shoulders. He stirred, very slowly.

"Hmm ... Wha ..."

"Where is he?" barked Jimmy's Grandad, who was the one doing the shaking.

"Who ... Where?"

"Jimmy? Where is Jimmy? He was supposed to be here with you. Wake up for pity's sake."

The scarred man lazily tried to pull himself up into a sitting position but yelped in pain as the syringe dug into his leg.

Jimmy's Grandad saw the needle. "Oh gods," he said standing up. "What happened? No, wait, don't bother explaining, there's no time."

"I'm sorry," mumbled the scarred man as he gripped the broken syringe, held his breath and yanked it out.

"No. It's my fault. I shouldn't have left this to you. It's my mess. It's always been my mess. I should have dealt with it a long time ago."

He helped the man to his feet, then walked to the doorway.

"I want you to stay here and get things prepared. If Jimmy sees you now, he will only run again. It's time to end this thing once and for all."

* * *

Midday marched onwards into the afternoon. When the clock ticked past two thirty, Jimmy sighed. "We should be down at the Centenary stage now, soundchecking," he said solemnly.

That was it for JoJo, the last straw. Her frustration boiled over and she began violently rocking and writhing against her chair, shouting at the top of her voice.

"Woohh. Watch it," yelled Jimmy, as his chair was tipped backwards along with JoJo's

281

At the last second he pushed his weight forward and brought both front legs down with a bang. As they hit the floor Jimmy's seat let out a long creak like a door that desperately craved oil. JoJo stopped dead. Jimmy craned his neck back to view the chair from behind.

They were made from wood and looked pretty solid, apart from where the back piece was attached to the seat and legs. It was only a single joint and one that had seen better days. He thought back to all those times as a kid when he and his classmates had been told-off for rocking on two legs, in case the chair would either topple over or snap. This particular chair had obviously seen some pretty good two-legged action in its time. Maybe, he thought, they had been sitting on the answer all the time. If they could do what JoJo had just done a few more times and make the back snap …

"It'll hurt if we go over the back," said JoJo, obviously on the same wavelength.

"Better than being stuck here," replied Jimmy.

She couldn't argue with that. So between them they shuffled round to make sure they weren't going to land on anything dangerous if, and hopefully when, the back broke, and grinned at each other.

"After three then," said Jimmy, "but not so hard that we go all the way over."

JoJo tutted. "Just count and let's get on with it."

They both leaned forward as far as their shoulders would allow and braced their knees. "One, two, thrrreeeeeee."

The two chairs lifted onto their back legs. Quickly they leant forward and brought them back down. A satisfying crack of wood on wood accompanied them.

They repeated the manoeuvre again and again. Every time the creak seemed to gain in depth and length. The joint was definitely working its way loose. Jimmy was panting. JoJo bit her lip in determined fashion.

Another push and this time there was tangible movement. The next one saw them almost topple backwards, but luckily they saved themselves in the nick of time.

"One more," breathed JoJo heavily. "One, more."

"Urgghh," grunted Jimmy, as all their weight went into the fraying joints. The two front legs lifted. The wood groaned like an old man's knees and finally, gloriously began to give way. For a second they were balanced perfectly centrally then the pressure on the joint grew … and snapped. A loud crack echoed around the room and Jimmy and JoJo hit the ground hard.

"Jeeeeezzzz," complained JoJo stretching her back, "that hurt a LOT. Are you okay?"

Jimmy's face was contorted in pain. "No. Ouch! I think … I've got a splinter in my bum," came the croaky reply.

JoJo burst out laughing. She couldn't help it

"I'm serious," said Jimmy indignantly. "I really think I've … Ouch, got a splinter in my bum. Either that or I've landed on a nail."

Tears were streaming down JoJo's face as Jimmy wriggled around trying to find some relief.

"Oh stop it," she snorted, dragging herself up. "Tell me. Should we head for the *rear* of the building to escape?"

"Oh very bloody funny," said Jimmy sourly.

"I'm sorry. No really I am. I shouldn't make fun of you when you got such a *bum* deal."

Jimmy sighed. "Is this going to go on much longer?"

JoJo giggled. "Not much. Another couple of hours should do it. And stop being so *stern* with me."

Just then the door to the laboratory swung open cutting JoJo's laughter dead. A man stepped in and glided around the front bench. He stopped when he reached the stranded pair. Staring hard, he lingered on JoJo.

"Well, well," he said, reaching into his pocket and pulling out a pack of cigarettes. He tapped one out and put it in his mouth but didn't light it. "Finally we meet. You won't believe how long I've been dying to talk to you, young lady."

He perched on a bench edge. "Please." He waved. "Find yourself

another seat. It appears the woodworm has had a field day with those."
He rolled the cigarette around his lips. Neither JoJo nor Jimmy moved.

"No? Very well, as you wish. I must say you look surprised to see
me. I don't know why. I would have hoped by now you would have
worked out why I'm here. But it seems from the dumb look on both
your faces that I will have to explain. I, children, am here to inform
you that your escape – such as it was – just got delayed. Permanently."

CHAPTER 49

SAY IT ISN'T SO

Jimmy watched with horror as the man he knew as the music manager Earl Cobs, stubbed out the cigarette he had never lit and retrieve something from within the folds of his long jacket. The something was a gun, but no ordinary human gun. With even Jimmy's limited experience he could tell it was a weapon constructed using Larian technology and it was pointed squarely at JoJo. Cobs was dressed exactly as before. His jet black glasses glinted in the sunlight as he eyed them with the menace of a tiger stalking its prey.

JoJo remained bold in the face of the weapon. All those feelings of menace and evil she had encountered at the Battle of the Bands when she first saw this man were back ... with interest.

"So," said Earl in a voice that seemed altogether deeper and more ... sinister than Jimmy remembered. "Finally I come face to face with the chosen one."

JoJo flinched. That was the name Lip Smear had taunted her with so many times at Nexus Hall. How did he know that?

"I must say, I was expecting somebody a little less ... oh I don't know, grubby."

"It's been a long week," said JoJo, tossing her matted hair out of her face.

"Then at least it is now coming to an end," he said chillingly.

JoJo shivered. The air in the room seemed to have dropped by a few degrees. Something here was very, very wrong. She felt as if she should know this man not as Earl Cobs, but as somebody else. What was it she was missing?

"Who are you? Because you're certainly no talent scout," she said.

Earl looked disappointedly at her. "You mean you still haven't worked it out. Tut, tut, and you being a straight A student. Tell me, rumour has it you are the best pilot never to have got into the academy. Better even than your traitorous Grandfather. Is that true?"

JoJo's face grew stern. "How do you know about my Grandfather?"

Earl smiled. "Oh he and I go way back. Forty years back in fact." He extended his arm and ran the barrel of the gun menacingly down JoJo's cheek. "And now here I am with the traitor's granddaughter before me, following in the family's rather dubious footsteps."

JoJo shook the gun off and narrowed her eyes. "Who are you I asked?"

"I, my treacherous little teenager, am your worst nightmare. The man your Grandfather betrayed forty years ago – the man with a very long memory." He turned his back and in an almost sing-song voice warbled. "Earl Cobs, Earl Cobs, mix up the letters and what have you got?"

JoJo stared unblinking.

Earl Cobs … Mix it up and what have you got … Forty years ago … Then it hit her. "My god," she said. "It's an anagram. You're … Obel Scar. Earl Cobs is Obel Scar."

Earl/Obel removed his glasses to reveal two eyes as black as the deepest abyss. "Very good. Not the most difficult of puzzles I'll grant you, but it kept me amused."

JoJo reeled backwards. "No, you can't be. You just can't."

"Oh I'm afraid I can be – in the flesh." He dragged out the shhhhh.

"But I thought you were one of the ……"

"Good guys? Aha." Obel laughed. "What can I say? History has been somewhat kind to me. You really should not believe everything you read, no matter *where* you may read it, JoJo."

Beside her Jimmy was beginning to look scared. "This has got nothing to do with JoJo singing at the Centenary Celebrations, has it?" he ventured rather dumbly.

JoJo and Obel exchanged eye contact. "Nothing at all, Jimmy," said JoJo quietly. "I think Damien was used as a stooge to get us here. Am I right?"

Obel nodded. "Correct. Such a covetous mind is easily made to do your bidding. You just have to know what buttons to push, like telling him that you were threatening to replace him in your band – sent him quite crazy with rage. When I told him I would sort it out, he was more than happy to bring you here for me"

JoJo sat straighter. "So now you've got us, what do you plan to do with us?"

"Oh I would have thought that was obvious seeing as I'm pointing a gun at you," he said.

"But why," she cried desperately. "What have I done wrong?"

"Wrong?" Obel screamed, his temper changing instantly. "You stand here on this wretched planet having placed the whole of Anilar at risk because of your selfish obsession and you dare to ask what you have done wrong."

JoJo was defiant. "But you can't just kill me. You'll never get away with it,"

"And why not exactly? No one knows you are here. You were very thorough about that. As far as anyone will know, you simply disappeared. A teenage runaway, never to be seen again. So you see, chosen one, you are going to die. And this time I will make no mistakes."

JoJo desperately fought her bindings, but it was no use. "What do you mean 'this time?'", she spat.

Obel perched on a stool and tapped the barrel of the gun on her forehead.

"Think girl. Think! Do you not remember the mystery of the green blip and the disappearing portal?"

"That was you?" she cried.

"Of course. And let me tell you, imitating a dimple probe and making an entire portal vanish takes a lot of work. You could at least have had the decency to smash into a rock like you were supposed to."

JoJo shook her head and thought back. "The grommets too I suppose?"

"An insurance policy. They were placed in suspended cryogenic animation with the re-animator set to thaw them out if ever your engines shut off. They would have worked too if it hadn't been for this meddling human jumping in, playing the hero."

Obel swung the gun around so it was pointing squarely at Jimmy. JoJo saw the fear in his eyes and the pure wave of hatred that was streaming from Obel.

"So all the time you knew I was coming here?" said JoJo, desperately trying to distract Obel's attention back to her.

"Correct, positively encouraged it in fact. You don't believe you could have really stolen a Star Seeker under our very noses do you? Surely not even you are that arrogant, or maybe you are. Your Grandfather certainly was."

All the time he spoke, the gun never moved. Keeping his eyes fixed firmly on Jimmy, Obel spoke to JoJo. "You know I'm going to kill him don't you? You can *sense* it."

JoJo tried not to show her terror for Jimmy's sake, but inside her heart was pounding as she watched him struggle against his bindings with hopeless futility.

"Oh dear. Poor little scared human," mocked Obel. "You know the best part though? It's all your fault JoJo. When he takes his last breath it will be because of you being here. I hope you remember that, JoJo. Goodbye, human."

Without pausing for breath, Obel fired the gun into Jimmy's chest. The air cracked and JoJo screamed louder than she had ever screamed before in her life.

It had happened so fast that Jimmy wasn't sure what actually had happened. Only when he felt the trickle of warm liquid tracking down onto his belly did he comprehend the horrific truth. He looked down and saw a hole in his shirt no bigger than his little finger. Around it a red stain was expanding. His eyes glazed with incomprehension as he realised it was his own blood. Like slowly closing the aperture on a camera lens, the light around him began to shrink until there was nothing more than a pin head visible.

That's when the pain came. Excruciating pain, mind-warping pain. Mercifully it was short lived because, as JoJo's screams became a distant beacon, an enormous sense of blackness and finality overcame him.

By the time Jimmy slid from the chair and hit the floor, he was already dead.

* * *

"Whhhyyyy?" screamed JoJo, beside herself with grief.

"He was a human," said Obel coldly.

"He was my friend." She spat.

"Well now he's a corpse. Get over it,"

With hatred burning through her whole body, she lunged at Obel, but he lashed his gun against her forehead sending her flailing back amongst the broken pieces of chair.

"Please don't do that again," he hissed aiming the barrel at her head. For a moment JoJo was convinced he was going to pull the trigger, but then he flipped the gun up.

"Not yet," he said, calm once more. "There's something I want answered first. How did you stop the plasma contamination? That CoyoteBot was reprogrammed perfectly to cut through those pipes."

"You re-programmed ScatterBot?"

Obel scoffed. "ScatterBot! Please. I re-programmed Pulp while he was out dropping cleaner bombs."

"PULP? But he …"

"Tried to kill you – yes."

"No." JoJo argued. "It had to be ScatterBot. Pulp tried to save me..."

Obel smirked. "ScatterBot is a useless bag of bolts. He couldn't cut through his own dinner never mind a plasma tube. Surely you didn't think...oh dear, you did."

JoJo thought back to the chaos. Was Obel telling the truth? Had she got it so wrong?

What if ScatterBot had caught Pulp in the act and raised the alarm, which in turn saw Pulp flee the scene and, in a bid to pin the sabotage on ScatterBot, return and attempt to destroy him before he could tell the truth. Rather than the selfless act of bravery she had believed it to be, had Pulp swallowed the Plasma purely by accident?

She cringed as she recalled ScatterBot's fading life-force. She had killed him thinking he was to blame. How could she have been so rash?

"Why are you doing all of this?" she cried desperately.

Before Obel could answer, an elderly gentleman suddenly stepped into the room catching them both off guard.

"I think I can answer that." He said softly. "Why don't you put the gun down Obel?"

Obel swung round. His eyes widened and the blood drained from his already pale face.

Seeing his reaction, JoJo stared at the new arrival. There was something in his features that she recognized. Could it be...? It was. It was Jimmy's Grandad, Obel's torturer from all those years ago.

"You," Obel hissed. "Yooouuuuuu."

Shaking wildly, he brought the gun around so Jimmy's Grandad was the new target. JoJo watched as forty years of pain and rage re-formed Obel's face into something not Larian, not human, just pure unadulterated hatred.

Jimmy's Grandad stepped into the room without so much as a care. He swept past, concerned only with one thing, his grandson's lifeless body. "You will at least allow him the dignity of having his hands untied." It wasn't a question.

Obel followed every step with the gun. "Like the dignity you offered my brother?" he spat viciously "You are dead. You are *dead*. I saw you die with my own eyes. I killed you."

"Clearly not," replied Jimmy's Grandad coolly.

As he knelt by Jimmy's side, his eyes burned with the most terrible pain of grief. He reached into a pocket and pulled out a pocket knife.

"Be careful old man," warned Obel.

Jimmy's Grandad sliced through the tough plastic bindings. Jimmy's hands slumped to the floor. Taking one in his own and with tears tracking slowly down his cheek, Jimmy's Grandad tenderly stroked his grandson's hair and kissed him just once on the temple. As he did so, unseen by the others he carefully pressed something into Jimmy's palm and closed his dead fingers around it. "For later," he whispered softly.

"So, Obel," he said getting to his feet. "You've come to take another one. Tell me, have the Admiralty changed their stance on the 'chosen ones' or is this another one of their 'publicity stunts'?"

"Be quiet," snarled Obel. "You have no idea what you are talking about. Tell me how you are here? I left you for dead, rotting in that festering barn."

"I know and that was no way to treat your best friend now, was it. Consider yourself crossed off my Christmas list."

Obel sneered. "There you go. Nothing changes does it? Always mocking. That's one of the things I hated about you."

"What were the others? My charm, my rakish good looks? You should try smiling once in a while Obel. It may help with all this hidden anger you have."

"I'll smile only when you take your last breath." Obel sneered.

Jimmy's Grandad glanced at JoJo. "See what I mean. Such rage, such melodrama. Do you think his Mummy didn't love him enough?"

Obel twitched his head. "Go ahead, make fun all you want. You're not the one with the gun."

"True, but at least I've got the brains."

JoJo frowned at the ensuing exchange. Something wasn't right. What did Jimmy's Grandad mean when he said 'Best friend?' How could these two people have ever been best friends?

Nevertheless, whatever Jimmy's Grandad had done in the past, he seemed to be on her side now at least. He was certainly all she had to help her out of this mess.

The two men were circling each other like duelers at dawn.

"Why is he doing this?" asked JoJo.

Never taking his eyes off Obel, Jimmy's Grandad replied. "Ahh, that's easy, JoJo. They are terrified that you may uncover the truth of what happened here forty years ago. So terrified, that they are quite willing to kill you to prevent the secret coming out."

JoJo slowly got to her feet.

"Stay where you are girl," Obel snapped fiercely. "Or else this touching family reunion ends right now."

JoJo stopped dead. Jimmy's Grandad stopped dead. Goose bumps rose like tiny volcano's on JoJo's arms as the room suddenly chilled.

Had he just said what she thought he had?

Obel sensed the mystification and tilted his head on one side curiously. He looked first at JoJo, then at Jimmy's Grandad. A knowing smirk grew slowly across his face. It was horrible.

"Oh now just hold on a minute here," he said. "Don't tell me that neither of you know who the other is?"

Jimmy's Grandad flinched.

"Oh I see. *You* do … but she doesn't."

Obel Laughed out loud. "Oh this is just precious. Absolutely precious." Smiling, he turned to JoJo. "Tell me Chosen One, why was it you risked everything to come here exactly?"

JoJo answered boldly. "Why should I……….."

"TELL ME WHY YOU CAME HERE!" Obel raged, his temper finally snapping.

"To find my Grandfather," she garbled quickly.

"Precisely. Well then, allow me to be the one to introduce you.

Chosen One, meet … can you sense the anticipation? – your very long lost Grandfather, Willum Havelok. Willum, say hello – and goodbye – to your granddaughter."

* * *

JoJo couldn't move. Her mind had gone into shut down. She couldn't take it in.

Somewhere in the room raised voices were arguing, but she could neither hear them clearly nor understand them. For her, the world had simply stopped turning.

After what might have been an age or just a few seconds, the gun was suddenly inches from her face and Obel's voice had drifted in from nowhere. He seemed to be enjoying himself. "And now, with this lovely reunion complete, it is time for you both to die."

His face was a mask of controlled insanity. Those pitiless eyes were the coldest, darkest thing JoJo had ever seen.

Obel smiled. "Consider yourself cleansed," he said.

Then he dropped unconscious to the floor like a heavy sack of gravel.

CHAPTER 50

BACK TO LIFE

THE BARN

The remaining members of Applejuice should have been at the Centenary field getting their equipment ready for the nights show, but they weren't. With Jimmy's disappearance and total lack of contact, they had remained at the barn and were now butting heads with a seriously annoyed Damien Dirt.

"Get it through your thick skulls," yelled Damien, tapping on Halfpint's head as if to indicate its hollowness. "Jimmy has chickened out, got cold feet, lost his bottle. He isn't coming so get over it."

"Stuff you Dirt," snapped Paige.

Damien grimaced. This was getting him nowhere. "So let me get this straight. You're saying that if Jimmy doesn't play, you're not playing? Does that about sum it up?"

"Got it in one Dirty boy," replied Paige facetiously.

He sighed. "Then I'm afraid you have left with me with little option."

He flipped open his mobile phone and speed dialed a number. A few moments passed while he waited for an answer then he said, "You have my authority to bring them down."

Paige and Halfpint looked at each other warily.

"If you would just care to take a look outside the window," said Damien in a self-satisfied tone.

They did and their jaws dropped.

Trundling down the hill was a line of four – no five – large yellow diggers. Their vast black wheels turned slowly as though they could hardly be bothered with the exertion, whilst their deep buckets stood aloft making them resemble armour plated elephants (albeit severely jaundiced ones).

"A little insurance policy I have taken out for just this very circumstance," explained Damien. "If you don't play tonight and look as though you're enjoying every minute of it, my men out there will reduce this place to scrap. Right now."

"You wouldn't dare," said Halfpint.

"Try me," said Damien, showing his best poker face.

"But you promised. You said Jimmy could have that lease."

"Oh promises smomishes. I don't see him here putting up a fight for them, do you?"

Paige looked disconcertedly at Halfpint who frowned at Cornelius. Damien Dirt had done it again. With the Star Seeker in the barn and Jimmy still missing since last night's snatch (2B had filled in the blanks for Halfpint), they couldn't possibly risk calling Damien's bluff this time. Whatever Jimmy had got himself into, he would be back, Halfpint knew it. He was just cutting it fine that was all.

"So what do you say?" sneered Damien. "Time is running out."

Halfpint reluctantly nodded.

"Excellent," smiled Damien clapping his hands together. "I'll tell them to turn around then shall I."

APPLE VALLEY HIGH. ROOM B12

Jimmy got to his feet tottering ungainly like a newborn gazelle whose legs were losing the battle against the weight of its body and the pull of gravity. He gazed down at his chest as his balance wavered and uncertainly pushed his index finger through the bullet hole in his shirt. He felt the skin underneath. It was unbroken and smooth. All the blood was dry. He felt like fainting.

Gripped tight in his other hand was something resembling a small can of deodorant. It was smoking slightly and venting an occasional blue spark into the air. His Grandad carefully prised it from his fingers.

"I'll have that. Welcome back son," he said, seemingly unsurprised by his grandson's Lazarus-like rise from the dead. He held the device for JoJo to see. "A Salton 3 disabler. Rather primitive and crude. I'm sure they've improved on the design by now. This one is rather old and … now broken by the looks of it."

He gazed at the stricken Obel. "Still, it did the trick. That shot should see him out for hours. Got him on the Achilles heel did you?"

Jimmy nodded blankly.

"That's my boy."

JoJo could not believe what she was seeing. Nothing that had happened in the last five minutes made any sense. On the outside she was desperately trying to retain an air of calmness whilst inside, deafening screams of perplexity were reverberating around her head shouting '*who, why, when, how, if, when, why,*' and '*Ahhhhh.*'

Jimmy was alive when he should be dead. Earl Cobs had turned out to be Obel Scar in disguise and definitely not the hero everyone thought he was, but rather a murdering monster. Whilst on the flip side, the murdering monster, Jimmy's Grandad, was not that at all – a murdering monster that is – but was in fact her lost Grandad, Willum Havelok.

Confusion didn't even come close.

"JoJo, you look terrified," said Willum softly. "Please don't be. Things will be all right now."

JoJo looked stunned. "All right? All right? I don't think I'm ever going to be all right again," she said staring hard into Willum's face trying to spot some kind of familial resemblance. "Are you really Willum Havelok?"

Willum nodded.

"*The* Willum Havelok. Commander of First Contact?"

"I realise it's probably a bit of a shock."

JoJo squealed. "A bit of a shock? I thought you were … Well never mind what I thought you were.

"And you!" She screamed at Jimmy. "You were dead. I saw Obel shoot you. You dropped to the floor, there was blood and everything." She paused. "I did see that didn't I?"

Jimmy touched his chest. "Oh, you saw it all right."

"Then how can you be alive? It's just not possible."

Jimmy didn't have an answer. His survival was as much a mystery to him as it was to JoJo. They both looked to Willum who cleared his throat like a man suddenly put on a very awkward spot.

"Right. Well, where to start exactly."

"At the beginning," said Jimmy.

"Yes. At the beginning. Very good place and all that. Um, right, JoJo, am I right in assuming that you recently came of age?"

JoJo frowned. "Yes. But what has that got to do with anything?"

Willum paused, fighting with the words he had to say.

"Because ... so did Jimmy," he said finally.

JoJo spluttered. "But how could he have. He's ..."

Her voice trailed off as the pieces of the puzzle began to click into place. If this was truly Willum Havelok, that would make Jimmy part Larian. A Larian/Human. A *Hurian*. That meant ... he would have the gift set too.

She gasped. "If you're alive when you should be dead that can only mean one thing, but it's impossible. There hasn't been one for generations." She shook her head. "You just can't be. You can't be a Healer ... can you?"

Jimmy, utterly shocked and confused, looked at Willum who nodded.

"Ohmygod," screamed JoJo excitedly. "Do you know how powerful they are? Do you know how *rare* they are? No, of course you don't. Well they are, sooooo rare I mean."

She turned her back on Willum and said eagerly, "Cut these will you?"

When she was free she screamed "Ohmygod" again and jumped into Jimmy's arms, hugging him tight. "I thought I'd lost you," she cried, "and all the time you were a Healer. It's unbelievable. It all makes sense. That's why my shoulder healed so quickly after the grommet attack. It was you who carried me to the Star Seeker that night, remember. And 2B! Wearing that explorer jacket for so long should have made him even more dopey than he already is, but it was you who put him to bed. You healed us without even knowing it."

"He's the first one to come of age for two thousand years," said Willum.

"Ohmygod," repeated JoJo.

Jimmy didn't know what to say. He felt quite sick. It was as though JoJo was talking about a different person. He didn't feel any different which was odd, seeing as he had just survived been shot at close range. All this talk of healing and special powers was making him quite ill.

Suddenly, as if she had just thought of something important, JoJo pulled back and punched Jimmy hard on the arm.

"Ow," he moaned. "Jeez. Why are girls always hitting me?"

"You took your time stopping Obel didn't you? How long were you awake before you decided to take him out? He had a gun pointed at my head. I thought I was a goner."

Jimmy rubbed his arm. "So did I," he said softly. "The first two times I tried zapping him, the thing didn't go off."

JoJo threw her head back and shrieked.

She turned to Willum. "Why did Obel Scar want to kill me?"

"Because he thought *you* were the Healer."

JoJo frowned. "But I'm not, I'm a seer. You knew I wasn't a Healer didn't you? Otherwise you wouldn't have given Jimmy the disabler."

Willum looked at Jimmy. "It's true. I've known ever since the accident that killed your mother. There was no way an ordinary child could have survived that wreckage. I was surprised even you did, considering your age. Also, you've definitely been showing all the signs of coming of age for days now. Those spots on your forehead are a dead giveaway. Larians only ever get acne once in their life – when they come of age."

JoJo touched the single spot on her forehead. Jimmy touched his, and fixed his Grandad with a terrified stare. "Did you let him shoot me on a purpose?"

Willum lowered his head uncomfortably. "I'm sorry son. It's not the way I wanted any of this to happen. I was always going to tell you man-to-man, but – well it never seemed to be the right time and when I got here and saw your predicament, I thought that letting Obel believe you were dead would give us the advantage."

"Bloody hell," cursed Jimmy. "You let him kill me. What if it hadn't worked? What if I hadn't healed?"

"But you did." Jimmy's Grandad said simply.

JoJo's mouth dropped open. "You mean he didn't know? All this time and you never told him anything? He really thought that he was going to die?"

Willum hung his head. Put like that it sounded pretty terrible.

Suddenly remembering, Jimmy reached into his pocket. He pulled out the envelope he had found in the outhouse, retrieved a letter from inside and handed it JoJo to read. "I knew some of it," he said. "It's all in there. Who he is, who I am, about my mother. I found it in the outhouse while I was searching for your necklace. I read it while I was outside the lab. I guess though … none of it really sunk in until now."

He looked at his Grandad hard. "This healing business though. I didn't know about that."

JoJo finished reading. "So how come you knew who I was?" she asked Willum.

Willum placed his hands tenderly on her shoulders and gazed into her deep blue eyes. "From the first moment I laid eyes on you at the Battle of the Bands there wasn't a doubt in my mind." His voice wavered slightly. "You see; you're the absolute double of your Grandmother."

He smiled tenderly and JoJo's world melted like ice cream in the sun. Ever since she was a little girl, people had told her how like her Grandma she was. And now her Grandfather, lost for forty years, was telling her the same thing. It was only then that she realised all of this was true.

Blinking back tears and without even realising she had moved, they embraced. JoJo buried her head in his chest. It was a strong Grandad type chest, the type she had longed for. It felt so right.

"There's so much I don't know," she said into his ribs, "and I want to know *everything*."

"And so you shall," said Willum holding her as if he was never going to let go, "but first we need to get out of here."

CHAPTER 51

HOW IT REALLY HAPPENED

So he did. Willum told her everything. The difference was, his everything was entirely different to the Admiralties everything. There was no capture by the human military, no systematic torture at the hands of brutal killers and no death-defying escape back to Anilar. There was only Obel Scar, a bottle of poison and a made up story. Oh yes, and two thousand years of secrecy.

The three of them were in his truck driving away from the school. They had cleaned up as much of the biology lab as they could. The chairs were write-offs, but at least they managed to wipe up the blood which had spilled from Jimmy's wound during the Healing process. Then Willum had carried Obel's still unconscious body from the school, tossed him in the back of the truck, thrown a tarpaulin over him and sped off.

His body exhausted from the Healing, Jimmy could do nothing but clamber into the back seat where he promptly fell asleep. JoJo was upfront. So far, since they set off she hadn't managed to take her eyes off Willum for more than a second, scared that if she did the next time she looked he may have disappeared like a holotrope.

"What do you know of the Vermese War?" Willum asked as the school disappeared in the rear view mirrors.

"The Vermese war? Wow, that's really going back in time," she said. "It was Anilar's last war but that was two thousand years ago. What's it got to do with now?"

"Everything, JoJo. Everything. It was two thousand years ago when spaceflight really began. Portals had just been discovered. The first Star Seekers were being flown and new planets were being explored. It was an illuminating time. A time of much progress, but like everything, for all the thousands of people who were excited by the promise of more and more discoveries, there were those few who were terrified of them.

"The Vermese war began after a man called Vermis Havel challenged the then leader of Anilar, Cubas, for power. Vermis was close to Cubas, one of his main advisors but, contrary to his leader, he had always hated the idea of venturing into the galaxy. One day Vermis claimed to have seen a vision sent by the gods. Yes. Larians still believed in such things back then, JoJo. In it he supposedly foresaw the destruction of Anilar and the slavery of its people by an outside world. Most shockingly, he claimed that this army of alien aggressors would be led by a Larian, a traitor who sought to claim Anilar for him or herself. The vision became known as 'The Prophecy.'"

JoJo grabbed a chocolate bar from the glove box, took a bite and welcomed the sugar rush. She hadn't realised until now just how hungry she was.

Willum continued. "Vermis gathered many powerful allies and was very persuasive amongst the people. His followers became galvanised behind the prophecy and, when they couldn't change Cubas' mind diplomatically, they began a civil war that lasted sixteen years.

"In the end Vermis triumphed but, unfortunately for him, by then it was too late. The space program had gathered momentum. Time could not be turned back. It would have been like trying to ban car travel here on earth.

"So he sought to control it instead. He chose six of his closest allies and called them the Admiralty. He gave them two roles. Firstly, they were to act as his generals, controlling spaceflight to his own agenda. Secondly, they were handed the secret task of searching for the traitor foreseen in the prophecy and preventing it from ever coming true."

302

"But how?" asked JoJo.

"By using the single clue they had. According to the prophecy the traitor would be ... a Healer."

Willum shifted gear and turned a corner.

"When Vermis died at the age of one hundred and thirty with no heir, the Admiralty took full control. Only, by then they had become even more paranoid than Vermis. They were not content to sit around and wait for a Healer to come of age and only then make sure he didn't get any foolish ideas. They began 'The Cleansing,' a program of selective *extermination.*

Despite it being quite warm in the truck, JoJo shivered. *Extermination*! Hadn't Obel said something similar to her before Jimmy zapped him? '*Consider yourself cleansed.'*" She remembered.

"Any child showing signs of possessing the Healer genes was killed or, to use their word, cleansed." Finished Willum.

JoJo was appalled. The Admiralty, murderers of children? It was too horrible to contemplate.

"But how have they got away with it for so long?" she asked numbly.

"By being very careful," said Willum, "and very secretive. They choose their friends well. Even now, no one outside the inner circle knows what I am telling you."

JoJo looked at Willum closely. Had he been part of the inner circle? Is that how he knew all this?

"How have they covered up so many deaths? Surely someone would have noticed."

Willum shook his head. "You're forgetting how rare the Healer genes are. There may be only one child born every five or ten years who carries the gift set. An accident here, a tragedy there, it doesn't take much covering up."

JoJo did a quick mental calculation. "One child every five to ten years. That's still ... a thousand murders since the Admiralty took control of Anilar." She was astonished – the sheer madness of it.

"Surely they still don't do it. Do they?"

Willum looked deadly serious. "As far as I am aware, you are the first person marked as a Healer to survive the coming of age since the Admiralty has been in power. If they truly believe you to be a Healer, JoJo, then you should be dead already. Either you slipped through the net and have only just been found, which I doubt, or you have some very powerful friends back an Anilar."

JoJo could hardly take it in. All this certainly explained why she had been given such a hard time from St Gills and Axel's brother. It was chilling to think that when she had been cast off that rock face two years ago, it might have been a genuine attempt on her life orchestrated by the Admiralty. As far as having powerful friends, it was the first she knew about it if she did.

"It doesn't explain why they let me go through the whole thing of coming here and then killing me if they are so terrified of the Blue Planet," she said.

"I thought about that. My guess is that they saw your coming here as an opportunity to combine your death with some more anti-Blue Planet PR of their own, just like they did forty years ago."

Willum checked the rear view mirror suspiciously. The road behind was clear, but forty years of hiding had taught him that it didn't hurt to be a little paranoid.

"When we found the Blue Planet, as much as it enthralled the people, it absolutely terrified the Admiralty. They thought it was the one. The planet Vermis spoke of in the prophecy."

JoJo scoffed. "But that's ridiculous."

Willum shrugged. "Maybe, maybe not. You've seen for yourself what humans are capable of. They have everything. Total superiority over every other life form, intelligence – although sometimes you wouldn't think so – and a truly wondrous place full of life and beauty to live in. Yet all they seem to do is look for new ways to kill each other and destroy their home. You can understand why that brought fear to the Admiralty."

"But humans can't fly more than a few thousand miles into space. Everyone knows that. How were they ever supposed to launch an attack on Anilar? It doesn't make sense."

"The human race learns fast. You'd be surprised. And don't forget, if the prophecy were true, they would be shown the way by a Larian. Maybe they thought that Larian was you."

JoJo laughed at the sheer craziness of that thought. *Her* – lead an army against Anilar. The idea was preposterous.

Willum continued. "Anyway, the Admiralty wished they had never found it. They certainly wanted 'First Contact' abandoned from the very first but this was the first real intelligent life we'd found in two thousand years of trying. The excitement it brought was unimaginable. If they cancelled the mission people would want to know why. They might dig too deep into the Admiralty's business. They may ask some very 'awkward' questions indeed."

"Like why have you been killing innocent kids for two thousand years?" said JoJo.

"That could be one of them," nodded Willum. "Rather than that, they let us go. Unfortunately, they didn't tell us that we were going to be the fall guys."

The deep hum of the diesel engine filled the truck like a swarm of bees trapped in a drum.

"So you're saying the Admiralty engineered the disaster and then made up a story that would terrify everyone into never going there again," JoJo asked eating the last piece of chocolate.

Willum looked grim faced. "Exactly. They figured what was the big deal? Five men dead to save an entire planet. You do the maths."

JoJo shook her head. It was unbelievable. "So everything they told us, was lies?"

Willum nodded. "All except the part about Obel taking his brother's dead body home. That was true, but I bet they didn't tell you that it was Obel who killed him!"

"Obel!" exclaimed JoJo.

"Mathius was never supposed to go. The crews had been long decided. I would lead the mission with Obel as my second in command. We knew each other from way back, it made sense. Each Star Seeker was to have a co-pilot and a navigator. Unfortunately, my navigator was taken ill at the last minute and I had to choose someone quickly. Mathius had just graduated. He was a fantastic flyer, a brilliant kid. I'd been his mentor through school so I knew he could handle the trip and he practically begged me to go. Of course Obel fought it, but I overruled him." Willum's face grew solemn. "It was a mistake. All I did was get him killed."

"But it wasn't your fault," said JoJo sympathetically.

"I should have chosen someone else. Someone … older."

Willum glanced over his shoulder. "How's Jimmy doing?"

JoJo stretched over her seat. "Still sleeping like a baby."

"Good," said Willum. "That Healing will have taken a lot out of him."

JoJo gazed at Jimmy a while. He looked so peaceful. "Does he never get ill like the rest of us?" she asked.

"Never had so much as a cold, the lucky beggar," replied Willum. "His body kills any infection before he knows anything about it."

She turned to face the front. There was something she had been dying to ask since she had found out about Jimmy. "Um, So when he had the accident, the one with his Mum I mean, could he not have saved her as he saved me?"

Willum stayed quiet for a moment.

"He was very young," he said eventually. "His powers were weak. Like I said, he barely had enough strength to heal himself. There was nothing left for his Mum."

JoJo sensed regret in Willum's voice. It was so sad. Jimmy's Mum was his daughter after all. But she knew Willum wasn't blaming Jimmy. It was no one fault what happened.

Willum sighed. "You see, people think that coming of age is the beginning of your powers. It isn't -quite the contrary in fact. It's the end of the beginning." Willum reached across and tapped JoJo's head. "It's always in there from birth, but it's uncontrollable. It's like the difference between riding in the passenger seat of your Star Seeker and actually flying it. Before coming of age, you experience the thrill of the flight, but get taken wherever the pilot wants to go. You have no choice. When you come of age, its as if you've suddenly stepped into the drivers seat and can go wherever you want. *You* control it, instead of it just happening. I'm sure if you think back, you'll remember times when you knew what someone was about to say, or knew the answer to a question before it had even been asked, or who was on the end of your communicator before it even rang."

JoJo smiled.

"You see, you've always been a Seer. It's always been there. Just like Jimmy has always been a Healer. He just couldn't control it. In a way that was good. If he could've directed it I'm sure he would have tried to heal his mother and sacrifice himself. They may have both died. At least I kept my grandson."

He turned another corner and headed down yet one more long, straight, tree lined road. He cleared his throat. "Anyway, I was telling you about Mathius.

"I believe the Admiralty's plans were simple. Everyone would die, except Obel. He was their inside man you see. The one sent to make sure everything ran smoothly. Obviously when Mathius came on board, things changed."

He explained how the Seeker's food and water lines had been infected with a biotic poison. It had been made up of genetically altered bacteria that once ingested, incapacitated the host by systematically shutting down every major organ, one by one eventually killing them.

"Gross," said JoJo.

"Quite," said Willum. "However, unbeknown to the Admiralty, Obel deactivated the poison in my Seeker and allowed us to land as planned. We had no clue what had happened on the other Seeker. Ratan and Sakuro were barely alive. We could do nothing for them. But Obel wanted Mathius on his side, so he told him everything. How he had been recruited into the Admiralty's inner circle of pilots and how he was doing only what was right for Anilar."

"What by killing even more people?" snarled JoJo.

"That's what he believed. He told him about the prophecy and the cleansings and begged Mathius to join him and fly back home victorious."

JoJo sighed trying to hide her relief. So that was how Willum found out everything. "But obviously Mathius didn't," she said.

"Obel may have been his older brother, but Mathius was a good man. He would never have been part of it. When he refused, Obel shot him dead. In cold blood. As calmly as if he were shooting a tin can. As calmly as he shot Jimmy."

He paused as if the pain of remembering, of re-telling the story which had remained untold for forty years, had finally caught up with him.

"Com … He ran at Obel and tried to stop him but Obel became possessed, shouting and blaming me for Mathius' death."

JoJo was about to say something reassuring, but figured it would be of little help. So, she just let him talk.

"After that, everything happened so fast. Com took a shot to the chest. I fled for cover. But I didn't make it."

"You were shot?"

"No, he missed and hit some kind of fuel tank. It exploded. My right arm and left leg were broken. I had more cuts and bruises than a heavyweight boxer, and it damaged my hearing. I was a real mess."

He breathed deeply. "The next thing I knew, Obel was standing over me grinning, his gun pointed at my chest. He told me how he wished things could have been different. That if Mathius had agreed to join him, he would have let me live." He let the words hang. "Then he pulled the trigger."

JoJo gasped. "How … How did you survive? Are you a healer?"

"Gosh no. I survived because Obel made one mistake. He aimed at my chest."

Willum slipped a hand under the collar of his shirt and lifted out a necklace. JoJo let out an involuntary squeak. He had been wearing it all the time. The other half to the Union necklace. He showed her the surface. Dead centre of the teardrop, just catching the bottom of the red letter 'S' was a dent.

"The bullet hit that?" she said completely amazed.

"Saved my life. Ricocheted off and caught me in the shoulder. Hurt like hell, but not fatal."

"Wow."

Quickly, she pulled out her own half of the union necklace, reached behind her neck and unclipped it. Gently she brought the two halves together and for the first time in forty years, they sealed and became one.

"It's waited a long time to be re-united," JoJo said joyfully.

Willum turned and looked at his granddaughter. Really looked. She was beautiful. True, she did look like her Grandmother, but she had her own beauty too: A beauty in her character that was all her own.

"Too long," he replied softly. "It's waited too long."

CHAPTER 52

THE SHOW MUST GO ON

Ten minutes later and Willum pulled the car to a stop on a small side road behind the back of Apple Valley's football stadium. Inside, the Centenary concert was in full swing. The muffled hum of music resonated through the windows of the truck as a band played.

Outside, the road was deserted. Willum had deliberately parked here, away from the main throng, so as not to attract any undue attention – they did have an alien's body in the back of the truck, after all.

JoJo tried to look into the stadium, but her view was limited to a sliver of space through which she could just make out the bobbing heads of a few thousand people.

It was perfect weather. The hot afternoon sun had given way to a balmy summer's evening. What a difference a day makes. Last night, it had rained so hard, you'd have been forgiven for thinking that somewhere, a bearded man was building an arc. Tonight the skies were clear, the moon was full and the stars were out in their millions.

Willum left the engine idling. JoJo looked across. She suddenly felt incredibly sad, sensing that goodbye was not far away.

"Wake Jimmy up and you two jump out here," said Willum.

"Why? Where are you going?" JoJo asked.

"To deal with Obel."

"On your own?" exclaimed JoJo worriedly. "Take me, I can help."

Willum shook his head unquestionably. "No you really can't JoJo.

This is something I must do. And you have somewhere else to be. Your place is not here with me on this Planet. It's at home with your family."

"But ..." she began, and stopped. She was going to say '*I don't want to go*' but that was not true. She missed her Mum and dad so much it hurt in the pit of her stomach. The truth was more, '*I don't want to go, without you*,' but she also knew that couldn't happen.

She tried again. "You're family too you know, and there's so much more I want to ask you. So much more I want to learn from you." She screwed up her face in anger. "It's not fair. I've only just found you, and now we'll never see each other again."

Willum put his hand gently on her shoulder. "Never say never, JoJo."

She turned away sulkily. "It's as good as never. There's no way I'll ever be allowed to come here again."

Willum sighed. He checked his watch. "Look, we have a few minutes. Why don't you ask me the question I know must have been burning in your mind since you found out who I was?"

JoJo looked at him closely. He knew, didn't he? She wondered if he too was a seer, because there was something she'd been wanting to ask. But it was difficult, and she wondered whether she had the nerve. Maybe it would be prudent to start with another question, and build up.

"How have you survived all this time?" she said. "If you were in such a bad way, who saved you?"

Willum smiled knowingly. "It was Jimmy's Grandma and her brother who saved me. I gather you know you landed in virtually the same spot as I did."

She nodded.

"Well, they had inherited the lease on that land from their father. They found me three days after Obel had left, and showed me kindness I could never have hoped for or imagined. They took me in, nursed me back to health and ... somehow understood about my reluctance to have any outside help or interference."

"Did you tell them who … what you were?"

"Eventually," nodded Willum. "The brother, Arthur, is a military man. A good man, but I still had to be careful. He could easily have turned me in. I'm sure capturing an alien life form would have been a great coup for him, but he never even considered it. He and I became best friends, still are. It was he who told me of your landing. He was in the radar room the night you crashed. He recognised the Seekers signature straight away. He couldn't fail really, I had talked about it nearly every day for forty years. And he'd been looking for it for as long. I'm sure he thought I was mad, but I always knew someone would come back, eventually. I just didn't expect it to be my own Granddaughter."

He smiled wryly and continued. "Arthur has been my eyes and ears on you and Jimmy ever since you landed. He was at the battle of the bands. I believe he guided you to the correct place to do your Vocalosis."

JoJo scrunched her eyebrows. "No one told me where to …" Then she remembered. The man at the door who wouldn't let her in. "That was Arthur?" she asked.

Willum nodded. "I couldn't let him contact you properly. If you knew that we knew then you wouldn't have been able to do the Vocalosis. So, he had to make you think that going to the balcony was your idea."

"Crafty," said JoJo smiling.

"We planned to tell you and Jimmy this whole story after the result. But seeing Obel disguised as some kind of music manager changed everything. There was no way I was going to let you become another one of his victims, so Arthur and I changed plans.

"When Jimmy came home, Arthur was supposed to give Jimmy a small sedative and keep him there until I returned to collect you. Unfortunately, Jimmy had other ideas. You told him I was a murderer, so when Arthur came for him it was understandable that he was scared. After that you were on your own, until now. I'm sorry, I'm afraid this

312

rescue has been mostly me making it up as I go along."

"Jimmy thinks Arthur's dead, you know. I saw it in his mind," said JoJo. "He won't say so, but he's really worried."

Willum laughed. "Hardly dead. In fact he's probably just had about his best twelve hours sleep in the last forty years."

Willum reached over and put his palm on Jimmy's forehead, checking his temperature. "It's been a long few days for the boy. I think he and I are going to need some time together when we get you off this planet."

"Will I ever get used to seeing inside people's heads?" JoJo asked. "Only I seem to be flipping everywhere. Into Jimmy's, then into the mind of a stranger passing by in a car."

"You'll get the hang of it. Just give it time."

"So why did you forget about my Grandmother on Anilar and marry Jimmy's Grandma then?" The words rattled out of her mouth before she realised she had said it.

"Ahhhh," said Willum. "Finally you ask the question. It's okay. You have every right to ask."

He took a breath. "You have to understand that I was left stranded. I sent a mayday the day after Jimmy's Grandma found me, and heard nothing. I took it to mean that I was on my own. It was the hardest time of my life. I'd lost everything. My family, my career. I was in a kind of mourning for a long, long time. Over that time, Jimmy's Grandma and I became close. Eventually, we fell in love. I won't apologise for it, but I will tell you this, a day hasn't gone by when I haven't thought about your Grandma and what became of her."

"She died in childbirth having my Mum," said JoJo softly.

Willum hung his head. "I'm sorry. I never knew she was having a baby, JoJo. If I had …"

They fell silent.

If he had have known, then what? There was nothing he could have done differently anyway, thought JoJo. He was here, his family was

313

there. She certainly knew how that felt. She had been confronted with the same emotions when she believed she and 2B were stranded here. It was a feeling that nothing can prepare you for. Your entire body fills with an emptiness so utterly and complete that not even dust or viruses exist in it. It's a dark emptiness, a sad and lonely emptiness. She couldn't even begin to imagine how much worse it would have been for Willum if he had known about his unborn child waiting back home. It would have been unbearable.

"It's okay," she said finally, her expression soft. "From what people have told me about my Grandma, I think she'd have been pleased that you found happiness. Besides, if you hadn't got together with Jimmy's Grandma, then I wouldn't have a long lost …" She looked at Jimmy. "What is he anyway?"

Willum shook his head. "Beats me. I think you're some kind of second cousins, just a hundred million light years removed." He smiled. "But who cares. It's just a name. You are to each other what you are. It doesn't need a name."

JoJo nodded. It was true. In Jimmy she had found something far more special than simply a new family member. She had found a true and special friendship – one that would last forever.

"You are wrong about one thing though," said Willum. "Jimmy's Grandma and I have never been married. You can understand how such a thing would be impossible."

He paused. "Jimmy doesn't know. I'd appreciate it if you didn't mention it."

JoJo smiled and nodded.

"Thank you. Now, if you're through," said Willum. "Will you get the heck out of here. You have a Star Seeker to go and rescue from your brother and *he*," pointing to Jimmy "has to play guitar in less than thirty minutes. I'm sure he'd rather be awake for the experience. It could be quite the show stopper."

JoJo seemed to suddenly snap to attention. "Oh my god, the Star Seeker, I completely forgot. Where is the barn, I have to get–."

"You don't have to get anywhere," interrupted Willum. "The Star Seeker is in that field." Willum pointed to a small piece of grass at the side of the football stadium. "I took the liberty of leaving SaRa instructions on where she should take 2B, as I wasn't sure you would make it to the barn in time. All you need to do, is get in there, get prepared, and when it's time for Applejuice to play, hover over that stage; as close as you can and stay there until they play the note. Then hopefully, you'll fly like the wind."

JoJo looked at Willum with awe. How did he know all this stuff about the cosmic boom and Halfpint's guitar note? Why couldn't she have met him sooner?

"And if you're wondering how come I know all this stuff," said Willum perceptively. "Then blame SaRa. She can be quite chatty when she wants to be. Particularly where you are concerned."

JoJo smiled softly and very reluctantly opened her door and stepped out.

"Oh and JoJo," said Willum suddenly serious.

"Yes Grandad." It was the first time she'd called him that. It sounded good.

"You may have a tough time when you get home. If they think you are dead and have spun a similar tissue of lies as they did forty years ago, they aren't going to be too pleased to see you back. To that end, you'll find some rather helpful documents in your cockpit drawer. Make sure you give them to someone you trust. They'll be your bargaining chip."

He winked. JoJo didn't need to be a seer to know that Willum had given her some kind of proof of his survival and the plot to kill the SpaceCoyotes. Maybe even something about the cleansings. With a lump in her throat, she jumped back in the cab and hugged him tightly around the neck.

"Thank you," she said.

"No, thank you. Meeting you has made these past years all worthwhile. Now wake sleepy head there, and go."

Reluctantly she released Willum and shook Jimmy until he opened his eyes. "Whassup," he said groggily. "What did I miss?"

JoJo glanced at Willum and grinned. "Oh nothing. Just talking about stuff."

Jimmy shook away the cobwebs and together they left Willum and headed towards the field where the Star Seeker was waiting.

"One final thing," shouted Willum as they went.

JoJo spun around. She was surprised to see his face like thunder.

"If you do anything as stupid as try and fly through another asteroid belt, you'll have me to deal with young lady. Got it? Oh yeah, and take a look in your pocket when you are in the Star Seeker – not before though." Then he smiled, nodded, put the truck in gear and drove off.

JoJo blew out a big breath as the truck disappeared. So that was that. Now it was just the small matter of getting home. What was the human phrase? 'Piece of cake.'

Yeah, she thought. *Piece of cake. Just like everything else.*

CHAPTER 53

RETURN OF THE MACK

BACKSTAGE AT THE CENTENARY CELEBRATIONS

"Don't wear your guitar like that. God you're thick. It needs to be lower. No, LOWER."

Damien was having a moment and, as usual, Halfpint was bearing the brunt of most of it.

"And *you*," he snapped at Paige. "Stop twirling your drumstick, you'll have my eye out with it."

"If only," whispered Paige under her breath.

They were fifteen minutes away from going on stage and the nerves were starting to show on them all. All, apart from Damien, were stood, silently contemplating the show ahead. Damien however seemed to have grown even more obnoxious than usual. Which really was saying something.

The Centenary Celebrations were going fantastically well. The whole day had been one long party with hundreds of stalls and fairground rides set up throughout Apple Valley Park. Huge barbecues had been burning since midday, selling mouth-watering burgers, ribs, sausages and steaks. You could get your face painted or have a temporary tattoo; slide down the water shoots and even skate on the huge patch of ice that had been created just for the day. The entertainment ranged from a magician who managed to saw not one, but a whole team of ladies in half, through to clowns whose stock in trade seemed to be falling over a lot. There had even been hot air

317

balloon rides and a fly past by the local military jets. All in all, people were having a wonderful time and the concert was proving to be the pinnacle.

Applejuice had been told that the crowd outside had swelled to nearly fifteen thousand.

In the dressing room, Damien cleared his throat. "Listen everybody. When we go out there, I don't want you doing anything stupid like moving. The last thing we need is for you lot to think you are the stars of the show or something. You will stand still. You will stand exactly where you are told and you will leave the entertaining to me. Understood?"

Paige gave him a grimace and a mock salute. "Anything you say master," she mocked.

"Exactly. Glad to see you've finally learnt where your place is Turner. Just keep thinking like that."

Paige turned away from him. "Idiot," she said quietly to Halfpint. "I swear when this is over I'm gonna shove this drum stick where the sun don't shine."

"I wouldn't waste it," said Halfpint dryly. "There's already a broom stick up there."

Two loud knocks rapped on their dressing-room door. "Ten minutes guys."

Damien snapped to attention. "Right. Everyone, around me now. Come on, don't slack. This is it. A final check for everybody."

Paige, Halfpint and Cornelius all sighed in unison. "God I wish Jimmy were here," said Halfpint.

* * *

Not that it was any help to them, but Jimmy was a lot closer than any of them knew. He had changed into a fresh set of clothes, which his Grandad had brought in the truck, and was currently with JoJo in what appeared to be a big empty field. In truth, above there heads was fifty tonnes of invisible Star Seeker, but only they knew that.

"I guess this is goodbye then ... cousin," said JoJo smiling.

Jimmy nodded. All this was taking some getting used to.

"So, how's it feel to be one of us? A Larian," she asked.

Jimmy shrugged. "How are you supposed to feel when you're suddenly told that you're a different species to what you thought you were? I feel like a frog who, after going through life quite happily, is told that he's actually a toad. I feel the same ... but different."

JoJo kissed him on the cheek. "You're the bravest person I have ever met Jimmy Green – next to me, that is. And luckily I don't see any warts." She laughed. Jimmy laughed too. "I, for one, don't care what you call yourself. It's who you are in here and here that matters." She tapped his head and his heart. "Who cares if your microscopic molecules aren't the same as everyone else's? You're still the same person you were yesterday only with ... added extras."

Jimmy smiled. "Added extras, I like that. I suppose if I can't get hurt, I will always have a career as a crash test dummy."

JoJo nodded thoughtfully. "Well you're half way there with the dummy bit anyway," she said.

"Hey," protested Jimmy, but his face was beaming. "I'm gonna miss you, JoJo," he said with genuine affection.

"I'll miss you too. It's been quite an adventure. Oh, wait, I nearly forgot. Don't go anywhere, I'll be just a minute."

JoJo jumped back and disappeared into the slight haze of the invisible turquoise beam. True to her word, she was back before sixty seconds had elapsed.

She handed him a small flat black disc about the size of a CD, but half an inch thick. "I wanted you to have this. It's called a holo-galaxy. You have to run your hand over it to make it work. Look."

Jimmy watched as a cloud of stars appeared between them, spinning and shining like a tiny explosion of silver dust particles. Briefly they appeared unorganised before they suddenly coalesced into a perfect miniature image of the galaxy. Just off-centre, amongst millions of silver dots was a single golden one.

"That's me. The gold one. If ever you want to know where I am, just look at this. It's so we can be close, even though we're so far away. It'll tell you the names of all these stars as well as a ton of other stuff, but I'll let you figure all that out by yourself."

Jimmy didn't know what to say. It was a truly beautiful thing. He would treasure it always.

"You will be careful when you get back won't you?" he said.

She saluted. "Coyotes honour."

As the music reached a peak around them, Jimmy hugged her tight and she hugged him back.

"Careful is my middle name anyway," she said ironically. "You go and kick some butt up there on that stage. Don't forget, I'm relying on you to get me out of here."

Jimmy let go. "You are going to do the Vocalosis thing again aren't you?" he asked worriedly.

"Don't worry, I'll be there for you," she reassured.

They stepped back from each other, and, although later if quizzed, neither would admit to it, a few tears escaped from both their eyes.

"See you," said JoJo

"Not if I see you first," replied Jimmy.

Like a phantom, the turquoise beam took her into the Seeker and she was gone.

Fighting a small but quite vehement urge to step in after her, Jimmy turned, checked his watch and made his way inside to find his band.

CHAPTER 54

GET THE PARTY STARTED

"Jimmy!" yelled Halfpint, as his best friend opened the dressing room door and walked in. "How the ... Where have you ... We thought ..."

"I know," said Jimmy simply, "But I'm here now that's all that matters."

Paige, Halfpint and Cornelius ran up to him as one, looking and touching, almost as if they were making sure he was real and not an illusion.

Damien however was a different story. He looked like the bottom had just fallen out of his ... well, bottom. As though he'd seen the ghost of someone he had killed. "You," he said, sounding not unlike the way Obel had greeted the arrival of Willum earlier.

"Yes me," said Jimmy, so utterly calmly it was scary, adding, "Are you ready to do this thing or what?", before turning and smiling at the guys.

Jimmy had been through a gamut of emotions and thought a lot about how he would react to Damien since discovering it was he who set JoJo up with Obel. His immediate reaction had been to want to hurt him badly. He had even imagined several horrible things in that regard.

All that was before. Before he had been shot. Before he had been dead.

When he awoke, lying on that laboratory floor, he had no idea that he was a Healer who had this bizarre DNA defect that made him virtually un-killable. He believed that, like every normal human being, when you are shot in the chest, it means you are likely to die. This changes a person, clears the mind of the detritus that smothers it. Makes you infinitely aware of what's really important in life.

Jimmy knew that from then on, should he survive, there were two paths he could take with regard to Damien Dirt. One was easy – the path of revenge. He could put all his energy into hating Damien and making sure he paid for what he had done, but where would that get him? There could be no real satisfaction in punching Damien's lights out, because people like Damien never change. He wouldn't feel remorse, or guilt, or sorrow for what he had done any more than an eagle feels pity for the rabbit it's enjoying for dinner. Put simply, Damien Dirt wasn't worth wasting any more time and energy on. Hate was debilitating and destructive, and could quite easily turn you into someone just as obnoxious as the person you started hating in the first place.

This left the much more difficult option of simply letting it be. Damien would get what was coming to him sooner or later, that was sure. Fate always seemed to have an uncanny knack of evening up the score. It just wasn't going to be Jimmy that dished it out. Besides, it would be fun to see how freaked out Damien got, the longer Jimmy acted as though nothing had happened.

To his credit, like all those blessed with supreme over- confidence, Damien rallied quickly. "I, er, yes I am indeed ready. Glad you bothered to turn up. I had you down as a prize chicken."

Jimmy let it slide.

"I was just telling everyone what I expect of them when they get out there. It's really quite simple, even for you. You stand in a row at the back, and do not move at all during the show. All the entertaining will be done by me."

Jimmy tilted his head. You had to hand it to the boy. He *truly* was a prize twerp. "Really," said Jimmy. "Is that what you *really* want us to do, Damien?"

For a second Damien looked unsure. Something about the look in Jimmy's eyes was obviously unnerving him, but again, he gathered himself. "Yes, yes that is exactly what I want you to do, and if you know what's good for you, you'll do it," he snapped. "Now I'm going to the stage. Meet me there in five minutes, ready for my grand entrance." He pushed passed the group and flew through the door as if he couldn't wait to get out. When he had gone, everyone relaxed.

"Where have you been?" cried Halfpint. "I've been texting and phoning you for hours. Are you all right?"

"Good as new," smirked Jimmy. "I'll explain everything after we get through this shambles. And I'm telling you, don't any of you dare follow his instructions. We do our show, our way. Stuff him okay."

He put his hand out. In turn, Halfpint, Cornelius and Paige put theirs on top. "To us," said Jimmy. "TO US," they shouted.

"All right then. Grab the gear. We've got some people to entertain.

* * *

In the Star Seeker, looking down on the thousands of people in the stadium, JoJo was ready. She was hovering exactly above the stage where her Grandad (it still sounded funny in her head) had told her to be, with Cat's cap in her hand. Everything was set for one more shot at Vocalosis. By her side 2B sat stoically, ready for the flight home, none the worse for wear after his ordeal last night.

Remembering what Willum had told her before he left, she felt in her jacket pockets. In the right one, her fingers surrounded a small folded piece of paper. Slowly, she pulled it out and took in the words Willum had scribbled in pencil. As she did, a wide smile grew on her face, and didn't stop until it hurt.

Oh this was perfect, absolutely perfect. She put the cap on her head.

The lights went down. The stage beyond was in utter darkness. The noise of the crowd hummed like a hundred trucks idling in a traffic jam. You could literally hold the tension in your hands. At the side of the stage Jimmy, Halfpint, Paige and Cornelius stood in a line holding hands in a show of unison. Damien stood alone, shaking himself down like an athlete about to compete in the one hundred metre Olympic final.

"This is sooooo scary," said Paige, nervously squeezing Jimmy's fingers. Jimmy just stared into the crowd. Funny, but nerves weren't affecting him at all. It seemed that after coming back from the dead, nothing fazed you anymore.

A bright light shone into the wings and Siegfried Dirt suddenly whisked past the four of them heading for centre stage. Anticipation swelled the crowd noise.

Dressed in a black dinner jacket, Siegfried coughed into the microphone to check it was working and then began to speak.

"Ladies and Gentlemen," he bellowed loudly. "So far tonight you've seen what the best bands in the world have to offer. Now its time to see what the best band in Apple Valley can do."

Loud cheers rang out. The hairs on Jimmy's arms prickled.

"As many of you know, this year's inter-schools Battle of the Bands contest had a very special prize – to play right here on this very stage, for you. The competition was won, I am very proud to say, by my own son's band, Applejuice."

"Oh Please," said Paige, eyeing a smug looking Damien. "Now it's his band is it? Let me go and push him into the crowd."

Jimmy gripped her hand tighter. "Leave him," he said calmly.

Paige frowned. "But he's stealing our band," she said through gritted teeth.

"No he's not," countered Jimmy. "The band is *us*, Paige. You, me, Halfpint and Cornelius. He can't take that away. Applejuice is just a name. It doesn't matter. We can think of a new one and start again after this."

Paige looked at Jimmy like he was, well … an alien.

On stage, Siegfried continued to address the audience.

"What can I tell you about my son? He's a huge talent as we found out in this competition. I must say even I was surprised."

Portions of the crowd laughed.

"However, tonight I have some rather sad news to bring you." His tone grew suddenly sombre. "Unfortunately, and much to his – and my – enormous disappointment, Damien will be unable to sing for you, due to illness."

Damien immediately stopped shaking himself down and stared unbelieving at his father. Jimmy turned his head to Halfpint. "Did he just say what I think he just said?"

"He said Damien can't sing."

"Well we all know that," quipped Cornelius. "But what did he mean?"

"Sshhhh," said Jimmy excitedly. "He's about to say something else."

Siegfried motioned to the crowd to calm down. "Please, this does not mean however, that the band are not going to play. Yes, I am happy to tell you that you don't have to go without your Applejuice tonight." He paused, waiting for any laughter to his pun. Some came, but much too late. Frankly it was more than the joke deserved. He carried on regardless "We have found, at very short notice, a replacement that I am sure will do the band … proud. So, without further ado, please welcome to the stage, Applejuice."

Jimmy, Halfpint, Paige and Cornelius stood stock still as if everything Siegfried had just said had been in Swahili.

As the stage lights dimmed and their opening music began to play from a pre-recorded tape, Siegfried marched towards them. Damien rushed him, his face fiercer than the worst bout of thunder the world had ever seen.

"What is the meaning of this father? How dare you …," he spat.

Siegfried put his hand up, silencing Damien immediately.

"*You*, be quiet," was all he said.

He turned to Jimmy. "You must be Green. I had an interesting chat with your Grandfather yesterday. I believe my son has something that belongs to your family."

Siegfried extended his hand towards Damien without looking at him. Damien knew exactly what his father wanted. Reluctantly, he retrieved the yellowing, tattered lease from his back pocket. Siegfried snatched it, and handed it to Jimmy, who could hardly believe what was happening. His whole body was shaking as he reached out and took hold of the paper. As he did, Siegfried grasped Jimmy's wrist – hard. Jimmy winced. Siegfried bent low, until he was level with Jimmy's ear.

"You may think that you have won young man. You and your … Grandfather, but believe me, there will come a time when you will wish that you never got involved with the Dirt's."

Siegfried stood up straight.

"As for your band, I won't have tonight turned into a circus. I promised the people the winner of the Battle of the Bands and the winner is what they will have."

"But, if Damien's not singing, who is?" said Cornelius.

Siegfried glanced over Jimmy's shoulder. "I'm told *she* will suffice."

Jimmy whipped around.

And he saw her.

His heart skipped a beat. Surely he was hallucinating. Could it really be?

"I understand, my son decided to take it upon himself to get my company to re-locate her father as far away from here as possible," said Siegfried.

Jimmy spun back. "You did it!" he spat at Damien.

Damien shrugged. "So, you love-sick imbecile, I told you didn't I? What I want, I get."

"Oh you are going to get it all right," barked Siegfried. "You have brought disgrace upon me tonight, a night which should have been my greatest success. This, my boy, is your punishment."

He turned, grabbed Damien by his collar and tried to drag him away, but Damien pulled back. "NO!" he snapped, "I will not have this. I am going to sing on that stage. *I* am the star, not these fools!"

"Fool is right," quipped Paige.

Damien turned to her, spitting fire.

"Don't speak to me you filthy, dirty, half-breed cow."

That was it. Paige's eyes narrowed. Her fist balled. Damien's nose exploded with blood and snot as he went down hard on his backside, yelping like a baby.

All eyes turned to Paige who looked shocked, then to Halfpint, who was rubbing his fist – the fist which had just floored Damien Dirt. "Prat," he said, before striding off towards the stage and his guitar.

On any other day Jimmy would have had no doubt that Halfpint punching Damien Dirt's lights out, was the best sight in the world. But today, there was one better.

Catrina Wickowski.

She walked forward smiling. Paige nudged Cornelius in the ribs and dragged him away onto the stage, where they took up their positions and joined in with the intro tape.

The noise in Jimmy's ears was deafening. He didn't know which was louder, the band or the cheers from the crowd.

For a moment, Jimmy and Cat simply stared at each other as something unspoken passed between them. No words could do justice to how he felt right now.

She looked amazing. Absolutely ready to stand in front of fifteen thousand people and sing her heart out. How he'd missed her. So much had happened this past week. Jimmy's life had quite literally changed beyond all recognition since she left. There was one thing that hadn't changed and when Cat smiled. Suddenly he was back at his tenth birthday party all over again – putty in her hand.

Someone broke the spell by thrusting a microphone into Cat's hand

and patting her on the back. "Time to go," they said urgently.

She looked at Jimmy. Out there, thirty thousand hands were pumping the rhythm to one of their songs. The feeling was electric.

Then she kissed him. Just once, on the cheek. Jimmy's heart triple flipped in his chest. "I love you," she whispered in his ear, but with the music so deafening, it sounded like 'mmm, mmm, mmm' Jimmy shook his head. "What?"

"I said, I …" She didn't finish because a sixth former from school suddenly stepped in between them and pushed a guitar into Jimmy's hands.

"Never mind," she shouted. "It will wait," and she gave him another quick kiss. Jimmy suddenly felt like a million dollars. He turned up his guitar and ran with Cat onto the stage. Finally, it was time to get the party started.

CHAPTER 55

FLY ME TO THE MOON

After five seconds it was as if Cat had never been away. The crowd lapped up every song. Now there was only one more thing left to do – make sure Halfpint hit the note that would send JoJo scorching through the atmosphere and into the galaxy.

It would come at the end of the final song. The big crescendo. And they were nearly there.

He wondered how JoJo was feeling up there, just sitting and waiting. She must be nervous. If it worked, she would be going home. If it didn't, she would be effectively sitting on a three thousand mile an hour bomb.

With sweat pouring from what seemed like every pore in his body, Jimmy dashed over to Halfpint to play guitar with him, back to back as they rocked out. Up front, Cat had the crowd eating out of the palm of her hand, whilst Cornelius and Paige kept a rhythm stronger than steel.

He watched Halfpint begin what would hopefully be the most dramatic guitar solo in the history of music, before taking up a position from which he could see high into the sky. One way or another, the next minute was going to be pretty spectacular.

* * *

Willum pulled into his garage about the same time as Halfpint was beginning his solo. The automatic door slid shut, triggering the light to come on.

Inside, Arthur was waiting for him. "Did he give you any trouble?" he asked, as Willum climbed out of the driver's cab.

Willum shook his head. "He's been as quiet as a mouse in the back there. Haven't heard a peep from him. That old Salton disabler packs more of a punch than I remember."

Arthur glanced tentatively into the back where the tarpaulin lay still. "Jimmy got to his concert okay did he?"

"Should be playing now," Willum said, flatly.

"You wish you could be there, don't you?"

"Of course," said Willum. "Who wouldn't? It's all he's ever dreamed of, Arthur. How many of us can say that we fulfilled our dreams, even partly. But some things are even more important, I'm afraid. This being one of them."

He nodded at the lump that was Obel Scar. Together they stared, unmoving and unspeaking. They had discussed this moment often over the years, even more so over the last few days and, always, they had been very clear what must happen next. The man under the tarpaulin was an alien. He didn't belong on this planet. He would not be missed or ever identified. Arthur had spent a lifetime in the military. He was privy to secret places. Places where people didn't ask questions or go snooping around. Places where bodies could be buried without fear of them ever returning to haunt you.

Deep down, Willum knew that it was the only rational thing to do. Obel Scar was a cold-blooded murderer, a man who would stop at nothing, even one hundred million light years, to achieve his objective. He was easily the most dangerous man Willum had ever met, Larian or Human. He had shot Jimmy, for goodness sake. Surely, if anyone deserved to die, he would be near the top of the list. But … but killing was still killing and the very notion did not sit well with Willum. Even now he was still hoping that at the eleventh hour, some other way would present itself.

They had everything they needed to do the job without pain or mess. The vials of potassium stood on the garage shelf. Administered in the correct dose, Obel's heart would just stop and never beat again. It was that easy. Just a simple injection. But ... Killing was killing.

Arthur, sensing his friends struggle said, "He will never change, Willum. You especially, will never be able to change him. Evil is evil, pure and simple. We must do this."

"I know, I know," replied Willum, uneasily.

They stood for another few moments, before Willum grasped one corner of the tarpaulin. Following his lead, Arthur took hold of the other corner.

"Shall we?" said Arthur.

Willum nodded, albeit in a resigned way. "We shall," he said and they yanked back the cover. As they did so, the still of the evening air was rudely shattered by a cacophony of fireworks exploding colourfully into the air. It was the signal for the end of the Centenary concert. Willum glanced briefly out of the window at the dramatic sight, before turning his attention back to what lay in the truck.

* * *

Halfpint hit the 'JoJo' note perfectly. The pitch, the tone, the volume, the duration; everything about it could not have been more ideal. The noise of the crowd erupted and was so loud Jimmy thought he could have touched it, as if it had become a real, living entity. It was a feeling of sheer ecstasy.

Instinctively he turned to watch the sky. Deep inside his chest he thought he felt a heavy, sonorous boom resonate his ribs, but he could have just been kidding himself, feeling what he expected to feel, rather than an actual sound.

The end of the show brought fireworks. They flew into the sky in their hundreds, adding their own thunder and colour to the moment, blanketing the darkness in blues and reds and greens and yellows and pinks. Jimmy knew that even if there was something to see, it would be impossible through the gunpowder haze.

But, as one gigantic red rosette exploded and expanded, he saw it. Way, way above where the fireworks were exploding, a blue/green streak shot across the sky, like a trail of fire, only the wrong colour. It lasted the merest of split seconds but it was long enough. Jimmy knew. It was JoJo. It had to be.

She and 2B had made it.

With the elation came a wave of sadness. That green streak was the last he would ever see of her and suddenly the thought of that had become all too real. Missing someone was a strange emotion. It was like a heavy, dead weight that sat as an unwanted guest in the pit of your stomach, whilst tears backed themselves up behind your eyes, waiting for that one single memory that allows them to burst forth. In a word it made you fragile. He'd felt it twice before. When his Mum died and when Cat left, and he was sick of it. But, like before, he would deal with it.

As they crashed out the final note and the music faded, reverberating in their ears, Jimmy was forced back to the reality of the stage. Together, the five members that were Applejuice joined hands, walked to the front of the stage and took their well-deserved bows. Jimmy had never seen Cornelius so animated or Paige so happy – except when she had just punched someone, that is.

"So all the troubles were worth it in the end," shouted Jimmy above the din of the crowd.

"What troubles?" yelled back Cat.

Jimmy smiled as they all bowed again. "Are you back for good?" he asked.

"Back for good," she beamed.

"Then I'll tell you all about it later."

They took three more bows and were finally forced by the enthusiastic crowd to play one last song. An encore! Jimmy could have burst with pride. Their first real show and they were playing an encore.

With Cat at the helm, and no pressure to launch an alien spacecraft into the galaxy, they played better than ever. They danced and jumped and threw their best rock star poses. They sang their hearts out and even got the crowd to join in during one chorus. It finished with a standing ovation – could life get any better than that? Jimmy doubted it, but he was definitely looking forward to it if it did.

* * *

In the Star Seeker, already cruising at full speed, JoJo and 2B had been joined by Occular, Janitox, Prickle, Pyro and Arachno, who, apart from having three of his eight arms bandaged together with Silicol tape, was doing remarkably well after his ordeal in the mud. JoJo sat back in her cockpit chair, passed full control of the flight to SaRa, put her hands behind her head and closed her eyes.

"Are you sure?" said the very surprised electric blue holographic girl. "This is indeed an unexpected honour and, may I say, not like you at all."

"Cut the cheek, fly girl, or I may rethink my position. Just take us home."

SaRa smirked satisfactorily. "It will be a pleasure, JoJo. Can I just say though, that that Cosmic boom was *the bomb* was it not?"

JoJo half opened one eye. "Are you trying to be hip, SaRa?" she asked.

SaRa grinned.

"Just fly this heap of metal and make sure it stays in one piece. Leave the stupid comments to 2B will you."

"Hey!" said 2B indignantly. Arachno beeped joyously and spun in a circle.

JoJo shut her eyes again. "You're right though, SaRa," she said. "It was the bomb."

Their laughter faded and JoJo thankfully began to feel the stresses of the last few days drift from her body. She and 2B had been through hell. They had survived because they were tough, because they had stuck together, and because they had found the most amazing four friends who helped them get through it.

She knew she was in for a rough ride when she got home. But, after surviving a week on the most dangerous planet in the galaxy, how bad could it be? Besides, she had the trump card. She had all her Grandad's evidence sitting in her Star Seeker. That should be enough to keep her wings at the very least.

With happy memories of Jimmy, the guys and her Grandfather playing through her mind, she finally succumbed to the one thing she hadn't had properly for a week – sleep. It was a deep dreamless sleep, one that she hoped would only end when they were once again flying over her planet.

Her home.

Anilar.

THE END